Crimes of War

Also by Neil Rolde

Real Political Tales: Short Stories by a Veteran Politician

Breckinridge Long: American Eichmann??? An Enquiry into the Character of the Man Who Denied Visas to the Jews

York Is Living History

O. Murray Carr: A Novel

Maine in the World: Stories of Some of Those From Here Who Went Away

Continental Liar From the State of Maine: James G. Blaine

Maine: Downeast and Different, an Illustrated History

Unsettled Past, Unsettled Future: The Story of Maine Indians

The Interrupted Forest: A History of Maine's Wildlands

The Baxters of Maine: Downeast Visionaries

Your Money or Your Health: America's Cruel, Bureaucratic, and Horrendously Expensive Health Care System

So You Think You Know Maine

Rio Grande Do Norte: The Story of Maine's Partner State in Brazil

Sir William Pepperrell of Colonial New England

Crimes of War

a novel by

Neil Rolde

Polar Bear & Company
Solon, Maine

First edition 2015
First printing: November 2015

Polar Bear & Company™ is an imprint of
the Solon Center for Research and Publishing
PO Box 311, Solon, Maine 04979 U.S.A.
207.643.2795, www.polarbearandco.org.

Library of Congress Control Number: 2015956505
ISBN: 978-1-882190-40-9
Cover photo by Dennis Nilsson
Cover design and author photo by Ramona du Houx
Manufactured on acid-free paper in more than one country.

Contents

Introduction

I f Saint Augustine were to walk through my doorway one day, what would I say to him? I have often pictured the scene. What would he look like, that North African? Like a Berber? My mental image of Berbers came from a picture magazine of my pre-World War II youth, glossies of our Foreign Legion fighting these fierce Muslim warriors in the Rif Mountains of Morocco: blond, blue-eyed "Berbers," resembling sunburned Bretons.

On the other hand, the first real Berber I ever met—he was a porter at the Limoges railroad station—looked nothing like them, mild not fierce, snub-nosed not hawk-beaked, and moon-faced, olive-complexioned, pudgy and black-haired, although mostly bald.

Or these other Maghrebians, who invest our country now—would Augustine resemble those Arabs? He was Tunisian, I believe, and—it goes without saying—at the time a Christian.

Yes, but for nine years he had also been a Manichaean, an archrival of the early Christ worshippers.

Still, despite that deviation, he finally answered his mother's prayers and joined the Roman Catholic Church. They made him the bishop of Hippo, notwithstanding he had fathered an illegitimate child. His fame as a clerical philosopher derived from his discovery—or shall I say *invention*—and propagandizing of the concept of "original sin."

We would certainly talk about such a dangerous notion, if he appeared.

And there he was! Saint Augustine had come to my unfortunate, martyred village, the place of my birth and upbringing, whose Romanesque *église* once bore his name but now remains a gutted ruin and part of a national monument. He had entered my remodeled fifteenth-century farmhouse, which lies just beyond the perimeter of Charniers-sur-Nys.

That my present abode was not reduced to a pile of rubble in June

1944 by the Boche was due to a Teutonic quirk, their finicky and often unimaginative penchant for correctness. I am now living just across a line of their field map that set off the hamlet of Bregonzac—not on the Waffen-SS's list to be obliterated, as was my poor Charniers.

I arose from my computer to greet this white-bearded guest.

He did not resemble a *beur*—which is our coarse slang for a swarthy North African. I once had an American "girlfriend," as the Yankees say. She taught me some colloquial English (we French would call it *américain*) and that *beur* corresponds to nigger—it has that much negative power.

"How would you translate *youpin?*" I remember asking her.

"Kike," she answered, and wrote it out for me and worked on my pronunciation. Her name was Nancy . . . She got me to say "Naansee," too, not "Nawnsee," like our city in Lorraine, with the same spelling of Nancy. She was a towhead blonde from Ohio, a student in Paris, while I was a professor there, and I often still think of her.

But I have digressed and am being rude as a host.

"Reverend Father," I don't know what else to call him—*mon cher saint* sounds awkward, "may I get you something? A coffee, perhaps?"

He regarded me uncomprehendingly. I had forgotten that his dates of 354–430 *Anno Domini* obviously preceded the popular drinking of this exotic beverage.

"Wine?" I then hastened to offer.

"I don't mind a glass," he said.

We dispensed with the question of red or white, and I served him a nice golden Sancerre.

He was dressed like a monk in a long-skirted, belted brown cassock. Who, I wondered, had told me wickedly in my youth that all priests were *pédés*, who took holy orders only so they could walk around in public in dresses? I flicked away such a naughty thought and remarked, "It's very nice of you to come, Reverend Father."

"You have questions for me, my son, do you not?" His voice was kindly and he spoke French without the trace of an accent.

Good Lord, what language did they speak in that part of North Africa before the Muslims? Numidian? Ancient Libyan? But Augustine had lived in Rome and Milan. Surely he knew street Latin. Since I'm the sole catalyst for this fantasy, should I not try it out on him in the Italianate tongue I studied for so many years in school or heard chanted on hundreds of Sundays throughout my boyhood? But why struggle with declensions? We will stick to *français*.

"*Oui ou non, Mon Père*, original sin is a monstrous doctrine?"

My brazenness did not extend to making this insulting utterance a categorical statement; it *was* put as a question.

"You are not sure," he replied adroitly.

His perception unnerved me. Had I been too rash? Would he get up and walk away?

Rather, he raised his glass, sipped and said: "This is an exquisite vintage."

I don't know why that sophisticated gesture made me angry. I knew he'd had a sybaritic past. But I'd been brought up to believe a saint should be a saint—sackcloth and ashes—not a suave habitué of the demimonde, and from Africa no less.

"Evil should not be inheritable," I said. "A silly woman's moment of weakness with a snake, a small fit of male disobedience, and we're all *foutu* forever. What kind of sadist is He who rules up in those heavens?"

"God is He who rules as the God of Love," was the vapid answer.

"*Merde*," I shot back. *Shit*, my Naansee had taught me was the equivalent in English. It seemed a very crass thing to say to a saint, I realized, but I was steaming. And thereupon the following tirade burst from me.

"You anger me, Father. Suppose I was a Manichaean, like once you were. The God of Love you're prattling about was to them a God of Evil. It was, as you know, their explanation for why evil existed in a world the Almighty supposedly advertised as good. How could evil exist if your Catholic God was as dominant and all-powerful as you insist. Your answer, to be sure, will be: 'It is simply the fault of those misbehaving humans in the Garden.' Generation after generation. To the end of time. Right? With your pernicious dogma, you jumped the Manichaean ship and became a well-rewarded hero to the Church of Rome. Will you dare to tell me my humble village of Charniers-sur-Nys and its innocent population had to be exterminated to prove your point?"

The saint, stone-faced, merely shrugged.

"And I suppose you're proud of the way your own Catholic Crusader bully-boys destroyed the Cathars," I fairly shouted at him.

His mask-like features above the flowing white beard unfroze. He looked perplexed. "Ca . . . what?" he asked.

"Latter-day Manichaeans," I responded. "Wiped out entirely eight hundred years after your death. In France and elsewhere in Europe totally massacred during the thirteenth century, the same as my poor martyred villagers here in 1944, slaughtered by Germans—although some of the SS killers were Alsatians, calling themselves Germans then, and now saying they're French."

"Heretics, I take it . . . how did you call them . . . Cathars?" Saint Augustine said airily.

"*Cathar* means pure," I answered him. "Some historians refer to them as Albigensians, because their religious reach went as far north as the city of Albi. Since they believed differently from the Church of Rome, it cost them their lives and property, to be cut in pieces by swords, skewered on pikes, burnt alive. Why should a God deemed good so abandon them?"

"God is the God of Love," he repeated stubbornly. "All can share His grace."

"*Certainement, Mon Père,*" I answered but argued: "The truth is your God didn't lift a finger to save the Cathars, nor to shield our humble, rural, devout Catholic folk here in the Limousin, minding our business during wartime, conservative to the core, nary a troublemaker among us."

Meanwhile, I contemplated adding a poignant detail from an exhibit the French government had constructed within the ruins beyond my door. It contained a child's severed hand, roasted a yellowy chocolate brown, the skin parchment-like, knuckles prominent, piteously small, presenting a reminder that the Germans not only burnt our women and children alive inside Saint Augustine Church, but blew up their charred remains with grenades afterward.

Meanwhile, Saint Augustine intoned, "If you believe in the God of Love, He will watch over you."

"You're joking, Father!" I exploded. "Take a walk through the ghoulish silence of our murdered village and see how well He cared for us, all believers in Him . . . The only one who did try to save us and lost his life doing so, for your information, was a . . . was a . . ."

"Yes," he demanded curtly.

"A Jew!" I screamed at him. "Imagine that. A Jew, no less."

He made a face. Then, a strange phenomenon suddenly happened. His features didn't exactly distort but rather imploded, melting one by one into nothingness. Remaining momentarily was a curled-lip smile. It vanished, too, as did the brown robe, the sandals he wore, the snowy beard fading last. I found myself alone in the peasant family room I had transformed into a sort of parlor, lined from wall to wall with books, which I called my study.

Of course I was alone and had been all along. I sat in my favorite leather armchair. There was another chair opposite me and a partly filled wine glass, indicating I'd been conversing with the ghost of a seminal superstar intellectual theologian of the fourth and fifth centuries.

To explain to myself and to you, I bent down and touched a contraption on the floor in front of my shoes. It was a tape machine. Pressing some buttons, I was able to rewind and play the dialogue just recorded.

You should have seen my head nod as if in tune to a rhythmic ethereal music. You should have seen the expression of glee on my face. It had worked, by God, it had worked! On the first try! The accent—St. Augustine's, I mean—was perfectly authentic, I thought. The amateur theatrical training I'd had in Paris many years ago had stood me in good stead for this experiment. I picked up the reel, stuck a blank label on it wrote "Saint Augustine" and the date. Fantasy had been turned into reality, although it was fantasy itself, this notion of interviews of the past as a way hopefully to exorcise the demons within me. Where might I go next, I wondered. After the success of tonight's trial run, I could proceed. It was no surprise to me whom I chose to appear next.

"Interview a Cathar!" I cried emphatically and heard the sound of my actual voice.

So I'd been talking to myself in both roles. No need to worry. Enough of the locals already think me mad, or at least eccentric.

"A Cathar leader," I added, still audible. "A woman, yes a woman! Esclarmonde de Foix! Voilà. PERFECT!" The irony of my spontaneous ending exclamation was immediately apparent. This noble lady was, indeed a "perfect," the title given to the highest clergy of her religion, *une parfaite*, in her case, *parfait* for males, since no distinction except grammatical existed between sexes in the Cathar priesthood. Esclarmonde was not only the equivalent of a Roman Catholic cardinal, but also revered ever since the thirteenth century as a martyred saint.

On the end table next to me was my own wine glass, from which I drank the rest of that glorious Sancerre, got up, drained the amount I'd poured for Saint Augustine, walked to a section of the bookcases, and paused before several shelves, dedicated to works about Gnosticism, Manichaeism, the tragic history of the Cathars in France, the Holy Grail legend, the Bogomils in Bulgaria, and other memoirs of the heretical, persecuted sect occurring at the same period in Italy, Catalonia, Spain, and Germany as well.

I read covers, picked several volumes, returned with them to my armchair and poured myself a fresh drink.

I

My apologies. It has occurred to me you don't even know my name. It is Desfosseux, *mon nom de famille*, and Eugène, *mon prénom*. I was named for my mother's father whom I never knew, killed in the trenches of the Great War, as it was known before we had to number our world wars. "Jalouneix, Eugène," read the engraving on the stone monument in the center of Charniers, an obelisk, perpetually draped with tricolor bunting of blue, white and red, and blown up by the Germans in their rampage a generation later.

I have a string of middle names, too, commemorating dead ancestors on either side. I'm only going to mention one, a name I truly hated— *Marie*—used in France for both girls and boys. There is an indelible memory I have of a group of maybe nine-year-old boys playing in the snow on an icy morning in Charniers (our village is high on the Massif Central and winters can be severe). Those other kids were farm boys, heavy-set, stupid-looking, and one of them began to tease me. Perhaps he had heard of my despicable middle name in church—I doubt it was in school since these kids didn't go to school much, if at all. "Marie! Marie!" this wise guy cried. "You're a girl. You're a girl." Incensed, I lunged blindly at him, knocked him down, rubbed his face in the snow, bloodied his nose, and he ran off crying. His companions just stood there dumbly. End of story. I never had any further trouble from those peasant lads, even becoming friendly with some of them in due course.

Not that I was a he-man, nor a Meaulnes, like the hero of the classic novel, *Le Grand Meaulnes*, an adolescent leader of epic stature. I wore glasses during early childhood to counteract a weakness of vision. I was gawky, scrawny, unlike my bull of a father, the mayor and regional physician who was all muscle. Worse probably, I was a "brain" at school. Years later in Paris, my Naansee introduced met me to an American slang expression of the period "queer bird," meaning an awkward, sissified fellow. But I was her "sweet darling queery bird," and thus my vocabulary was enhanced by a term for which there is no equivalent in French except possibly *pédé* (homosexual) and I was no pédé, I assure you.

But enough personal biography for now. Fortified by my research last night and during the morning and afternoon today, I am about to embark on my second experience in spectral history—a difficult test. I will attempt a woman's voice. Esclarmonde de Foix will be my interviewee. I have visited the small city of Foix, nestled in a valley in southern Languedoc at the foothills of the Pyrenees. The castle of her father Count Roger Bernard I of Foix continues to loom above the site. Incidentally, Languedoc means the "language of Oc"—referring to Occitan, a tongue with a lot of Spanish in it. In her native region, she was therefore *Esclarmonda de Fois*.

Translated, her *prénom* means "Light of the World," and she was also called *La Grande Esclarmonde*, and is clearly the most notable of the Cathars, whose memory has come down to us throughout the centuries. I also intend to interview the last surviving member of the Cathar clergy—Guillaume Bélibaste—called simply Bélibaste.

There are numerous likenesses of Esclarmonde de Foix, in paintings, in sculpture, in drawings, rendered by artists as they thought she should be portrayed. Many variations exist. One striking picture could have been an advertisement, showing a young woman, her amazing blue eyes boring into the viewer, her blonde hair in shoulder-length braids, a white dove cupped in her hands. Esclarmonde was also imagined with a single, long, black braid and a glittering crown on her black-haired head. In addition, she has been represented with ragged, reddish hair and brandishing a sword, as a full redhead with luxuriant, curly hair, as a blonde without braids, sultry as a movie star, and in a Joan of Arc style sculpture, where she wears a full-length fashionable gown and carries a spear. When the last major Cathar fortress, Montségur, fell to the Roman Catholic crusaders from the north in 1244, a white dove was noticed flying away from the smoldering ruins. Legend has it that this was Esclarmonde, having been dead for at least two decades, assuming the shape of a dove and carrying the Holy Grail to safety. Otto Rahn, a Cathar aficionado and also an officer of the Nazi SS in the 1930s, confirmed he'd been assured by Montségur shepherds with whom he'd talked that "a white dove escaped, and it was Esclarmonde de Foix." Yet another legend is that after having refused the blandishments to convert back to Catholicism by Saint Dominic, the founder of the Inquisition, she eluded men sent to kill her and "ascended into the sky in the shape of a dove."

Lest you think we are totally in fantasyland, she was indisputably a real woman, born in 1161 and sixty-four years old at the time of her death in 1215. When she was thirteen years old, she dedicated herself to the Cathar religion. Persecutions of Cathars by the Roman Church had already begun as early as 1143 in Germany, where a number of Cathars were put to the torch. By 1163, (little Esclarmonde was only two years old), a council led by Pope Alexander III met and decreed all Cathars were to be deprived of their possessions and worldly goods. On the heels of this action, the Third Lateran Council took place, again presided over by Pope Alexander III, who condemned "heresy" and approved the use of force against the Cathars. Esclarmonde de Foix was twenty years old in 1181, when the pope's Albigensian Crusaders attacked the Languedocian towns of Castres and Lavaur. Not yet an important leader in her chosen faith, which would have bound her to celibacy, she first married Jourdain de l'Isle Jourdain, and had four children by him. He died in 1200. Four years later, Esclarmonde became ordained in the Cathar priesthood, which accepted men and women on an equal basis.

Eh bien, the sun had set outside my windows, and the witching hour had begun, the same way it had the previous evening for my chat with Saint Augustine. The recording device was primed to start. I had turned on the electric lights in the study. Alas, no wine tonight. Cathars were, as Naansee would have said, teetotalers. The one thing missing was my leading lady.

But promptly Esclarmonde entered. So what did she look like? Blonde, yes, but close-cropped hair (no braids) turning silvery in patches. She could be, at this point, maybe fifty-five, maybe sixty years old, her ravishing good looks no longer fresh, yet not entirely lost to age. She had been the mother superior of a Cathar convent, yet she didn't appear forbidding. She wore the simple homespun gown of a poor female of her day, and she was carrying nothing, no dove, no spear, no sword.

"Ah, my dear lady, make yourself comfortable," I greeted her, and she sat opposite me after smoothing out the floor-length skirt of her simple dress, with eyes like twin sapphires.

A moment of tension, of excitement, followed. She opened her mouth to speak.

What if it just sounds like a high-pitched masculine me?

However, I had a model in mind. Our area of France still holds a smattering of aristocrats. In fact, above my humble abode rises the venerable ivy-covered château of the Counts of Bregonzac-Chastain. During my adolescence, the reigning Lord of the Manor was Count Charles François III whose august family dated back to the time of Charlemagne. He had a daughter my age, Chantal. A breathtaking beauty: what an unapproachable icon she was for a daydreaming schoolboy to worship from afar. I only saw her at Saint Augustine Church. She had perfect diction, an elegant sound, redolent of some high-class school for girls, smacking of Paris and snobbery and haughtiness until you got to know her.

Enough. My visitor spoke. At once I knew I had been successful, the Chantal-type tones feeling exactly right and feminine enough.

Esclarmonde's gestures were aristocratic, too, as she pointed to my bookcases and said, "I see you are a scholar."

I had to admit I blushed.

"A few of those books I wrote, myself," I volunteered, trying not to seem boastful. "My future plan is to write someday about your people, the Cathars."

"You must have questions for me?" she responded.

"Many," I said. "Foremost is—" I gave a little chuckle. "If you don't mind, did you . . . in reality . . . fly away from Montségur in the form of a white dove with . . ." again I hesitated due to a certain nervousness, "with . . . er . . . the Holy Grail . . . to keep it from the Crusaders?"

She answered primly, "Old wives' tales never go out of fashion."

"Is that a yes or a no?" I asked.

"More toward a no," she replied—then flashed a grin, a ladylike smile, somewhat mischievous and beguiling even at her years. "But I have my image to protect."

"Let's talk about Montségur," I went on. "My understanding is that you organized and led the effort to fortify the Château de Montségur."

"Correct, Monsieur. Also with the help of the de Pereille family, well known as adherents to our holy religion."

I replied: "When I was much younger, I went to Montségur. I climbed up alone on the path to the top. It was so scarily steep. Once at the ruins of the fortress, I couldn't imagine how the heavily armored soldiers of Simon de Montfort could climb that veritable crag, never mind conquer such a towering, well-placed, well-defended position. Up there, you can well imagine someone flying off into the sky, so breathtaking is the view of the adjacent mountains."

"There is also a meadow running down one side, a grassy slope," offered Esclarmonde. "You know about the meadow, don't you?"

Those blazing azure eyes fixed on me. It was impossible not to notice pain in them.

"That's where the monument is," I volunteered.

"That's where the bonfires were," added Esclarmonde. "My people marched singing into them until they were turned to ashes."

Not only did this gracious lady break into song the next moment, a hymn of defiance, but she did something else—she became a conjurer. I could hardly believe my eyes. One wall of the renovated room we were in had been left free of books, its plaster white as a movie screen. Which was what she used it for, while her gaze turned, as it were, into a projector.

The scene came alive. The mighty bastion of Montségur had fallen. Down the precipitous incline from the stony grey peak streamed sword-waving Catholic Crusaders, scarlet crosses on their shields and tunics, guarding a roped line of prisoners, men, women, and children, mouths opening and closing, who kept singing even after they caught sight of the first pyres that had been set alight.

There was no background music, simply the motion-picture-like image.

Ten seconds, twenty seconds—as long as she stared, the effect remained: black smoke rising, flames engulfing the initial batch of victims. Once she turned her head finally to regard me, the horror of cheering killers and roasting martyrs diminished and died out.

"There were three hundred and twenty who refused to abjure," Esclarmonde boasted.

"Interesting," I commented. "Our numbers of those burnt to a crisp—the women and children here—were about the same. And among the men . . ." I hesitated. How could I explain machine gunning to her? "Wounded men were covered with straw and set afire," I added.

"Your numbers, did you say?" she asked.

"All told, more than six hundred dead. Didn't you notice the charred church, the shattered stone walls of old barns and houses, the gutted buildings, nearby on your route here?" I replied.

She shook her head but a pout showed on her lips. "So atrocities are happening now, too!" A flash of anger accompanied her indignation. "The Pope of Rome never gives an inch."

"No, not precisely," I hastened to say. "It wasn't Catholics killing heretics."

With what I would call an aristocratic snort, Esclarmonde absorbed my bit of information, as if she were about to say, *Imagine!*

I quickly responded. "We were offered no alternative. The Germans came to kill us deliberately. No innocent civilian from our innocent town was to escape death."

"They wouldn't at least allow you to abjure. How barbaric!"

"We were singled out to be doomed."

"But *you* are here."

"I escaped. Thanks to a friend—" I cleared my throat. "He was a Jew."

"I knew Jews," was her response. "They were called heretics like us. Sometimes, too, they were burned, unless they would bow down to Rome. Stubborn people, though."

"God's chosen, they claim."

"The God we Cathars see as evil," was her response. "Otherwise, how do you explain the persistence of evil in the world?"

While we were talking, I kept eyeing the bare wall on which she had projected her images. It had gone blank again. I kept wondering if I could do the same thing—gape and illustrate our horrors in Charniers-sur-Nys.

Consequently, I asked what secret she had used, saying I'd like to show our story to her.

"Simple," she said. "Concentrate. Then blink."

I did as she told me. In my case, it was not wholly unlike turning on a television set. The shiny whitewashed surface turned grainy. But the next moment, expecting a scene of the Church of Saint Augustine in flames, disgorging oily smoke, I was shocked. Portrayed in color against a blood-red backdrop was a large black swastika.

"I know the hooked cross!" she exclaimed. "It's from India. Were you attacked by those dark people?"

"No, by these light-skinned murderers," I retorted. Without realizing what an enormous strain it was for me, I conjured an action picture of the camouflaged Waffen SS trucks and armored vehicles entering Charniers-sur-Nys.

Thoroughly exhausted, I relaxed my intensity and the wall screen went blank again.

"Are you feeling all right?" Esclarmonde demanded. "You seem out of breath. I have experience in caring for the sick, you know."

"I'll be fine," I said. Candidly, I was surprised she hadn't vanished, already. If my encounter with Saint Augustine was any indication, she should be gone at any minute.

Reading my mind, Esclarmonde inquired: "Do we have anything else to talk about?"

Really I had decided I didn't want her to go. Rather desperately, I sputtered: "Domingo . . . Domingo Guzman. You debated him."

"A wily, unscrupulous cruel Spaniard," she said. "The pope made him a saint—Saint Dominic."

"I understand you were sensational when you disputed the saint on religion at Pamiers."

"I was no docile nun."

"He must have been stunned by your performance."

"One of his henchman had the nerve to yell at me while I was arguing with him: 'Go back to your spinning, Madame. It is not proper for you to speak in a debate of this sort.'"

"And your response?"

"I yelled back at him: 'Shut up, you *criminal*.'"

"Touché," I cried. "Bravo!" What a fetching grin I received. She made a little la, la musical noise in her throat.

I said: "While you're here, I have another question. It's about Guillaume Bélibaste. You know who I mean?" She nodded, rather grimly I sensed. "A few writers have called him 'the last of the Cathars.' Most say he's 'the last of the Parfaits.' Which is correct?"

"The latter," answered Esclarmonde. "But be careful with him. He was not an ideal example of a Parfait."

In truth, my intention had been to *interview* Bélibaste this very evening along with Esclarmonde de Foix.

That impulse had died, however. Tomorrow night would have to do. I needed a respite. Ironically, the instant I had that thought, Esclarmonde's image commenced unpeeling, vanishing quickly, just as Saint Augustine's had.

Slumped in my armchair, I closed my eyes. When I opened them a few minutes later, surprise! Perched on the chair that Esclarmonde had vacated was a perky white dove, examining me with its bright button black eyes.

"That's you, isn't it, Madame Esclarmonde!" I exclaimed.

For an answer, I received a musical cooing, using the notes of her la, la trill.

The song, if that's what it was, lasted about thirty seconds. Those wings of the dove lifted and the pure white of the handsome bird body was instantly airborne, flying toward the wall that had served as a projection screen, merging right into it, and disappearing like the last frames of a film.

Sinking once more into the leather padding, I rested long enough until I felt like arising. But before I headed to my bedroom, I walked over to inspect the bare wall. No feathers. No splat. No sign of anything. Silly me. I actually detoured to my front door, opened it and tried to discern a white spot in the sky. The familiar shadows, the smell of night, the crenellated ivy-covered towers of the Château de Bregonzac-Chastain against the darkened sky—all these sensations greeted me. For the minutes I stood outside, sniffing the dampness, the immediate déjà vu of memory shifted to the many times I had waited on the stoop for my faithful black poodle Jacques to return from doing his "business." Poor doggy. There was a marked grave in the fruit tree orchard where I had buried him in back of the house. Mercifully, he'd died of natural causes, unlike most of the previous human inhabitants around here.

II

At least once every day, if I can, I take a solitary walk through the preserved ruins of the community where I grew up. In former times, I would always bring Jacques with me on his leash. Poodles are a nervous, high-strung breed, German in origin, but achieving fame as the "French poodle." *Somewhat like Alsatians*, I often thought, except my curly black-haired pet had all the earmarks of an expensive French canine, somewhat dandified yet genuinely good-natured and friendly. As I trudged today without him at eventide, I no longer had any spring in my step. Indeed, I shuffled, using a cane, a lonely, aged, white-mustached male, entirely absorbed in his memories. By this hour, few if any tourists were still wandering about the mounds of rubble amid the silence of former streets and houses. The busloads had left. Thus would I stand by the broken World War I memorial in the town square and gaze all around. Visions would prick my brain, causing my mind to configure the structures in every direction and who had lived in them.

Our family house was located on the rim of the "marketplace," so-called because once a week a market day had been held there since the time of the Romans. Otherwise, it was a simply a center of the rural community with a traffic island in the middle upon which the local officials in 1919 had erected the World War I monument. Automobiles, quite rare during my boyhood, would carefully navigate their way around the circle and disappear into one of the several side streets that poured in like streams disgorging into a river. As a kid, I loved to watch these shiny machines from an upper window, that of my bedroom, which faced the square.

The Desfosseux home was a two story edifice in French Provincial style, with ten rooms, having been bought by my parents in the expectation that the young doctor and his bride would produce a large brood. Alas, my mother's illness precluded anyone but me. After her death, we remained in the big house, Papa, myself, a housekeeper, and a procession of dogs (not poodles but mongrels) that my father, I sometimes felt, seemed to like better than his only child. Papa *was* gruff, but this mannerism concealed a kindlier side. He would openly weep when he lost a patient he thought he could save. The decease of a pet would visibly sadden him.

Papa was also a bit of a jokester. He called our place *Maison Crapaud*—Toad House—since he insisted he'd been born atop a peak in the Vendéennes Hills, the Puy de Crapaud, instead of at Pouzauges, the major municipality in that region of the rugged Vendée, where he actually had seen the light of day. "Am I not a toad?" he would ask sarcastically whenever I tried to get him to rectify his fib. He would puff up his cheeks and under the illumination in his office reveal a pockmarked complexion, the result of some childhood disease. He made noises like a toad, so droll that I could not help laughing. Ever since, I'd convinced myself that my ability to mimic had been directly inherited from him. Strangely enough, he never had tried to hide his skin disfigurement with a beard. A handsome bushy dramatic dark mustache served him just as well. He would frighten cranky children by taking off his glasses and staring at them through his beady deep brown, almost blackish, eyes. Only then, after their whimpering ceased, would he start making toad noises, sending them convulsing into giggling hilarity.

The sun was starting to set this evening. What do you call it—*crépuscule*—twilight? It was generally at these hours I took my lonely strolls, accompanied now only by my faithful cane, clumping along slowly until I reached the heart of the ex-town. From there, I would summon a visual resurrection of my actual birthplace. In my mind, the bourgeois dwelling was draped by the back-lighting of the end of day, deepening reds and gilded glows behind the stately roof. Its blue-black slate shingles reflected its owner's wealth and high social standing rather than submission to the pedestrian orange tubular tiles of all the other housetops in sight. The closest complementing show of architectural richness was exhibited on the towers of the Count de Bregonzac's château. Papa most likely was consciously or unconsciously emulating him.

As always, our home the way it flashed onto my mental screen, stayed long enough for me to see the side entrance on the left, used for Papa's patients, and the ell on the right he had had built to serve as the *mairie*, the town hall, once he'd been elected *maire*, upon achieving the earliest of a long line of victories. Gone soon, like the visions in my study, the familiar stone walls dissolved. I would find myself gaping at gaunt, shattered sections of scorched rubble, still left upright after the raging fire and phosphorous grenade explosions.

Tonight, I lingered a few minutes longer since a particular thought had come to me. Not for the first time at the scene of such wanton destruction, the words "general massacre" had popped into my mind. From there it went to a memory of Papa's telling stories of the Royalist rebellion of the Vendée against the armies of the French Revolution. The "massacre at Pouzauges," not much remembered now, occurred in 1793. Some authors say, like Papa, that four hundred women and children were burnt alive. Men were shot, too, by firing squads of the "infernal column," a force of *les bleus* dispatched by the triumphant anti-Monarchist government in Paris. The Royalists, *les blancs*, centered their failed counter-revolution on the Vendée. French killing French again more than three centuries after the slaughter of the Cathars.

It was growing darker. There were no street lights in the ruins but I could still have walked home like a blind man. My house was fifteen minutes away. But what quickened my cane-assisted pace this early evening was excitement, not trying to outrun the shadows.

Guillaume Bélibaste is coming! I exclaimed to myself. I could hardly wait to meet him. In fact, I hastily gulped down the supper prepared for me before rushing to my study.

It took a while for Guillaume to appear. I could tell solely by looking at his rough-hewn, towering frame (two meters tall at least), red face, jutting jaw, that he was a cantankerous individual. I had to remind myself he was the last of the Parfaits, the upper priesthood, the sainthood, so to speak, of the Cathar religion.

He was dressed like a fourteenth-century shepherd. That is, he had disguised himself as a shepherd when he had had to flee precipitously from France into Spain. Or so the story went. There had been a brawl. Bélibaste had killed his opponent, a bona fide shepherd by the name of Barthelemy Garnier, a native of the town of Villerouge-Thermenes in the wild Corbières Mountains (the site incidentally where Bélibaste was later immolated by the Inquisition in 1321). This guest of mine tonight projected the air of a ruffian, but had actually been born to a rich peasant family in the nearby village of Cubières.

My initial question to him was a stinger. "Is it true that you were once in the act of fornication with your mistress Raymonde, when you were interrupted and shouted at the intruder: 'You bastard! You have just disturbed the work of the Holy Church!'"

His answer: "Everything told about me is true," A sly smile then materialized and he added: "Or isn't."

Enigmatic fellow, I thought to myself. *A trickster maybe.* Speaking to his puzzling response, I quickly asked: "Did you kill that shepherd with a dagger or pummel him to death with your fists?"

They were large, raw-boned, powerful fists, I had noticed.

He suddenly stood up and exclaimed: "What is this, an Inquisition! And in that case, Monsieur, they tortured me first."

"All right, sit back down," I told him. "I concede you hate being probed. What did you wish to say to me, if anything?"

He didn't sit down but simply declaimed like a Roman orator. Conceivably his earliest relative in France had been a Roman soldier.

Initially, I endured a long diatribe delivered by him as he restlessly paced back and forth in front of me. "They pretended to be servants of God," he started off. "Those damnable Roman Catholics, spawns of the devil, the priests and especially the grinning monkeys, the bishops, who had me executed so painfully. I can feel your question coming. *How is it you're not simply a mass of charcoal?* My dear Monsieur, let me point out that we Cathars, from the lowest to the highest, were made exclusively of spirit, although we can assume human form at will. Our God is spirit, all spirit. He dwells at the top of the heavens and watches over us, but never intervenes. The world is inhabited by the scum that massacred us. Fallen angels, led by the monster Satan, framed the universe and populated it with people of their own kind, vile, evil, money-grubbing cold-blooded murderers, thieves, full of hypocrisy, untrustworthy . . . Take Arnaud Sicre, the swine who betrayed me to the Inquisition. A man I'd befriended. He persuaded me to return to France from Spain, telling me an old woman I knew was dying, had requested the last rites, the *consolamentum*, our most sacred prayer, and I was the only one who could administer it because I was the only Parfait remaining. Did their God punish this lying piece of *merde?* No, his misdeeds made him rich. I was the end of the line of the *bonshommes* who set an example of peace and purity to our followers. However, four demons ruled in Languedoc. I curse them one by one. King Philip IV of France, Jacques Fournier, the bishop of Pamiers, Pope Boniface, and Bernard Gui, a vicious interrogator. May they all drown in their own urine. I defecate on their souls. For centuries more, let them twist and turn in their agony. How about a hot poker up their rectums? I'd be glad to provide one." At length he came to the final remark of his tirade. Sounding like a gurgle, he said: "I could easily strangle such beasts with my bare fingers."

I bade him sit down again, which he did. Between us, there was a passage of silence for maybe two minutes.

I cleared my throat. "You seem like an educated man," I told him, "but very, very angry."

"Wouldn't you be?"

His snappy answer irritated me somehow. "What do you think?" I snapped back. "You Cathars are the only ones who suffered? There are crimes that have nothing to do with religious persecution."

"You are a Roman Catholic, I believe,"

"No longer," I answered.

With that exchange, I felt we both were striving for a rapport, a brotherhood of victims. His hardened defensive manner seemed less aggressive. In our further discussions, we could say things to each other in a more affable fashion. I even dared to bring up his sex life again and the rumored charge of adultery against him.

He merely laughed. "Rumor!" he snorted. "Contrived is more like it. *Un ménage a trois.*" Suddenly he slapped his knee and literally giggled. "Adultery? With my beautiful Raymonde, who I got pregnant. Then, I persuaded my closest friend, Pierre Maury, to marry her so the child would have a name. After the birth, Raymonde and I resumed our liaisons. Technically, this was now adultery . . . That is how the tale was told." He looked positively gleeful. "Remember," he said, "everything written about me has been the work of my enemies."

His fierce green eyes abruptly flashed, as if he had spotted something I couldn't see.

Previously, I had often wondered if I *could* handle two interviewees at once. Even mix up figures from different periods of history. Believe me, the last specter I ever anticipated attracting was the blondish young man who now materialized alongside Guillaume Bélibaste. This fellow was dressed as a Nazi officer in a black SS uniform, swastika armband, runic insignia, silver hafted dagger, black leather-holstered pistol, death's head, etc. Had such a mirage come from my own subconscious?

Bélibaste seemed as surprised as I was. "Who the Christ are you?" he demanded of the intruder in his coarse peasant manner.

"Rahn, *Obersturmführer* Otto Wilhelm Rahn," the sensitive-looking, pink-skinned German introduced himself, clicking his heels. "I am the author of a noted book about the Cathars, whose title is: *The Crusade Against the Grail.* And another work *Lucifer's* . . ."

"Utter nonsense," Bélibaste cut off the Nazi.

Otto Rahn stiffened. I noticed his hand reaching for the hilt of his ceremonial dagger.

Bélibaste spied this movement, too. He carried a dagger with him also. I saw his hand slipping inside his shepherd's cloak for it.

Suddenly, our Nazi lieutenant relaxed his facial muscles, smiled ingratiatingly and waited for the tension to ease. "Monsieur Desfosseux—" Again he addressed only me. "I believe you have read *The Crusade Against The Grail*, if not *Lucifer's Court*, as well. I feel you know my story. How Heinrich Himmler, himself, sent me to Montségur in 1937 to locate the Grail." His French was excellent, revealing barely the faintest trace of accent.

Left out of the conversation, Bélibaste groused impolitely, as if talking to himself, but likewise to me, muttering: "Why listen to this pédé in his fancy get-up?"

An obvious cloud of puzzlement darkened Otto Rahn's feature. "Pédé? What is pédé? Is it French?"

"*Pédéraste*," I answered.

Instead of acting insulted, the German seemed amused. "Yes, I was accused of that deviation," he said, talking to both of us. "For punishment, because of an alleged incident, my superiors made me do guard duty at concentration camps—Dachau and Buchenwald—gruesome places. But I assure you fellows, I became married to a fine beautiful woman before my death."

"Your death," I interjected, "A mystery never totally explained."

"The usual tale is I committed suicide, purposely freezing myself by lying exposed on a glacier in Austria, in the style of the Cathars—" Rahn nodded to Bélibaste—"which you know as the *endura*."

Bélibaste nodded back, his hostility seemingly diluted.

"Another version," I offered, "was that you, yourself, ended in a concentration camp and were beheaded there."

The Nazi laughed. "Do you see me carrying around my head under my arm?"

Bélibaste laughed, too.

Hiding the fact I was a bit miffed at their joking, I declared: "My understanding was you made a fuss and complained the SS censors had inserted anti-Semitic material into your *Lucifer's Court* publication. As a result, Himmler went after you."

"Bosh," he said.

"Nice pistol," I finally commented, indicating the handsome leather holster on his belt. "It's a Luger inside, isn't it?" I recognized the handle and the shape.

"We SS officers have to wear such weapons at all times."

"Did you ever encounter Sturmbannführer Horst Heinrich Durchmann of the Waffen SS?" I asked. "He commanded the company that destroyed our village."

"I was in the Allgemine SS," Rahn answered. The Waffen SS was the military branch. Durchmann and I would not have known each other."

"The name Lammerding—does it mean anything to you? A Division Commander."

"Sorry," said our Nazi visitor, still on his feet due to the fact of no chair for him.

And a moment later, he wasn't there, anyway, breaking up without warning, dissolving.

Guillaume Bélibaste hadn't departed. How much longer would he stay seated opposite? But seeing him about to rise, I cried: "Wait. If you're going, I have a final question."

On his feet, he lingered.

"We were talking about anti-Semitism," I quickly said to him. "Is it true you once announced the Jews had the worst faith because the Devil gave them the law in the form of a cow or a calf, perhaps the Golden Calf."

"Words to that effect."

"Were you an anti-Semite?"

"Yes, I suppose so."

"Me, too," I told him. "When I was quite young, eleven or twelve years old, thanks to hearing my father rage about certain of them."

"At least the Jews didn't burn me," he replied.

"Good point."

But there was no response because Guillaume Bélibaste was on the verge of coming apart. The rough character in the medieval shepherd's outfit left one last thought behind before he faded entirely. "Remember Satan and Lucifer, the tweedledum and tweedledee of evil, make the world go round," he shouted, "and it is ever thus."

III

It's time for me to take a break from my self-engendered theatrics. I feel I need to fill you in much more about me, my late family, my late surroundings, my curriculum vitae, etc. This exercise will not necessarily be chronological and will make room for additional episodes of the historical re-creations you have just witnessed.

Right now, I am back in the kitchen. You will remember I paused there earlier, gobbling the meal—featuring an ordinarily appreciated tasty *pot-au-feu*—left in my oven by Arlette Arnaud, a young married woman, mother of two children, who lives with her clod of an alcoholic husband in the New Charniers. Ever the didactic historian, let me explain that after the massacre of June 1944, General Charles de Gaulle and the postwar government he installed in Paris decreed the old Charniers-sur-Nys would remain exactly as the Waffen SS had left it—a blackened ruin. The charred, torn bodies were buried and consecrated, the mountains of debris tidied up to an extent, a makeshift museum erected full of exhibitable artifacts of this perpetuated war crime and signs exhorting visitors familiarly to *Souviens-toi*—Remember.

Not far away, abandoned farm acreage was converted at national expense into another Charniers—not exactly a replica, since it was all modern concrete construction. Survivors and close relatives of victims were offered homes at no cost. I declined to accept one, and not solely because I had determined to live in Paris. I was being sentimental. The feel of the substitute village wasn't right.

Consequently, once I retired from my career of Professor of French History at a branch of the Sorbonne, I gravitated to Bregonzac, the tiny hamlet next door to Charniers, spared by the Boche, which had kept its ambience of the old-world Limousin.

Finding that the Phillipon family farmstead was up for sale, I purchased the property. The Phillipons had for centuries been tenants of the counts of Bregonzac-Chastain, from whom in the nineteenth century they bought for themselves the plot of land and an age-old neglected building on it. At any rate, I had modern improvements made to the rundown house and attendant sheds, converted the attached barn into a garage for my automobile, and at last moved in permanently.

All right, a word about Arlette Arnaud—whom you might say is my housekeeper and cook. Her grandmother was the famous Madame Blanchard—famed locally, that is—particularly for her cooking skills. She worked for my father, lived in our household and was like a second—if not first—mother to me. My own *maman*, always sickly, died when I was nine years old. That wonderful Blanchard woman, loved by everyone in Charniers-sur-Nys, perished in the Nazi onslaught here. Her own children had moved elsewhere in France and did not share her fate. After the war, Arlette, alone, of the third generation returned to Charniers and I hired her. Three times a day, she fixes meals for me while once a week she cleans my quarters.

The perennial bachelor I'd always been (except for the years with Naansee) suited me fine. Financially, I now had a decent pension, but much more substantially, being an only child, I was sole heir to my medical doctor father's not insignificant wealth. Unlike my paternal Vendéen forebears, I didn't hide my nest egg under a mattress but invested it with professional advice. Whenever the needs of my work struck or if I yearned for a change of scenery, I traveled. At one time or another, I've visited every continent except the two poles. However cosmopolitan, though, I could not escape my past. My memories always drew me back, pondering deeply what had happened to us in France and to the world. I ceased writing the academic books that had won me neither fame nor fortune and only a small amount of pin money in royalties. Still I never wanted to stop expressing myself about—to quote André Malraux, a favorite author of mine—*La Condition humaine*—*Man's Fate*.

Even before I went to Paris and lived in the Quartier Latin, I knew I had a talent for mimicry. There, I even went on stage, throwing my voice to a dummy like a ventriloquist. Thanks to vivacious Naansee, I ended up among a group of her ex-pat American actor and actress friends in amateur productions, mostly in English (improving my use of that language exponentially) and occasionally in French. In the latter case, I most often played a major character and my acting ability was not without its strengths, I was told.

Photos of my childhood and youth all went up in flames when the SS set torches to our household. All my school papers, all my books, all my letters—puff, gone in smoke and fire. The same for pictorial and other memoirs of Papa and Maman. Accordingly, on occasions when I gaze into the mirrors in my bathroom and bedroom these days, I hunt for signs of how I must have looked and how changed I am now.

If you stood behind me before the looking glass in this twilight of my life, you would observe a thin old fellow, always well-shaved, but who left room for a now-white mustache that he tended like a beloved plant. I am long-jawed, a trait inherited from the Jalouneixs on my mother's side. Like her, my original hair before it turned old and skimpy, could be called—and was—"straw-colored." I stand not quite two meters tall. My eyes are murky hazel. They were always weak and requiring thick spectacles until I matured. I never had much of a chin, and the aquiline nose I sported the family dubbed "Roman." Because currently I bend a lot over my faithful cane, it can also be confessed that my posture was always slump-shouldered. Luckily, I've never had much of a protruding belly. Papa made sure my teeth were good, thanks to his friendship with dentists in Limoges. Of athletic ability, I had very little, except I could run fast and I'm proud to say never ducked a fight, whether with fists or, in the war years, guns.

Wiry, I guess you'd call me "wiry"—*dry and nervous.*

The following morning, I slept late. Arlette had silently left me a breakfast of croissants, cheese, *confiture*, and coffee. Included, too, was my Americanized habit (even pre-Naansee) of *jus d'orange*—orange juice. Quite without thinking, I wandered into my study after putting my dishes in the sink. No sign of last night's adventure, no folding chair, no recording apparatus.

Settled into my comfy armchair, what did I do for the next ten minutes but stare fiercely at the blank wall on which the imagined picture show had played the evening before?

I began experimenting. I stared hard at the space left blank. I wanted to re-create Papa. I awaited his hulking, pock-marked, slightly neanderthalic figure with his flaunting, flamboyant dark mustache. Nothing happened, alas. The section of wall remained utterly bare.

A pertinent question would have been why had that area been left open? The answer I must admit is a bit *compliquée.* I had had a crazy idea. A prized possession of Monsieur le Docteur Desfosseux had been a set of colorful prints that had decorated his private office in the clinic at our home. After World War I, during which Papa had served in the medical corps, he'd done a year of postgraduate medical work in Alsace, in Strasbourg, since France had regained its lost province. These lithographic illustrations had been bought there by him. They depicted incidents of the Franco-Prussian War of 1870. How often he lectured me about that previous French military *débâcle*. But he adored the picturesque cavalry in their dashing uniforms, the smiling Alsatian peasant women bringing bread to French troops, the unsuccessful generals in their braided kepis surveying the results of Prussian bombardments, etc. Thus my desire to devote one wall of my renovated study to hanging his favorite mementos. But naturally they'd been destroyed in June 1944. I thought surely I could buy copies at the kiosks on the quays of Paris. I never found them, but always hopeful I kept the space in readiness.

Hence, *voici*, another trait of mine: an unseen gritty stubbornness.

In fact, this morning, I tried several times in vain to summon a moving picture recording of Papa I had formed in my mind: Papa with his black medical bag on a house call; Papa wearing his mayor's blue, white and red sash of office presiding at an event; Papa drinking marc brandy with his cronies at the village bistro . . . But the screen stayed obstinately empty.

Discouraged, I opted to go for a stroll.

Rather, I suddenly longed for fresh air, for Nature, and where else could I find it close by within walking distance but on our lovely river, the Nys.

Its stream of absolutely unspoiled water was cold, fast-running, and, in deep swirling pools, full of wild rainbow trout. Ever since I was old enough to hold a *canne à pêche*, I began casting and catching my share. More often than not, I was able to supply our entire household, Papa, myself, Madame Blanchard, Emil, the gardener, and occasional dinner guests with delicious repasts. Those memories of the firm pinkish ultra-fresh trout flesh and the delectable sauces Madame Blanchard provided can still make my mouth salivate.

The Nys runs north and south on the eastern edge of Charniers. Two stone bridges connect the two parts of the village. In the distant past, the smaller portion had had peasant homes and farms in it, but since the early nineteenth century they have been replaced by untended forest and brush. It was this far side that had the best angling under a canopy of total green. In the summer, after the annual spring run-off, eddies formed around the bridge foundations and we boys jumped from those moss-stained structures into the depths they had created. Our favorite plunge was from the Pont Neuf, the New Bridge, the southernmost of the two sites. As you might expect, the "New" Bridge was at least five hundred years old. The "Old" Bridge, the Pont Vieux was, indeed, more aged yet, by about two hundred and fifty years.

One question perhaps teasing you is: why didn't the Germans destroy these venerable bridges as they blasted or burned every other human-built construction in the town? The simple answer is: I don't know, nor do I expect we'll ever find out. We have proof, though, that they posted sentinels along the river. After these left, a young woman's corpse was found in the water, riddled with rifle bullets, unburned, one of the few non-singed victims among our martyrs. She was Paulette Malinvaux, a pal since elementary school . . . sweet, harmless, affectionate Paulette, a little bit of a thing, the first girl I ever kissed. Since her body had caught on a snag, we were able to retrieve her remains and bury her with friends, relatives, and a few lovers to boot.

One of the reasons I had for some time restricted my strolls through the ruins to the later hours of the day was the increased influx of tourist traffic to Charniers-sur-Nys—mostly busloads that would depart by the afternoon. While I appreciated the interest of other French people and even foreigners including Germans in our martyrs, it almost seemed to me subjectively that these wandering crowds were dancing on my coffin. Or distracting my memories when I clomped alongside what to them simply constituted past history—over and done with, cleansed of personalities, sterile, albeit horrifying in its impact. They hadn't lived in that devastated town. They had no idea how it had really been.

On this particular midmorning, it wasn't so bad. More likely, too, I experienced a sense of concentration that allowed me to ignore the figures walking around and so by the time I reached the former key center, the *Champ de Foire*, Fairground, I could envision the old Charniers of the 1930s coming alive.

Even in the bourgeois quarter of town, the *fumiers*, the manure piles, were once again at various street locations, abuzz with flies. Farmers led oxen past our big house. The excitement I saw was of people thronged with their baskets and bundles on market day. These were mostly women, while the men crowded around the *alembic*, a portable still, to which they brought their rotted fruit to have it distilled into *marc*, a fiery but cheap eau-de-vie liqueur in several flavors that my papa loved. I approached the ramshackle Malinvaux abode, sheltering ten children, poor as church mice. Paulette was sitting on the broken front steps, looking wistful and amorous. I waved; she waved back with a grateful smile. A short distance farther on, I stopped before Saint Augustine Church. Experts had called it "the perfect example of the Romanesque style." It occupied somewhat higher ground atop a hillock. A belfry, jutting from the orange tiled roof, although of Gothic design, gave the grey stone massive, thick walled building a further sense of supplicating for its parishioners. The Romanesque features were, above all, the curved arches, the curved windows, the rounded shape of the turrets and a recessed carving, Christ on the Cross, filling a triangular lintel outside its heavy wooden doors of Limousin oak. So sturdy a structure was Saint Augustine's that most of it, the collapsed roof and bell tower an exception, still stands despite the Nazis' frantic attempts to demolish the place.

In the past, whenever I passed by the fourteenth century structure, I would, out of childhood habit, make the sign of a cross. These days, I no longer did, but since the church was a living memorial to the Charniers-sur-Nys murder victims, I always allowed myself an inner bow of respect as I approached the site.

Wait! Those doors are opening. It is a Sunday and the end of morning Mass. The worshippers are departing in bunches. I always sit (and/or kneel) in a back pew nearest the exit. Thus, I am already out in the fresh air when certain of *mes copains*—my buddies—join me. We are an unruly group, cracking jokes, referring to the women in mourning, dressed from head to toe in funereal black, as "crows" or "nuns." We are beginning to experience the pangs of attraction to the opposite sex. We are convulsing ourselves with stupid remarks and jejune laughter. Last out from their exclusive box down front is the Count Charles de Bregonzac-Chastain and his beauteous daughter Chantal. There is, too, the bratty younger brother, also Charles. *Les grands huiles*, as the French say, "the big oils." Accompanying the count is the new priest, Father Hibert, and the two of them are conversing. Chantal and her sibling are a few steps behind. As she approaches, I say to myself: *Oh, God, if she looks at me, I'll die!* And a moment later, I think: *Oh, God, if she doesn't look, I'll die.*

Chantal did neither. As she came abreast of me, she was having an altercation with the little boy beside her. What an adorable girl, with her shoulder-length chestnut hair, her pale blue eyes, the touch of first lipstick, and she was wearing silk stockings! I noticed her fetching attire, the Scottish-plaid skirt, the frilly white blouse, her dark velvet jacket. The aristocratic party was headed toward a parked, black Citroen touring limousine and its attendant chauffeur in uniform. The count, while taking his leave of the priest, shot a frowning glance back at his still-warring children and they immediately fell silent.

Count Charles was a majestic man, although quite bald. His face was ruddy, his posture erect, his bearing that of a king. I knew he had been an officer in Indo-China, fighting Native rebels and in French Equatorial Africa, as well. A male adolescent's hero, needless to add.

Back in the present momentarily with the ruins all around me, I wondered amid the tomb-like quiet: *Why not choose to do Chantal tonight?*

Equally mum, I rejected the idea. *Not yet*, I reasoned. Although I had her voice down pat, there were other considerations. Returning to the long-ago Sunday in my mind, I believe I was thirteen years old. The trolley car—did I mention we had an electric trolley connecting Charniers with Limoges? Crowds thronged from the city on weekends, determined to enjoy *an outing in the country*. With much clanking, the vehicle went back and forth starting from the earliest morning hour. Ahead, I soon can make out the near-distant riverbank and its park on the far side in which families spread out their picnics, men fished, children raced about, women gossiped and lovers sauntered hand-in-hand. Before I attain my goal, which is to sit on a certain stone balustrade of one of the bridges and contemplate the world, other visions attract me. I am now about to pass the Hôtel Mayon, whose open terrace is jammed pack with holidayers. This was the only eatery and hostel in the region, and rightly famous for its trout. The owner, roly-poly Monsieur Fernande Mayon will be noted circulating among the diners, shaking hands and exchanging pleasantries. His collection of wines was, as the adults said, *impeccable*. We kids never failed to elicit a laugh among us when we called the enterprise Hôtel Mayonnaise.

Before long, I observed the Pont Neuf and headed for the perch where I intended to sit. Surprise, shock, I have the image of a familiar red-headed figure in front of me, proceeding briskly in the same direction. I know where he's headed and who he is—Jean-Luc Mueller— going precisely to the spot where he and I had sat side by side for hours, deepening our friendship with fascinating talk.

He was an Alsatian my age and had arrived in Charniers in the fall of 1939. We had two whole busloads of kids from Alsace, sent by the French government out of the war zone that our northeastern-most province had become on the heels of the German invasion of Poland.

I don't intend to dwell here on the irony of accepting Alsatian refugees in our town and the role of Alsatians in the SS in the "massacre." Besides, in my reverie, I've got to pick up my pace in order to catch up with Jean-Luc. It was plain, nevertheless, he would get to the Pont Neuf before me. His back was all I could see, but his carrot-top mane was unmistakable.

Alas, he was long gone by the time I got to our stone perch. I had returned to reality.

My disappointment was brief. I had been sitting there alone without Jean-Luc for many, many years. The place was relaxing for me. I dangled my feet over the edge, facing upriver. The gurgle of the waters never changed. The bird songs were the same as they had always been and I couldn't identify a single damn one. Jean-Luc had tried to teach me their tunes, but I have no musical ear despite my talent for imitating human sounds.

All around me was quiet defined by natural noises. The setting was restful, filled with mixtures of green. Growth—untamed growth—had provided copses of trees, mingled among thorny thickets. I wish I had listened more intensely when Jean-Luc did lessons on tree species. Oak, maple, beech—it was all the same to me. The grass in the old park had attained unaided the height of hay. Beyond was *La Jungle*, into which most of the local kids were afraid to go—the den of the ogres who ate people, augmented by genuine things to fear—a few lurking small poisonous vipers and ferocious wild boars.

Let me state we never set eyes on such dangerous creatures. In due time, Jean-Luc and I and eventually Chantal—the Trio—rode our bikes torturously over the trail through the undergrowth, headed for our favorite secret place—*La "Cav"*—The Cave.

France is full of caves. The most famous among them, those at Lascaux, world-renowned for their magnificent wall paintings, were only discovered in 1940, a painful year for poor France. Before they were put off limits to the public in 1963 because of feared degradation of the art work by the breathing of hordes of tourists and subsequent bacterial contamination, I had been privileged to visit the site. For artistic quality, the depiction of animals at Lascaux—horses, cave bears, rhinoceroses, aurochs (or black bulls) and even a *megaloceros*—an extinct deer related to the giant Irish elk—has never been equaled. The world-famous art find is in a portion of the Dordogne region of thirty-seven caves and rock shelters containing meritorious prehistoric illustrations. A picturesque winding river, the Vézère, has cut a valley through this home of Paleolithic populations. The center appears to be a town of less than one thousand people whose tongue-twisting complete name is Les Eyzies-de-Tayac-Sireuil, ordinarily reduced to Les Eyzies.

One of my postgraduate programs was a course in the prehistory of France. As a result, I traveled to Les Eyzies and my particular interest was piqued in learning that French paleontologists had unearthed proof of two distinct species of pre-humans who had lived cheek by jowl in the area and interacted with each other. These were the Neanderthals and the Cro-Magnons: the former, a somewhat junior complement in abilities to the latter in the development of the genus *Homo* starting 350,000 years ago.

It was not solely a private joke to mention the Neanderthals in relation to Papa's physique. The adjective *costaud*—hefty, strapping— often applied to my father, was for me an indication of such a possible descent. I was fascinated to learn more about these crude ancestors . . . for example, how due to certain aspects of their facial structures, they could only speak with great difficulty. The Cro-Magnons, conversely, had the complete panoply of skills of our modern species, *Homo sapiens*, whose very classification indicates these later folks were *knowledgeable*, enjoying the same brain power we do.

There have been scientists who posited that one of the reasons the Neanderthals ended up extinct was the result of an overt early example of genocide. The Cro-Magnons had wiped them out entirely, apparently acting even more efficiently in this regard than the Nazis toward the Jews. An accompanying theory, however, has fingered interbreeding as the cause of their wholesale demise. The DNA of various humans today has Neanderthalic traces. Quite possibly this was true in Papa's case—his bandy legs, his lack of neck. To investigate that intriguing thought as thoroughly as possible, I resided in Les Eyzies—staying in a hotel, still extant, called the CRO-MAGNON. Among other searches, I went to the nearby cave at La Ferrassie where the remains of eight Neanderthals from 35,000 years ago had been found. And it was in Les Eyzies, itself, that five corresponding Cro-Magnon skeletons were uncovered, individuals described as "much rounder than Neanderthals." A French paleontologist Marcellin Boule in 1912 first expressed the genocide explanation: Cro-Magnons versus Neanderthals, and as if backing a Cro-Magnon superiority dictum, he called the creatures they allegedly wiped out "brutish, bent-kneed and not fully erect bipeds."

La Cav, on the outlying boundaries of Charniers-sur-Nys, boasted no artifacts, no paintings, no signs of biped habitation. Animal bones were scattered about, but mostly those belonging to contemporary bats whom we only saw sleeping since we, on trips there, never stayed the night. Essentially, the location was so hard to get to that we always had the place to ourselves.

The *we* had begun with Jean-Luc Mueller and myself. Soon added was the third member of our "Trio," none other than the lovely Countess Chantal de Bregonzac-Chastain. More on the formation of our clique is to follow. But not right now as I sit, a solitary old man with a cane on an abutment of the Pont Neuf.

My one decision at the moment was that neither of the other two members of the Trio would be subjects for tonight's entertainment and elucidation. I would need much longer preparation time—emotionally, that is. Thus, oldster that I was, I slid back down from the bridge abutment to the roadside. An old cracked tarred road had brought me to the Pont Neuf and also ran to the far bank of the Nys. I had a plan to traverse the bridge carefully toward the grass plot trampled by generations of anglers. Once there, I warily kept an eye on the rippling waters alongside the path while my trusty cane was put in use for prodding my finicky legs so I didn't trip.

Suddenly, I froze. From the riverbank, the thrilling sight of a gorgeous, fat, roseate, speckled fish that must have weighed two kilos had stopped me in my tracks. It was a granddaddy rainbow trout, and hung in the glassy near depth, either oblivious to my presence or knowingly showing off.

Two thoughts raced into my mind as I stood transfixed, staring down. One seemed only mildly relevant, a newspaper filler I'd read stating France was the world's third largest exporter of rainbow trout. The other was a memory connected to Jean-Luc Mueller. At approximately this same spot, we had noticed a still patch of water and fish rising and snapping up insects. "Trout!" I yelled to Jean-Luc. We jumped off our bikes and rushed to watch.

After a minute or two, I laughed out loud.

Naturally Jean-Luc asked me the cause of my merriment.

"Freckles," I said. "Look how freckled he is. Like you."

Wrong thing to say, I realized too late. To be sure, Jean-Luc had those blotchy facial marks in profusion but he also had a redhead's temper. We didn't know each other very well then. He flushed a shade of pink. "So you think I resemble an *onchorhychus mykiss*," he snarled and made a fake lunge at me from which he pulled back at the last moment. "You know I can throw you right in there with your chums," he snapped. I suspected he easily could. He was a lot more muscular than me. Defiantly, however, I stood my ground. "But you won't," I said.

"Oh, really, why not?"

I waited a moment before answering. "Because I would be the first *oncoronky kiss kiss* you ever threw back."

Success. I received a jovial roar of laughter, an appreciative nodding smile and a pat on the back for my cleverness.

We went back to fish watching a few minutes longer. *Hélas*, we hadn't brought our fishing rods with us.

You can be certain I never compared Jean-Luc Mueller to a *truite* again.

For the moment presently, I was standing absolutely still, my gaze fixed on the huge trout which was as motionless in the water as I was on the land. Then, as if tired of posing, he (I assumed it was a male) flinched and turned into a sliver of motion, disappearing like a slash into the darker deep below.

I could dare to move then, and deem how truly alone I was, and also marvel, as I always do out in Nature, of how wondrous creation always strikes me. Not in any religious sense, I must admit. To me, it was like admiring an ingenious invention, wrapped in an array of mysteries that humans were continually unraveling, only to find new amazements emerging from behind the discovered ones. Thank God, I always thought, the Paris government had included these wild places in the memorial they were preserving. Rather, thank de Gaulle, I would always secularly correct myself.

The route I had laid out today had two goals to accomplish. The first, already achieved, had been to go to the Pont Neuf and engender a touch of nostalgia regarding Jean-Luc in order to fortify my instinct that I didn't want to interview him (nor for that matter, Chantal) tonight. The second quest had to do with Papa, specifically with his burned-out automobile the Nazis had left in this mostly unpopulated part of our town and was a seldom visited relic of the massacre memorial. I had reasoned the sight of it again might stir up memories of my father and signify whether or not I wanted him to be my next interviewee.

My trajectory was to take me downstream from the Pont Neuf to the Pont Vieux and cross back over the Nys to a small hamlet known as Les Prevot, a cluster of half a dozen homes with adjoining farms that now lay desolate after their visit from the SS. One extended family, the Prevots, had lived for generations at this location and their habitations had been leveled once the inhabitants had been herded into central Charniers to their deaths. The several barns they had owned had not been used by the Nazis for execution sites, presumably because they were too remote from the Champ de Foire.

The answer of how Papa's Renault happened to be abandoned out here was explained on a placard erected beside the incinerated wreck.

"Four Waffen SS men, drunk on stolen liquor, commandeered Mayor Desfosseux's vehicle for a pleasure ride through the burning village.

Here, on soft ground, it sunk in the mud. Finishing their binge, they set it afire before returning to their unit. *Souviens-toi*. Remember."

The long since discontinued make of the automobile had been given by Renault the bizarre name of a *Juvaquatre*. Papa called it his "Zhuva darling." He had owned the sturdy four-seated sedan since 1937 and during the war, Vichy had allowed him plentiful gasoline rations so he could continue to make house calls over the rutted rural roads throughout the district.

As I gazed at the pathetic hulk, crusted by the heat of flames to a uniform burnt brown now thoroughly invaded by rust, I noticed a glint of something shiny in the surrounding grass. Going closer to investigate, I saw shards of glass amid the nearby undergrowth. *Broken windows and headlights*, I had always thought. Amid this debris close up, I only spied the remainder of smashed wine bottles. Miraculously all these years later, the print on a piece of labeling on one of them was decipherable. I decoded "Sancerre" among the vintage's designation.

"*Par exemple*," we would say. What a coincidence! The same white wine I had symbolically poured for Saint Augustine. My favorite because it had been Papa's favorite. Like an excited treasure hunter, I searched for further clues that those SS bastards had helped themselves to Papa's liquor. Remnants of a certain Cognac container confirmed my suspicion. Another conjecture was that the louts who had done this were Alsatians. If Germans, they would have commandeered beer.

Did that discovery in any way influence my decision whether to choose Papa as my subject for this evening's foray into the past? Sooner or later, I knew, I would have to bring in contemporaries—people I had lived with like Papa, Jean-Luc and Chantal—and not simply figures of non-personal history such as Saint Augustine, Esclarmonde de Foix or even the recent brainy SS man Otto Rahn whom I simulated—biographical strangers in other words.

I did not yet feel secure about confronting my feelings toward my all-imposing parent. Shouldn't Papa be put off for another time?

The answer: Yes, resoundingly. Plus moments later, I had a new inspiration, an idea that popped into my mind unbidden and caused me to chuckle.

Not far from Papa's poor "Zhuva" was a patch of ground near an abandoned orchard where the earth had been fairly torn up. The damage, it was plain to see, had been caused some time ago by a wild boar. Those dangerous lumbering beasts were rarely ever sighted in our environs, especially if you were carrying a shotgun, yet one of them—maybe young—had been rooting around in an area where the Prevot family had plantings that possibly still went to seed. Now what in the world does this have to do with my choice of a Neanderthal and a Cro-Magnon tonight rather than Papa?

Here's how. When I was a kid, I would dig in the dirt, and not simply for extracting bait worms. I loved to watch all the tiny creatures that emerged. Years later, studying biology, I learned about the importance of these itty-bitty members of our environment and even became able to identify a few of them. Many were invisible to the eye. It was the same in water—salt and fresh alike. These "bugs" were the underpinnings of our populated world. In history studies, too, I was fascinated by hidden origins. My dabbling into prehistory in the Dordogne was a beginning. Neanderthals and Cro-Magnons. Had genocide been born in their long-ago era?

Investigating this subject would set me up for later examining Papa at length, I convinced myself.

Besides, I would have some fun.

IV

I can't say I haven't been creative. Because I harbor a bit of the temperament of a ham, I couple it with the disciplined adherence to actual facts of an academic historian. In the writing of my books of history, I often chafe at these "handcuffs." Nonetheless the recent "shows" in my study, the images I have dragged out of me still have to contain not only coherence but conformity with the mode of dress and style of speech of whatever era they inhabited.

With tonight's Neanderthals and Cro-Magnons, the opportunities for sheer invention will be tempting.

To reach my Bregonzac abode, I had to cut back into the central ruins of Charniers and turn off. I passed more tourists during broad daylight than I had encountered in months. Unlike a number of the locals, I did not resent their presence. They brought money to the area. Those who weren't mere day trippers on buses often stayed overnight in New Charniers where they used our facilities, ate in our restaurants and left donations for our efforts. When I say "our," I mean the National Association of the Families of Martyrs of Charniers-sur-Nys—the NAFMCN. For many years, I had been one of its officers, despite living in Paris.

If I hadn't been so inwardly excited about tonight, I might have tarried to chat with a visitor or two. In the early days, I had often done so. As you've seen, currently I exhibit aspects of a hermit (or vampire), since I come out mostly at dusk. I don't seek to communicate then except exclusively with myself and phantoms.

Very well, onward to the Neanderthals and Cro-Magnons.

Following a quick lunch à l'américaine—a sandwich and drink—I brushed up on my knowledge of these two prehistoric entities. For example, the myth that Neanderthals, because of physical throat impediments could not speak but only grunt. Untrue, experts reported.

Their voices, though, were high-pitched and nasal. The question of whether they could literally communicate with Cro-Magnons has been left in the air. They could interbreed and certainly did. "There were probably plenty of matings and hook-ups," one scholar has written. For more than several thousand years, the two species co-existed in Europe, often neighbors. Or were they indeed separate species? The Cro-Magnon are clearly of the same classification as modern humans—*Homo sapiens*. Yet *Homo neanderthalensis* has been recognized in some quarters as *Homo sapiens neanderthalensis*.

The conventional wisdom is that female humans (i.e. Cro-Magnons) interbreeding with Neanderthals, could produce babies who would survive and reproduce themselves. However, female Neanderthals who cohabitated with Cro-Magnons couldn't produce viable offspring. This quirk of nature lends support to the theory that Neanderthals became extinct through miscegenation rather than deliberate genocide committed by our human ancestors.

Anyway, that's enough science for now. The event I have devised for tonight, albeit rooted in actuality, relies on imagination, too, if not snippets of out-and-out fiction.

Therefore, let me open the curtain—so to speak—on the evening's entertainment.

In the two folding chairs I have set out opposite my own comfy armchair sit two—shall we say *persons*—a young male and a young female. Attached to the backs of their seats are cardboard signs on which I have black-crayoned N and CM. At a glance you could tell without the labels that the masculine figure was a Neanderthal and the feminine type a Cro-Magnon. Disconcertingly, the Neanderthal was quite naked except for a furry *cache-sexe*. The girl alongside him, with long, limp, dark, unkempt hair, yet pretty even by our standards, wore a primitive dress made of animal skins.

The two had moved their chairs closer together and, touchingly, were holding hands.

I studied them both for a few minutes until something caught their attention and together they both turned sideways. The Neanderthal boy most interested me. He was old enough to have grown a small beard, his scraggly whiskers a deep brown reddish color like the hair atop his head. The only resemblance to Papa, I thought, was in his build and posture—highly muscular thighs, thick legs, a stooping sort of stance and very like *mon père*, a powerful hairy chest. One noticeable trait gave me a jolt. Monsieur Neanderthal had no chin to speak of.

My two unusual guests were conversing with each other. It sounded like language, anyway, but I could not decipher a single word. It wasn't as sing-song as Chinese and to tell the truth, their verbal communications crackled like plain noise instead of speech.

Once they stared off at the "Screen" of the blank wall space, I followed suit. Had they discovered something I couldn't see? Were their senses finer than mine?

Wrong. Before any images showed, there was a blast of distinctive music. In my childhood, I had originally experienced French Pathé News when Papa took me to the movies in Limoges. I remember mostly scenes of war—in Ethiopia, in Spain, in China. Papa said the Pathé Company was started in France by a Monsieur Pathé, and had spread to England and the U.S.

Tonight, the announcer's voice (in French) aroused those types of pictures from the past. But the grainy, black and white newsreel war scenes now looked much different.

The screen was full of men marching with spears and bows and arrows. Separate columns of near-naked Neanderthals and skin-clad Cro-Magnons strutted for the camera. These tableaux then caught them clashing with each other. The river below could have been the Dordogne. Fat Neanderthals, stuck with arrows, collapsed and expired. A Cro-Magnon, his skull crushed by a stone axe, lay slumped on the ground. A phalanx of his comrades rushed past him, chasing unclothed warriors who fled in droves. Some Neanderthals could be seen surrendering.

The narrator's voice declared pontifically: "Victorious Cro-Magnon troops herd their prisoners." The camera focused on a knot of dejected captives guarded by spear-wielding Cro-Magnons being led to an unknown destination.

Would they be massacred?

If they had been, the camera didn't record the slaughter. Had it done so, it might have documented the world's first instance of a cold-blooded war crime.

With a whining whirr, the screen darkened and the "newsreel" ended.

My two guests of the evening turned their heads back toward me. They also began chattering. Needless to say, I still did not understand and waited for subtitles or dubbed voices. Yet nothing happened. They had disappointed expressions on their faces and stood up, seemingly ready to leave.

Noticing a bulge under the front of the girl's dress, I called to her: "Are you having a baby?" both in French and English.

Whether they understood, I could doubt, but the Neanderthal male patted the stomach of the Cro-Magnon female until moments before, like all my other interviewees, they underwent their break up and dissolution.

But I wasn't left totally deserted. After several disbelieving blinks, I discovered one of the abandoned folding chairs was occupied.

"Hello, my friend," said a ghostly masculine voice.

"Cro-Maritan! Mon Dieu!" I exclaimed. "I might have expected you'd crop up."

"Simply to remind you of my eternal presence."

One more blink and that figure of my fancy also had vanished. The glimpse I'd had was of a stick figure, a seven-year-old's drawing in black crayon, but life-sized. I'd originally done a sketch of this character in my mind. I'd named him Cro-Maritan after reading about Cro-Magnons in a kiddy's history book and hearing the Bible story of the Good Samaritan at church. Since childhood, Cro-Maritan would appear at key moments in my life.

Totally alone finally, I remained in my comfy armchair, staring up at the ancient beams of my favorite room. This theatrical bit with the Neanderthals and Cro-Magnons affirmed a conviction that genocide had never taken place between them, only interbreeding. But I wasn't ready to go to bed. And my reminiscence juices had been stirred.

A memory of Jean-Luc Mueller shot into full focus. Red hair was a subject on which we one day discoursed, riding back from the Lycée in Limoges aboard the trolley to Charniers. In class, we had been discussing the prehistory of France. I was smart enough not to tease Jean-Luc again about red hair and freckled complexion. Sounding innocent, I merely asked if he thought he had inherited any Neanderthal traits to account for his hair color.

"Do more reading," my newfound Alsatian friend scolded me. "There is absolutely no correlation" (he liked to use big words). Equally as glib as when spouting the Latin species name for rainbow trout, he liked to belabor me with scientific terms. I did memorize *Melanocotta Receptor Allele*, the "ginger gene," a mutation not found in humans. In what context Jean-Luc used this exact term, I'm a bit fuzzy, only that the upshot of his argument was his definite conclusion he had nothing Neanderthalic in his background.

Moving backward in chronology, maybe five months earlier, I also have kept sharply in mind Jean-Luc's arrival in Charniers.

I know the date was in September 1939 several weeks following the outbreak of World War II. A contingent of Alsatian kids we were sheltering in our village had already arrived. But Jean-Luc, I soon learned, had not been among them.

It so happened I was in my bedroom, passing the dormer window that looked upon the town square in time to see a sensational-looking automobile drive by the World War I monument and turn in the direction of our house. This long black chauffeur-driven limousine resembled the vehicle owned by Count Charles de Bregonzac-Chastain. Was Count Charles coming to see my papa? More to the point, though, were my next two self-queries. *Would Chantal be inside? Could I get a glimpse of her?*

Except I no longer felt sure, as soon as the luxurious town car parked below, that it was the same make as our local squire's. Of German or English manufacture possibly, although the license plate was French.

Its chauffeur—who wasn't wearing a driver's livery but only a chauffeur's visored cap—jumped out and opened the rear door. A female did emerge but hardly Chantal. Dressed entirely in black was an older woman and the most compelling feature of her somber costume was the wooden crucifix worn around her neck. It was the largest I had ever seen.

A nun? I asked myself. *A mother superior?* She stood on the sidewalk, a regal figure. *Taking someone sick to see Papa* was my next explanation.

The woman, herself, appeared quite healthy, spry, youthful as well, although old enough to have been my mother. Or was the ailing party the other passenger who vacated the back seat? All I really noticed was a boy about my own age with reddish hair who joined the lady before these two visitors set off for the entrance to Papa's clinic.

Since Monsieur le Docteur Desfosseux never spoke about his patients—that was that. I abandoned the window after one last admiring glance at the exotic automobile parked below. The chauffeur stood on the sidewalk smoking a cigarette. In other words, I wasn't overly interested and didn't even go to the window when the car drove off.

That Sunday morning at Mass, a few days later, I had taken my usual seat by the door when I saw the two, the woman in black and the red-haired kid, enter and walk up front toward the altar. This was a bit of a surprise but nothing like the shock of noting they were situated in a front row pew adjacent to that of the count and his family.

Yet another offhand contact occurred the next week. Hanging around the village square with my friends, I spied the redhead amid a group of Alsatian refugee kids. So he was one of them! They were chattering away in their own language, which sounded, I thought, like German. We French locals felt none too kindly toward the strangers. Big Freddi—Frédéric Lemire, the Notary's son—claimed there were Jews among them.

I kept noticing this redheaded kid in the following days but nothing more of the woman in black with the outsized crucifix. Among the young Alsatians he appeared to lead the others. I overheard him speak French in the *boulangerie* one day when the group went to buy bread. His command of our language was absolutely perfect, absolutely flawless, if anything too cultured for us country bumpkins. He reminded me of *Meaulnes*, the youthful protagonist of the famous novel, and like the fictional character, was physically taller than the rest of his compatriots.

Admittedly at the time, I knew little about Alsace. Coupled with Lorraine, it was best known as the part of France taken from us in the Franco-Prussian War but returned in the peace treaty ending World War I. One evening Papa had discussed his military prints bought in Strasbourg and hung framed on his medical office walls. A grandfather of his had fought in that losing conflict. He never wanted to forget. Papa also never had a nice word to say about the Second Empire and Napoleon II who'd provoked the mess and lost to the Prussians.

My father's political views must be brought up now because of their bearing on the overall story of relations between Jean-Luc Mueller and myself. No, Dr. Desfosseux was not a friend of the Second Empire, nor was he anything except a diehard enemy of the Third Republic.

In short, Papa was a Monarchist. Like many natives of the Vendée, he sought to put a king back on a throne ruling France.

To that end, he was a devoted follower of *l'Action française*, a Royalist movement led by the outspoken journalist and litterateur Charles Maurras. On Papa's desk was an elegantly presented photograph of a pinch-faced prissy old man with a white goatee, who had autographed the likeness to his "dear friend and supporter, le Docteur Desfosseux." One more salient fact concerning Maurras: he was an outspoken anti-Semite, always complaining about Jews and how they were responsible for all of the ills besetting France.

Papa never echoed such bigotry. But I ingested it when I browsed the columns of the newspapers Papa left on the breakfast table, also called *l'Action française*, usually containing editorials written by Maurras himself. His consensus was the Jews were ruining France and no more of the foreign ones from eastern Europe and the German ones escaping Germany should be allowed in the country. I had never known any Jews nor would I have recognized any, but out of loyalty to Papa I shared his mentor's sentiments. They were *les youpins*—bad people.

Hitler, in Germany, was saying the same thing. But I never heard Papa praise him.

Plus the war was going on. The German *Führer*'s forces conquered Poland in a month. We combated them but to paraphrase the title of a famous German novel, "All was quiet on the Western Front." Our mighty Maginot Line, we all thought, had stymied the Boche.

The first snows arrived. The Alsatian refugees were still with us. There was talk they would soon head back home to our northeastern-most province since the danger of a German invasion appeared moot.

Suddenly back in the present, was I simply getting *chicken*, as Naansee would say, afraid of the next scene that fit in here chronologically?

For the most searing event of my young life took place then at Papa's office.

I was summoned from my bedroom while awaiting dinner on a late wintry afternoon by Madame Blanchard.

"*On t'demande*," she told me from my doorway." No need to say who was ordering my presence. The expression of silent pity exhibited by the kindly messenger told me everything. I was in trouble with Papa!

What sin had I committed? Stopping to figure it out would get me into even more trouble. . I hurried downstairs to his medical office.

Patient hours were over. His door was open. I could see him behind his desk.

"Close the door behind you. Sit down," my father commanded.

My beloved *père* had big, brutal hands. I braced myself for an eventual *gifle*—an unlovely French custom where an angry parent, usually the male—smacks his child across the face. I had been a recipient of those stinging blows and knew how much they hurt.

These later years (he had reached fifty) Papa had begun wearing glasses for reading. He held a sheet of paper in his hand and said: "I have here a written complaint about you. Would you like to hear it?"

He was not expecting an answer. I sat frozen in any event. Some peccadillo from school, I suspected.

"I will read the charge against you," he intoned, as if he were a judge or the mayor of a community, which of course he was. The missive had been addressed to him in that capacity.

"Monsieur le Maire, on Thursday last, your son Eugène Desfosseux committed an unpardonable assault upon a boy—a guest in this village from Alsace—several years younger and much smaller than he was. Physically, he knocked the boy into a snow bank and rubbed his face in the snow. To add insult to injury, he repeatedly called his victim 'a dirty Jew.' You should be made aware that Emile Wasserman is an Alsatian of Protestant denomination. His father is a *pasteur* of an Evangelical church in Strasbourg. At a time when the French nation is in peril, such behavior borders on treasonous. I earnestly hope you will take corrective action."

Papa put down the document. "Explain," he barked.

"That Jew boy hit me with a snowball," I shot back.

"I have since had a chance to discuss this grave matter with your accuser," Papa said. "I also learned that you and your pals started the snowball fight. That you acted like a complete bully and . . ."

I actually dared to interrupt him, crying: "Papa, I thought he was a Jew. He had a long nose. Big Freddi said he was a Jew."

"So what if he was?"

I pointed to the photo of Maurras on his desk. "Doesn't M'sieu Maurras say Jews are *chameaux*?" Camels, in English—one of the worst insults we French can use in our language. Maurras had openly called Prime Minister Leon Blum *un chameau sémitique*.

"You must be deaf." Clearly irritated, Papa raised his voice. "Emile Wassermann, the younger boy you mistreated, has no Jewish blood. The Alsatians came here to be safely away from the Germans. We invited them as guests."

"Those Alsatians have such funny names, Papa," I interjected. "French *prénoms*, German *noms de famille*."

"Alsatians are French. Don't you ever forget it."

"Who wrote that letter, Papa? Was it the redhead?" By then, I had heard around town his name was Jean-Luc Mueller, a perfect example of the mixture of nomenclature I was talking about.

Papa did not answer me. Quite deliberately. Instead, he regarded me balefully with those deep, blackish, beadyish, toad eyes of his plainly visible behind his spectacles. The imposing tips of his flamboyant dark mustache seemed to quiver. Eventually, like a Grand Inquisitor, he inquired: "Do you deny the accusations?"

At my age then, I did not know to plead *extenuating circumstances*. In this instance, it had to do with the anti-Semitism I had imbibed from him and *l'Action française* newspapers. "M'sieu Maurras . . . doesn't he say: 'Attack the Jews?' Don't the *Camelots du Roi* do so for him?"

I should have added my secret ambition in the future was to become one of *l'Action*'s Monarchist bully boys in Paris, beating up Jews, Communists and even supporters of France's Third Republic. However, Papa intervened, stating: "Allow me to correct you about M'sieu Maurras position vis-à-vis the Jews. His is not an *antisémitisme de la peaux*—of the skin—but an *anti-sémitisme de l'état*—of the state. He wants them out of the government and high places. He wants a king in

France again. He is no Hitler."

Genuinely, I was puzzled and it showed in my expression.

"If you don't understand, you need a lesson," Papa declared, standing up, coming out from behind his desk toward me, unloosening his belt. "Lower your trousers and bend over the chair you're sitting in," he ordered.

To my utter astonishment, I didn't budge. "No," I said, astounded by my disobedience.

"What?"

"No!" I fairly shouted.

The next thing I knew, he struck me . . . *une gifle*—the back of his right hand swatting me across the face.

Correct, it hurt as it always did, physically and emotionally. But previously, I had never felt such pain. I reached to the cheek he'd struck and felt wetness prior to discovering my fingers covered with sticky redness and finally I noticed the steady drip of blood falling to the floor.

Through the dizziness his blow had caused me, I heard Papa mutter "*Oh mon dieu.*" Yet within moments, Dr. Desfosseux became his professional self again, staunching the bleeding, disinfecting the wound, applying a bandage.

Not a word passed between us. Ultimately he made a signal dismissing me.

It was only much later I learned what I suspected had happened. Papa had forgotten to switch the ring he always wore on his right hand to his left hand before he impulsively hit me. It was not a wedding ring, by the way, not a mere band, but an opal ring (his birthstone) my mother had given him after they were married. He considered it his most cherished possession.

All this I had confirmed when years afterward he very belatedly apologized. The incident had shaken him as much as it had traumatized me. He had brooded upon it all the while. Perhaps I had always sensed the regret he felt. The actual remorse only occurred in the spring one night after he had had several drinks of marc brandy and was feeling sentimental. Did he have an inkling of his own mortality that evening?

It was the first of June 1944.

V

The story of the bloody gifle, as you might expect, had an aftermath. For the better part of a week, I went around with a bandaged cheek. To all inquiries, I merely answered blandly I had slipped and hit the side of my face. Nothing was said at home, but I believed Papa was grateful I hadn't "ratted" on him. He was particularly tender, I thought, in caring for the wound, changing dressings, applying antiseptic, examining how it was healing. When he finally pronounced me cured, my usually phlegmatic parent allowed himself a touch of humor. "*Bon*," Papa said. "No scar. I didn't want you looking like a German dueling student." It was a little joke that had to be explained to me.

Meanwhile I was plotting dire revenge against the redheaded Alsatian. Despite Papa's injunction that the refugee kids were our guests, this wise guy *had* "ratted" on me. My dislike for him was further inflamed when I noted him at church on Sundays being chummy with the beauteous, unapproachable (to me) Countess Chantal.

There was something mysteriously suspicious surrounding the fellow. I kept brooding about it the first moment I'd laid eyes on him when he followed the crucifix-wearing woman out of that ritzy limousine. Had they seen Papa on something other than a medical visit? What did Papa know about them? I was afraid to ask.

Also, the matter of the church seating arrangement disturbed me considerably. The pew they'd taken—and Jean-Luc kept—had once been Papa's, where he and I sat along with my mother when she was alive. That I now sat on a bench in the rear of Saint Augustine's was due to a spat between Papa and the local priest and his relinquishing the coveted place. In fact, he ceased going to church altogether. This boycott most likely happened during the period after his idol Maurras was excommunicated by Pope Pius XI for differences with Vatican policies.

However, his dictate to me remained that I was to attend Mass every Sunday. Honoring my devout maman's memory.

Thus I chose a Sunday to spring my plan of teaching Jean-Luc Mueller a painful lesson. My confidants were two of my *copains:* Big Freddi Lemire, whom I've already mentioned, and Mario Cioffi, the offspring of Italian immigrants in Marseille whose father had been transferred to run a branch insurance agency in Charniers. The three of us would accost the redhead once he had exited Saint Augustine's and invite him to a rendezvous in the woods below the house of worship for a confrontation. If he declined, we would warn him, he forever would be branded a coward and no better than a Boche, which he probably was.

Another of the unexplained quirks about Jean-Luc was that although obviously the leader of the Alsatian contingent, he did not live with them, but rather boarded by himself at the home of the widow Pochard who lived not far from our Desfosseux residence. The rest of the group were sheltered by the French government in an annex of the Hôtel Mayon farther down the main street. About half were Protestants (like Emile Wasserman) and half Roman Catholic (like Jean-Luc), reflecting the religious makeup of our recovered province. The woman in black, I had realized, after that one Sunday had not re-appeared nor was her limousine spied again.

On subsequent Sundays, I noted how Jean-Luc would join the Count de Bregonzac-Chastain and his family in the honor of first to leave the church. He would walk side by side with Chantal, the two of them chatting. I would slink down in my seat as they passed by me. Then, slipping outside, I would track the redhead's movements after he bid adieu to the count and his children. Big Freddi and Mario would join me when we followed our Alsatian quarry from a distance and saw his destination was Madame Pochard's.

After three Sundays, this pattern was unexpectedly broken. The count and family were away visiting relatives in Burgundy, I was told. Therefore, Jean-Luc, in sole occupancy of his pew, politely waited for everyone else to exit ahead of him.

Our perfect chance, I whispered to my pals once we'd gathered outside on the stoop, ready to confront our intended victim. Most, if not all of the parishioners had dispersed by the time Jean-Luc Mueller crossed the threshold of the church interior.

Behind him, the sexton and his assistants were arriving to shut the massive doors of solid Limousin oak. The three of us kids had set our embuscade to occur just outside those portals. Seeing us blocking his path, the Alsatian didn't falter. He smiled to himself while continuing to walk briskly. Within a few meters, he said coolly: "Gentlemen . . . Messieurs . . . Can I help you?"

Big Freddi jumped the gun. It had been agreed I would do the speaking. Yet from his loud mouth, we heard: "Take a little promenade with us, youpin-lover."

Ending his insulting threat with a flourish, Freddi jerked his thumb in the direction we would take. Mario pointed, too. It was toward the slope leading down from the grassy rear of the round Romanesque stone building. "There's a quiet spot where disputes are settled," the big guy added.

"Unless you're ready to run away" was my contribution.

Unfazed, Jean-Luc brushed away a few strands of hair from his freckled forehead. "I am at your service, Messieurs," he answered, as if in the midst of some nineteenth century dueling scene.

Like a cortège of captors leading a prisoner to execution, all four of us descended. Never will I forget how I glanced up at the stained glass panels of the apse and observed Christ on His cross in magnificent Technicolor, but seen from the back.

We had to march through a dense copse of evergreens to reach our destination. The piney scent of needles was another sensate impression I still summon to this day.

When we entered a small level plot of ground amid the thickly grown forest area, Jean-Luc halted and asked: "By the way, do I have to fight you together or one at a time?

His brazen, pugnacious attitude offhandedly delivered, was a bit unnerving.

Big Freddi and Mario looked to me to give him an answer. "One at a time, it goes without saying," I responded, sounding quite gallant, I thought.

Jean-Luc acquiesced with a nod. He proceeded to remove his Sunday jacket and tie and hanged them on a nearby low branch.

The three of us followed suit.

I said reproachfully to the Alsatian, "You got me into trouble with my father."

Again he concurred with another nod.

"You deserved it," he retorted. "You should apologize to that boy— and not because you called him a Jew in your ignorance."

"Maybe he is one. Did you see the nose on him?" Big Freddi interjected.

"*Ça suffit* . . . That's enough, Frédéric," I snapped.

In the middle of this glade a small patch of earth showed where the grass had been tamped down by decades of surreptitious fisticuffs here. Jean-Luc stepped into the center of this makeshift arena, his fists ready. The redhead was tall, but my friend Freddi topped him by half a head, it seemed. The Notary's son was a giant among us schoolkids. "Are you sure you want to fight, youpin-lover ?" he taunted. "I'm an experienced boxer. I'll mash you to a pulp."

Jean-Luc smiled in his cocky manner. "We'll see," he said. "My boxing lessons started when I was eight years old."

That much was obvious the moment the two battlers started throwing punches. Freddi missed with two roundhouse rights. Jean-Luc simply sidestepped. His foot work was fast. A left hook to the stomach had our not-so-gentle giant bending double, the breath knocked out of him. From there, Jean-Luc easily landed an uppercut to my friend's jaw; another a second later and Freddi collapsed in a writhing heap.

Hot-blooded Mario was never one to shirk from a brawl. He rushed at Jean-Luc, swinging wildly. More agile footwork came into play. Dancing away from these ill-aimed blows, the redhead almost seemed bored. Within half a minute, he feinted with his left, plowed a right onto Mario's jaw and the latter went sprawling and couldn't rise up on his feet.

My two companions watched with trepidation as I came out to box.

Neither of us said anything but circled each other warily. A red spot on my right cheek still showed where Papa had cut me. I must say I surprised myself by managing to block Jean-Luc's jabs, realizing finally he was trying to avoid the side of my face where he'd no doubt seen me wearing a bandage. Good sportsmanship. But the end result was inevitable. Jean-Luc's hands were small, not like Papa's huge mitts, yet when he finally landed a haymaker to my chin, it felt ever so much more powerful than Papa's blow. I staggered, fell and briefly must have been unconscious. Sitting up finally, I kept shaking my head from side to side.

Jean-Luc knelt beside me, offered his hand and pulled me to my feet. "You fought well, Desfosseux," he told me. "You might have possibilities." Whereupon he retrieved his jacket and tie and sauntered away, disappearing into the dense *sapin* woods.

We three didn't see him ahead of us while eventually climbing back up the church slope because it took us ten or fifteen minutes to fully restore our senses.

The Alsatian's last statement lingered in my mind. I appreciated his remarks. Little did I dream those words of encouragement were the opening gun of a grand friendship.

Such reminiscences of mine are a means of trying to get at the problem of absolute verisimilitude. My nightly interviews are sheer theatre, to be sure, but with the intent of offering entertaining insights rather than the clogged footnoting of academia with the annoying aim of proving its "scientific" veracity, as well as demonstrating how many erudite—and the more obscure the better—sources you've quoted.

If I sound full of cynicism or sour grapes, it's because I am. Or is my attitude due to a streak of Vendéen independence I absorbed from Papa. From my mother in the short time I was with her, I gained a modicum of forbearance and stubborn optimism. So I sit tonight in my Bregonzac study armchair, during the twilight of my life. What I have just finished remembering of Jean-Luc Mueller, etc., is simply inner flashbacks. There has been nothing projected onto the "screen" of the blank wall. Apart from the VSOP cognac I am sipping, I find myself alone, a bit drowsy, and about to call it a night.

Plus at this point, I should also disclose I have been keeping a written paraphrase of what has been going on in my memory and transcribing on paper the recordings of these interludes of reimagined history.

I slept late the next morning. Arlette, who'd prepared my breakfast, had come and gone before I'd gotten out of bed. The food she'd left me was warming in the oven: delicious home-baked croissants, a tasty cheese omelet, plus my indispensable *jus d'orange* and coffee in a thermos, kept nice and hot.

On occasion, I tend to be impulsive. Naansee had a saying in English about "having a bee in your bonnet." Hard to translate that into French. But because of all this thinking of mine about Papa, I had an intense urge to revisit his association with the Maurrasians of *l'Action française* who later gave such aid and comfort to the German occupation.

There is a locked drawer in my bedroom inside a rather worn, once elegant commode that I picked up cheaply from a local *brocanteur*—secondhand dealer. In it, I keep items of special importance to me, sentimentally if nothing else.

This morning, I knew exactly what I sought to find inside. Producing the key, I opened the "treasure chest" and extracted a newspaper excerpt brittle with age. I had also attached the cut-out masthead to identify its attribution. It was from an edition of *l'Action française*, the mouthpiece for Maurras' Royalist movement, dated September 7, 1937.

The article bore the headline: LA MAGNIFIQUE FÊTE DU SOUVENIR VENDÉEN À CHOLET.

I had discovered it and clipped it while doing research on the *l'Action française* organization and Maurras for an article. Papa was a guest of honor at the culminating banquet of the get-together, attended by more than five thousand Maurras adherents. He sat at the head table between Damaillacq, the mayor of Cholet and an unidentified professor from a Catholic University. Moreover, a biographical sketch of my father was included in the write-up.

Although it bears the title of "Military Capital of the Vendée," the small city of Cholet actually is not in the Vendée, itself, but on its outskirts in the Département of Maine-et-Loire. Yet here on October 17, 1793, the final battle of the counter-revolution of the Royalists and ardent Catholics against the French Revolution ended in the rebellion's defeat. The disaster's memory haunted Papa as it had his family for generations. His attraction to Charles Maurras was absolutely understandable.

Maurras, incidentally, was not able to attend that giant *fête* in Cholet.

As visual artifacts will do, a glance at this reminder of the Royalists revival in the early twentieth century induced real scenes in my mind. The signed Maurras photo on Papa's desk, for example. Under the Republic, naturally, Doctor Desfosseux had to temper his anti-Republican enthusiasm while in truth serving the Republic by being Charniers' mayor, wearing a blue, white and red tricolor sash of office instead of the old monarchy's *fleur-de-lis*.

Reading again about this long-ago political gathering primed me for my newest innovation. Bring back Papa for a *daylight* interview. This morning, actually.

The newspaper article was finally returned and the "treasure chest" re-locked. Into my study I went. Out came the recorder. A chair was unfolded for my guest. There would be no motion picture newsreel on the wall. Nothing elaborate.

I was not afraid, waiting for my parent. Papa could never strike me nor so much as upbraid me in the short period I would let him stay.

Neither was I nervous. I felt in control, no sooner had I set eyes on him.

His lumbering "neanderthalic" walk propelled him to his seat in brisk strides. True to his Frenchman's character, he had a lighted cigarette in the corner of his mouth. A *Gitane*—its pungent tobacco odor soon sniffed in the room. Playing with one end of his immense mustache, twirling it, he sat ponderously opposite me—*Le Grand Crapaud*.

"So?" he said.

The doctor's white coat had been discarded. Monsieur le Maire, sashed in the Republic's patriotic colors, wearing a vest with his decorous suit and conservative tie, awaited my response.

"Papa, we don't have a minute to spare," I commenced. "This is an experiment."

"In that event . . ." From a side pocket of his jacket, he took out a leather case and put on the pair of reading glasses he'd been wearing the day he'd swatted me. Simultaneously, he continued puffing on his cigarette, which now hung on his lip unattended.

"I suppose you have a document for me to sign," he inquired. "Some stupid legality about your inheritance?"

"No, Papa, I simply have a few questions. Do you remember the great banquet in Cholet?"

"Of course," he said. "Cholet. The big rally we had two years before that fool Hitler marched into Poland.´

"Did you have any sense then that one day your Maurrasians would help Hitler?"

"Charles Maurras would pair with the Devil to bring the Republic down. He called Herr Hitler's victory over France 'a divine surprise.' He was delighted. He backed Vichy to the hilt."

"You did, too, Papa."

"I liked Pétain. He whipped the Boche in 1914–1918."

"But he collaborated with the Germans, kowtowed to Hitler."

As if not hearing me, Papa went on to say: "After 1940, I could openly display the *Maréchal*'s portrait in my offices . . . a huge one behind my desk. Pétain had the right ideas . . . but he was too old. Laval, I didn't trust. A slimy *Auvergnat*. Vichy was full of pygmies like him."

"De Gaulle?" I asked. "Did you pay attention to de Gaulle?"

"I understand some *député* in the Chamber once said, 'de Gaulle has the character of a pig.' And another one answered, 'But at least he has character.'"

"De Gaulle was always for the Republic. The Third, the Fourth and the Fifth. You didn't live to see the later governments. And he fought the Germans."

"Look where it got us in Charniers."

'Papa, I have something very painful to report to you. You need to know you are a hero in all of France for defying the SS commander when he demanded you name thirty hostages. You only offered yourself. Unfortunately a few evil tongues here have blabbed that if you hadn't made such a fuss, the Nazis wouldn't have wiped us out.

"You survived," he answered.

"Only because of Jean-Luc Mueller."

"Ah, the Alsatian redhead kid . . . I saw the Germans strike him down . . . He was yelling something at the commander in German. They had him carried unconscious to the Phillipon barn. They propped him up alongside us. We were facing machine guns. The rest ends there."

"God, Papa. What a horror!"

"Where were you, incidentally, when we were all on the Champ de Foire?"

"I'll try to explain. You see, the Trio . . ."

But it wasn't useful for me to continue. Still puffing smoke, still fiddling with his mustachios, Papa silently and swiftly disintegrated.

Slunk in my leather armchair, I wanted to cry.

VI

Because of my aborted morning interlude with Papa and its emotional impact on me, I suspended any further notion of preparing another phantom colloquy for any time that same day. Relax, however, I couldn't. Although the exchange of dialogue with Papa was entirely my own invention, the immediate memory of it acted like a genuine happening. Thus getting into Papa's mind, while a guessing game, became a formidable experience. The story of what happened on the *Champ de Foire*, the Fairground, in Charniers-sur-Nys once the SS arrived has been told so often that I can picture the setting in the wink of an eye.

But why not have the real thing as a model? The site was a five minute walk. The Nazis didn't dig up the grass or burn it. Grabbing my cane, I was happy to leave a house that seemed so mournful to me after my failure in interviewing Papa. If I needed my imagination to populate the scene of that sunny June day, I had images to fall back on. Where had *SS Sturmbannführer* Durchmann stood? Where was Papa opposite him? I know a phalanx of bodyguards surrounded the Nazi company commander. They wore bucket steel helmets and camouflage brown, green and yellow smocks. They seemingly had no faces and must have looked as sinister as Martians. One of them, I later learned, had corn-silky blond hair. Their utter immobility was countered by continuous action on the field. Groups of civilians were being herded in and the women and men separated. On the fringes of the Champ de Foire were parked the military trucks that had transported the bulk of 2nd Company, 1st Battalion, Das Reich Division, Waffen SS to our town. At the end came the schoolchildren, their teachers trying to stem the little ones' fears. Meanwhile Papa and Durchmann parleyed.

No doubt Papa had turned his head more than once seeking sight of me. This had to be the case after he saw Jean-Luc arrive, shrieking in German like an SS drill sergeant. By June 1944, Jean-Luc and I had become bosom friends for nearly four years practically inseparable.

Where is Eugène. Where is my boy? is how I read Papa's thoughts. Followed by: *What am I going to say to this Kraut bastard in front of me?*

An interpreter—an Alsatian SS man naturally—abetted the conversation between them.

Papa—survivors testified afterward—was cool and unintimidated. He was a brave, very French figure, wearing his sash of office and on occasion he has been so portrayed in book illustrations. Nor was he smoking his usual Gitane cigarette.

Now, more than half a century later, tourists were criss-crossing the village green while I tramped here and there on the grass, estimating the placements of the actors and acted-upon in the awful drama. I had brought a pad of paper, took notes and even drew a primitive map . . . until eventually I trudged back to Bregonzac. Arlette would have brought my major midday meal and a light supper for afterward, *un sandwich de jambon de Bayonne* and fruit.

Living in southwest France previously, Arlette had learned to make a most delectable version of my favorite dish—*cassoulet*—the traditional stew from the land of Oc. This was my main meal today. No goose, *hélas*, yet the duck, pork sausage, lamb and white haricot beans were more than sufficient. A special trip to my wine cellar procured a luxurious red Bordeaux, a Pomerol, to accompany this delectable feast. For almost two hours I gorged myself, ending with several heavenly cheeses.

Logy with the food I had consumed, I left the dishes for Arlette and entered my study. I continued to reminisce at some length. The setting was of an unforgettable celebration in Charniers-sur-Nys, full of good eating and good cheer.

Nothing like it had ever occurred in our humble village. It was early November 1939, I believe, when word came to Papa from Paris that the Alsatian children were soon to go home. They had been in the Limousin practically two months. The Ministry of War or whoever was in charge had decided a threat to Alsace no longer existed. Our Maginot Line had proved its worth.

The first time I knew something was up was when I looked out my window, as I did each morning, and saw Jean-Luc Mueller leading a group of Alsatian boys and girls to the houses surrounding the village square. They were leaving flyers of a sort on the doorsteps. I followed the redhead's movements while he guided his charges off into side streets, continuing their task.

During his exile from Strasbourg, Jean-Luc had not been going to school. Rather, we heard, a tutor visited him at Madame Pochard's. Every now and then, he and I would cross paths in town, shake hands, exchange a polite word or two and go our separate ways. There appeared to be no hard feelings from our fight but no friendship either.

I hurried downstairs to the front door stoop to discover what message had been left us.

Unfortunately, that copy, which I'd kept, went up in flames with everything else in our house. Naturally, I can't quote its exact wording . . . To the best of my memory, the affiche read:

"To the *très gentils citoyens* of Charniers-sur-Nys. In loving gratitude for your kindness to your compatriots from Alsace," I winced a bit, remembering Emile Wassermann, "we wish to thank you before we return to our province. Therefore, as a token of our esteem, we invite you as our guests to a *fête* we will prepare. We hope everyone in Charniers will attend."

Beneath was the date, the time, the place (Phillipon's barn), and in capitals, the theme:

ALSACE THANKS CHARNIERS-SUR-NYS
ONE FRANCE FOREVER

ALSATIAN FOOD. ALSATIAN FOLK DANCING. ALSATIAN MUSIC AND ART.

I recall bringing the handbill to Papa, seeing him nod and hearing he knew all about it. He told me he had been visited a day earlier by Jean-Luc Mueller who had delivered a personal invitation, hoping he would honor them with his presence at the head table.

"I told him I would attend so long as I didn't have to make a speech." Papa handed me back the flyer with the statement, "That rascally redhead is certainly *à la hauteur*—on top of everything. You and I will both go together."

Parenthetically, Phillipon's barn had been built by a branch of the same family from whom I'd bought my house in Bregonzac. Located near the center of Charniers, it mostly stood empty until needed for any large communal event.

La Grange Phillipon was a short walk from the Desfosseux domicile. Curiosity, as well as appreciation for the refugees' gesture had almost all of our inhabitants on the chosen evening headed in the same direction. Not far behind Papa and me was Madame Blanchard and her family, husband, sons, their wives, her daughters, sons-in-law and grandchildren. Our gardener Emile plus family could be seen coming from a different direction. Old and young, rich and poor, we had a much bigger crowd than turned out for Bastille Day.

In addition to his mayoral sash, Papa wore his service decorations from the Great War, and I had on the suit and tie I normally wore only to church.

The sight greeting us inside the open barn doors is forever engraved in my mind.

The interior had been transformed. No stored farm implements were in view. The rough wooden floor was covered with tables and chairs, draped by the decorating Alsatian colors of red, white and black. Streamers of identical hue hung from the rafters, intertwined with similar banners of our blue, white and red French colors. On walls were blown up posters of Alsatian communities: Strasbourg 's glorious cathedral, Colmar's picturesque canals, quaint preserved Riquewihr, and emblems of the province on the Rhine—storks on rooftop nests, Vosges Mountain scenes, *Haut-Koenigsbourg*, the famous fortress, rolling vineyards and evergreen forests.

Indeed the piney scent of sapins—the firs—penetrated everywhere because on each seat a souvenir bag of balsam needles had been deposited.

Delicious cooking smells immediately assailed our nostrils. No, the youngsters were not acting as chefs. Cooks had been imported from Strasbourg and so had musicians and professional organizers who had arrived circumspectly in several carloads the night before.

Who paid for all this? No one asked then. Nor since. Yet the image of the limousine that had brought the redhead to town flashed into my mind temporarily.

This Jean-Luc Mueller who greeted Monsieur le Maire and his son as soon as we crossed the barn threshold, was in costume. His outfit—a black broad-brimmed hat, a white cotton blouse, black trousers, hose and shoes, and a bright scarlet red waistcoat with gold buttons—was traditional folkloric wear for Alsatian males. He escorted us to the head table set on a raised platform at one end of the building.

Imagine my surprise when I learned I was to sit up front next to Papa. When I expressed the thought to him, he whispered jokingly: "That's so I can keep an eye on you and assure you don't abuse *any* of these nice Alsatian kids." It was good to find my papa in such a jolly mood.

Upon Papa's entrance behind Jean-Luc, spontaneous applause burst from the groups forming at the tables. Papa smiled and waved, clearly pleased, no longer his usual somber self.

Not long afterward, another roar of approval and respect broke out. Clapping vigorously, guests were on their feet, and the men doffed their hats. No one had expected the Count de Bregonzac to attend, but there he was with his daughter, Chantal, being escorted by Jean-Luc to the head table a few seats away from Papa's and mine. It's funny. I did not feel a single twinge of jealousy noticing Jean-Luc sit down next to that adorable beauty and converse with her before returning to his supervising duties. I could always think—not that I could do anything after it happened: *Within a few days, my rival will be gone, ha, ha, ha.*

I must mention that Count Charles was in the military regalia of a high-ranking Foreign Legion officer—having been called back into service during the general mobilization in September. With his ramrod Saint Cyrian posture, his tanned features, his affable smile for everyone, he made a popular handsome figure despite his baldness, which he unselfconsciously revealed when he briefly lifted his heavily braided *kepi* to dab his handkerchief to his brow and remove a bead of sweat. Chantal, for her part, looked every bit the storybook princess to me.

The presence of the count was not the only oddity. The master of ceremonies, it turned out, was none other than fifteen-year-old Jean-Luc Mueller of Strasbourg. But then again, as Papa expressed it to others later, the boy had proposed and overseen this entire amazing farewell, written the advertising and arranged for the professionals. It turned out he had won prizes in Strasbourg for his speaking ability.

Accordingly, the redhead left his seat next to Chantal, went to a microphone and called for quiet—in French—and next in the Germanic-sounding Alsatian dialect. His gracious speech of welcome— in both languages—was cleverly linked with the printed theme of ONE FRANCE FOREVER. Like a smooth professional impresario, he pointed out the tables of his Alsatian comrades, also in colorful costume, who thereupon stood up and waved signs on which they had painted MERCI CHARNIERS. Waves of applause exploded and hand-clapping continued while Jean-Luc introduced the head table—even me. (I glanced furtively to discover if Emile Wassermann had joined in the applause—he had, I noted).

Once the meal was served—waiters had been hired from surrounding towns—Jean-Luc took center stage again and explained his region's specialties to the diners. I've remembered writing them down: *backehoffe,* a stew of pork, lamb, beef and potatoes; *choucroute* or sauerkraut with sausage, ham, etc. cooked in champagne; *knaepfle* or *spaetzle*, small buttered dumplings, accompanied by delicious Alsatian white wines and plenty of Alsatian beer, ending with desserts, *kugelhopf*, a sweet cake and memorable Christmas cookies, with holes like donuts, through which they were strung in bunches.

His culinary lesson was succeeded by one more announcement. *Une chose encore*," he said but abruptly changed over to *Elsaesserditsch*—Alsatian. After he finished in that language, the expectation was he would repeat what he said in French. The guests waited several moments and he didn't say anything. A voice shouted from the audience: "*En français!*" Immediately, Jean-Luc banged his forehead with the palm of his hand. "*Oh, je m'excuse!* I forgot!" French flowed from him but not of his accustomed elegant upper-crust variety. It was the Limousin argot and accent heard around Charniers and he was perfect at it. As Naansee would say, "he brought the house down." The local folks laughed and laughed and gave him a standing ovation.

The message he had delivered in both tongues was an invitation to peruse several large books of drawings displayed in certain corners of the room for those interested. They contained the works of a patriotic Alsatian satirist who had drawn anti-German cartoons while Alsace and Lorraine were under Prussian occupation from 1870 to 1918. The artist was called Hansi or Uncle Hansi to children and revered for his merciless lampoons of the invaders. Before the World War I victory and Alsace's return to France, he was jailed by the Boche but escaped to France to fight with us. Now in 1939, he was still alive, living and working in Colmar. Jean-Luc exhorted the crowd to pay homage to this outstanding French patriot whose real name was Jean-Jacques Waltz.

Folk dancing would begin shortly, the young emcee announced. Tables were moved by the waiters to clear a space for the performance. Jean-Luc explained the symbolism of the refugees' costuming, especially the girls. "Note their headdresses," he said. These were outsized ribbons they wore sticking up in their hair like giant ears and recognized as typical Alsatian ceremonial dress. What we didn't realize was the significance of the colors they bore: black for Protestants, red and other colors for Roman Catholics. Our host was quick to add that both populations, the former in the north of Alsace, the latter in the south, lived together in harmony as an integral part of France.

The musicians, also costumed *à l'alsacien*, who had serenaded us upon arrival with oomp-pah-pah tunes, were readying to strike up again. The dancers were in place.

However, at the last moment Jean-Luc held up his hand and said: "Messieurs, mesdames, I have a special treat for you. A poem has been composed for this occasion and dedicated to you by Elsa Leibart, one of the young people to whom you have given haven. Elsa Leibart is thirteen years old and lives in the picturesque city of Selestat where there are many charming old buildings. Mademoiselle Leibart, please step forward and read us your words of gratitude."

A hush fell over the room. The poetess, a braided blonde slip of a girl approached the microphone. I had noticed her around town among her compatriots. She had a nice intelligent face but she was not very good-looking: skinny, gawky, flat-chested. Her voice was chirpy as a bird's. Yet you could hear a pin drop.

I am hereby setting down the opening stanza as reprinted from a back number of the *Voice of the South West*, a regional weekly that wrote up the Charniers fête at the time.

"Mesdames, messieurs, it is Alsace who is talking to you. We will sing you the beauties of my birthplace. We will bring you the gurgle of rushing mountain streams unloading their force and foam to form still wider flows, toward Selestat, my native city, toward Colmar, through Strasbourg and into the Rhine. We will chant the holy magnificence of the great cathedral in our largest community. We will offer you the greetings of our half-timbered houses, reeking of the Middle Ages, their smiling exteriors unchanged since then. Feel the shadows of the Vosges peaks overwhelmed by the changeless greenery of forests of sapins. We, your countrymen, most endangered by the Hun, cried to you for help and you answered: "Come stay with us. We embrace you, fellow French!" (loud applause).

The local newspaper's editor, I've reasoned, was smitten by the lyricism of her opening and printed all her words in full. There was further lyricism, I remember, devoted to the Limousin and "dear, incomparable Charniers-sur-Nys." The curtain call she took drew a torrent of appreciation that made her blush, blowing kisses and curtseying, before she flounced off in her wide pretty skirt and frilly blouse to join her comrades and I even noticed her big headdress was red, meaning she was a Catholic like most of us in the hall.

The Alsatian youngsters put on their dance show and Jean-Luc added narrative to introduce the typical Elsaesser waltzes, mazurkas and polkas.

Roundly cheered, the kids went back to their table and general dancing commenced. Contemporary French melodies abounded and modern steps displayed. Not by me, I admit, usually so embarrassed on the floor at local celebrations that I always sat out most numbers like a—Naansee taught me the American word for it—"wallflower." I somehow prefer that expression to our own—*"faire tapisserie"*—merge into the tapestry.

Jean-Luc asked Chantal to dance and they went off hand in hand, I noticed.

I also caught sight of a scene that dismayed me. Poor homely Elsa Leibart sat inconsonantly by herself. Her hands were folded in her lap, her wan smile greeted any male who came by, her cheeks had been rouged and maybe for the first time in her life, she wore lipstick.

My heart has always gone out to those unfavored members of the weaker sex. Despite her poetical talent, she was being ignored as a female.

Before I knew it, I rose impulsively from my chair and headed toward her. Never had I done anything like this. Upon approaching, I bowed and using words of German I'd learned at school since I didn't know Alsatian, said: *"Wollen zie tanzen, gnadige fräulein?"*

She appeared startled. Repeating my request in French, she seemed better to understand. Her pointing at the moving bodies nearby was like a question. I nodded. And that unspoken response brought forth a broad, sweet smile. Mind you, there was nothing tepid about her acceptance. She took my arm and I led her into the melee.

Dancing, I don't have to tell you, can be very strenuous. I've forgotten how many numbers we participated in before fatigue sent us back to the seats. But I didn't desert Elsa. I drew up a chair and we talked, despite the continual din while the musicians played on.

The one part of our conversation I've retained ever afterward occurred when Elsa asked me if I'd seen *La Grande Illusion*.

I must have looked blank, for she added: "The French movie by Renoir, not the artist but his son Pierre . . ." She smiled and she did have a nice grin. "They filmed part of it near Selestat."

Soon I heard all about this heralded work and Haut-Koenigsbourg, the real-life fortress where the ending was shot. For Elsa, *La Grande Illusion*, with Jean Gabin and Pierre Fresnay, was an all-time masterpiece. For me, too, once I got to see that incomparable film.

My talk with Elsa was finally interrupted by Jean-Luc who stepped to the microphone, holding up his hand for quiet. Gradually, the hubbub diminished. "It is growing late, messieurs, mesdames. The buses for Alsace will leave early tomorrow. We have time for one final number."

Then a suspenseful pause. "This tune is known as *Chant de Guerre pour l'Armée du Rhin*" and was written and first sung in Strasbourg. Some people call it *La Strasbourgeoise*."

His signal to the musicians was a downbeat. At once, there burst out the stirring, martial, immortal opening bars of the *La Marseillaise*.

Delighted, the crowd jumped to its feet.

Jean-Luc intervened for the final time. "You see, *messieurs, mesdames,* our national anthem began in Strasbourg and was picked up in Marseilles. So, to honor our French solidarity, let us all sing: "*Allons enfants de la patrie. Le jour de gloire est arrivé . . .*"

The very rafters seemed to reverberate with a lusty roar as every voice pitched in. I have often heard *La Marseillaise* sung, magnificent renditions, too, but never with such fervor as that night. Verse after verse was repeated before the partyers grew exhausted. Many a cheek, male and female, had tears streaming down them.

The fête was over.

I presently faced the ticklish problem of saying good-night to Elsa Leibart. I was as awkward as she was, it seemed. We settled for a decorous handshake.

Papa, as always at the end of these events, had a crowd surrounding him. I hurried to his side and when at last he stopped gabbing to his cronies, he signaled it was time for us to walk home. The barn had been quickly emptying.

Immediately outside, torches illuminated a path toward the center of Charniers. But there, streetlights were on, the "miracle," townspeople still called it—the most up-to-date electric glows in what would have been solid darkness a few years earlier. My Royalist father had pulled some strings in higher places and voilà, Charniers had joined the twentieth century. It always struck me that in municipal matters, he was as much Papa to the community as he was to me.

I was up early the following morning. I wanted to see the buses off and most particularly to bid good-bye to Jean-Luc. I would congratulate him on the great job he had done the previous night. Many of Charniers inhabitants had come to say farewell to our guests. Folks were milling around on the Champ de Foire and I did catch the figure of Jean-Luc, rushing hither and there, exhorting his compatriots to occupy their seats. One bus was already full. Bedecked with flags and patriotic colors, it would lead the cavalcade, including a few private cars back to Alsace. The drivers had started to warm up their engines. As I sauntered alongside, a bus window opened and someone called to me. It was Elsa. She appeared much less timid than the night before. Leaning out as I paused, at least to utter bonjour, she asked without a quaver: "Would you mind . . . would you mind awfully if I wrote?"

I instantly and loudly let her know how pleased I'd be and would write back. Behind her, I was certain, were sounds of girlish giggling from her friends.

As I moved on, I realized Chantal was nowhere in sight. I had certainly expected she might wish to bid good-bye to . . . should I name Jean-Luc her "boyfriend." Or had their parting happened the night before?

I saw Jean-Luc hurrying past to the lead bus crying "*En voiture, tout le monde!*" and continuing down the line to the second bus behind me, which I assumed he boarded. The motors of both vehicles revved up. The column started forward. Flags were flapping. Windows had been lowered and the refugees were shouting: "*À bientôt*" The Alsatian girls had been given bouquets of flowers by our local women. Horns were honking. The kids started singing *La Marseillaise*.

When I turned around, I could scarcely believe my eyes. Jean-Luc stood amid the cluster of onlookers from Charniers.

He spotted me and instead of settling for an off-hand wave, started in my direction.

Without a word, we shook hands.

Meanwhile, I had figured he was waiting for the flashy car and the informal chauffeur to arrive and transport him home. Maybe the woman in black wearing the big crucifix would arrive, too. I had guessed she must be his mother.

Prior to my saying a word, he told me: "You know you did a very nice thing for that dear sweet girl last night."

How sensitive of him to have noticed. A bit embarrassed, I answered: "She's very intelligent. I enjoyed talking to her." All of a sudden, my nerve was back and I asked him point blank: "How much longer will you stay in Charniers?"

Laughing, he responded: "Until the end of this stupid war."

Seeing how taken aback I was, he promptly added: "Tomorrow is not a school day for you. My tutoring ends around noon. Let's do some bike riding together in the afternoon."

"*D'accord*," I agreed, surprised but enthusiastic.

We arranged a time and place to meet.

So ended my long midday reverie these many years later.

Back in the study, I stared at the blank wall. If I expected anything on the white plaster like newsreels or other pictures from my mind, I was disappointed, *at least for now*, I told myself.

VII

Amazingly, although my "Screen" remained blank, my mind kept reminiscing on. Into its purview appeared my distant cousin Cyprien Desfosseux. His home was in the Vendée, yet our family had never ventured to see him because he resided apart from Papa's native region of the Vendéenes Hills and lived on the island of Noirmoutier off the Vendée's small segment of Atlantic coast.

He had passed away quite a few years ago. What I did recall of him in the present centered on a visit he made to Charniers after the war.

He asked me to use his initials, C.D. in addressing him. I had received a phone call he was in Limoges on business (he dealt in seafood) and had left time for a side-trip to the now nationally important memorial of Charniers-sur-Nys and acquaint himself with a long-lost relative. I expressed my delight and hoped he would stay with me, which he did for two days.

Almost at once, conducting him around the ruins, I was his "Vergil, guiding him like Dante through Hell's inferno." Businessman to be sure, he also had a literary if not a classicist's bent. We were to have stimulating if sometimes argumentative talks.

The first occurred on the evening of his arrival after we had spent most of an afternoon tramping about the martyred village. At the apéritif hour, we retired to a café-bistro in New Charniers and indulged ourselves with glasses of Byrrh and a plate of hors d'oeuvres. C.D. was a corpulent fellow with a full belly and a compelling belly laugh. He teased the *patron* and his wife, made contact with other imbibers in the establishment and if I can be literary myself, was somewhat Falstaffian. But he soon had a serious moment.

Suddenly, he said to me: "You haven't asked my thoughts about your Pompeii."

"Pompeii?" I replied quizzically. "That was an act of nature. This is the handiwork of man."

"But both have ended up looking identical," he answered. "These carefully preserved relics could exist anywhere, from any cause, any century. I'm sorry to say I didn't feel any human connection and therefore no empathy for the victims, even including your father."

I swallowed my shock over his remarks yet didn't contest him frontally. "But doesn't the presence of the Alsatians in the SS unit add a new moral question—what is a man's responsibility for murder committed by him even under duress?"

His reply was: "I suppose the Roman Legions had soldiers who weren't there voluntarily but killed innocent civilians, anyway." As if aware his unfeeling words had hurt, he switched the subject. Rather bizarrely, I felt. "Don't you think it ironic that you and your father bear the name Desfosseux," he interjected.

Was this one of his jokes? I hardly suppressed my anger. "How so?" I curtly demanded.

"*Fossoyeur*," he answered. "Gravedigger. I'm sure your ancestors and mine—the Desfosseux clan in the Vendée—buried people for a profession.

"I did it unprofessionally," I retorted. I had been in a burying party after the massacre.

"Charniers? Do you know the meaning of the term?"

"I didn't know it had a meaning," I responded.

"I understand there's another Charniers nearby in the region."

"Charniers-sur-Vare. On the Vare River, like we're on the Nys. Much bigger town.

"If there are two Charniers close together, what does that suggest?"

Honestly, I was beginning to be provoked although I hid my annoyance. "Dear cousin," I said sweetly. "I'm not a mystery solver—unless it's about French history."

"In a sense it is," said Cyprien Desfosseux. "I suspect you understand some Latin. *Carnale* . . . from *caro*—flesh. Old French, *carnel* . . . Charniers . . . *charnel house* . . . a site in the Middle Ages where they heaped dead bodies."

"Would you call it the same as a hecatomb?"

"A great slaughter, so said the Greeks. I suspect your ancients in the Limousin had an overflow of corpses then. Thus a second Charniers, one practically next to the other."

Another reportable incident took place when I walked back from

New Charniers with my relative. We were passing the cemetery—the original village burying place, not the site where the 1944 victims are buried and a monument raised. I wasn't paying much attention when C.D. stopped abruptly. Coming toward us from the ancient cemetery's iron gates shambled a bent-over old woman, wearing the somber black of widow's weeds that would have earned her the title of "nun" from us saucy kids in other days. She carried an empty flower basket in the crook of her arm while manipulating two canes. We could see her snappy jet black eyes giving no sign she noticed the two men in front of her. Nevertheless Cyprien doffed his hat in a gesture of respect.

The instant she was beyond earshot, I said to CD: "That person is Marie Malinvaux. She is a walking miracle, the only survivor of the *hécatombe* in the church where all the women and children were slain. Once a day, she puts fresh flowers on the graves of all her loved ones— eight children and a host of other family members."

His hat back on, Cyprien said—as much to himself as to me: "Now I can declare I have genuinely experienced the inferno of Charniers-sur-Nys."

After he returned to his Noirmoutier-en-l'Île, we did write each other on occasion.

In one letter, he enclosed a tinted postcard of an antique armchair, explaining it was a display in the local château that paid homage to General Louis d'Elbée, a leader of the Royalist forces in the Vendée's war against the Republic. Badly wounded, captured at the battle of Cholet, d'Elbée was transported to Noirmoutier and, unable to walk, carried in this armchair to his execution by firing squad in the town square. "A bit of French history," Cyprien wrote. Not long afterward, I learned CD had been diagnosed with cancer and the last news was a black-edged funeral card. Had I been alerted earlier, I would have made an effort to attend his funeral. I liked the guy from the start—a bright, irritatingly outspoken, yet sensitive man.

With thoughts of Cyprien still in my mind, I suddenly entertained a "brainstorm." Why not now go to New Charniers, to the same bistro where CD and I had sat so many years ago, and have a drink or two? The establishment was called Le Nid (The Nest) but previously had been Le Cygne Noir (The Black Swan), and when that had seemed too lugubrious, Le Cygne Bleu.

About New Charniers, I've already revealed my distaste. In my case, it was partially because its official name remained Charniers-sur-Nys, not New Charniers, which we old timers had dubbed it. But also its ambience was so unlike the past—all concrete structures—a sameness of architecture that even included the botched attempt at re-creating a Romanesque church. On occasion, when I did not feel like driving to larger towns like Nieuil or Saint-Junien, I would patronize the *supermarché* within its confines. The main square was only a short walk from Bregonzac although I rarely ventured in that direction on foot.

Ah, here's a change of pace, I told myself. It would give me a chance to sit at a sidewalk table, relax with several glasses of Byrrh, and mindlessly watch the parade of traffic and pedestrians. It might happen I would encounter an acquaintance of mine or possibly my great friend Octave Bois who lived nearby and kept an office in the ersatz community.

Off I went. Along the footpath, the sights, sounds and smells were of an almost full-blown spring. Enough foliage had sprouted so it was mostly impossible to identify the birds whose mating songs I was hearing. I had invariably envied Jean-Luc his talent in this regard. His attempts to enlighten me, I'm afraid, most always fell on my musically deaf ears. With his coaching on identification, I could generally name whatever I saw on a branch by its plumage coloring, beak size and shape, and eventually its mode of flight.

But today my mind was on my destination and I didn't even turn my head whenever I heard a rustling in the leaves. Before I almost knew it, I was on a paved street leading to the main square. It was a bit early for the apéritif crowd. So I had no trouble finding a sidewalk table outside at Le Nid. The Byrrh I ordered had the traditionally attired (in black and white) waiter seemingly confused. Byrrh was an old-fashioned no longer quite popular fortified wine. I had to write out the name for him. I recognized the moment I heard his accent that he wasn't native French. His origin was Reunion in the Indian Ocean. I'd been there, I told him, doing research on French overseas history. In the next hour or so, we exchanged comments about the DOM-TOM—*départements d'outre-mer* and *territoires d'outre-mer*. Reunion had opted to remain with France when our "Empire" had officially ended.

Meanwhile, as soon as the viewing of cars, noisy motorcycles, bicyclists, shoppers, strolling lovey-dovey couples, etc. had become a bore, I entertained myself by giving a silent lecture to the ghost of Cyprien Desfosseux as if he were in the vacant chair next to me.

"You saw Marie Malinvaud," I began my unheard lecture. "Until you did, the tragedy at our original Charniers-sur-Nys held no reality for you. But you recognized the inferno in Marie's mere gaze. Let me tell you her horrific story."

"You have to remember," the silent monologue to my late relative continued, "that Vichy was still in power in this region as the puppet of the Nazis during June 1944. The *Libération* hadn't yet reached us. Understandably, the massacre at Charniers-sur-Nys was played down by the official Pétainist newspapers and spokespeople. Marie Malinvaux's incredible escape from the holocaust inside the church received only peripheral coverage."

"On the grassy slope behind Saint Augustine's, Marie's motionless body was found alive by a Red Cross rescue unit. Periodic moans had been heard from her inert form. Much was made of the fact that she lay directly beneath the shattered stained glass window once depicting our Savior's agony on the Cross."

"When discovered, Marie was so blackened by smoke from the fires the Germans had set inside the holy sanctuary with their phosphorous grenades that the leader of the salvage effort exclaimed: "I didn't know there was a negress in Charniers.""

"All of the little hands of her youngest children had been let go inside the blinding chiaroscuro of suffocating fumes and flashes of white hot exploding phosphorous. She knew all the children locked inside with the women, her own included, had already perished. Sheer instinct drove her as she stepped over bodies past burning pews to the altar beyond the nave. Climbing up onto it was likewise an instinct. Rudimentary stairs ran up a side wall she had often seen used by handymen climbing to the belfry. However, her goal was the casement once sheltering the much admired stain-glass depiction of Christ crucified. How she wedged herself through the broken shards to reach open air provided a lesson in stoicism. Her hands were cut, burnt where they'd touched heated metal, and yet—although not a thin woman—Marie urged on her body without thinking. A piece of good fortune awaited her. Squeezing herself onto a still-intact section of rooftop, she found a drainpipe leading to the ground. But shimmying down it, she lost her grip halfway and with a piercing cry, dropped at least twenty meters."

"Luckily the two patrolling SS men alerted by her shriek were tipsy from drinking a bottle of brandy they'd stolen and their aim wasn't sharp. Only two bullets hit her as she lay crumpled with a broken leg and neither struck a vital organ. In testimony after the war, the Germans said these gunmen were Alsatians. The Alsatians countered that the would-be killers were Rumanians drafted into the Waffen SS, as they had been."

Here I paused, as if out of breath. The vision of myself as a solitary disheveled old Frenchman sitting alone and nursing a drink intruded on my narrative.

Chargez les valises was an expression I always found amusing.—"getting crocked," to quote Naansee's English. *Why not?* It had been a long time since I'd gone on a binge. Who could blame me?

After I signaled the waiter, I downed the last of my first Byrrh and ordered another. But being a cautious old Frenchman at heart, more conservative than I'd care to admit, I asked for a plate of cheeses to go with my second drink. Once I started eating the reblochon, brie, and chèvre with slices of baguette, I amused myself by mentally repeating Charles de Gaulle's witticism: "How do you govern a country that has four hundred and forty-six different cheeses?"

Images from my narrative to invisible cousin CD were woven into bits of mute talk.

"It was a Saturday and, as you know, a school day in France."

"The clickety-clack sound of kids in wooden shoes on cobblestones of the town center."

"The mass of women and children crammed among the church pews."

"Frightened youngsters crying and soft voices trying to console them."

"SS men lugging in large black boxes that had fuses hanging from them. These infernal machines were used to produce smokescreens. With cigarette lighters, their wicks were set ablaze and exploded into dense black smoke . . ."

That's enough, I finally decided. I believe I must have uttered the phrase aloud for several people at nearby tables glanced quizzically in my direction.

But only momentarily. I ignored their stares.

Let them think what they like. Little did they know where my mind was heading next. My most ambitious nighttime escapade to date!

How or why the idea appeared to me at that moment, I'll never know. It was of an extravaganza based on recent French history before, during, and immediately after World Wars I and II.

Commanding a third (and final) Byrrh, I used my waiting time to triage among various outstanding personages of the era. There were to be multiple interviews. Arbitrarily, I limited myself to seven.

Before the waiter arrived with the bill, I had made my choices. Colleagues of mine in the world of academic French history would certainly have quibbled over my selection. *Tant pis.* I would be unbending.

My super-interview of the seven was to be left until tomorrow evening. That gave me all the rest of this evening and most of the next day's morning and afternoon to prepare. The finalists in my mind were—in order of appearance—Georges Clémenceau, André Maginot, Charles Maurras, Leon Blum, Pierre Laval, Joseph Darnand and Paul Raynaud.

The attack on this selection, I expected, would open up with: "But where is Philippe Pétain . . . and where, oh where, is Charles de Gaulle?" The honest answer that followed from me could only be: *I doubt my ability to portray them accurately: Pétain already senile in the 1940s and de Gaulle a figure larger than life.*

Runners-up, incidentally, were Jacques Doriot, Jean Moulin, Maurice Thorez, Admiral Jean-François Darlan and Albert Camus.

It would be a test of all tests of my mimicry abilities and require thorough boning-up on these personalities. My aim was to draw a composite picture of what led to the tragedy of France's downfall, which for me peaked in my retrospection with the imagined motor sounds of those SS trucks and vehicles pulling into Charniers-sur-Nys on a hot June Saturday.

When I finally paid the bill at Le Nid and headed for the path back to Bregonzac, I knew it would be a cliché to declare I felt like a new man. Rather, it seemed tantamount to changing jobs, overcoming steep odds, and, if successful, ridding myself of the moral confusion into which I'd been plunged.

I could hardly wait to get started on the research I had to do.

My new *baccalauréat*, I told myself, a crucial test.

VIII

The lights in my study—overhead fluorescents and a pair of reading lamps on stands flanking both sides of my comfy armchair—were not extinguished that evening until at least midnight. There was a fairly copious section of biographies among the crowded bookshelves. Eventually stacked on my nearby desk were nine books carefully extracted from the stacks. They covered the first three of the personages I had selected: Clémenceau the Tiger, Maginot the alleged defense expert, and the highly controversial Jewish Socialist politician Leon Blum. Taking continual notes, I made a dent in the knowledge I would need for quizzing seven former big shots on the French political scene. When I decided finally to call it a night, I felt satisfied by this initial research stage. The following day, I would have daylight enough not only to complete the other four subjects but with time still left for accumulating additional information.

Confessedly, I became invigorated by this awesome task I'd assigned myself. Loneliness had never been a problem for me as long as my mind kept active. Scaling a mountain—I'd never done that physically, only mentally, and in my writings on French history. For years, I had worked on the mammoth subject of France's reach beyond the *Polygon*, the home country in its present shape. I had traveled the world over, including dangerous sites, to trace materials I could use. This late-blooming enthusiasm of mine for theatrical representation was a slight deviation. Infusing me was something of a playwright's skill. Remember, I once had been an amateur stage actor in Paris.

Helping out was the fact the characters conceived in my interviews had well-known traits. My experiences with Saint Augustine, Esclarmonde de Foix, Bélibaste, and Otto Rahn the Nazi Cathar-lover, were structured upon real living figures even if their distance in the past lent them a modicum of poetic license. With the chosen seven I would be encountering mostly contemporaries visible during my lifespan.

Then, too, I had to answer the question: do one at a time, or all seven on stage together?

For reasons you can surely understand, I chose the former mode. Separate interviews, yet seven chairs on stage, to which each would repair after completing his talk, and then all would reunite for a finale—a feat I could project intellectually, albeit while worrying chaos might ensue.

In the midst of my arduous ruminations, there was a knock at my study door. It was a timid rap, and thus I knew it was Arlette.

"Come in," I called.

Just as timorous as always, the thin, careworn-looking young woman shyly entered. "*Excusez-moi, M'sieu le Professeur* (she never addressed me in any other fashion), we will run out of eggs, butter and milk by the end of the week."

There! She had gotten the words out with an obvious effort. Whenever I gazed at Arlette, I could see something of her grandmother's features—those of Madame Blanchard, our martyred family housekeeper.

"Thank you, Arlette. I will see to it we are re-supplied," I assured her.

I did not mean to sound so business-like. Preoccupied as I was, I would have welcomed a conversation. But from experience, I knew it would be one-sided. Poor Arlette, mother of three youngsters, was the eternal victim of a drunken husband, and her Catholic upbringing would not permit seeking a divorce. More than once I'd seen her with dark glasses, no doubt hiding a blackened eye from a beating the brute had given her.

Having delivered the message and received an answer, she promptly vanished. A sardonic thought bubbled up: *Not all victims in Charniers are war victims.*

She had provided me a delicious boeuf bourguignon for my midday meal, and since she had also included a croque-monsieur for supper, I could go ahead and set up my operation in the study since she would have no need to return until the following morning.

From a utility closet, I picked out seven folding chairs and arranged them side by side opposite my favorite brown leather armchair in which I would sit tonight. I inserted a fresh tape in my recording machine and had others ready. I also set up the ledger into which I would later transcribe the dialogue I had contrived—for myself and my projections alike.

What an undertaking! I amazed myself that I had so much energy at my age. The boeuf bourguignon was consumed. Further research continued until eventide. Then with the croque-monsieur devoured, and my will fortified with several glasses of red wine, I was finally ready for the ambitious drama I had planned.

The first test was Georges Clémenceau. This son of the Vendée, a standout in French public life since the 1890s days of the Dreyfusards, had been nicknamed "The Tiger" due to his fierceness in the political arena. Still, his career had ups and downs, until he rose to immortal stardom in France after taking charge as premier in 1917 and turning defeat into victory. His toughness was even more apparent after the war, when he represented our country at the Versailles Treaty negotiations.

Concentrating furiously, I started things off by projecting a newsreel quality onto my plaster wall "Screen" that depicted hero Clémenceau, following the Armistice of November 1918, on a visit to Alsace, the lost province that his legendary stubbornness had returned to the mother country. Ecstatic crowds cheered him on the streets of Strasbourg. In front of the Cathedral, he was greeted by a phalanx of costumed little girls with huge ribbons in their hair. Moving in the jerky rhythm of films of that era, the old warrior, with his huge, drooping white mustache, bent down to kiss each little darling on the cheek while they handed him bouquets of flowers. The caption read:

THE TIGER TAMED BY FRANCE'S RETURNING CHILDREN

The last shot was a close-up of the premier's craggy squint and tears in his eyes.

When I turned my head to the array of folding chairs in front of me, Georges Clémenceau, himself, was entering stage left and settling into the first seat he reached.

His cane was deposited across his knees. It was plain to see he liked it close to hand. I could well picture him raising it in anger to bash an opponent.

Because I learned he had been born and raised in a small village in the Vendée called Mouilleron-en-Pareds, not far from my father's native community of Pouzauges, I instantly saw a resemblance in my guest's muscular build: his Neanderthalic thrust of body and imposing presence which so reminded me of Papa.

But George Clémenceau was no reactionary Vendéen Royalist. He was a Republic enthusiast to the core. In younger days, he had strongly upheld the innocence of the Alsatian Jewish French military officer Alfred Dreyfus who had been falsely convicted of treason. In fact, it was on the front page of a newspaper, *L'Aurore*, owned and edited by Clémenceau, that he published Emile Zola's immortal incendiary article, "J'accuse . . . !" which led to Dreyfus' exoneration. Nor was this Vendéen a devout Catholic, like most of his neighbors. His own father was an atheist, and he probably was as well.

"Good evening, honored Sir," I began. "You remind me of my father. He was also from the Vendée."

"Your family name?" I was curtly asked.

"Desfosseux . . . My father was Étienne Desfosseux of the Desfosseux family of Pouzauges. He was a medical doctor and the mayor of this martyred town . . . one of the martyrs, himself, I must add."

"Mort pour la France."

Immediately I recognized the politician's instinct behind this patriotic benediction.

"I have to be honest," I said. "You might not have liked my father. A Maurras disciple."

Never had I felt a pair of sharp eyes rake me like his did. "Maurras," he literally spat the name with contempt. "That pygmy ass-kisser of nobility. That goateed gnat. An intellectual piss-pot." Ferocious language had always been a hallmark of Georges Clémenceau.

But so was intelligence and mental quickness. He regarded me intensively before asking: "Did you say your late father was a medical doctor? I studied to be one. Maybe I should have stayed in the Vendée where I was practicing."

"Poor France would have been much the unhappier," I said rather obsequiously.

Again those gimlet eyes bore into me. "What is your *prénom*, Monsieur Desfosseux?"

"Eugène," I said. I wasn't going to give him my other names."

"Hah," he declared. "I am Georges *Eugène* Benjamin Clémenceau."

I have to admit I was not happy with this dialogue. It seemed petty and awkward, two old codgers chit-chatting and quite possibly both eager to get away from each other. Here I was with one of the greatest men in French history, and I was wasting the short time I had with him.

"Cut to the chase," was another of Naansee's American slang expressions.

"Let's cut to the chase, Mr. Prime Minister," I said in English, knowing he spoke the language. He had lived in exile in New York City for a number of years, and his first wife was an American, a student of his when he taught in Stamford, Connecticut. "I want to talk to you about the Treaty of Versailles."

Those heavy white eyebrows of his lifted a bit. "*Pourquoi?*" he demanded to know, refusing to join me in English, it seemed.

"I am trying to reconstruct a trail," I answered him in our native tongue. "It leads to the obscene ruins just beyond my door. Your part in it, if any. Some of my historian colleagues say you were too tough on the Germans at Versailles. Inadvertently, you gave Hitler the ammunition he needed to rise to power."

"Poppycock," That archaic expression was the only English I heard from him.

It was explained (in French) that he had learned this old-fashioned term during discussions at the peace conference in English with Lloyd George, the British prime minister, and also U.S. President Woodrow Wilson. Thus he launched into a vigorous defense of his own campaign in 1919 for harsh measures against Germany. "They should have listened to me," Clémenceau insisted. "We needed a buffer state between us and the Boche. We needed to strip them permanently of the Rhineland and the Ruhr and the Saar. I wanted to defang them completely. The only reason I accepted Wilson's fourteen points was because of one point— that Alsace and the parts of Lorraine the Huns had occupied would be returned to France. I was too soft, not too hard, and I overestimated Wilson's ability to speak for the United States."

We then touched upon an event right after the opening of the Versailles talks that made the Tiger even more admired by the French: a failed assassination attempt on his life. Most remembered was his bravado about the gunman who shot him. "The coward fired his revolver at me from the back at point-blank range. He should have been jailed for his carelessness in using a dangerous weapon. He missed me six or seven times from a few paces away. He should be condemned to eight years of training in a shooting gallery."

Nevertheless, one bullet did hit his shoulder blade and lodge in his lung, and no one believed he could survive. But two weeks later, he was back at work with the other Allied leaders. "I was seventy-eight years old," he told me, "and the bullet stayed in my body until I died in 1929. Too much of a risk to remove. Have you ever been shot, Eugène?"

"Shot at," I immediately retorted. "When I fought the Nazis in the Resistance."

"That madman Hitler. I could see even in the late 1920s he'd be trouble."

We were at the nub of my query: "Who's to blame for the *débâcle* of

May 1940?"

"*Débâcle* is the right word." Clémenceau nodded in approval. "The débâcle of 1870." I thought of Papa's Strasbourg prints. "The Dreyfus débâcle. *Les débâcles* in 1914 and 1917. The Versailles débâcle . . ." It seemed the white-mustachioed old gentleman would go on and on.

But I interrupted him. "Was it primarily hatred for the Republic that undermined us?"

"No, frankly Maurras and his gang of Camelot thugs were nothing but an itch, a pinprick, Royalist puke . . . do you think the French populace would die for a restored king and queen and a horde of sycophantic nobles and social climbers who would eat them out of house and home, pay no taxes and snottily tell people to eat cake when they were starving . . . the final, the ultimate, débâcle, it goes without saying, was the defensive mindset."

Picking up the conversation again, I said to the ex-premier: "You wrote a book in the late 1920s answering Maréchal Foch and others who'd attacked you for your handling of affairs during World War I and afterward. *Grandeurs et Misères d'une Victoire* caused a sensation. You attacked the threat of German rearmament. You even accurately predicted 1940 would be the year when we felt the full effects and . . ."

Now he interrupted me. "I didn't live to see that book in print, unfortunately."

As if completing his thought, I stated: "I know. The publication date is 1930."

Still furthering his theme, the Tiger declared: "By 1930, our occupation of the Rhineland ended five years earlier than I'd agreed. So we built thick walls around France. The Boche built tanks and planes to pierce them."

In a stage play, this would have been the perfect cue for the next appropriate character to enter. Consequently, I decided to put Georges Eugène Benjamin Clémenceau to sleep . . . not break him up and have him vanish. My guest, still sitting down, then slumped, the cane on his lap rolling onto the floor with a low clatter. It was as if Clémenceau became wrapped in a transparent cocoon. The limelight left him and moved to the empty chair adjoining his.

On my one bare wall, new versions of a grainy film had appeared. Massive barbed wire was shown, behind it a concrete pillbox with a monstrous cannon poking out, a subterranean train with open cars carrying immense shells for that powerful artillery piece, soldiers underground eating in a spacious mess hall and above ground, a delegation of high-ranking French military officers led by a nattily dressed civilian, a middle-aged man of imposing girth and height. The caption:

FORTRESS FRANCE.
FORMER MINISTER OF WAR MAGINOT INSPECTS HIS HANDIWORK.

Since André Maginot had seated himself by the time I looked away from the introductory newsreel, I did not see his famous limp. The cane he needed to maneuver was already placed by his chair. Unlike Clémenceau, however, this infirmity was not from age, but the result of a knee shattered at the battle of Verdun. It ended his fencing career, a gentleman's sport at which he was quite adept for such a physically large man.

His military career in World War I had followed a most unorthodox trajectory. Before 1914 he had gone from the bureaucracy (assistant to the governor-general of Algeria) to an elected député in the French Assembly and from then on to undersecretary of war. While retaining his number-two position in the army command, Maginot enlisted as a private, became a *poilu* of the infantry in the trenches of hell holes like Verdun. Because of his "coolness and courage," he was soon made a sergeant. At the same time a top army brass, General Maurice Serrail, sought out this non-commissioned officer, showed him an authorization on paper to evacuate and asked what he should do. The undersecretary (not the sergeant) simply tore up the document. Verdun's defense held and, many Frenchmen think, saved France.

Returning to politics after having won the highest decorations—the *Croix de Guerre* and the *Médaille Militaire*, the war hero was a shoo-in for re-election to his old seat from the Département of the Meuse. In short order, he became a full cabinet minister—first of Pensions, then of Overseas France and eventually minister of war in the 1920s and early 1930s.

It happened in Maginot's case that the Meuse Département contained his family's ancestral home in a part of Lorraine the Prussians had left to France in 1870. But he was born in Paris.

So *Parisien* was my instant thought, observing Maginot take his seat. He was dressed impeccably in a pin-striped business suit, a watch chain on his vest, cufflinks on his sleeves, gleamingly polished expensive shoes, a conservative tie, a rosette in his button hole, neatly trimmed brown brush mustache, not a hair on his head out of place. Here he was the very model of a debonair Frenchman planted in the upper crust of the bureaucracy.

Therefore my opening question to André Maginot was: "M'sieu le Ministre, you spent your formative years in Revigny-sur-Ornain in Lorraine. How do you consider yourself? A big city sophisticate, or rude country boy?"

Maginot's answer reflected the years he had practiced a politician's art of not committing himself right away.

"Maybe sophisticated peasant," he replied with a good-natured laugh.

I suggested: "It has been said that your prime motivation for the Maginot Line was the bombing of your family's residence in Revigny by the Germans in World War I."

His features lost their amiability. I imagined he was picturing the ruins of a small town château he had loved. "Yes of course I am a Lorrainer. We know what it's like to be invaded by the Boche."

My follow up was: "Your idea I have to agree was admirable, making France safe from our enemy beyond the Rhine." And I added: "You had seen the advent of Hitler."

Retorted Maginot: "Even while the Austrian was thought a crackpot clown, I still worried about these successors to the Prussians. I was minister of war when the so-called Führer and his gang attempted their putsch on November 9, 1923. Unlike many of my colleagues, I had doubts the Nazi defeat in the streets would mean the end of them. Hitler turned a disaster into a triumph by his performance in court. Should I go on?"

"By all means," I said.

Chock full of facts, the ex-war minister continued with a grouping of rhetorical questions. "Who now remembers the Ruhr occupation of 1923 by French troops? Who remembers the Weimar Republic had welched on its reparations payments to us? Who remembers the short-lived Rhenish Republic, an attempt by the inhabitants of the Rhineland, with pushing from the French, to establish a new nation independent of the Reich?" In this flow of words from him, there was a patina of authenticity. He had been there, he had participated and he had taken away a lesson. "We had to arm ourselves against the Teutons," Maginot declared in summation. "I saw that as my sacred duty."

"Ah, the defensive mindset!" I exclaimed. Clémenceau called it "The Final Débâcle."

"With all due regard for the Great Clémenceau, the 'Father of Victory'," Maginot began a spirited defense of himself. "The immortal

Tiger did not have my problems. To be sure, he let Wilson and Lloyd George wear him down at Versailles, but nothing could have changed the downward slide of France's population. It would take us several generations to make up our losses of 1914–1918. The French are lovers but there is a limit."

A *bon mot*, this last quip of his, proper for a Parisian drawing room. The veteran politician was grinning after he spoke.

Next Maginot laughed aloud, causing me to ask what had struck him so funny.

"How I got 3.2 million francs voted by the legislators for the *ligne*. They were, regardless of party, ready to shut my indefatigable mouth about the need to protect our frontier with Germany. I bored them to death in speech after speech. On the whole, the right wing was all for military expenditures. But on the left, they were mostly pacifists, the Communists as well as the Socialists. So I played the employment card. It was a time of widespread *chômage*, and any new jobs were joyously welcomed. Believe me, the Maginot Line created lots of work, which prompted the left to join my parade. Then, again, I also could put forth an argument that the string of forts was purely defensive. France would neither attack nor threaten the peace."

"Pétain was one of your strongest supporters, wasn't he?"

"Correct."

I had the impression from Maginot's curtness that he didn't want to argue the matter further. "And no one was listening to de Gaulle," I added disapprovingly, "except the Germans, who pored over his treatise about tanks and their use as weapons on the offense."

"De Gaulle struck us at the Ministry as a nuisance—a junior officer overstepping himself."

"There was certainly the inescapable problem of Belgium. Was there no thought in the Ministry of extending the Maginot Line to cover that flank?"

"We had a treaty with Belgium to assist each other if either were attacked along with the belief the Ardennes Forest on the border was too tangled a wilderness for the Germans to penetrate."

"All false assumptions," I commented.

Momentarily, M'sieu le Ministre looked a bit crestfallen. Then, again, he brightened and said: "At least we fortified La Ferte, which is practically in Belgium."

The silence between us for the next minute was awkward. I broke it by saying chattily: "In doing my research, I happened upon an amusing report on what the *poilus* manning your fortresses had for meals. The monotony of canned beef. First day, lunch, beef miroton and green beans; supper, cold beef vinaigrette and rice; second day, lunch, chopped beef and lentils; supper, beef sauce Robert and green peas; and so on. Even French culinary genius couldn't make such a diet palatable day after day."

"I hope the wine was good," Maginot laughed.

But once more, his fine features clouded over. "Eating," he said, "that was my undoing."

"A bad oyster, wasn't it? You caught typhoid from it."

"*Exactement.* How much better I would have been—maybe France, too—had I stuck to the rugged peasant fare of my dear Lorraine. Those elegant Parisian restaurants absolutely seduced me. The *belons* were always so delicious, but lurking in one was a fatal germ."

"You died in 1935," I said. "You still receive praise. An American author wrote that your 'shining honesty, singleness of purpose, lack of personal ambition . . . found no single parallel.' Your beloved Revigny has erected a magnificent statue of you, a street there bears your name and so does a school. At the Verdun battlefield, another majestic monument to you overlooks the graves, and yet . . ."

"And yet?" he mimicked me.

I continued: "In 1936, Hitler marched his troops into the Rhineland, announcing his decision to re-militarize in violation of various treaties. France stood by helplessly."

"Are you suggesting if I had been in office then, I would have abandoned my preference for defensive action only?"

"You know Hitler, himself, admitted: 'If the French had marched into the Rhineland, we would have had to withdraw with our tails between our legs.' Later, his number one tank commander Guderian said that had the French intervened, 'Hitler would have fallen.'"

"A lost opportunity, to be sure," was André Maginot's smooth but meaningless reply.

Instinctively, his silky manner upset me. I wanted to shout at him: "Your miscalculation on dealing with the Boche cost me my father, my family home, my best friend, my town and its people!" But rather I had a better idea. I put the former war minister into the same condition in his chair as the slumped Clémenceau alongside him.

My routine had become to direct light onto the next unoccupied chair and swivel around within my own armchair to gaze at empty wall space for a newsreel introducing the next interviewee. At once a caption appeared, under a photo of a grey-goateed man:

EX-IMMORTAL SENTENCED TO LIFE IMPRISONMENT.

On screen was Charles Maurras dressed in the ultra-elegant uniform of the French Academy.

This outfit was only worn by the forty Immortals of l'Académie on special occasions. They had life tenure once elected by their peers. However, membership could be terminated for misconduct. Interestingly, when Maurras received his invitation to join France's most prestigious institution, he had just been serving an eight-month prison term for threatening the life of French premier, Leon Blum. It wasn't the first time. A decade earlier, he had let loose his waspish tongue at then Interior Minister Abraham Schramek. "We will kill you like a dog," Maurras declared and received a suspended sentence and a one-thousand-franc fine. These two men he verbally slashed were French Jews in high office. In addition to insulting Blum as "a camel of an old Semite," *le Maître*, as he liked to be addressed, had threatened Schramek, "You should be whipped while awaiting the kitchen knife." Those years 1936–1937 found the inveterate rabble-rouser also cooling his heels in a cell. It seemed incredible the Academy would accept him in under such circumstances.

Yet his credentials were unassailable. The *Académie*'s purpose was the furtherance of Literature and Letters in France. Maurras had a host of published books credited to his name, starting in 1895 with *Le Chemin de Paradis* and continuing with works like *Anthinaea*, a travelogue about Greece, and *Les Amants de Venise*, the love story of George Sand and Alfred de Musset, and less literary, political ideas like *Enquête sur la monarchie* and *L'Avenir de l'intelligence*. Not only poets, novelists, biographers, etc. were in the Academy but political types, too. Pétain, for example. After World War II ended, both Pétain and Maurras were removed from their Academy seats.

Off screen, I now had an opportunity to examine Maurras in his full regalia. The spectacular apparel is referred to as *l'habit vert*—the green costume. The dark coat, dark trousers, dark shoes, dark cocked hat—all in Technicolor would be of the deepest forest green. The complicated braid covering on his bicorn Napoleon-style hat has been identified as "greenish-gold leaf."

As if at a fashion show, the progenitor of *l'Action française* showed off his finery. He also wore a scabbard attached to his belt, containing a ceremonial sword.

One last description—of the man, himself—showed more facial hair than in Papa's desk photograph. An ample greyish mustache accompanied the signature goatee and he presented the image of a stern, gaunt, prissy, aged person whose fierce eyes betrayed his inner fanaticism yet still conveyed the image of a boulevardier. His ubiquitous cane was visible as well. The canes of his bully-boy Camelots actually were weapons, lead-tipped for smashing heads in street brawls. I have never found any indication Maurras participated in the rough stuff, most of which had been inspired by his waspish tongue.

In gilt and deep dark green, Maurras made his way to the place I'd set out. Before he sat, he cast a decidedly unfriendly glance in my direction, then daintily lifted the tails of his Immortals dress coat before pushing aside his sheathed sword and plunking himself down onto the folding chair.

"Welcome," I greeted the Immortal, which was the only civil thing I felt I could say.

Charles Maurras glared at me, his angular face a frozen mask. So supercilious was he in his silent demeanor that I wanted to punch him right on his aquiline nose. Nevertheless, I unclenched my fists, reasoning he *had been* a friend of Papa's.

Consequently, remembering he had become almost deaf at twelve years old, I literally shouted: "I am the son of your loyal supporter, Doctor Étienne Desfosseux!"

This time, his features unfroze. Another stare of his raked me up and down. "I couldn't hear you completely," he said. "Doctor somebody?"

The voice I heard when he did speak had been halting and squeaky but not the odd accent of the average mute who learns to express words.

"Do you not remember Doctor Étienne Desfosseux?— DESFOSSEUX!" I shouted for emphasis. "He was the mayor of the village of Charniers-sur-Nys that lies in ruins nearby this house."

"A mayor . . . and doctor . . . ? That must be Doctor Desfosseux."

"He was my father."

There was significant strain on me, while tensing to catch his next word. That is, until I noted he was reading my lips, and I lowered my decibels from then on.

In conversational tones, we entered a discussion in which I planned to focus on the role he had played in France's 1940 defeat. I agreed with Clémenceau that *l'Action française* was strictly small potatoes. Statistics I'd unearthed revealed that during its heyday in the 1930s. Maurras' group had thirty thousand members and its newspaper one hundred thousand readers. Comparatively, the Croix de Feu of Colonel de la Roque, another right-wing operation, had three hundred thousand adherents.

When I pointed the statistic out, he rolled his eyes in a gesture of, *I've listened to all this before.*

"Brasillach, the poet, called La Roque 'an old cuckold of the Right,'" Maurras cattily reminded me.

I rebutted: "Brasillach was shot as a traitor following the Liberation. You're a poet who collaborated, too. How did you get off so easy—set free after five years of a life sentence?"

"To die misunderstood," complained Maurras. "I was always against the Boche. Anti-Nazi, too. When Hitler sent his goosesteppers into the Rhineland in '36, I screamed at our government to drive them out. You know what Hitler said would have happened if they did?"

"I'm aware of it," I said coldly." To which I added: "Your anti-Semitism helped them send thousands of Jews to their deaths with French help."

"I swear I thought they were only deporting foreign Jews back to their countries." The old goat seemed a bit frantic now. "French Jews were different. Some were very good friends of mine. Daniel Halevy. René Rosenstein, an Alsatian businessman . . ."

"Dreyfus was Alsatian."

"Dreyfus had to be guilty to save the army's honor."

"Second-rate Saint Cyriens sacrificing another pushy Jew," I wisecracked.

Maurras wasn't amused. He wrinkled up his nose as if sniffing a bad smell.

But as he sniffed again, I thought mischievously: *Maybe it's just the mothball scent of his Académie uniform he took out of his closet.*

Once he sniffed yet again, I really deemed the latter was the case. The gaudy gilded outfit did appear a bit ragged and past its better years. He had donned it in 1935.

That was a year after the infamous riots of 1934 in Paris when a mob of right wing fanatics tried to invade the National Assembly. This overall "revolt," some claimed, might have succeeded had Maurras swung the full weight of *l'Action française* movement behind it.

He didn't, however.

Was his reward an election to the Académie the following year? I could only speculate.

Or was his reluctance to support other right wingers a sign of weakness? In 1926, the pope excommunicated him due to his writings and he lost thousands of devout Catholics.

Ah, here was another subject for him to sniff at. Charles Maurras, the ultra Catholic, kicked out of the Vatican church!

I said to him: "You know 1926 was the year after I was born."

No sniff. But a doleful expression.

"I went back to adherence to Rome twenty years later," he alibied.

"My father stayed with you people," I told him. "As long as my mother lived, which was only a few years, he kept attending Mass, going to confession, taking communion. Once she died, that was all over for him, though it was still forced on me."

"Doctor Desfosseux was of the Vendéen strain that was much more devoted to Vendéen autonomy than to Catholicism. My first love was also Regionalism. Regions ran their own affairs under the king. I am a Provençal first and foremost."

"The Land of Oc!" I exclaimed snidely, "where Catholics wiped out the Cathars."

Once more, Maurras sniffed. "The Cathars, a dead-end religion," he snickered. "But the troubadours had something to them. Like my friend and mentor, the great poet Mistral."

"Frédéric Mistral!" I exclaimed anew. "The Félibres."

"He and five fellow poets organized groups in Provence and even in Catalonia, Spain. *Félibre* means 'free' in the Occitan language."

"As if I didn't know. Here in the Limousin, we had a famous troubadour, Bernart de Ventadorn. I've always liked one of his lyrics about a lady love: 'I wish to remain at her feet until she, as a sign of mercy, admits me where she undresses.'"

With this last line, I wondered if I would get a rise out of Maurras. It has been argued that with his mannerisms and dainty appearance, he feared he would be called effeminate, so he had a number of well-advertised affairs with women while remaining a bachelor.

Yet Maurras didn't go after the bait. His visage remained frozen.

Subsequently, I tried another lure. "Did you know that *félibre*, translated into Greek, means 'friend of the Hebrews'? Some friend you were."

This time I struck home.

"I called anti-Semitism of the flesh a stupidity," he defended himself.

Shaking my finger, I railed: "You inspired Darnand, he was one of your Camelots, the head of the Milice during the war. We have them partly to thank for what happened to us here. Your bully boys nearly beat Leon Blum to death . . . But you'll see him soon enough."

There was alarm in Charles Maurras' tinny voice. "What do you mean?"

"Leon Blum will be here any minute to join you and Clémenceau and Maginot."

"I will not stay in the same room with that youpin!"

"Oh no?"

Seconds later, I had him slumping down in his folding chair, sword and all. Before turning away, I observed his ceremonial gold-leafed bicorn hat. He had been wearing it front and back like a superannuated admiral. But it had slipped and now slanted horizontally on his head like Napoleon wore his. *Un Bonaparte manqué*, I thought, sinking back into my own armchair, momentarily mentally exhausted.

IX

I must have dozed off right afterward. It was pitch black outside my one window in the study when I sat up and realized I had fallen asleep. The spotlight trained on the fourth folding chair had kept it illuminated but not yet occupied by my next invitee, Leon Blum.

The "camel of an old Semite" had been waiting in the wings. Once my head lifted and my eyes focused, he became visible walking slowly and ponderously past the other three seated unconscious forms. Leon Blum was indeed "old." Moreover, the terrible beating he had received from *l'Action française* thugs in 1936 had affected his physical being evermore, not to mention additional damage from years in concentration camps.

Just before Blum seated himself, I sought to see if my newsreel had reappeared. It had—in the shape of a blown-up photograph on a 1936 cover of the American magazine, *Time*. The future premier of France was shown in a hospital bed, his skull swathed by bandages. The caption broadcast against my wall proclaimed:

OUTRAGE IN FRANCE: THE ASSAULT ON LEON BLUM.

The kindly, white-haired, white-mustached gentleman of advanced age who now took his seat opposite me *did not look Jewish*. Anywhere in France, you would have encountered his like. In fact, he had been born in Paris, although his ancestors were Alsatian Jews who likely had emigrated from Germany decades earlier. It was the success of this highly articulate lawyer in French politics that had so aroused the ire of Charles Maurras. How dare an Israelite rise to the highest position—of premier?

I do admit after studying him closely that his cleverness showed in his facial features, particularly his intelligent eyes, which he proceeded to hide with a pair of spectacles removed from the vest of his nice suit and

thus armed, examined me closely. *Something foxy*, I told myself silently—
silver foxy, given the hoary hue the years had colored the hair on his head
and his pointed mustache.

He said archly: "I suppose you would like me to start by elucidating
the incident illustrated on your wall, by my wounds.

I volunteered: "The date, if I'm correct, was in February 1936, two
years after the right-wing battles in the streets surrounding the Assembly."

"I was not prime minister in 1936. But I was a député, a Socialist
from the interesting seaside town of Narbonne. Imagine, an Alsatian Jew
representing an historic community in Languedoc—land of Mistral . . .
and . . . his disciple Maurras, my nemesis. Yet the real irony was Narbonne
had once been an important Jewish center in the Middle Ages, that is,
until their expulsion in the thirteenth century."

"You were the *second* prince of the Jews of Narbonne," I said jokingly.

"So you've heard of that obscure figure," said Blum. "Naturally, you
are a French historian. But did you also learn this so-called Narbonne
King of the Jews was simply a mocking title given to the Israelite whom
the reigning *Seigneur* had placed in charge of the considerable population
of local Jews?"

A grin followed from the *sympathique* old camel.

I smiled, too.

"Where were we?" Blum asked rhetorically. "I assume, Professor, you
know Paris well."

"For a country bumpkin from the Limousin, most certainly I do."

"And you are acquainted with the Boulevard Saint-Germain, *n'est-ce
pas?*"

"I lived near Odeon."

"*Bon*. I do not have to describe the geography of the attack". The
next moment, he launched into a play-by-play recital of how the brutal
trauma he'd suffered had occurred.

"I was leaving the Assembly building at the end of a day of sessions
with my Socialist colleague Georges Monnet and his wife Germaine. Our
means of transportation was Georges' Citroen. He drove while Germaine
and I sat in the back seat. A right turn put us on the Boulevard Saint-
Germain. It was a route I had taken hundreds of times in my life into
the heart of the famous Quartier Latin. We passed the world-renowned
Saint-Germain-des-Prés—"

Pausing, Blum caught his breath. "Now the incredible phenomenon
of coincidence . . . Jacques Bainville, a founder with Maurras of *l'Action
française*, had managed to die a few days earlier. He lived on the Boulevard

opposite the Ministry of War. I'm sure you know the spot. Not quite at Odeon."

I nodded my head.

"Bainville's funeral was being held in his home. A like-minded crowd of fascistic rightists had gathered to pay homage to the departed littérateur. They spilled over into the Boulevard. Too late, Georges Monnet saw they were essentially barricading the way. He sought to drive through them. Impossible! Trying desperately to turn around, he was likewise blockaded. Someone spotted me in the back. The cry went up: 'We've got Blum, come quickly!'

Others began chanting: 'Better Hitler than Blum! Blum to the stake!' These hooligans pulled me out of the vehicle. Their blows rained down on my head—lead-tipped canes, wooden cudgels, bare fists. It didn't take me long to black out. Their hate-filled faces faded. Their howls against the Jews grew dim. I fell into total darkness. It was afterward stated that only the intervention of police officers guarding the War Ministry building saved my life."

"Finally, we may cry *Vive les flics!*" I joked, undoubtedly much too insouciantly.

Blum continued drily: "Four months later the Popular Front I organized rose to power and I became the premier of France."

I said to him: "In June 1944, when the massacre occurred in Charniers, you were in Buchenwald concentration camp. Obviously you couldn't have known of our Armageddon. When did it come to your attention?"

Blum looked thoughtful before he answered: "I believe it was in an article—I can't recall the source—it had gruesome pictures. During 1946–47, I was briefly premier again. I had planned an official visit to your hallowed site but my time in office was too short, only two months." He smiled self-deprecatingly at me. "Blame age," he said. "I can't for the life of me remember why I never went on my own."

"You died in 1950," I replied. "Not long enough to witness the trial in 1953 of the few perpetrators who'd been caught, mostly Alsatian draftees, as you know."

"I was aware they'd been involved."

"Do you consider yourself Alsatian?"

"No, French of Alsatian Israelite heritage. Our family was prominent, right up with the Dreyfuses, the Weills, the Meyers, the Rosensteins—"

"The Rosensteins—" I interrupted. "Did you know that R. R.—René Rosenstein, the department store king—despite being Jewish, had been a member of *l'Action française?* My father knew him in the 1920s when

Papa, also an early member, studied in Strasbourg."

"René was smart," Blum remarked. "He sold his stores and left the country for Switzerland. It happened in 1938 when I was briefly again premier. I've since learned about your father's own bravery when the SS arrived here. That more than atones for any lack of political wisdom on Doctor Desfosseux's part."

"Thank you," I said.

I felt triumphant. Papa had now been absolved of guilt by leaders of both the right and left. His heroism would remain heralded for decades to come.

"Let's talk about Riom," I said to Blum. "Where Vichy put you on trial."

"In the Auvergne. Laval country," Blum declared. "The Nazis had prodded the Vichyites to take judicial action against certain leaders of the Third Republic. Their goal was a show trial to prove France had gone to war against Germany, not vice versa. Allegedly, we had so weakened our country's defenses that France had no choice but to attack. Pétain and his henchmen were only too happy to back up such nonsense."

With a handkerchief, the ex-premier wiped his brow before adding: "Myself, my successor Edward Daladier, Paul Reynaud, his successor, Georges Mandel, a fellow Jew and former interior minister, General Maurice Gamelin, chief of the army, and several other military figures were indicted. We had undermined France's defenses, Vichy charged. It was even absurdly claimed that my success under the Popular Front in creating a forty-hour workweek and paid vacations for France's labor force had caused our country's downfall. Before we entered the courtroom in Riom, Pétain, for reasons best known to himself, dismissed cases against Reynaud and Mandel."

Another dab at his temples and Blum picked up the thread again. "Foreign reporters were allowed to attend and the proceedings went worldwide. At that time in February 1942, Vichy and the United States still had diplomatic relations. I even received a birthday card from Eleanor Roosevelt and a favorable editorial in the *New York Times*."

"Daladier and I conducted most of the rebuttal," he went on. "We proved the worst cuts in France's defense budget came from governments in which Pétain and Laval served. I noted the Popular Front had boosted military expenditures by the highest amount since 1918. I also lauded a one-time Communist opponent of mine, executed by the Germans, who died singing the *Marseillaise*. The whole fiasco at Riom embarrassed the Nazis no end."

"Therefore Hitler stopped it."

"Yes, and Daladier and I went to Buchenwald, but to a special section where they treated us halfway decently."

"Hmmm." My tone was skeptical.

Blum added: "It was very likely I was actually saved by falling into German hands. The Boche would have killed me eventually, I realized. But had the fascists in the Milice gotten their hands on me, I would have been torn to pieces. My poor friend Georges Mandel was 'taken for a ride' by Darnand's killers."

Did I have the heart to tell the lifelong humanitarian Leon Blum that he would soon be sharing the stage with the executed traitors Pierre Laval and Joseph Darnand, heads of Vichy and the Milice respectively?

Subconsciously, I caved. Leon Blum took off his grampy spectacles, closed his eyes and receded into the same sound sleep as his silenced confreres in my occupied folding chairs.

Pierre Laval entered next.

"The Auvergnat."

This was a title he bore in his long career in French politics. It was not exactly complimentary nor merely geographical, in that his roots were in the Auvergne, as distinct a region of France as the Limousin or Alsace. Rather, Auvergnat peasants were renowned for their guile and duplicity. Laval had brought these attributes in plentiful quantity to Paris.

"The Auvergne RAT," we referred to him when I was in the Resistance.

Anyone who has seen a photo of Laval knows how much he resembled a rat—his sleek dark hair, beady eyes, twitchy nose, runty size, et al. However, the man's whiskers didn't flare out like a rodent's; they formed an ordinary mustache. Conversely, this mousy character was no ordinary man. He also possessed a diabolical intelligence, few scruples, and the gift of gab.

Needless to say, he began his career as a lawyer—and an ardent leftist.

He was born into a petty bourgeois family in a small Auvergne town the size of Charniers called Chateldon, where his father ran a café, was the local butcher, postman, and owned a vineyard and horses. This rural community was located between Riom and Vichy, which may have stirred rumors he'd had a hand in choosing the famed watering place for the site of Pétain's government. Chateldon is also noted for its locally bottled mineral water.

From ardent Socialist to Nazi collaborator was quite a climb. Nor was Pierre Laval lukewarm as a humanist when he joined the French Socialist Party in 1903 and followed the footsteps of the famed pacifist

Jean Jaures. In 1909, back in Chateldon, he married the daughter of the local mayor. The couple moved to Paris where Laval set up a law practice and vigorously defended strikers, trade unionists and left-wing agitators. He dubbed himself "a comrade among comrades, a worker among workers . . ." On the eve of World War I, the CGT, the major union, persuaded him to run as a Socialist from the Seine district, a *Parisien* suburb, and he won.

Outspoken in his opposition to France's participation in World War I, he was kept under surveillance yet never arrested. His quick wit in one debate in 1917 won him widespread publicity. Édouard Herriot, the minister of supply and no friend of Laval's, when blamed for the coal shortages in the country had the misfortune of pompously declaring, "If I could, I would unload the coal barges myself." Laval's popular riposte, which even received the approval of Clémenceau, was: "Do not add ridicule to ineptitude."

Laval had already seated himself in chair number five before I let any images appear on my primitive screen. It happened that I had an unpleasant surprise for him.

Offscreen, a drum roll: French soldiers wearing forage caps, rifles slung over their shoulders, are marching rather nonchalantly on a cobble-stoned street. Cut to a black prison van pulling up before a prison gate. French officers in their kepis surround it. A prisoner is hustled out from inside and escorted through the now opened gate and into the gloomy building. Cut to an empty courtyard in the middle of which stands a lone stake, with ropes attached. Cut to riflemen filing into the courtyard and forming a firing squad. Cut to the prisoner tied to the stake. He shakes his head when offered a blindfold. Cut to an officer, sword raised, then dropped as he yells "Fire!" The caption in bold red letters blares:

EXECUTION OF A TRAITOR.

Rifle smoke briefly obscures the scene. The slumped prisoner is held up by his bonds.

I watched Laval opposite me flinch when the officer gave his command and he positively shivered in his folding chair as the bullets hit him onscreen. To add to my deliberate cruelty, I said: "You actually preferred poison like Goering and Himmler except the vial of cyanide you'd secreted on your person was so old it had lost its potency."

Laval shook his head. "No, in my haste, I didn't swallow enough of it," he corrected me. "I got my stomach pumped and only delayed the procedure by several hours." Then he angrily inquired: "Why on that film didn't you hear me shout *Vive la France!* at the last instant?"

The aggressive defense lawyer at work instinctively, I reflected.

"You made your point, Maître Laval," I conceded.

His weaselly smile showed he was pleased at my according him his judicial title. In his career, this four-time premier of France had become an important person worldwide. I remembered he, too, like Leon Blum, had been on the cover of *Time Magazine*. He was chosen as their Man of the Year for 1931.

It was interesting if not deliberately coincidental that he picked up our conversation again by stating: "You know the American press named me the Man of the Year of 1931."

I allowed him his bit of exaggeration before replying. "*Time Magazine*, I understand, chooses the person who caused the most trouble in those prior twelve months, not an individual they found most admirable. You certainly kicked up a storm in 1931. Some historians believe you set the Great Depression in motion by blocking an international loan for an Austrian bank about to go bankrupt. Leon Blum said of your government "it was "like a night bird surprised by the light because it merely imitated Tardieu's defeated conservative policies."

Laval simply answered: "I never listened to Leon Blum even when I was a Socialist."

"But if your Milice boys had gotten hold of him, you would have had the satisfaction of seeing the old Jew torn to pieces."

"The Milice was not my Militia. It was Darnand's."

"You were its official commander."

"Only nominal."

"The Milice helped trigger the destruction of my town, the murder of my father, my best pal, and many friends and neighbors. I hold you in part responsible."

"Nonsense." Laval made a dismissing motion with one hand.

"Your Chateldon was a small town like ours. Your attachment to it was very strong. You bought its finest building, Castle Chateldon, showing off your success. How would you have reacted had the Germans razed your home and surroundings to the ground?"

"If you're insinuating I collaborated with the Boche, you're wrong."

"Oh really? In one instance, you acted worse than the Nazis. The Jewish children under the age of sixteen sent to death camps by your orders—the Germans would have spared them."

"I believed children should remain with their parents. I was under the impression they were all deported to work camps."

"Liar!"

"They were only foreign Jews, anyway," he snarled. "Pétain had me arrested, if you remember, for standing up to him in order to protect French people better."

"Pétain's enmity to you, he said, was because you were slovenly and blew smoke in his face at cabinet meetings. Nevertheless, released and back in power, you were worse than ever. The STO—you can't forget the *Service du travail obligatoire* you promoted. Forced labor."

"I got Hitler to compromise. One French prisoner of war released for every three French workers who arrived in Germany."

In reply I said satirically: "Perhaps we of the Resistance should have given you an award for creating that return to old-style slavery. It was our best recruiting tool."

"I knew it! *Un résistant!* Communist, no doubt. Terrorist, definitely!"

"Traitor!" I roared at Laval. Seconds later, I was aware the newsreel had come back on. The dead prisoner had been untied from the stake and laid on the ground. The commanding officer approached the inert body, pistol in hand. He fired it into Laval's head, the *coup de grâce*, making absolutely sure of the condemned's demise.

I looked up. My virtual Laval, still intact, had sunk back on his chair, eyes closed, asleep.

Almost immediately, the spotlight shifted and Joseph Darnand hurried to seat number six.

I won't say he goose-stepped, although in the course of World War II, he not only served as the chief of the Milice created by Laval in 1942, but also held the rank of Sturmbannführer (Major) in the Waffen SS and took a personal oath to Adolf Hitler.

His stride was unmistakably that of a military man despite the fact he was wearing civilian clothes—coat and tie—not the hated navy-blue Milice uniform he had designed. His baggy attire might have been the outfit he had on when he, like Laval, faced a firing squad. I noticed he wore no decorations on it nor rosettes in the lapels, notwithstanding he had won important medals and citations for bravery as a French soldier in World Wars I and II.

It was said Darnand's failure to win an officer's commission in the regular French Army after 1918 forever embittered him against the Third Republic. Thus, his attraction to Maurras' *l'Action française*, until he tired of the Monarchists' *inaction* and their fixation on restoring a king. This pugnacious, out-of-work veteran soon found himself drawn to the *Cagoule*, the "hooded ones," an out-and-out fascist organization inspired by Mussolini. These were underground terrorists who indulged in political murder, bombings and sabotage. Due to his organizational skills and command ability, Darnand next set up his own group, *Service d'ordre légionnaire* using a nucleus of combat veterans who became the forerunner of the Milice.

After Darnand sat down, I recognized he still bore his Hitler-style brush mustache. Moving images reappeared on the wall. The caption was in bold black: THANKS TO THE MILICE, THESE SCENES HAPPENED. What we were soon seeing was a montage of grim and gruesome pictures. Gaunt blackened house walls of torched, gutted buildings, grey empty streets, abandoned trolley wires and tracks, a leadened sky, and charred, crispy bodies, some armless, legless, bones sticking out, laid on torn-off window shutters pockmarked by grit. The roving camera panned in silence over the devastated landscape. Another caption surfaced:

CHARNIERS-SUR-NYS. SOUVIENS-TOI!

"What is all that crap?" Darnand, barked. "Pure propaganda."

"Look out my back window. You'll see an example of your Nazi handiwork."

"Charniers." When he pronounced the name, it sounded like a snort. "An SS officer was murdered there. Sturmbannführer Lange. I knew him well. A good man."

"No, you imbecile. An SS officer was captured near Charniers-sur-Vare. He tried to escape and was shot when he failed to halt."

"You were all bandits here in the Limousin. Charniers-sur-Merde, Charniers-sur-Con. What does it matter? Outlaws! We were the legitimate government."

The din resumed as soon as I caught my breath. "Little children were roasted to death at this location! Were they terrorists?" I shouted.

"Arms were hidden in this Charniers!" he shouted back.

"Yeah, old farmer Duglos had a shotgun."

"German soldiers were found mutilated."

"Yeah, one of them got hit by a falling brick."

"The SS taught the Jews a lesson in Russia. Too bad you had to learn it in the Limousin."

"Burning humans inside locked buildings. Sturmbannführer Durchmann's specialty."

"Durchmann! Horst Durchmann! I knew Durchmann well, too. A *very very* good man."

"He killed my father, among others. My father, a lifelong member of *l'Action française*."

"Tant pis."

"You're like those thirteenth-century killers of Cathars in Occitanie who slaughtered Catholics, too, at Beziers with the excuse: 'God will sort out his own.'"

"What do I care about the Limousin? I'm from Coligny, Rhone-Alpes."

"Coligny. Indeed. A small town the size of Charniers. Laval, your boss at the Milice, also came from a small town. I asked him how he'd like to see his birthplace leveled and all of its inhabitants murdered. So I'll ask you: how would you like to have seen Coligny obliterated?"

"What did Laval answer?"

"He didn't answer."

"Then, I won't, either."

Darnand got on his feet to stand up for the rest of our shouting match.

"Sit down again!" I ordered like a drill sergeant.

The Milice *führer* obeyed like a good soldier. Moments later, he was off to slumberland. The spotlight switched to the final seat in the row.

This time the newsreel focused on an elegant automobile speeding down a road lined by plane trees somewhere in France. At the wheel was a compactly built, short, slim, clean-shaven man, quite expensively clothed, and beside him in the passenger seat a not-so-nicely dressed woman, unattractive, nervous and likewise small. She was jabbering about something as he drove. Abruptly, the vehicle swerved and went crashing into one of the adjoining trees. Once the dust cleared and wreckage was clearly seen, it seemed no one could have survived the accident. Yet when the ambulances arrived and crews extracted the victims, the man was declared alive and the woman dead. The caption:

OUSTED PREMIER FLEEING SOUTH CRASHES CAR,
COMPANION DIES, HE MAY SURVIVE.

Before ending, the newsreel flashed a head and shoulders photograph of Paul Reynaud, the last head of government of the Third Republic.

Then Paul Reynaud, suave and normal, was making his way to my seventh folding chair. Before sitting, he shot me a quizzical glance, no doubt wondering why I had chosen him.

To forestall his asking, I said: "M'sieu le Premier, I hope you may be able to round out the mystery of what forces led to the war crime that destroyed my native community."

He answered glibly: "I am well aware of the tragedy of Charniers-sur-Nys. I was still a prisoner of the Germans when it happened but later you know I returned to government service in the Fourth Republic. General de Gaulle's proclamation declaring your martyred town a national memorial had my deep approval.

I had to think: *What a master politician.* So rather than discuss his discourse, I took a different tack. One might name it an historian's bent.

"De Gaulle was a protégé of yours, was he not?" I blithely inquired.

Reynaud was a bit taken aback but answered: "I supported the colonel in his ideas about tank warfare. I made him a general and undersecretary of war in my cabinet in 1940. He was the only one of our commanders who gave the Germans a bad beating that fateful spring." Obviously thoughtful, the dapper little man stared right at me and remarked: "You imply had we been more forceful in 1939, gone on the offensive, we could have prevented the *débâcle* of 1940? In that case, logically there could have been no atrocity at Charniers-sur-Nys."

I responded: "I'm conscious you struggled against France's surrender. But you finally resigned the premiership." After a pause, I posed an exceedingly delicate question to Reynaud. "Would you admit the Countess de Portes had anything to do with your eventual submission?"

Surprising me, Paul Reynaud showed no emotion at the mention of his mistress. She was a married woman cuckolding her aristocrat husband with a married man.

His response: "I realize it has been stated Hélène de Portes argued me into resigning and thereby accepting the Armistice. But other factors of pressure were more persuasive. You may have forgotten I even supported Churchill's offer to unite the UK and France into a single country or have our Government, after I moved it to Bordeaux, depart for North Africa to continue fighting the *Boche.* I was one of eighty députés who voted not to accept Pétain.

"Yet you often gave in to Madame de Portes." Whereupon I produced a sheet of paper and said: "I will now read you a conversation you once had with François Mauriac, an outstanding journalist and author, whom I'm sure you respect."

What followed was a verbatim passage from Mauriac's book, *The Tragedy of France.*

Mauriac: "One day I had criticized in Reynaud's presence a particularly unsuitable political appointment made by Daladier" (then Reynaud's boss and bitter rival)

Reynaud: "It was not his"—Daladier's—"choice. It was *hers*," Hélène de Portes'.

Mauriac: "That was no excuse, I said."

Mauriac: "He [Reynaud] sighed. Ah, said he: 'You do not know what a man who has been hard at work all day will put up with to make sure of an evening's peace.'"

Mauriac to Reynaud: "Do you remember that exchange?"

Reynaud: "Perfectly."

Mauriac: "And you didn't resent it?"

Reynaud: "Hardly. It showed how powerful she was. Daladier had no love for me but he bowed down to Hélène."

What I hadn't included was Mauriac's portrayal of the countess as *slightly mad, excitable, meddlesome*—and *dangerous*. Others called her a *chattering middle-aged woman, unattractive, slovenly, a busybody, who acted like a sovereign and at times like a fishwife*.

Pressing Reynaud further on the subject of his mistress, I asked: "Is it true the countess presided over the General Staff, invaded the Supreme War Council, broke up cabinet meetings, prepared State papers, dismissed generals and reproved ambassadors?"

"Perfectly true," the former premier conceded. "I knew she was not chic. She was not particularly intelligent. But I needed her. That was all."

In that regard, he used a term in French—*egérie*—with which I was unfamiliar. It had derived from Egeria, an ancient goddess who was a female advisor and counselor to male kings.

"It was later charged that when you and the countess had your cataclysmic accident, you were en route to Spain, fleeing the country after turning it over to Pétain."

Hardly reacting with gentlemanly composure, he pantomimed he was going to spit. "Calumny. Pure calumny. It was almost a week after the cowardly Armistice while driving to my property on the Cote d'Azur. We were outside of Sète when I somehow lost control."

"You survived. A medical miracle, they say."

"And the moment I healed, Pétain and Laval sent their goons to arrest me."

"They were going to try you at Riom. But relented. Why?"

"You will have to ask Pétain. In any event, Blum made them look like fools at Riom."

"And you ended up in German hands. Yet you survived."

"Maybe they misplaced me. I don't know. The Americans liberated us from the Waffen SS at Castle Itter in Austria before they could murder all of us. *Special* political prisons."

"Is it true you married again at age seventy-one to your new mistress, Christiane Mabire, and fathered three children."

"My greatest accomplishment for France."

Paul Reynaud, grinning, stood up, bowed and slumped back into his seat while the spotlight on him immediately dimmed.

There is always the unexpected. How true it was in regard to these nightly interviews of mine. My intended finale had been to bring all seven resuscitated guests together and have them mix and mingle. They would do silly things such as engage in sword duels and for a rousing finale, form a chorus line of hirsute can-can-can beauties dancing to Offenbach's *Gaîté Parisienne*. But when I looked again, all seven had vanished from their seats

However, on the blank wall a caption extruded, simply stating:

DE GAULLE

It was followed seconds later by a well-known photograph of Charles de Gaulle wearing the gold-leafed kepi of an upper level French officer. His commanding presence, despite a recessed chin, was already discernible.

That image faded. Replacing it was a series of cartoonish drawings under the title:

LE GRAND CHARLES

From a hospital in Lille (where de Gaulle was born) a man and a woman are carrying home a newborn baby. The infant is so lengthy it takes the two of them to carry him. His face sticks out beyond the swaddling clothes, his long nose, anemic chin and big feet at the other end . . . Caption:

WHEN EVEN A BABY—HE WAS GRAND.

Cut to a sketch of Notre Dame Cathedral. During his boyhood in Paris, de Gaulle loved to climb the interminable steps to the top . . . Shown is a profile of young Charlie posed alongside a gargoyle, looking much like it . . . Caption:

GRAND IN HIS LOVE FOR FRENCH HISTORY

Cut to a parade of marching cadets at Saint-Cyr Military Academy. De Gaulle towers above his classmates who call him:

LE GRAND ASPERGES—THE GREAT ASPARAGUS

Focus on de Gaulle's proboscis, even longer now . . . But his fellow cadets do not label him: *le grand nez*—large nose. They prefer:

CYRANO

Cut to de Gaulle in the trenches of World War I . . . "Get down," his men yell at him because he is standing above the parapet. "I am down!" he shouts back. Bullets are whizzing . . . Caption:

THE GRAND TARGET

De Gaulle on a stretcher, his head and feet hang over its edges . . . Caption:

DE GAULLE, THE WAR HERO

GRAND, GRAND, GRAND—the encomiums continue.

Cited are his *grandeurs* in proposing tank warfare on the offense, which were rejected; his courageous attempts to hold back the Nazi tide in 1940; his flight to England; his stirring radio address of June 18, 1940, to the French people, exhorting them to resist; his creation of the Free French Army; his insistence that the Free French and Resistance liberate Paris; his shaping of the Fifth Republic; his presidency of France, his ending the Algerian War; his crushing the Revolt of the Generals; his stubbornness in maintaining France's prestige; his vetoes of England's entry into the European Union; the uproar he caused in Québec; etc., etc.

The next iteration for his grandeur, for good and bad, was a floating series of cartoon heads with balloons coming out of their mouths containing noted quotes.

Franklin Delano Roosevelt: "The greatest cross I have to bear is the Cross of Lorraine."

Winston Churchill: "He had to be rude to the British to prove to French eyes that he wasn't a puppet of the English."

Harry Truman: "I don't like the son of a bitch."

Pictured is Notre Dame Cathedral at the time of the Liberation. De Gaulle arrives to attend a Victory Mass. German snipers fire from up around the gargoyles. His followers plead with de Gaulle to stop walking upright and take cover with them on the ground . . . His withering reply: "The regeneration of France cannot begin in the gutters of Paris."

De Gaulle on why he allowed Laval's execution to take place . . . that it was "an indispensable symbolic gesture required for reasons of State."

De Gaulle's "certain idea of France" likened to an old painting of a Madonna and how France could not retain its stature without "a policy of grandeur."

Their ultimate tribute: "General de Gaulle is dead. France is a widow."

Postscript: de Gaulle's father taught the subject of France's past at a Catholic college. The family's ancestry went all the way back to the Celts. Their surname is said to have derived from the Gaullish language meaning "oak," a tree sacred to the Celtic Druids. The general's uncle, also Charles, was a passionate Celticist. One can hardly go deeper into the roots of France.

It was still dark within my study but hints of light were visible in the east beyond my single window. Already the de Gaulle finale to my excursion into the Third and Fourth and even Fifth Republics was succumbing to increasing illumination.

Exhausted, I sunk back in my armchair. It would not be long before I heard a rooster crow. This had been my daily reveille from earliest childhood. I knew the cry was a macho aggressive sex symbol, and yet the moment his cock-a-doodle ceased, an immediate and magnified sense of peace took its place. Another day had been heralded in the placid countryside.

Thus I went to bed, after having returned the folding chairs to their closet, along with the recording device and any other indication of what had happened throughout the night.

If Arlette peeked into the study this morning as I lay still sleeping in my bedroom, she would see everything was in order.

X

Someone was knocking at my front door. That pounding, not masculine poultry cries, brought me out of a dream, which eased away like quicksilver and carrying off images I knew I could not reproduce.

Arlette had a key. Did she misplace it?

This silent wonderment accompanied me to the entrance hall. I had donned slippers and a robe over my pajamas. "I'm coming, Arlette! I'm coming!" I started yelling from a short distance away. On the other hand, I realized my words couldn't possibly penetrate the massive Limousin oak. Fumbling, I turned the key, but also unloosed an iron bolt that gave me added protection, not because I feared intruders, but out of big city Parisian paranoia, now a habit. At last, the door was opened. On the threshold stood not an embarrassed Arlette, but a smiling fat woman about my age—*perpetually cheery*—I recalled in my groggy state, going back to childhood.

"Mathilde!" I exclaimed. "*Quelle surprise!* Come inside." She carried a small wicker basket in one hand.

"Bonjour M'sieu le professeur," said Mathilde, almost making a curtsy in her ample skirt. "*Je m'excuse.* I had to come this morning in place of Arlette who is indisposed. I have your breakfast with me." Then she further excused herself for arriving late because to obtain fresh croissants, she needed to go to—she jerked her thumb a bit contemptuously such as old-timer Charniers people did in the direction of downtown New Charniers. Further, displaying her arthritic hands, she added: "I no longer can make them myself."

Therefore I remembered her late husband had been the village baker—machine-gunned during the massacre. Sheer luck had saved her—shopping in Limoges when the SS struck.

Mathilde brushed past me and made a beeline for the kitchen. By the time I caught up with her, she had her basket emptied, a place setting for me on the table, the tea kettle boiling and an omelet cooking. This latter, sprinkled with parsley was served within a few minutes, accompanied by a glass of orange juice, slices of cheese, the heated-up croissants, and the *thé citron* she knew from Arlette that I preferred to coffee.

"Sit down, Mathilde," I said to her. "Visit with me."

"My dear Professor," she said (wild horses couldn't have gotten her to call me Eugène as she had when we were kids together), "I have so many things to do. *Je suis désolé.*"

"But tell me at least. Is Arlette sick?"

"No, but badly bruised. This time, her good-for-nothing drunkard has gone too far. The police have him in custody. May he rot in jail." Her tone was only momentarily bitter. Once more, her affable, chatty self, she went on. "Poor Arlette is in the *Clinique*—overnight for observation. Her little ones are with me. That's why I mustn't linger. A neighbor's daughter, only eleven years old, is watching over them. But I need to check that everything is *comme il faut.* And I have other errands I must run."

As I walked her to the door, she rattled off a list of chores involving families whose names I would know from the past. Mathilde did let me kiss her on both roly-poly cheeks when we bid adieu and I watched her waddle off in the direction of New Charniers where she lived on the outskirts of our original village's not always popular replacement.

Back at the breakfast table, I finished eating while remembering Mathilde was related to Madame Blanchard, had the latter's "robust" features but not the same formidable demeanor, meanwhile savoring our quiet interlude of communality from olden times. It brought back the gossipy talk in the kitchen of Madame Blanchard and her cronies, in which there had often been disapproving mention of local wife beaters and drunkards. Those miscreants, too, along with these good folks, had perished in the massacre, I thought to myself.

Once I had put the dishes in the sink, I decided to return to bed.

After I laid my head on the rumpled pillow at my bedstead and pulled the covers over me, I dozed, yet awakened within maybe ten minutes, retaining a vivid memory of a dream.

A statue stood in the middle of a rural village. The medieval architecture surrounding it looked French. But puzzling me, it lacked patriotic tricolor bunting, nor was there any evident on any part of the pedestal despite the fact the ramrod stiff figure bore a strong resemblance to General Charles de Gaulle—the same big nose, the same towering height, the same *hauteur.*

A closer view revealed the personage was wearing a flowing white gown. I instantly recalled de Gaulle had told Churchill he was a "reincarnation of Joan of Arc." Could a touch of transvestitism be at work here, a satire? On second thought, though, men wore such frocks—even skirts like the barbaric Scots—in the yesteryear. Around the elongated head was a tight-fitting wreath of oak leaves, and the tousled hair was hardly military with ringlets cascading down to broad shoulders. A golden belt became visible along with sandaled feet. It was de Gaulle—de Gaulle as a Druid priest—no doubt one of his distant ancestors.

Druid! Druid! Druid! I sat straight up and, in the penumbra of a half-awake, half-drowsy state, devised a ridiculously lengthy title in bold mental lettering:

THE OPPIDUM ADVENTURE (AND ITS AFTERMATH) OF
THE AMAZING *TRIO*—
THE STRASBOURG WHIZ, JEAN-LUC MUELLER;
THE ALLURING LADY OF THE CHÂTEAU, HER HIGHNESS
CHANTAL DE BREGONZAC-CHASTAIN; AND
THE MAYOR'S SON, EUGÈNE MARIE OF THE GRAVE-
DIGGING VENDÉEN DESFOSSEUX CLAN—
ON THEIR MOST MEMORABLE BICYCLE EXCURSION IN
LATE MARCH 1940.

By the end, I was out of bed, re-donning robe and slippers, hurrying to the computer in my study and pecking away furiously like some mad genius in throes of a magical inspiration.

The completed result is now before you in printed form transposed from the word-processing screen.

Dear readers, please remember the morning in October 1939, when the Alsatian children, who had taken refuge in Charniers-sur-Nys, left for their home province by bus. If you recall, Jean-Luc Mueller stayed with us in Charniers. Without taxing your memory further, let me remind you of his inviting me to go bicycling with him, which I promptly did.

In this fashion, the Trio began as a Duo. We were soon a common sight around town—Jean-Luc with his flaming red hair and myself with a mop of straw-colored—inherited, I was told, from my mother's people, the Jalouneixs. In short order, however, a third color was added— brown—the luxuriant chestnut coiffure of our only recruit, Chantal. It was no surprise to me that she joined our ranks. I had watched her and

Jean-Luc interact in church on Sundays. Their obvious mutual attraction caused me no pain, I swear. Rationally I had no basis to be jealous since I had no reason to expect anything. In no time at all, Chantal became like the sister I never had.

Fast forward to Thursday of the last week of March 1940. No school for me, of course, on a Thursday, and Chantal was privately tutored, and the redhead had promised a special treat on what turned into a sunny, blue-sky, balmy, spring day. All he would allow us to know was we would be undertaking our longest bicycle trip ever.

The other two had speedier bikes than mine. Chantal rode a girls' model without a bar, allowing her to wear a dress or skirt. Like riding sidesaddle, I used to think. Woe betide any female in our world in the 1940s who wore long pants or shorts in public. Even an illustrious countess! In any event, she and Jean-Luc often had to stop and let me catch up to them. We'd all wait a minute or two and—presto!—were off again.

The starting point for the Trio that morning and all other times was my family home in the center of Charniers-sur-Nys. Since the place where Jean-Luc boarded was closer to Bregonzac, he and Chantal would arrive together. By March 1940, France had been at war for seven months. You'd never know it from seeing three adolescents on a holiday jaunt. The small hamper Chantal had attached behind the seat of her bicycle would be full of hard-to-get delicacies we would devour at our midday picnic. Jean-Luc had a knapsack containing more mundane items like baguettes and usually plentiful cheeses and plates, silverware, etc . . . and I on the other hand had wine in my carry-all—red table wine—siphoned into bottles by Madame Blanchard from the cask of *vin ordinaire* Papa had in his cellar.

The route of the mystery tour led us first, like many others, to the old Pont Neuf stone bridge over the river Nys. Sure enough, Jean-Luc and Chantal beat me to that venerable structure. However, neither of them stood alongside their bicycles, ready to push right off once I arrived. They had dismounted and were sitting on one of the parapets.

"Chantal has a special treat for us," Jean-Luc greeted me. I then noticed our beauty had a colorful little package on her lap.

"What is it?" I asked stupidly, halting in front of the two.

"I have no idea," Jean-Luc declared.

With a twinkle in her lovely green eyes and a cat-like grin, Chantal turned to her *ami* and said: "*Chérie*, I need a flourish." Her hands had begun undoing the gift wrapping.

"Tah-dah! Tah-dah!" Jean-Luc imitated orally the blast of a trumpet. Her present to the Trio consisted of three pennants—triangular miniature flags—with strings attachable to our bike handles.

Watching her tie on the one she'd kept for herself, Jean-Luc examined the object in his hand. "A tricolor of our own!" he exclaimed. "Red, brown, blond. Chantal, you are a marvel. Wherever did you find them? Red head, brunette, straw-haired—the exact order en route."

The teenage countess was beaming. "I had them made," she answered. "Jeanette, one of our kitchen girls, is a genius with a sewing machine. But the design was from me."

"Our Trio's private coat of arms," I commented.

"Perfect, Eugène," said Chantal.

Once more en route after Jean-Luc and I affixed our banners, we went in appropriate file across the bridge to a path that took us through a wood on the other side. It led to a dirt road and eventually a paved thoroughfare on which we biked seemingly for several hours.

Our midday destination was at the top of a punishing hill where they waited for me at the entrance of a copse of evergreens. The view was beautiful all around, several rivers cutting through grassy dales, agricultural land stretching up to forests, the quaint roofs of hamlets here and there, a sapphire blue pond tucked away in the distance. I wondered whether this was the *treat* Jean-Luc had promised, but didn't ask.

Our red-haired leader finally conducted the Trio onto the needled floor of a group of firs, an amazing profusion of balsam-smelling full-grown trees luring us like children in a fairy tale into not a haunted wilderness, only a benign and luxuriously natural one. Jean-Luc obviously had scouted the area. We walked our bikes until we arrived in a luscious green glade lit by sunlight filtered through barely swaying tops of these tall *sapins*. Within, there was a rude table with benches in the opening. We would have our picnic in absolute privacy, punctuated solely by the tweets of birds we couldn't see.

Was this the *treat*? Still I didn't ask.

We had a sumptuous meal. Especially welcome was the jambon de Bayonne, the king of French smoked ham, and a reblochon cheese the best I had ever tasted. All of these and other goodies came from the larder at the château in Bregonzac, long ago provided by Chantal's father, the count, now away in the army, leaving his fourteen-year-old daughter in charge. We could argue we weren't breaking any rationing regulations by consuming provisions bought in peacetime.

My contribution of *vin rouge*, although not of famous vintage, was good enough for table wine to elicit compliments. I blushed like a damsel at their praise.

Finally, the mystery of the *treat* was solved. I still didn't ask. Chantal did. "Is this lovely place and marvelous *déjeuner* the treat?" the countess inquired?"

"Hardly," Jean-Luc said. Both Chantal and I evidently showed puzzlement, for the Alsatian went on. "Do either of you know what an *oppidum* is?"

I looked at Chantal. She looked at me. We both looked at Jean-Luc and shook our heads.

"It's a Latin word," he said. "But not pertaining to the Romans. It means city or town."

As Chantal and I pondered this cryptic retort, Jean-Luc continued. "Once we digest our food a bit more," he said, "we are going to visit an oppidum." He added comfortingly: "Geographically, it's not that far a ride. Yet historically, we will be going back to a very ancient period in France, to the Celts and the Druids, *nos ancêtres* in ancient Gaul."

This oppidum that Jean-Luc took us to visit was tucked in a valley not more than three kilometers from the luncheon site. We left the mass of evergreen foliage and soon entered a region of different trees—mostly a tangle of gnarled old giant oaks—finally debouching into a small valley through which ran a babbling brook. Above was a height of considerable steepness and at its base a ragged, thatched-roof hut and a sign in front featuring an arrow drawn in black pointed upward and in hand lettering, also black,

TO THE OPPIDUM

"We leave our bikes here and lock them," said Jean-Luc, pointing to a set of unoccupied posts having chains to attach, "and we climb."

What else do I remember of Jean-Luc's introduction to the oppidum? Such Celtic ruins exist throughout Europe and as far away as Asia Minor. The one we were about to reach consisted of grey stone walls running along the perimeter of the peak for seven kilometers. Maybe ten thousand Celts had lived there in the Iron Age. And, yes, the Druids! They were the priests—philosophers and scientists, too. Julius Caesar and other Romans claimed they practiced human sacrifice and burned captives alive inside giant wicker effigies they set afire—ideas later dismissed by some scholars as merely imperialistic Roman propaganda. "In truth, Druids were revered for their piety and goodness," our leader assured us.

With the news we were in a holy place, albeit a pagan one, our trek upward to the remnants of the Celtic city commenced.

We ascended in the usual Trio order, red hair, brown hair, straw hair. I would say it took us half an hour to approach the summit. At several places, Jean-Luc had to give Chantal a hand to get over a particularly steep section. As if to compensate for these moments of feminine weakness, she turned frisky as a colt when the terrain became more forgiving. After all, she was the daughter of a courageous, much decorated French officer. Twice she actually passed Jean-Luc. The second time, the countess called down to him: "I'll race you to the top." Already we could see the tree line just ahead. Instead of accepting the challenge, Jean-Luc waved her on. "Nature is calling me," he shouted back and stepped behind one of the larger oak trees still at the altitude we had reached. "Me, too," I added, hiding myself in some bushes.

"You men," she cried scornfully and with a giggly laugh resumed climbing.

She was out of sight once Jean-Luc and I reappeared on the last stretch of the trail.

We had gone only a few more meters when we heard Chantal shriek and yell for help.

Upward, we raced and to this day, I will never forget the sight that met our eyes.

On the flattened table top much like the brink of a shallow volcano, Chantal stood frozen while a bizarre figure, his unruly hair flying in snake-like locks, cholerically red-faced, frothing at the mouth, dressed in a long dirty white gown and brandishing a lethal-looking stave, was bearing down on her. As Jean-Luc and I clambered up and rushed at him, this creature was screaming imprecations in a totally indecipherable language, which all of a sudden he translated into a weirdly-accented but understandable French. "Do not be afraid, my beauty. I am not going to eat you, only sacrifice you to my Gods—" to which he quickly added, "I am Lugus, one of those Gods."

I bent to grab a good-sized rock. Jean-Luc, who had a hunting knife at his belt, whipped it from its scabbard and ran past me shouting: "Back, back, or a you're a dead Druid!"

The stave was lowered as Lugus drew away from Chantal. Jean-Luc sped by her, too, and thrust his blade in the style of a sword, ready to run the apparition through the throat, I came chomping up alongside, ready to brain our nemesis on his oak-leaf garlanded skull.

"Careful, you guys," Lugus said in French. "I'm a powerful Druid priest."

"You're just a shitty actor, Lugus," Jean-Luc yelled at him. "Who told you to scare this poor lady like that? I sure as Hell didn't."

"Simply having a little fun, Jean-Luc," he said.

"Look at this poor girl. She's still trembling," the Alsatian replied. By now, he had Chantal in his arms, comforting her.

"No, she was actually very brave," argued the so-called Druid. "She didn't try to run."

Now it was the countess's turn to speak. "I would have kicked you in the—(anatomical expletive deleted), if you'd taken another step."

That remark drew a burst of laughter, first from Lugus himself, then from Jean-Luc, then from me and eventually from Chantal who had left her *ami*'s protection.

"Meet the real Lugus behind the *faux* Lugus," said Jean-Luc. "Michel Fontaine, *un acteur manqué*. Watch out, he really is quite *fou*, haunts the oppidum, preys on tourists and lives in that grubby hut below."

We were introduced and hearing that Chantal was a countess, he kissed her hand and declared: "I am Michel de la Fontaine, milady, an aristocrat, too." More laughs ensued.

"We will just call you Lugus," Chantal said.

"Better a God than an aristocrat," Jean-Luc quipped.

The countess rather un-aristocratically stuck her tongue out at the Alsatian.

Festively then, we went on a tour with Lugus. Needless to say, we did not inspect the full seven kilometers of greyish stone walls encircling the original settlement. The perimeter was in fact like that of an ancient cut-off volcano so that the lost Celtic city lay just below its inner edge. The thespian Druid led us down a set of natural steps onto a plateau containing one-time streets that criss-crossed in an urban pattern. Neither houses nor ruins of houses remained. Yet there was still one building. It was a close replica of the ragged thatched hut we had encountered below. In front were billboards featuring drawings of what this ancient Celtic fortress-town must have looked like when it was populated two thousand years ago.

Lugus stopped by the doorway of the shack.

"You are about to enter my hallowed museum and—I make no apologies—tourist trap and workshop through which I make my living. The other admittedly shabby facility by the brook is my abode, my home, where I spend my evenings. One would think there might not be robbers or other miscreants in this remote location but remember the Druids were very powerful individuals hated by very powerful spirits." The actor climaxed his little theatrical speech with a trio of winks at the three of us.

Reaching into his voluminous once-white robe, he withdrew a key hung on a leather lanyard and proceeded to unlock and open the hut door.

"I must warn you, Countess," he said, bowing to Chantal. "Expect gruesome sights."

What the actor seemingly had been referring to were rows of severed heads that decorated the walls of these quarters. They were extraordinarily realistic and gory.

The open-mouthed, wide-eyed horror of having one's head cut off was aptly expressed on distorted faces of men (only men), some of whom wore Roman-style helmets.

Standing in front of a pinned up map (which could be purchased) illustrating the different Celtic tribes and sub-tribes in their respective territories of ancient Gaul, Lugus lectured us again. Offhandedly referring to the displayed heads, he explained: "I make them myself out of papier-mâché. These grotesque objects are my best sellers. Barbarism isn't dead in our day and age, as the daily newspapers testify."

"Were the historic Celts really actually headhunters?" I asked once he paused.

"Do you consider yourself Celtic, Eugène?" he answered me with a question.

"I don't know," I replied. "My papa's family came from the Vendée. My mother's was from here in the Limousin."

"You could not have been a Sequani," he said. "The Sequani settled farther north up as far as Alsace." Our momentary mentor pointed out the different color-coded Celtic tribal areas on the map. "The Sequani most certainly *were* headhunters. They believed they could assume powers from the brains of enemies whose heads they preserved by pickling. They hung their ghastly trophies on the walls of their houses and dangled them from the necks of their horses to advertise their fierceness. They fought other Celts and Romans and German Huns. By the way, Alsatian that Jean-Luc is, he probably has descended from the Sequani. I would watch this redhead very carefully, Countess Chantal and you, too, Eugène."

"Ah, but the Sequani were also intellectuals and scientists and decidedly brainy leaders," Jean-Luc argued." You haven't mentioned the Sequani Calendar they invented."

"True. Druids were expert professors. They could measure the moon, stars and sun. They could tell exact time. They set up a system of learning among their illiterate society that included natural studies, poetry, religion, and so forth."

Chantal interrupted next. I was surprised at her interest, popping a string of queries: "What were some other major Celtic tribes? When did the Romans appear on the scene? Did Caesar fight these warriors? Why were Celts also called Gauls? Were there a lot of them?"

"Three hundred varieties in France, alone, Mademoiselle," the actor answered. But as Lugus started to enumerate a few, Jean-Luc cut him off. "It's getting late, my friend Michel. We need to get back before dark."

Once we turned to start leaving, we were greeted by: "Aren't you forgetting something, Jean-Luc, my friend?"

"Oh, yes, the admission charge," said the Alsatian, taking out his change purse and handing the Druid three five-franc coins.

"And a *pourboire?* A tip for your humble servant?"

Three more similar coins were thrust at him. Plus: "We will leave you leftover food we haven't touched by your cabin door and even an unlabeled half-bottle of a quite decent red table wine." Our exit right afterward was somewhat hurried as was our descent.

The return bike ride struck me as shorter, too, and we arrived at Charniers in front of my home while the sun was just starting to set.

Prior to the other two's departure for Bregonzac, Chantal announced she had an important thing she had to say to us.

"Out with it, young lady," Jean-Luc said.

"I want to have a party at the château," she declared. "A special kind of party."

Jean-Luc and I both appeared confused, it seemed.

"A Druid party, you sillies."

Her tone was strictly girlish, not dignified nor aristocratically standoffish.

"What a superb idea!" I exclaimed. "Everyone dressed like ancient Celts!"

"Our roots!" Chantal cried enthusiastically.

"This Sequani agrees," Jean-Luc finally joined in the approbation.

After deciding to plan the event for the immediate future, the Trio thereupon dispersed.

XI

Unlike Charles Dickens who began his epic novel, *A Tale of Two Cities* by calling its period "the best of times" and simultaneously "the worst of times," our teenage Trio's own encounter with a turbulent France before the end of the *Drôle de Guerre* felt absolutely halcyon at times. Witness our glorious adventure of the oppidum trip and its aftermath, the Druid Ball, which was a *succès de scandale*, or in Naansee's American English "a smash hit."

Lest you reckon the three of us a trio of shallow, pleasure-seeking, selfishly indifferent youngsters, know that we perused newspapers, listened to radio news broadcasts and had our own opinions of Hitler, French politicians, racism, ethnic conflict and rampant anti-Semitism, not solely in Germany. Chantal let us know her revered father condemned the Nazi persecutions strongly due to the splendid Jewish comrades he'd had in the French military. On another occasion, discussing a magazine article detailing how beastly the Nazis had been to *their* Jewish comrades from the Great War, Jean-Luc had spoken briefly of persecutions of Jews during the Middle Ages all over Europe, and of a certain French count in the nineteenth century named Gobineau who wrote a notorious anti-Semitic tome.

It was on the Sunday after the oppidum adventure that the three of us met following Mass at Saint Augustine's to plan the Druid Ball.

The sleek black limousine in which Chantal, her father, and brother had been driven to church services was now on blocks in an unused stable on their estate. War time—gasoline rationing—the count was adamant an officer's family should not be seen indulging in luxury. Colonel Charles had thus cautioned his daughter and she was only too happy to ride her bike to church. Frère Charlot had to do his devotions in the château's chapel with the staff's help. I well remember gazing into that gorgeous shrine where the de Bregonzac-Chastains had worshipped for generations. From the age of seven, I was taken to the château by Papa on his mayoral visits to the count and allowed to play with Chantal while our fathers closeted themselves. Although the count was an outspoken supporter of the Republic, he and my Monarchist father got along perfectly. Finally, once his wife's mental illness became so severe she was institutionalized permanently, he started taking his children to the village church in a show of solidarity with the pious townsfolk.

Meanwhile, at that time I had the company of a charming little girl my age and we fairly much had free run of the castle—a labyrinth of hallways, elegant rooms, artwork, statuary, portraits, armor displays, and, what else, a secret passage. Chantal led me to explore it after pressing a hidden button that revolved a section of wall and staircase, on which we tiptoed up to the rooftop battlements and took in the magnificent views in four directions visible from its turrets.

That clandestine climb was one of the strongest memories of my entire childhood. Another major imprint happened when the cherubic imp guiding me during a later tour entered a darkened tunnel on our way to the playroom.

"Shh," I remember she told me when I scuffed my shoes inadvertently. "Spirits are about." So saying, she switched on a rank of floodlights. Grotesque paintings leapt out in a flash. They were frontal portraits of rough ugly men from past centuries. In retrospect these many years later, I realize I was having my first glimpse of surrealist art. Although they were not as scary as Lugus' severed heads, I hid the fact that I was shaken.

"Don't be frightened," Chantal had said. "These are my relatives." Promptly, she went down the row of pictures, laughingly identifying each brute. "This is Uncle Pouf-Pouf and Uncle Pish-Tosh and Uncle Pettipatapon and Uncle Ron-Ron and Uncle Mouche and Uncle Touche." Amazingly, I can still reel off her names for them in exact order.

But to get back to the Druid Ball arrangements years later: we three, returning from church, walked our bikes up the steepest part of the château entranceway and left them on the front steps. A side door to which Chantal had a key was opened and allowed us into a courtyard and then a huge reception hall, hung with huge (and priceless) tapestries.

Where were we headed? Out in the main corridor I noticed us approaching the count's private office where Papa would always veer off and I continued following a servant to the children's quarters.

"Where will we be working?" I finally asked Chantal on the present occasion.

"The Billiard Room," she said.

After a few meters, we reached the alcove where the weird artwork had been. I waved at the blackness. "Bonjour Uncle Pouf-Pouf and Ron-Ron and Pish-Tosh and . . ." Before we had gone past, I called out all Chantal's silly names for them.

"You cur. You remembered." Chantal turned on me, though without sticking her tongue out. *A private joke*, Jean-Luc no doubt thought. He remained expressionless as we continued our trek on the marble floors.

The large billiard parlor we entered had a most familiar look. How many times had I witnessed Papa and the count indulge in games of billiards after their work.

There was only the one billiard table on the parqued floor. As we went by it toward three wooden chairs set out for us, I spied a rip in the expensive green felt covering. "Someone didn't know how to handle a cue stick," I commented to Chantal.

"My darling brother did that in a rage," she told me. "I left it unrepaired for the colonel to see when he comes home on leave."

In addition to the chairs, pads of paper, pencils, books on Druids, etc. had been laid out by the staff plus a portable blackboard on a stand.

"Jean-Luc, you're in charge," Chantal commanded the moment we took our seats.

And forthwith, a simmering dispute between my two companions revealed itself.

Put simply, their problem boiled down to a single question: should they inform the count by letter of the elaborate entertainment they were contemplating at his family residence?

"I consider it a matter of simple courtesy," Jean-Luc argued. "Sooner or later, even in the bowels of the Maginot Line, your father will hear about this fantastic Druid affair."

Chantal countered: "I have been granted his full permission to run this household."

Her slightly waspish tone did seem to befit an annoyed aristocrat but immediately she retreated. "Suppose I write him, Jean-Luc," she said. "But we go ahead, of course."

"*Bien sûr*," the redhead agreed. "I've given our plan a good deal of thought."

He took a sheet of paper from his shirt pocket, unfolded it and proceeded to the blackboard. With a squeaky piece of white chalk, he wrote out questions he had prepared.

"How many guests?"

"Only kids, or kids and adults?"

"Only Druid costumes, or Celtic dress as a whole?"

"Only Celts in France, or include the British Isles, Ireland, Scotland, Wales, Brittany, even Spain and Italy?"

"Only ancient Celtic clothes or modern, too, like green leprechaun Irish outfits or up-to-date Scottish plaids?"

"Only Celtic music or popular French tunes, as well?"

"Unlimited attendance? Admission fee?"

I suspect we spent two hours making decisions. Chantal emphasized she had money enough to pay for all the arrangements. She had so enjoyed the Alsatian event when everyone in town had been invited. Jean-Luc opined that making it a costume party might limit attendance. I came out strongly for a costume ball but not limiting the Celtic dress to France nor ruling out modern adaptations. I also made a plea about broadening the taste in music.

We discussed caterers, too, and hiring musicians. No dinners, we decided unanimously, but hors d'oeuvres, cheeses and wine. Publicity we could handle ourselves. Chantal would design the posters. I could take stories to the local press, something I did for Papa.

Always cogitating, Jean-Luc said: "We need to work out a justification for having a party when our country is at war, so it will have to promote a patriotic theme."

"What do you propose, *mon chéri?* Chantal asked in her sweetest feminine manner.

"Exactly what you should tell your father. We want to evoke thoughts about the very roots of our French civilization. The Celts fought the Germans, the same Huns the colonel is facing. This is a patriotic act that can bring everyone together—Republic supporters, Royalists, Socialists, Vendéens, Burgundians, peasants, bourgeoisie, the upper crust. One single French heritage to celebrate . . . besides . . ."

He paused.

"Yes?" Chantal prodded him.

"Everyone is so gloomy these days. We could certainly use a good time."

Chantal effusively added: "In my father's last letter, he wrote he thought the war would be over by Spring. This could be a pre-celebration."

Our upbeat mood after we set up a timetable for doing our chores finally led us to leave the Billiard room and visit the ballroom where the event obviously would be held.

It had not been the site of an entertainment, we learned, since Chantal's mother had departed permanently for her private asylum. The idea crossed my mind that the present teenage countess was subconsciously grooming herself for the hostess role her *maman* had performed so well when she was in her right state of mind. Throughout several earlier centuries, this polished dance floor had known many an elaborate soiree. The de Bregonzac-Chastain grandparents had been noted hosts but only to *les grandes huiles* or Jean-Luc's "upper crust." Invitations to nights at the château were then highly prized. However, the present colonel initiated a once-a-year open house for the entire surrounding population.

An inspection of the gleaming floor underfoot revealed the original oak planking was as sturdy as ever. The giant carnelian red drapes and other plush furnishing had been brushed free of lint and shone like new despite their age. The chandeliers when we turned on the lights glistened. No spider webs to be seen, no mouse droppings. We could go to work without needing any repairs to bedevil us at the start.

Thus done for this day of our initial meeting, we headed for the front steps and our bicycles. But first of all, Chantal stopped us outside the darkened alcove containing those weird although artistic portraits of the "Uncles" and flipped a light switch. Once more, those grotesque faces leapt out at us. I gasped, as I undoubtedly did when I was a little kid. "Look at these works again, Eugène," Chantal said to me. "You remembered all the funny names. My maman painted each and every one of them. If they scared you, she must have scared the art world in Paris when she studied painting there. But the colonel wouldn't throw them out once she got terribly sick. He just hid them here . . ." Chantal asked the redhead: "So how do you like my relatives, Jean-Luc?"

"They're Cubistic," he commented. "Plus a touch of Les Fauves. Braque. Picasso . . ."

"Know-it-all," Chantal sniped at him light-heartedly.

"Besides, I was going to say, a unique *je-ne-sais-quoi* style of her own raw talent."

Chantal added: "In Paris after the Great War, Maman was very much on the art scene and the social scene. She mingled with famous painters. She hoped to emulate them. Then along came my father, a handsome war hero and she was swept away. I was born. Charlot was born. And then . . ." With her hands thrown up, she made a gesture of momentary futility. "Come. I want to show you both something special."

As if on tiptoes, we followed her silently down a Persian rug carpeted adjoining corridor to a door she unlocked. The interior was a *boudoir*—a woman's intimate bedroom.

Solemnly, our hostess announced: "This was Maman's inner sanctum. No one has been allowed in here since her absence except the count and myself. Here is my refuge when I am melancholic, I lie down on her bed and weep. Over there . . ." She pointed to a full length oil painting, "you can see the beautiful lady as she once was—a self-portrait."

Jean-Luc and I turned to regard a chestnut-haired beauty with extraordinary blue eyes whose resemblance to Chantal (and Chantal's to her) immediately struck the eye. The coloring of the evening gown was the same carnelian red as the ballroom curtains and the whole canvas was suffused in varieties of paler red. Madame Eulalie de Bregonzac-Chastain was slim and statuesque and although she had reproduced her person with an amazingly realistic appearance, a certain surrealism hovered about the picture.

"Did your mother know Pablo Picasso?" Jean-Luc asked after concentrated study.

"She often spoke of meeting him socially with his wife, who was a prima ballerina."

Then Jean-Luc noticed another painting on the wall next to the old-fashioned canopied bed. "Isn't that—It's a Picasso, isn't it?"

"Shhh. You can't say anything to anyone. It's worth such a lot of money. My father bought it for her when it was still affordable. But it will never be for sale."

After ushering us out, Chantal locked the door and said: "There you've seen my hideout when I am sad."

"Thank you for trusting us with your secret," said Jean-Luc.

"But now I'm happy. So excited this house will come to life again. Thank *you*, my Trio friends, for helping me indulge my fancy."

We had only a few hang-ups from then on. The most serious was a conundrum Chantal raised. She confessed she was elated over the new letter from her father that approved our event. But a certain line in it had prompted a pressing question before we started.

Taking the missive from a pocket of her dress, she said: "The colonel mentioned another colonel he met named de Gaulle, a tank man, and how he impressed he had been by him. They were both Saint-Cyr graduates, although in different classes. But the point is . . ." She read from the page. "This patriot's name de Gaulle is ironic. Takes you to the very roots of France." Her striking blue eyes went from Jean-Luc to me. "Which came first, the Celts or the Gauls?"

"They're both the same. Interchangeable," answered Jean-Luc.

"So what do I put on the poster I'm supposed to design?"

"Good question," I remarked vapidly.

"Celtish-Gaulish heritage?" asked Chantal.

"Too formal," Jean-Luc objected. "No, stick to Celtic. The Romans called us Gauls."

Per usual, the Alsatian's wisdom carried the day. This Solomonic decision also convinced me he had Celtic ancestry, not merely Germanic traits of an Alsatian. His freckles, red hair, fair skin, now also made me think of typical Irish and Scots I'd seen in geography books.

The blackboard soon filled up with further chalked decisions we reached.

1. Anybody could wear a Druid costume.

2. Anybody could dress like a Celt, either of the Iron Age period tribes or up-to-date Celtic wear, such as Chantal's Scottish clan's plaid skirt.

3. The music would be a mixture: traditional French tunes, modern favorites, waltzes, patriotic airs, etc.

4. *Oppida* would be explained and pictures of these ruins exhibited. There would also be an explanation of the Celtic-Gaul confusion and a drawing and story about Vercingetorix, the first French hero-martyr.

5. Costumes of enemies like Germans and Romans would be acceptable.

6. Special guests like public officials need not wear costumes unless they so desired.

7. Emphasis would be on French patriotism, support for troops at the front, fueling up optimism, a morale booster.

8. Food and beverage to be decided by Chantal.

9. Local people would be hired to assist the château staff.

Immediately, there was a stir in the region. The young Countess de Bregonzac-Chastain and her friends were preparing a *fête* at the château. Mutterings were heard these kids were much too young to pull it off. Others argued Chantal was so much like her mother in the good old days—excellent at whatever she undertook. I was deputized to get Papa's approval and assure we weren't violating any wartime regulations. To my surprise and delight, he not only offered us full cooperation, but declared he would attend himself as mayor but not in costume.

It seemed a miracle how easily Chantal made arrangements. Before long, everything was set: hors d'oeuvres, drinks, the musicians, decorations for the walls, a repolished dance floor, etc. Entertainment was hired, including a bagpiper to play Celtic themes, some singers, a mime, and a mystery guest. Jean-Luc would be Master of Ceremonies since he'd performed so brilliantly at the Alsatian farewell. He would also cover the history of early Celtic tribes in our region. I would do the overall Celtic populating of the rest of Europe and elsewhere. Not too much speechifying though. The main intent was having a good time.

Finally, the magic night arrived. We three had donned our costumes. Jean-Luc, needless to say, was done up like a Druid priest, but in contrast to Michel the actor, his robe was snowy white, his oak leaf cluster freshly green, his belt and sandals shiny gold. He had toyed with the idea of donning a wig of snake-like locks over his flaming hair. Chantal and I urged against it. "The audience won't recognize you," I warned. "I'll miss the real you," Chantal facetiously echoed me. So he relented.

Our beauty's outfit, designed by her, was a stunning sleek ball gown composed of Celtic patterns, a mixture of gorgeously colored plaids. The countess wore a tiara that had been in her family for generations. If anyone asked, she instructed us, the stones were mere glass, not diamonds and emeralds (which wasn't true).

In regard to me, I was one of about a dozen males trying to impersonate the Celtic war leader Vercingetorix. I was a pretty poor facsimile, scrawny, relying on leather to resemble armor, a weird helmet on my head, an axe at my belt, a cardboard shield and sword, a tunic made out of a lady's frock and thongs crisscrossing my calves.

I joined my fellow Trio friends on stage for the opening ceremonies. The size of the crowd was well beyond our expectations. It seemed party-goers had come from near and far. There were as many unfamiliar faces as neighbors we knew. The patriotic theme and need for a good time if only for an evening had the effect we hoped.

The musicians struck up a fanfare. The attendees milling about quieted. Jean-Luc arose and strode to a microphone. He first addressed the crowd in a gibberish like the language Michel/Lugus had greeted us with at the oppidum.

"Messieurs, Mesdames," the Alsatian then immediately reverted to French. "I have just saluted you in an extinct tongue called Gaulish. It is an underpinning of the heritage that makes France the magnificent country it has since become. It is the root of our fighting spirit. It is the basis of Vercingetorix's war cry!" (loud cheering).

I won't repeat the rest of his opening remarks nor quotes from the dignitaries who spoke. Jean-Luc had been adamant they keep their words short. My papa, who hated public speaking, led the way. "Amuse yourselves, everyone," he simply said and sat down. The applause he received for his brevity had its effect on the other big shots. Thus, the eating and drinking and socializing soon began.

Tables had been set around the perimeter of the dance floor. Local folks, wearing the simple homespun of the Celtic tribes acted as waiters and waitresses, carrying trays of canapés and wine to the guests. There was also a bar if you wanted something else. They served beer too.

On my way to my seat with a beer, I passed a muscular, heavy-set man seated alone at one of the tables. He was drinking an absinthe. Like me, he was costumed as the barbarian hero.

"Hail, beer-swilling Vercingetorix," he greeted me, patting an empty chair beside him. "Come sit and talk to an absinthe-swilling Vercingetorix."

Shyly, I accepted. Did ancient Celts shake hands? We two Frenchmen did and I had to admit he made an extremely authentic Vercingetorix. Rugged, commanding, no doubt fearless, tough as nails—all these descriptions would fit "Paul the Gaul," as he told me to call him.

"It was the damn priest," he said. "That pious fraud refused to baptize me with the name my parents wanted for me. Guess what it was."

Before I could answer, he spat out, "Vercingetorix."

"Seriously?"

"A Catholic boy had to bear the name of a saint, not a pagan," he insisted. "So my mother and father fixed him. They called me Paul."

"After Saint Paul?"

"But the joke on *l'abbé* was: Our family name was Paul. This baby became Paul Paul."

The raucous laugh he emitted showed gaps in his teeth. I felt he was already a bit drunk yet I made no move to leave the table. I sensed an intelligent and friendly quality in him despite the rough edges of an apparent, pot-bellied, brawling type. My new companion went on: "Paul Paul le Gaul the kids at school teased me, teaching me to use my fists and at the same time learn all about my fighting Celtic ancestors. God bless you three kids. It's what we needed. By the way, Monsieur Desfosseux, I know your father. He's a good man, although I detest his politics. Me, I don't know what I am . . . Communist, Socialist, Radical, but no prissy Monarchist . . . no thanks."

He delivered pretty much a soliloquy as I sipped my beer, telling me how he, too, lived in Charniers—that is, the other Charniers—the one on the Vare River—twenty kilometers away. In the machine shop where he was the foreman, he had forty men under him. His wife was bossy or tried to be. They had no children but a faithful dog.

"Guess what I named him?"

"Vercingetorix," I offered.

"You're a smart kid. A genius." He gave me a congratulatory slap on the shoulder. "Come see me in *my* Charniers. I'll show you the best tool makers in France Bring your gang, especially that gorgeous female creature on the stage with you two, her highness the countess. Oh, and bring the redheaded kraut, too. For his age, he's a wonder."

"We will. Only don't ever call him a kraut. Big as you are, he'd take you on."

"Merely kidding, *mon vieux*. That Alsatian kid is all right."

Following another slug of the absinthe, he said: "Now run along Monsieur Desfosseux the younger. Find yourself a pretty girl to charm."

Feeling some trepidation, I nodded. Indeed, probably the main reason I'd gone off to the bar was I had noticed a certain person among the "wallflowers," waiting to be asked to dance. You've witnessed my gallantry to Elsa Leibart at the Alsatian event. Now this girl in question you could easily deem "pretty," not shy and homely like the *alsacienne*. If anything, she was shamelessly forward. I'm speaking of Paulette Malinvaux, the unlucky Paulette, whom the SS patrol was to shoot and kill four years later. En route to the bar, I noticed she had already grabbed one fellow and was in his arms, waltzing to a popular tune by Offenbach.

I wished she still had been with him. I could see Paulette not far off, searching for a new partner. When I glanced behind me, thinking retreat, whose eye caught mine but Paul the Gaul's. With a hand gesture, he urged me on, no doubt thinking I was a shrinking violet with girls.

Some violet! One more snuck glance of Paulette was accompanied by a mental picture of the two of us alone in the hay at the Malinaux barn—*frequently*—and too frequently for me because I didn't want our little *affaire* to continue.

But gazing about again, spying Freddi Arnaud a few meters away watching the dancers, I suddenly had a brainstorm. I observed the big guy for a moment, his puffy face spoiled by the nemesis of youth—splotches of pimples—his demeanor falsely haughty and genuinely pompous, and I quickly rushed over to the Notary's son.

"Freddi, my pal," I cried. "Thank you for coming. And are you in luck, *mon ami*. Paulette was just asking for you." A pure fib, I confess.

"She was?" His expression of incredulity was almost instantly succeeded by: "But aren't you two . . ." Frankly, it wasn't always easy to keep a secret in Charniers, especially with a chatterbox like Paulette.

"She's tired of me," I said, another utter fib. "Go to her, old pal. Ask her to dance. You won't regret it."

Go to Paulette Malinvaux, Freddi did. I had the added pleasure of seeing them together the rest of the evening while I was busy dancing with at least half a dozen other partners. If she stuck with Freddi out of spite, *all the better*, I thought.

There was a finale, to be sure, we had planned for the fête.

The best had been saved for last.—as advertised, an entertainment component. The drinks and hors d'oeuvres had produced a mellow audience. Having quieted the crowd, Jean-Luc next introduced the performers who were standing behind him, waiting to do their acts.

The Scotch bagpipers in their plaid kilts were a decided success as they marched around the ballroom, squeezing their instruments and providing several catchy numbers. Despite the squealing quality of the sounds, people were tapping their feet to the rhythms. A harpist representing Wales was the next interlude and her songs, which she sang while seated and playing, were some of the most melodically haunting music I have ever heard. Afterward, we had Irish jig dancers, all in green, and they were like a chorus line, men and woman, whose intricate steps were enthusiastically received. Watching them jig their way off stage, we three planners knew what was coming next.

One man in the audience—we had planted him—commenced yelling: "And where is Brittany, our own Brittany!" From his pocket he took a small black and white Breton flag and waved it. Those standing a few meters to either side of him, held up black and white placards with BREIZH printed on them. The upshot of their mini-demonstration was that the promised mime appeared, clothed in black and white.

This performer's routine was most unusual. To his simple costume he added accessories, an ancient Celtic helmet, a sword, a buckler and with these engineered a sword fight with an opponent who was also himself. On the one hand, he acted the good guy, the Gallic hero Vercingetorix, with big V's on his helmet and shield and changed to the evil alter ego, who had horns on his headpiece and B's on his equipment and BOCHE labeling him—the eternal enemy, the Hun, now German, When the enemy was visibly vanquished, the mime lifting his sword in triumph, the symbolism of his Celtic victory was not lost on the attendees, who went wild.

After this highly talented man disappeared backstage, Jean-Luc stepped to the microphone, holding up his hand for silence.

"Mesdames, Messieurs, on our posters we promised you a mystery guest. We haven't forgotten. But first an introduction is necessary. Although I am dressed as a Druid priest, many of you know I am an Alsatian—(pause) and *French through and through* (loud applause) and proud to represent the section of our homeland once occupied by the Sequani tribe of Celtics. They were French. The Arverni were French. The Aedui were French. The Helvetii were Swiss but a goodly portion of them speak French. The Druids were the leaders of these ancient Celtics. Not warriors, but men of science, sages, discoverers of great secrets, powerful pagan priests who sought to do right. Despite the propaganda of their enemies, they were good and often benevolently magical. Tonight I am going to introduce a genuine Druid God. He lives in an oppidum not far from us. I hope all of you have seen the pictures of the oppida we have displayed. Thousands of Celts once lived in them. Some experts have called these abandoned settlements 'milestones in the urbanization of the continent.' Today, this Druid God you are about to meet watches over the memory of our ancestors who formerly inhabited the Limousin, who laid the foundations of French history. Welcome Lugus, the Druid God."

Behind the redhead a flash of zigzag lightning amid artificial stage smoke erupted and out of it stepped—no surprise to us—Michel Fontaine in his Druid costume. What did turn out to be surprising was the quality of his get-up—as snowy white and glittery gold and oak green as Jean-Luc in his regalia.

Lugus headed to stage front to the microphone holding two plants, one in each hand. He identified them as holly and mistletoe.

"These creations of nature were sacred to Celtic mortals," he declared. "But for Gods like me, they are the basis of our magic. Behold!" After mumbling some more in what conceivably was authentic Gaulish, Lugus tossed the green holly with its bright red berries into the air above the onlookers. His immediate second round of abracadabra produced another flash of smoke and light and instantly—"*as if by magic*" (people actually said it) boughs of holly appeared everywhere in the ballroom. Spontaneous applause arose.

"Ah," the Druid deity sighed. "Don't forget the magic in my other hand. You men, you know mistletoe's powers." He made a lewd but not indecent gesture (guffaws broke out). "Ladies, you know, too" (female titters). "Fecundity. Fertility. In its presence, you have to embrace the opposite sex. Don't hold back. France needs children." And accompanied by more gibberish, out from the same concoction of light and smoke a rain of mistletoe descended onto the crowd and alighted on doorways, windows and even the chandeliers. Exuberant applause and cheers greeted that trick.

Calling for silence, the Druid God said: "I don't see any kissing," then quickly added: "On second thought, better wait until you get home." (heavy laughter).

Finally Lugus stood by the microphone and just as expressive as the mime, displayed an absolutely forlorn image. But he spoke:

"Alas, poor me, I am a lonely God. I am without a Goddess." After a very exaggerated and lascivious wink, he made an aside heard by everyone. "Oh, but I can be tempted by a mortal. Is there not a charming demoiselle who would like to keep company with Lugus."

He put his hands to his forehead to shade his eyes. "I'm searching," he cried. "I'm searching. I see possibilities." Next those hands went behind his ears. "I'm listening. I'm listening . . . Wait! What am I hearing?"

A young woman's voice cried. "Monsieur Lugus! *Moi.* Would I do?" Standing up was an exceedingly attractive brunette in a fetching skirt and blouse of Celtic colors.

"*Mais oui, ma pigeonne.* Approach. You would do very nicely."

She headed for the stage but hesitated at the bottom of the steps before turning to the audience and asking: "Should I?"

Along with shouts of "Mais oui!" and "Pigeonne!" the burst of clapping seemed to decide for her.

"*Embrasse-moi,*" Lugus said once she'd mounted the stairs and sashayed toward him. He puckered up his lips for an exaggerated kiss.

"Catch me first," she giggled.

Everybody loves a chase. Everybody howls at a pratfall. Everybody in France adores accordion music. We might as well have been at the Gaietee or the Follies. Or on a village fairground, watching Judy beat Punch over the head . . . But back to Michel and his brunette.

My Naansee would have called the end: *A boffo finish.* The game of flirtation continued. Michel would catch the enchanting *mignonne* and she would slip out of his grasp before he could hold her firmly until he ultimately did grab her, whereupon from under her skirt she took out a stick and began hitting him to fend him off. At that point, he shouted "*Ça suffit!*" and made one of his magical signs while spouting his magical gibberish. She froze. "Aha!" the Druid God exclaimed lasciviously and kissed her passionately. She awoke. She kissed him back. (loud applause)—Then, the stick she was holding turned into a broomstick. "*Une sorcière!*" Lugus cried. The witch nodded, then invited him to join her straddling the wooden steed.

The workings of the "special effects" that went into play from then on were never explained to me. Thus I had the same reaction as everyone else when the mounted couple commenced to lift into the air, higher and higher, circling around, and after a few more circumlocutions, to a blasting crescendo from the orchestra, they sailed offstage, throwing kisses while they flew.

The curtain came down. Rhythmic clapping signaled not only an ovation for the show, but curtain calls for everyone who'd participated. In the order in which they'd appeared out marched the Scots, danced the Irish, bowed the Welsh harpist, sword fought the Breton and last, but certainly not least, the Druid God and the sexy witch.

When only Michel was left on stage, he turned to the seated dignitaries behind him (and this *was* rehearsed) drew the Trio out of our chairs as if bewitched and he snapped his fingers and introduced the three extraordinary young people who had put on this event and we received a hearty accolade. There were cries of *Vive le Trio!* and we two prompted Chantal to go forward and Michel could yell "She made it possible!" Pandemonium almost ensued. *Vive la comtesse!* erupted from hundreds of voices. *Vive le comte! Vive la famille Bregonzac-Chastain!* Tears of happiness welled up in Chantal's beautiful blue eyes and once she rejoined us, Jean-Luc and I put our arms around her shoulders.

There was also a *final* finale. To another fanfare, strings of flags descended from the balconies, recognizable as Celtic banners—from Brittany, Wales, Scotland, Ireland, even Cornwall in England where some people still spoke Cornish—and an outsized French tricolor, the biggest blue, white and red *drapeau* I'd ever seen was lowered. The musicians had their cue to strike up the Marseillaise. Never had I heard it sung more fervently.

That excitement I shall savor to my dying day, yet I shan't attempt to describe the feeling in words. When everyone else had left, we three exhausted elated souls had retired to the Billiard Room. We flopped down on a sofa and seconds later, after a rap on the door, it was shyly asked by the head of the live-in staff if they could come in to congratulate us. Mostly woman, long-time servants, several also teary, they offered expressions to Chantal of "You are your mother's daughter," "You've made this house come alive again. God bless you"—a very moving scene. Eventually alone again as the Trio, Jean-Luc suggested we were too tired to do a post-mortem and could save it for another day. Since I had to go home to Papa anyway, I took it as a hint and the Trio soon became a Duo.

With kissing on both cheeks, we parted. One of the male attendants let me out the front door. I saw my bicycle had also been brought out of its rack in the barn and laid on the steps. But before I mounted, I cast a glance up at the château façade. The building had not been lit up as it ordinarily would have been for a party (wartime you know, although the idea of Nazi aircraft scouting over Charniers-sur-Nys seemed the height of absurdity)—but under moonlight the handsome ancient castle retained its radiant, many-turreted magnificence. It made a fitting image for all of France—civilized and indestructible.

XII

The French film, *Jeux interdits*, is among my all-time favorites. It opens with a devastating scene of refugees fleeing northern France right after May 10, 1940, and being terrorized by the notorious German Stuka dive bombers, strafing and blasting helpless civilians clogging the roads. One pretty little blonde girl, maybe five years old, wanders off into the countryside after her mother has been killed and ends up in a home of French villagers nearby. This rural setting could also have been Charniers-sur-Nys, off the beaten track.

I saw the movie alone first in Paris. Later Naansee went to see it with me and she, too, was deeply moved by the story. One striking feature, I should add, was the absolutely haunting musical score. I find myself even now as I'm writing silently humming its unforgettable melody.

But more ineradicable in my mind is the powerful visible opening shock of the *débâcle* in progress when the upper half of France's humanity desperately sought a perceived refuge in the country's south.

We in Charniers were effectively insulated from such terrifying scenes. Life in our region of the Massif Central went on as placidly as ever.

Since the beginning of the school year, Jean-Luc and I had been commuting to the Lycée in Limoges. We took the trolley that stopped in Charniers and walked together to and from the station. The Alsatian to a certain degree had been adopted by the other Limousin kids, most of whom were from the city. They saw in him a leader, a spokesman, not an alien from the north. That his French was more polished than theirs was not a cause for jealousy. His articulate use of our tongue made him an ideal intermediary with teachers. He could also kick a ball farther and straighter than any of them plus run like a deer. And those fists! Once a bully in an upper grade had tried to torment Jean-Luc by calling him "a pig of a Boche." Smilingly, Jean-Luc invited him to go off school property to a secluded place and see if that was correct diction for him to use.

"No, right here," the bully yelled, grabbing the redhead by the collar. "I'll teach you diction!" and he raised his big fist. Our friends were ready to turn away from the ugly sight of a fearsome beating they expected their comrade would take. Instead, they saw me smiling, too. I told them: "Don't worry yourselves . . . watch."

They were in time to see Jean-Luc land his first blow, right to the bully's chin. The big kid staggered back but didn't fall, lifted his fists again while our hero simply took two steps forward and hit him in the stomach. Gasping, he bent over, as if paralyzed. Ending the fight was Jean-Luc's upper cut that sent his opponent sprawling onto the ground and writhing.

Our classmates rushed to Jean-Luc. One held up his arm and shouted "*Champion de boxe, notre Jean-Luc!*"

But rather than act triumphant, the "Champion" walked over to his fallen foe, helped him to his feet and said: "I'm French, born in Paris, *mon copain*, raised in Strasbourg, which makes me doubly French. You're French, too. We are French brothers, unbeatable when we are inseparable."

Jean-Luc waited a moment before asking: "*D'accord?*"

The ex-bully nodded, still a bit winded.

They shook hands. We all applauded, including the upper classmen.

This happened in April 1940, a month seemingly so peaceful that I quipped to Jean-Luc on the trolley ride back to Charniers how his battle was "probably more action than they've had on the Western Front today." My companion in the next seat flashed me an amused smirk and said: "Only don't say so to Chantal."

I nodded understandingly. "You mean that you were in a fistfight."

"Hardly. It's just not so peaceful as people believe where her father is. She's learned he *has been* in action there. Patrol clashes."

"I see your point."

Soon we were disembarking in Charniers and retrieving our bikes. Always Jean-Luc rode with me to my house, and then would go off to the quarters where he roomed, closer to the château. On this particular April afternoon, he reminded me that two days hence, after church, the Trio was scheduled for a trip to *La Cav.*

The coming Sunday would be our third visit in the month of April to this remote area. We took picnic lunches there, too, and felt assured enough of privacy to sit on the smooth rocks outside the cavernous entrance while we ate and relaxed before casually exploring the interior. We had high-powered flashlights and their play of yellow beams against the rock walls inside and into depths below gave us an eerie feeling. Nothing scary, like I remembered from an American movie Papa had taken me to see in Limoges, *Tom Sawyer*, with a boy and a girl chased in a cave. Still, we had to watch our footing carefully while descending.

The key to our enhanced number of visits to this hidden place was a short cut Jean-Luc, ever the adventurer, had found by himself. The new straight path had been tracked by the redhead through a bewildering run of forest we could enter near the château. In ancient days, a road had penetrated what had been an agricultural area. Abandoned centuries ago, the unused land had grown up to a jungle of trees and shrub. Yet Jean-Luc unerringly led us on our bicycles and once out of the woods we followed him through grassland onto high ground and up to the huge spreading rock formation itself.

What I first always squirmingly remember from the third April 1940 trip was how it marked the end of Chantal's ability to supply us with jambon de Bayonne. Any type of ham was getting hard to come by because of rationing. Jean-Luc commended her for all she was able to do despite difficulties, peaceful though it might seem to us in the Limousin. I remember he mentioned the German invasion of Norway and Denmark earlier in the month and how French troops had been dispatched along with the British to help the Norwegians and a battle was continuing.

If there'd been any concern at all on these excursions, it had happened on our second April trip—a concern for our privacy. Both times, we'd come on a Thursday—a no-school day. Jean-Luc with his boy-scout-trained eye, had spied the nub of a cigarette in a crevice. It hadn't been there, he was positive, the week before. He'd picked it up, smelled it. "A Gitane," he announced. "Let's see if the guy left anything else around." With the charred object deposited in the trash bag we always carried out, he led us on a search of the grounds. "We'll check inside, too. He may have camped overnight."

But whoever the smoker was, he hadn't left a trace. "Just a passerby," I'd suggested to Jean-Luc. "A hunter maybe."

"There's nothing to hunt in this area."

"Maybe a dumb hunter."

That had brought a laugh from my friend and seemingly broke whatever tension there was.

On the Sunday outing the next week, I observed the redhead seeking other hints of a human presence. I said nothing and enjoyed our truncated (no ham) lunch. Despite the Alsatian's nervousness, I looked forward to the exploring adventure awaiting us. We had gone fairly deep into the bowels of the main grotto previously. Today, Jean-Luc advised, we would go actually to the bottom. He admitted he was on the trail of a discovery.

His confession perhaps explained his jitteriness. A lot of mystery still hung about Jean-Luc Mueller. However, no new evidence of any interloper materialized, neither out by the flat boulders nor in the darkness beginning underneath the lip of the cave's overhang.

The opening was more than high enough for us to stand upright and also more than wide enough for us to move side by side when we climbed down on a set of smooth limestone slabs that lapped each other like a set of gradual petrified waves. Our flashlights gave us adequate illumination. The spread-out Trio had the two males flanking the female. Our only danger, really, was of tripping on a billow outcropping underfoot or turning an ankle. We had known enough to bring sweaters because the lower we progressed the cooler and damper was the air.

Although we weren't in our usual single file formation, Jean-Luc remained our leader. At the bottom of the cascading limestone escarpment, he bade us stop momentarily and succeed him onto a ledge that offered room enough for us to stand. "Sweaters," he commanded. While we took these warmer garments out of our knapsacks and donned them, the redhead also extracted a sheet of paper from his own sack. Chantal held the light for him to read it by. I peeked over their shoulders. It was a hand-drawn map.

"This isn't a hunt for hidden treasure, Eugène," Jean-Luc said to me. "I copied it from an old newspaper article in the Limoges library."

"But of the interior of La Cav, isn't it?"

"Yes, only a different kind of mystery here," chimed in Chantal.

"You might say I'm holding the blueprint of a hoax," added Jean-Luc.

"I'm listening," I said "And utterly confused."

Since we appeared to be in no hurry, Jean-Luc took pains to elucidate, as he obviously had with Chantal. No, it wasn't an adventurous tale with romantic embellishments. It was historic research in action and I've believed ever since, the spark that ignited my own lifetime interest since in probing the past.

Voilà! Here's Jean-Luc's narrative: as we huddled around his flashlight-lit, crude drawing: "Approximately forty years ago, a Professor Achille Forestier of Paris, an archaeologist, arrived in Limoges . . ." La Cav, like caves do, magnified the speaker's voice with a hollow echo. "The scientific era was discovering constant new finds. Cave paintings had surfaced in Spain and near the Dordogne valley in France. Somewhat of a showman, Forestier announced he had come to study the La Cav formation, which he claimed was similar to other sites that had yielded fabulous art work attributed to Neanderthal and Cro-Magnon hunters. The regional newspapers of the time had photos of him alongside a local guide named Gueret. After the two of them spent several days exploring the cavern, they emerged and Forestier claimed, hélas, nothing had been found. But as soon as the Professor had left for Paris, there were new headlines. Gueret declared Forestier had lied. It was in conjunction with this uproar that Gueret provided a map . . . the map I've copied . . . supposedly the location of a secret grotto filled with fabulous primitive artwork."

Interrupting his narrative, Jean-Luc pointed to a small dark blotch in one corner of the map that our direct illumination turned into a miniature sketch of a sort of furry elephant.

"Chantal can tell you I'm a bad artist," Jean-Luc said to me. "Gueret was a good one, and you can easily see it is a woolly mammoth he depicted. Meanwhile Forestier had returned to Limoges to defend himself. Such a hue and cry arose that an expedition of scientists and local authorities was formed to go back into La Cav and investigate Gueret's charges."

Picking up, Chantal interposed: "And Jean-Luc, you said Gueret was complaining he wasn't paid by the Parisian who insisted he had only agreed to pay if they found anything."

"All this brouhaha was in those yellowing newspaper pages," Jean-Luc confirmed. Writers from the press went on the second search, which found the grotto, but no paintings."

"Imagine the anti-climax," Chantal editorialized.

"This Gueret did have a reputation as an *escroc*—a swindler. He disappeared fast. Forestier stayed a few days and took the train back to Paris."

"But the Professor didn't intend to stay away," volunteered Chantal.

"Chérie, you'll spoil the suspense."

"You told me he died."

"Fell over dead. *Crise cardiaque.* Getting into a cab at the Gare d'Orleans."

Did I need to ask how all this discussion related to the three of us? Or would Jean-Luc reveal his denouement? I waited. Finally, he took me by the arm and turned me half-around in another direction. "*Regarde*, Eugène. Can you make out a bit of light?"

I could. It seemed like an inverted cone of indistinct whiteness filtered from above.

"It's where we're headed," the redhead confirmed. "The grotto of no cave wall paintings."

Memories of the route we traversed to that point of light are of treading on a natural rock bridge with chasms on either side and pools of impenetrable darkness and a distant rumble below of flowing water. Enough width existed on the walkway so we were easily accommodated side by side although visions of slipping and tumbling an endless drop into nothingness tormented at least one mind—mine. It was a relief when we reached a solid floor and saw the grotto, receiving brightness from an opening in its vaulted ceiling ahead—an easy trek.

Inside, I commented finally: "No woolly mammoths."

"Monsieur Gueret might be thought to have played a nasty joke on Professor Forestier, which had backfired on him," Jean-Luc said. "Rather, I believe the two were in cahoots to hide the fact the Professor *had* found something."

"Show him," said Chantal.

Jean-Luc moved us to the section of the grotto illuminated by sunshine penetrating from on top. Moisture on the limestone mass was clearly visible. Yet closer up, one section, unbelievably, seemed manmade, quarried blocks put together by human hands.

No doubt, Jean-Luc had suspected my skepticism. He, too, must have felt he was in a dream world when he first made *his* discovery. Letting me into the secret, he said: "We both know about the hidden stairway in Chantal's family's château, a revolving wall. She had clever ancestors in the Middle Ages. So were the Stone Age people who once inhabited this site."

Distracted, perhaps, I didn't then catch exactly what Jean-Luc was up to there in the grotto. Nothing less than pressing some lever that in this instance, so help me God, caused those fused blocks of limestone to revolve inward.

Beyond was a passageway, immediately lit up by the redhead's flashlight and soon joined by Chantal's beam.

"Enter Sesame," a smiling Jean-Luc invited me.

"No, that's Open Sesame," I corrected him.

"Come on, pedant. We have a lot to do."

But once on the other side, I glanced back, worrying if the hinged contraption would swing shut, entombing us.

"It's all right," Jean-Luc had read my mind. "Chantal and I have been here before. And so has someone else. We have a surprise to show you."

Maybe thirty meters of walking through a tunnel brought us to the entrance of another grotto. The so-called "surprise" turned out to be nothing but an ordinary ladder. We had to go deep into the grotto to see it at the farther end.

"That ladder has been in that same position in for nearly forty years," Jean-Luc said. "Professor Forrestier and Gueret brought it, planning to come back and use it." He shined his flashlight onto the topmost rung. "Look carefully up. Do you see anything?"

I moved up to stand beside him, squinting. "A hole in the wall?"

"I've climbed it," the Alsatian answered. "So has my brave countess. Now we want to introduce you to our find."

As an aside, I must state that on these excursions to La Cav, Chantal scandalously wore trousers. She merely changed clothes once were out of sight of the château; and vice-versa, changing back at the end of our return.

Thus going below her on the ladder was therefore not a matter of eye-averting delicacy. Our order was slightly different on this occasion. Chantal went first, then me, then Jean-Luc taking up the rear. He joked he'd catch us if we plummeted.

In the same order, we entered this upper grotto that was as spacious as the others. But it was better lit by the daylight from above and much airier. What's more, after Jean-Luc arrived, he took us on a tour and pointed out *cave paintings!*

To be honest, they were nothing to get excited about. Most of the images were stick figures. With a few exceptions they were black, as if done with indelible charcoal. A few were of red ochre, Jean-Luc said. But there *had* been attempts at actual animals. The results were hard to identify—horned bulls, a bear, a deer, even a barely identifiable woolly mammoth.

We still had provisions in our knapsacks that we hadn't eaten at lunch. After all our exertions it felt good to sit on the stone floor, drink water from our canteens, munch leftover cheese and bread while putting together the pieces of this adventure.

The basically preposterous tale of Professor Forrestier and Gueret had lain ignored for four decades. That Jean-Luc had come across it was due to an interest he'd developed in La Cav when the Trio had first biked to the site. The superstar of cave paintings, Lascaux, hadn't yet been discovered (not until six months later, in September 1940). But fusses over wall art had been common since prior to the turn of the twentieth century.

To quote Jean-Luc or paraphrase him: "We are now in a situation like the climax to a detective story. The sleuth is summing up at the end. All the hullabaloo caused by Forrestier was to cement one verdict in peoples' minds—locals as well as scientists. La Cav was bare. No pictures. Forget about it."

"For how long? I asked. "You said he and his henchman put the ladder where it still is. They must have climbed it before they left it."

"You might make a good sleuth yourself, Eugène. You've realized they discovered these scratchings we see around us."

"They're not very artistic," Chantal got in her opinion, the same as mine.

"If you know anything about scientists, Eugène, especially about professors," Jean-Luc went on. "Their main goal is to make exclusive discoveries like Darwin or Cuvier."

"I know who Darwin is," I said. "But who's Cuvier?"

Jean-Luc's erudite reply was: "The Baron Georges Cuvier. The greatest geologist and zoologist of his day. Late eighteenth and early nineteenth century. A founder of paleontology, the study of fossils, *paleo* from the Greek word for old—in this case old bones. And a foe of Darwin. I'm surprised, Eugène, the Church didn't teach you about his theory of catastrophes they employed to battle the heresy of evolution."

Chantal seemed amused and even sympathetic to me, indicating her *ami* next to her and saying archly: "Isn't he a wonder, Eugène, a fountain of knowledge?"

If her countess-like remark was meant to take Jean-Luc down a peg, it had no effect.

"Professor Forrestier's intent, I have no doubt, was to try to become world-famous by announcing he had discovered *Neanderthalic cave figures*. Most drawings already known by then such as Pont de Gaume in the Dordogne were attributed to *Cro-Magnons*."

"Maybe we could call these Faux Magnons," I wisecracked.

"Or Neanderfigures," the Alsatian parried and we all three chuckled at our silliness.

Jean-Luc said to me: "We apologize, Eugène, we did so much exploring by ourselves. So we have another surprise for you, although we think you'll like it. We do not need to go back the way we came. I sensed you were leery the wall might close back in on us."

"No, not really," I answered blithely. "All right, maybe for a second or two . . ."

"Take a final look for today," Jean-Luc said upon consulting his watch.

"Remember, this is the Trio's hiding place if ever any of us need one."

The "easy" return trip out of the labyrinth required we actually do some additional climbing. Jean-Luc led us to a natural stairway in the rocks that rose toward the afternoon sunshine and emerged into a summit out in broad daylight. We were on a scrub-covered *(maquis)* plateau. Three sides of it were sheer cliffs. Jean-Luc's next revelation was a type of natural chute, hollowed out by rushing water, slippery on its surface and angled gently enough so sliding to the ground below on our buttocks could be likened to a toboggan ride. Whooping and hollering, we took off at intervals to avoid crashing into each other.

Once on the bottom, Jean-Luc pointed out the sluice we had used in order to impress on me—something I had already determined—how we couldn't return by it. Going to the hideaway could only be done from the front. "Those Neanderthals knew about making themselves impregnable," he said. Then, he pointed out a rock-strewn area we would have to cross to reach La Cav's entrance and the bikes we had concealed inside its darkness. Continuing, the redhead stated: "The early inhabitants also left a legend that to walk around to the entrance, clambering over dry, craggy field of rocks, would mean encountering an abundance of snakes, poisonous asp vipers. Some few still exist in the Limousin.

I must have winced or shown my innate horror of such reptiles, venomous or not.

"Don't worry," my pal patted me on the shoulder. "Chantal and I have walked there twice and never seen any sign of serpents, did we Chérie?"

"I would have shrieked," she added.

Consequently, we light-heartedly made our way through to the major cave opening and retrieved our bicycles. But before mounting, we leant them against nearby oak trees and policed the area again. No vestige of our presence was left.

On our bike seats, ready to pedal, Jean-Luc said: "Since today's Trio excursion was really our doing, Chantal, Eugène should pick out our next destination. *D'accord?*"

While Chantal nodded in agreement, I thought a moment before replying. "It just so happens," I told the other two. "We've been invited to visit Charniers-sur-Vare. Paul the Gaul whom I met at the Druid Party wants to show off his town to us. I'll contact him. D'accord?"

"D'accord. D'accord."

With that understanding, but naturally no date set, we started home.

XIII

April had almost turned into May before I was able to arrange for Paul the Gaul to receive us at Charniers-sur-Vare. I'd half suspected he'd been so drunk at the Druid Ball he had forgotten his offer. Not so. His delay in answering the message I'd left at his workplace was he'd been sent to Lyon to confer on matters pertaining to the Radical Party, a left-leaning political entity. He had abandoned the Communist Party because of the Hitler-Stalin Pact. This *superfluous information* was contained in a handwritten letter the village postman delivered to me personally. He would expect us the last Thursday of the month. Come at lunch hour.

Papa talked to me about Paul the Gaul. He had no objection to the Trio's visit. The man had leadership qualities, he said, and was very intelligent although not well educated. His fierce French patriotism and anti-Boche sentiments were appreciated. His record in the Great War had been exemplary—a Croix de Guerre for bravery. His new devotion to the Radical Party and its chairman, a fellow mayor of Papa's, Édouard Herriot (of Lyon) was better than his going with the Socialists and "that Blum."

During these years of my *jeunesse*, my father and I did not have a lot of interaction. At breakfast, he invariably immersed himself in his newspapers. Originally, *Le Figaro* had been his favorite national daily— "conservative in an old-fashioned style," he told me—until François Coty the Perfume King, bought it and used its pages to push his own fascistic political career. That left Papa afterward relying temporarily on the regional press and, of course, his beloved *l'Action française* daily. When the Vatican banned Maurras' journal and excommunicated him in 1926, Papa stubbornly kept on reading the condemned publication. After 1934, when François Coty died, *Le Figaro* was seen in our house again.

Occasionally, if an article interested him, he might let me know his thoughts. In this slack period prior to the May 10 blitzkrieg, I do remember his ranting about what a mess the Third Republic had made of the war in Norway. But our exposure to one another was always brief. Soon he was off into his medical office and closeted with patients all morning. While at grade school in Charniers, if I came home to eat at midday, Papa was invariably out making house calls. He had hospital duties, too, in Charniers-sur-Vare on certain days. His presence in the evening was more regular. Occasionally, though, he would dine with his cronies at the Hôtel Mayon or hold court at the Café Coq d'Or. Sundays there might be a festive feast with Jalouneix family members who hadn't moved away.

Mayor Desfosseux's municipal role, while nowhere near as taxing as his medical routine naturally took time away from me, too. Now and then, he had to attend ceremonial suppers at which the mayor's appearance was *obligatoire*. His signature was always needed on heaps of official papers. Local projects were initiated by him. On trips to Limoges to confer with the *préfet* (technically his superior), he would take me along and we might dine out and go to a movie (he liked American Westerns) and once or twice he took me to visit workshops and collections of the world-famous Limoges enamels.

The later years when I went to the lycée in Limoges, I saw even less of Papa except for matters of discipline but he never hit me again after the infamous *gifle*. Regarding his anti-Semitism, he had thoroughly taught me the fine distinctions of his idol Maurras. Papa rarely spoke ill of the Chosen People as a whole. If an individual Israelite had acted badly, he might use the word *youpin*. He still insisted Dreyfus was guilty. But compared to Maurras' bellowing editorials, M'sieu le Maire Desfosseux was a model of discretion vis-à-vis Semites.

That Papa never remarried was something I never questioned, except in retrospect. To my knowledge he never had a mistress nor off-and-on *amies*. Francine Jalouneix remained his one and only love. In the Vendée, he had been brought up to revere saints. She was in his memory as holy as the Virgin herself. To me, she was a memory of softness, of cuddling, of goodness, of warm affection. With her gone, Papa's natural inner coldness had conquered his being. No woman could ever take Maman's place.

The site in the house where her portrait hung was in his bedroom. I believe he talked to her when troubled. I was nine years old when we lost her. Returning from the funeral, he brought me into what had been their bedroom and where he had placed the painting formerly in the parlor and made me swear never to forget her. He also gave permission, if Madame Blanchard accompanied me, to enter the room without him and pay my respects and love to his *Francine, ma bien-aimée mère*.

Now for the Trio's excursion to Charniers-sur-Vare . . . I have no hesitation in writing this was the last of our truly carefree outings before the May 10th catastrophe. Not that we disbanded afterward. On the surface in our remote corner of the Massif Central, we experienced little change. Vichy was not far geographically but the Pétain government that emerged there tried hard to maintain an air of normalcy. At least at first.

On the trip to Paul the Gaul, I felt nothing except we were on a fun excursion, kids ready to enjoy ourselves. We didn't even have to carry provisions. Our host had invited us to lunch at a certain café in the center of town.

In every way, Charniers-sur-Vare was larger than Charniers-sur-Nys. You could say it was a small city or on the verge of becoming one. It had shops, stores, a gas station, several garages, a TABAC selling cigarettes and other tobacco products and the aforementioned hospital where Papa was on the staff and I was born. There was a train station, a choice of hotels and cafés, a well-known restaurant, light industry (where Paul the Gaul worked), parks and a riverwalk. A *sous-préfecture* had been located at this site by the Paris authorities. It was on a *route départementale* (D20, I think) that the Trio bicycled to Charniers-sur-Vare on the last Thursday of April 1940 (the 26th). We arrived at the Café Bon Temps at the noon hour. The spring weather was lovely, balmy enough for tables and chairs on the sidewalk. Awaiting us was Paul the Gaul, indulging in a glass of white wine.

Quite possibly his imbibing had begun earlier in the day. The ruddiness of his cheeks, the blood lines around his nose, were marks of an inveterate drinker. Yet not the slightest slur marred his welcome, nor the merest hint of unsteadiness when he got up to greet us. Hearty handshakes for the two males and an old-fashioned propriety as he took the countess's hand and kissed it. Then we were bade to sit down and join him.

The *garçon* in white-and-black waiters' dress code was by our side within moments. "The *choucroute d'Alsace* is *formidable*," Paul said to Jean-Luc. "I believe the chef is *alsacien*. But naturally his other dishes are *formidable* also."

"You are a gourmet, I see, M'sieu Paul," Jean-Luc diplomatically replied. "I will gladly accept your recommendation."

Chantal and I followed suit. M'sieu Paul also ordered the same dish, declaring: "Unanimous. *La France unie.*"

When we all had red wine before us (we'd be eating meat), we drank a toast to a united France. A warm, friendly ambiance had been created by this dynamic individual who was to surprise us—and continually overturn our expectations throughout the visit—by his displays of sophistication and knowledge. After all, he was a workingman, albeit now in a supervisory role, and made no bones about his having been a French Communist Party member. From our table seats, we could view the rushing waters of the Vare River running under several graceful stone bridges constructed, Paul told us, during the *Ancien Régime* of Royalist control. "My praise is in honor of your father, young Desfosseux," he informed me. "They did do some things right during the monarchy."

Once having eaten (Jean-Luc pronounced the *choucroute* to be superb), we were like privileged tourists seeing his community through Paul the Gaul's eyes. It must be mentioned that wherever we went, and while we were at the Café, he could easily have been crowned King of Charniers-sur-Vare. It was a rare person that he didn't know. Some pretty scary characters who hastened to greet him were obviously his cronies.

We did go to his workplace before we left. It was on the outskirts. The thirty machinists were each introduced and we toured the premises, which made war material for the French Army. The sole time I noticed Paul assume a hard, tough mien was when he brought up the subject of strikes the CGT, the Communist union, had threatened while France was at war.

"Ass-kissing their Nazi-Soviet Pact sweethearts," he grumbled disgustedly. "None of my *gars* would dream of walking off the job while *la patrie* is in jeopardy."

What a study in contrasts. The burly, ex-revolutionary atheist from the working class, to be one and the same with a sensitive, knowledgeable soul who had an appreciation of history and religious art. The most memorable of the landmarks he showed us was the Church of Saint Benedict, Romanesque like our Saint Augustine's, in its conglomeration of square blocks and curved turrets and—a significant difference—a gothic spire. Paul the Gaul introduced us to the frescoes on the inner walls depicting the life and crucifixion of Jesus Christ, relating how such imagery was used to teach the illiterate native peasants the New Testament story they couldn't read. In his inimitable style of the self-educated descendant of such folk people, he reported to us in a slightly humorous style how Saint Benedict Church got and kept its title.

He said: "It was an article of faith for many centuries in *our* Charniers that relics of the original Saint Benedict had been stolen in Rome and brought here. But why are they not available now for you to see? We believe they were robbed from us and in actuality turned up in the church of Saint-Benoît-sur-Loire in the village of Fleury where they remain to this day. What most interests me is that Fleury was named "the navel of Gaul" by none other than Julius Caesar. Benedictine monks built their church over a pagan shrine where the Druids of Gaul congregated once a year. Nearby was a Gallic sacred spring dedicated to the Goddess of Fertility. Then, with a wink, Paul added: "We have nine kids together, my wife and I.""

Before we left Saint Benedict's to tour his home and meet Madame Paul, he told one more story about the Charniers-sur-Vare church. After the Revolution had in effect closed all churches and the Restoration had opened Saint Benedict's again, his grandfather had sought to substitute the name of Saint Martial, the patron saint of the Limousin. It was Saint Martial, called the "Apostle of Gaul," who had been sent by Jesus to convert the Celtic tribe of Lémovices, who were to give their name to Limoges and the Limousin. Their name derived from two words in Latin—*orme*, meaning elm tree whose hard wood they used for their lances and *vices*, standing for: those who conquer. "We are warrior folks," Paul reminded us. "Don't you forget it."

The home Paul led us to was a former farm house within the urban confines of his town. His wife, a stout woman, once quite handsome, looked like she might be a match for her husband. Of the nine children, four still lived at home; others had surrounding houses so it was like a compound where they resided. The farming was now truck gardening and there were orchards and even a vineyard. We had to sample some of Paul the Gaul's *marc* brandy that he made from his fruits. "Strong enough to kill a horse," he joked while he poured each of us glasses. "Be grateful you're not horses."

The *pièce de résistance* of this home visitation was to inspect his collection of Vercingetorix memorabilia. He had it closeted in a special room that was a shrine to the heroic, albeit tragic Gallic hero. Whatever Paul had found of articles, pictures, models of helmets, swords, shields, etc. were lovingly displayed and annotated. In the same fact-filled manner in which he'd explained Saint Benedict's to us, he enlightened the Trio on the legend of the immortal Celtic leader who had risen from the Arverni tribe to take on Rome and Julius Caesar in a lost cause.

We ended the trip, I've said, with a final stop at Paul the Gaul's machine shop. He handled the metal products his men manufactured with the same delicate care he gave to his Vercingetorix artifacts. The explanations Paul gave of each finished product's use were too technical for my mind but Jean-Luc seemed to understand and asked intelligent questions. While we were saying good-bye and thanking Paul, Chantal contributed her gratitude for his support of the troops and by implication her colonel father in delivering a great big kiss to his cheek, at which the rough-tough guy actually blushed.

It had been a full afternoon for the three of us, one of our most enjoyable and unforgettable. We pedaled back the twenty-odd kilometers to our admittedly smaller enclave in high spirits.

Two weeks passed in which nothing of note that I can remember occurred.

On Friday, May 10, 1940, everything changed for France!

The breakthrough of the Germans at Sedan was as much a psychological blow as a physical occurrence. All of French military thinking was, as they say, "in the toilet." No German units, we were told, could penetrate the Ardennes Forest and its tangle of trees; their tanks would be useless; their formations of infantry dispersed by nature alone. The truth: the Boche marched a million men into and out of that clutter of roots and branches. Monstrous armored vehicles more powerful than anything we ever imagined had simply crunched their way through. The Maginot Line was outflanked. France's deputy prime minister, World War I hero Marshall Philippe Pétain, incessantly called for an armistice—a negotiated surrender.

Today, we can look back at old newsreels or the re-creations on the movie screen such as in *Forbidden Games* at the panic that eventually overtook the northern part of the country. In Charniers-sur-Nys, we did not for some time witness any effects that followed the German breakthrough. The fighting went on for more than a month. Franco-German battles were fought at unremembered places like Gembloux, Hannut, Perbais and Chastre in Belgium and the town of Sonne in France. De Gaulle's outmoded tanks won victories against superior German armor but they were short-lived. While France still had a million men in arms, the defeatists did their undermining. On the political front, the holdouts against capitulation like Paul Reynaud, Georges Mandel, Jean Zay and Leon Blum were vitiated. On June 16, 1940, Reynaud gave in to the pressure and resigned his leadership of the Assembly. Pétain took his place as prime minister. The government, which had fled Paris for Tours, then for Bordeaux, ended up in the watering spa of Vichy. On the following day, June 17, despite continued French resistance, Pétain radioed a broadcast to the nation, saying: "It is with a heavy heart that I tell you today to end the fighting." A day later, Colonel Charles de Gaulle, who'd escaped to England, radioed a plea to the French nation, urging his countrymen to keep resisting. However, within four days, on June 22, an Armistice was signed. Charles Maurras declared the German victory "a divine surprise."

What of the Trio during this turbulent period?

First of all, Chantal. She was her father's daughter, brought up on military stoicism and aristocratic aplomb. No handwringing, at least not in front of anyone. The count was a soldier. He had been in battle before. Even the shock of Sedan didn't seem to rattle her. When photos of the long lines of French prisoners of war being marched off by helmeted German guards appeared in newsprint, she did remark how high officers would be treated differently, just a hint she secretly hoped he had been captured. It was not until July before she received word from the Vichy War Department that Colonel Charles de Bregonzac-Chastain was listed as missing in action. Nor had she received a word from the count in the interim.

Jean-Luc . . . it was an upsetting time for him, too, although you'd never have known it. The problem was Alsace. Once the Armistice was signed, the Germans re-occupied the territory they had been forced to give up in 1918. It had been Jean-Luc's thought beforehand that Alsace would be incorporated into Germany, his citizenship would change and he'd ultimately be forced to serve the Nazis. Such an outcome, unthinkable earlier in 1940, had actually been behind the exploration we did of La Cav to lay out a secure hiding place if ever necessary. As for the crucifix-wearing woman in black back in Strasbourg, his mother, he never talked about her.

Concerning myself, I kept my feelings secret, too. While Papa's idol Maurras exulted over the defeat of the Third Republic, juridically extinguished by a 596-to-80 vote of the Assembly in July, Papa had to be pleased. No king from the existing monarchical families was given a throne but Maréchal Pétain was the next best thing. The grandfatherly-looking, distinguished white-haired and white-mustached octogenarian began using the *royal We* in his official discourse—*Nous, Philippe Pétain, Chef de l'Etat française*—that is, the *régime* established by the so-called National Revolution. At the head of this agglomeration, Pétain was said to have held more power than any Frenchman since Louis XIV. Behind Papa's desk in the mairie, there was soon a large head-and-shoulders, blown-up, framed photograph of this generalissimo. All over Charniers-sur-Nys, the picture was displayed. It was the first visible evidence for us that something had very much changed.

Also seen was an emblem of the *francisque*, an ancient Frankish double-bladed battle axe, still bearing the Republican colors of blue, white and red, yet with the motto of the Vichy dictatorship superimposed—

TRAVAIL, FAMILLE, PATRIE

replacing,

LIBERTÉ, ÉGALITÉ, FRATERNITÉ.

The francisque mimicked Mussolini's use of the ancient Roman *fasces*. Otherwise, the rhythm of our village didn't alter. Agriculture was important—mainly *élevage*—the raising of food animals. It was a daily occurrence to see beef cattle in the streets. Farmyards had pigs and lambs besides beef cattle and an occasional ox and inevitably chickens and often ducks. Horse-pulled wagons were still in use. Automobiles were rare, although we had a garage and mechanic to fix them along with a blacksmith. The smell of the country, including manure, reached downtown. People had fruit trees in flower as an opposing scent. Life was slow-paced. A *boulangerie* supplied us our daily bread; an *épicerie* allowed us to pick up needed groceries. A trolley stop. One hotel. One café. A doctor's clinic and a mayor's office.

To me, this was the familiar picture Charniers-sur-Nys presented on the day of my first consciousness. In our case it was *Unoccupied France*. There wasn't a German uniform seen within many kilometers.

Yes, once—but this was months later in the fall. Jean-Luc and I saw two obviously high-ranking Nazi officers of the SS in an open car on the main street of Limoges accompanied by several high-ranking French officers of the standing army of one hundred thousand men the Armistice had left Vichy. The driver was French, we noticed, when we stopped our walk from the Lycée to let them turn in to the prefecture building's driveway. They were obviously on a business visit to the prefect. It was a chilling sight, viewing in actuality those SS runes on their tunic collar tabs.

Jean-Luc and I had moved on in stunned silence. Yet back in rural Charniers, it was possible to imagine we had only seen an ugly mirage.

Intrusions from the outer world occurred infrequently. The first after the news from Sedan penetrated was de Gaulle's now-famous radio broadcast from London heard three times on the BBC in June, 1940. Chantal heard it on the 22nd, because one of the young maids came to her in a flurry. Another of the maids had a radio that could pick up the English station. They were going to listen to her father's friend General de Gaulle who was addressing the French people.

His message, the same on all three broadcasts, has since been called "one of the most important documents in French history." His simple ringing words asked rhetorically: "Is defeat final?" His answer was a rousing: "*Non!*" He flatly stated: "This war isn't over as a result of the Battle of France." He invited all French military personnel who had escaped to Britain to join him. And his finish was: "Whatever happens, the flame of the French resistance must not be extinguished and will not be extinguished."

Jean-Luc and I were not in the château when Chantal listened. Even had Charles de Gaulle not been a friend of her father's, the girl's spunk and heritage would have immediately made her a Gaullist. In the next few days, she spoke to convert the other two of us to her point of view. It wasn't a strong sell for Jean-Luc and me to agree. Only I cautioned I had to be circumspect because of my father's allegiance to Maurras, who had joined the Vichy government. Papa was likewise an admirer of Pétain. Like millions of the devastated French, he saw the aged Maréchal as the "Savior of the *patrie*," even though the Armistice had left only two-fifths of France free from the heel of the German boot.

On August 2, 1940, a Vichy court-martial sentenced Charles de Gaulle to death in absentia.

That summer, a preponderance of the Trio bike trips were to La Cav. We naturally kept our Gaullist sympathies to ourselves and, indeed, our visits to the isolated cavern remained secret . . . especially since we were also engaged in hoarding. It wasn't easy work since it had to be done in small increments in our backpacks—stocking up a place for Jean-Luc to hide if ever necessary. Other supplies like canned goods, batteries for flashlights, sleeping material, towels, etc., were transported. At least once a week, we would pedal the short cut and to date, in August, we had not encountered anyone, nor *signs* of anyone else in the area, not even a cigarette butt.

We thought it possible we would never have to activate our plan. There was no indication the Germans were hunting for Alsatians in the Unoccupied Zone. On the contrary, they were expelling French Alsatians and Lorrainers to the Vichy territory. Quite a number of these exiles were Jews: French Jews, as well as immigrant Jews. Limoges was one of the cities to which more than a few migrated.

We knew of at least one Jewish family settled in Charniers-sur-Nys. Their surname was perfectly French—Labelle—and the father was a decorated hero of the Great War. Nobody seemed to mind they had come to live among us.

It was in October 1940 when Vichy showed its true colors in regard to anti-Semitism. Initially, this was done within the distinction drawn by Charles Maurras—his "anti-Semitism of the State," not of race, and approved, as I knew only too well, by my own father. A national law, promulgated by the decree of *We, Philippe Pétain, Chief of the French State*, was issued on October 3rd. This *Statut des Juifs* was soon afterward posted publicly. I will never forget Jean-Luc and myself stopping en route from the Lycée to catch our trolley and perusing the *affiche*. We browsed it quickly, not wanting to miss our ride. At an extended glance, it was apparent that Jews in the *zone libre*, as it was called, no longer would be able to hold any positions in French government and were restricted from working in private industries that received public funds. They could no longer be teachers because teachers were paid by *l'état*. They could not be military officers. The first article of the statute defined who was a Jew—anyone with three Jewish grandparents or two Jewish grandparents if married to a Jew.

Jean-Luc and I read this notice in a solemn silence lasting until we were seated in our transportation to Charniers. One might say we were blasé because the law didn't apply to Catholics like ourselves. Still, although we switched to schoolboy talk, I sensed both of us shared an uneasiness, which instinctively we preferred not to discuss in the open.

Less well-known was another decree issued the following day, October 4th, ordering the internment of all foreign-born Jews in France.

October was also a directly cruel month for the Trio when word finally came from the War Ministry to Chantal that Colonel Charles de Bregonzac-Chastain had been confirmed by witnesses as Killed in Action, although his body had never been recovered.

MORT POUR LA FRANCE . . . the communication ended, offering consolation to an officer's family.

The same afternoon, Jean-Luc and I had returned from the Lycée and arriving at my house where he had left his bicycle we were met by Madame Blanchard who said Chantal had sent a request we go immediately to the château. I grabbed my bike and we both set off, pedaling furiously. Our third Trio member received us in the Billiard Room. She was amazingly composed, holding the official telegram in her hand, dry-eyed, greeting us gratefully, thanking us for responding so promptly. Then, she read the contents aloud.

This was a prelude to a gathering she had called of all the servants. With the two of us by her side, she gave them the news. The genuine sorrow and tears of the family retainers did not visibly affect her although she later confessed to Jean-Luc how badly she wanted to break down and blubber. Little brother Charles was brought in. When told his papa had gone to heaven, he'd sort of just grinned in his usual malevolent manner. Once the Trio was alone again, Chantal asked our help in arranging a religious service in the family chapel.

She told us quite frankly she did not want the present priest at Saint Augustine's, l'Abbé Pierre, to officiate. Her relatives in Burgundy had close ties to high Church officials who could prevent this but she did not want it to appear she had meddled. "Could either of us help—you, Eugène, through your father or you, Jean-Luc, through your mother at the convent in Strasbourg?"

I will not go into the intricacies of the matter at this juncture. Jean-Luc volunteered and true to his habit of being on top of things—*à l'hauteur*—succeeded in having Monsignor Solignac of Limoges agree to do the memorial Mass, with the assistance of Father Pierre, who was to keep his reactionary mouth shut.

Nor will I dwell on the details of this farewell to the count. It was confined to Chantal's relatives—particularly those impeccably-dressed wealthy ones from Burgundy, who managed, through pull, to obtain passage into Vichy territory—the Trio and the château's faithful hired help. It was held in that gem of a chapel within the château's walls, a dignified celebration with religious sacraments before a photograph of the colonel in full uniform and the portrait of his wife. Little Charles, for once, behaved himself.

I think it was a week later Jean-Luc told me the Trio had to have a meeting the next day—it was on Thursday, no school—in the Billiard Room. I was to come at 10:00 a.m. sharp.

When I asked him what it was about, he merely said all three of us had to be present. He didn't have to *add* how terribly important it was for me to attend.

XIV

Without an audience, is a drama actually drama? The setting, the mise-en-scène, always has a role. At 10:00 a.m. on the dot, I was back in a comfy place—the château's billiard room, yet anxious. This place had become the Trio's unofficial headquarters. We often played billiards here after Chantal had taught us that intriguing contest of making ivory balls carom off each other. At the far end, where we had planned the Druid Ball, we once again gathered in three close together leather-backed chairs and talked.

The moment I assumed my usual place in our little circle, Jean-Luc, more serious than I had ever seen him, said: "Chantal knows my secret. Now you must know it, too."

He leaned toward me and, not wasting any time, let the words explode. "You see, my dear friend, I am a Jew."

My reaction? I was more bewildered than stunned. I literally wanted to argue with him. Church attendance every Sunday, taking communion, kneeling in the confessional with Father Pierre, but I also immediately recognized how this could be camouflage.

The Alsatian's voice was softer as he said to me: "My life is in your hands, Eugène."

Chantal seized the initiative. "Are you with us, Eugène? Are we still the Trio?"

"Of course," I said, not hesitating for a second. "Always."

Un-countess-like, beaming the most radiant smile I have seen in my life, Chantal rushed out of her chair to hug me. Jean-Luc followed to shake my hand and put his arm around my shoulder. The three of us stood in a sublime moment of wordless euphoria.

As we were getting back into our seats, I voiced a reflective thought. "If my father ever learns . . ." I started to say.

But Jean-Luc cut me off. "Your father already knows," he said.

Puzzlement upon puzzlement. It took the next half hour for some riddles to be unraveled. Although Jean-Luc was the main narrator, it was obvious Chantal had been briefed already.

First of all, a basic fact: Jean-Luc's *nom de famille* was not Mueller; nor was his *prénom* Jean-Luc. He was born Jean-Marc Rosenstein. If the name Rosenstein sounds familiar, you will recall it was mentioned by Leon Blum in our interview as one of the major French Jewish families in Alsace. Jean-Luc (I will continue to call him that) was the third child and only son of René Rosenstein, the famous R. R., the Department Store King. The boy's two older sisters were married and living in the United States. His parents had separated. The woman in black, his mother, a convert to Catholicism, did not countenance divorce. His perspicacious father, frightened by the rise of Hitler in Germany, sold his businesses in Alsace and other parts of France and moved to Switzerland where he also had stores, significant influence, and was easily able to buy himself Swiss citizenship.

"He wanted me to stay with him," said Jean-Luc. "I would live in the lap of luxury, be sent to an exclusive private school around Geneva. Except I refused."

"Why?" I asked.

"The same question I asked," Chantal volunteered. "Listen to his answer."

"Remember the *affiche* we read together in Limoges not long ago," he started. "In my case, I had *four* Jewish grandparents. The cover story for the Gestapo would be that I was in the United States with my sisters. The reason I'm in hiding here was that my mother wanted me to remain in France near her. She still had hopes she could convert me to her adopted faith."

Why Charniers-sur-Nys? The connection was with Papa who had met René Rosenstein while working as a young doctor in Strasbourg in 1919. They were both adherents of *l'Action française*. A few French Jews did follow Maurras, did believe in monarchy. A famous example was the writer Daniel Halevy, of an old revered Israelite family, whom Maurras advertised as a dear personal friend.

According to Jean-Luc, R. R. contacted his old *copain* who had since settled to practice in his wife's hometown of Charniers-sur-Nys. Thus, the precocious redhead since September 1939 had been under the secret protection of M'sieu le Maire Doctor Desfosseux.

That explication should have satisfied all of my curiosity. A few more details were provided later when the two of us Trio guys went trout-fishing in the Nys while Chantal was away visiting relatives on the Cote d'Azur. This was in the spring of 1941. Those intervening months, since the "confession" saw no change in the status of Jean-Luc Mueller. Life continued for him exactly as before except, due to the death of her father, Chantal had him often remain with her overnight in the château, although he still kept the quarters Papa had arranged in the house of the widow Pochard, chosen, I now realized, for her reputation that she never gossiped.

The budding love life of Chantal and Jean-Luc was not really a subject for village tittle-tattle. If anything, it was suffused with the romantic, unreal aura of a fairy tale—the princess in the castle and her commoner admirer who is ultimately revealed to be a prince in disguise . . . amid predictions they would live happily together ever after.

It was again a Thursday when Jean-Luc and I biked down to the local river to try our luck. Because the Nys was so fast moving, it did not ice up much in the dead of winter. Now the crescendo of thaw run-off had passed and increasing warmth in the water had those finny beauties stirring and hungry. We were not fly fishermen and used worms and our *cannes à pêche*—fishing poles—were decidedly primitive. Nevertheless, in a short period of time, we had landed ourselves the ingredients for a nice repast of *truite* that Madame Blanchard would cook for us with her inimitable culinary skill.

I had a sixth sense, once we had ceased casting and hauling in, and lay luxuriating in the sunshine of the river bank that Jean-Luc had something he wanted to confide in me.

To a certain degree, I had sensed such an urge on his part not infrequently since his "revelation" in October. Indeed, when we two were out of earshot of anyone, "a course in Judaism," as I called it, would commence. The "curriculum," you might say, was based primarily on the wisdom and knowledge imparted to Jean-Luc by a single individual—his maternal grandfather—Marcel Cohen, who, he said with a laugh, had legally changed his first name to Max "because it sounded more Jewish." In a very real manner, while Max's daughter Jeannette kept trying to convert her son Jean-Marc Rosenstein to Catholicism, Grand-Père Cohen, his mentor and steady companion, was re-converting him back to his Israelite roots.

I could soon understand the tension in Jean-Luc. He intended to tell me what so far he had not dared tell Chantal. Consequently, I was sworn to silence.

Once I'd pledged my fealty, Jean-Luc asked me: "I've made you aware of Zionism, have I not?"

"Correct," I answered. "The idea of a Jewish homeland in Palestine."

"But I've never told you my dream to emigrate to the holy land and help make it into a country for ourselves."

His revelation caught me by surprise. Why was he confiding this startling news to me?

"It may happen someday," he continued. "The message can come. I will have my certificate to go to Palestine. People will risk their lives to transport me. I would like the advice of a disinterested friend, and you have become such a friend."

I was immensely flattered. He then spoke of a boyhood pal of his in Alsace whom he had often mentioned to us. Those two had been inseparable growing up in Strasbourg. This fellow's name was Lucien Veynachter, a curious nom de famille, meaning "Christmas" in the Alsatian dialect of German. His father was a Protestant pastor. I remembered that at a recent Trio meeting Jean-Luc had wistfully said: "I hoped to bring Lucien here this summer, so we could become the Quartet—a couple of stalwart Catholics and two heretics, a Jew and a Huguenot."

At that moment, from his wallet he impulsively took out a snapshot he hadn't shown either of us until then. "I jokingly nicknamed him the Aryan," he explained as we gazed at the image: a slightly younger Jean-Luc next to a handsome, extremely blond teen with fine intelligent facial features, but looking like a poster boy for the Hitler Youth.

"Good thing you didn't bring him," Chantal teased her *ami*. "He's gorgeous."

"He only likes blondes," Jean-Luc teased back.

"I'd dye my hair," the countess retorted mischievously.

It was in recalling this playful exchange, overshadowed since July by the darker knowledge of an Alsace firmly in Nazi control, that I now asked Jean-Luc how I could take Veynachter's place as a confidante. "What advice can I give you?" I asked.

His dilemma, he asserted, would not climax immediately. Maybe it would never happen. His father still held out for him to emigrate to Switzerland. His mother, strongly opposed, kept on fantasizing he would abandon the religion of the Cohen family and save himself spiritually and in the eyes of the Nazis through conversion. In agreeing to allow himself to hide out in Charniers, Jean-Luc had contemplated a stay of no more than a few months. That, it goes without saying, was before he laid eyes on Chantal. At the present moment, it was more than a year and a half since he'd come to the Limousin.

"I never realized how much Chantal needs me with her now that the count is gone." Thus commenced his airing of their relationship. "Should the message be sent to me, 'Pack your bags,' frankly I would turn to stone. What should I do? How could I act? Agonized. Torn. Love versus duty. An eternal conundrum . . ."

Once he paused, I got a word in edgewise. "You plan, I assume, to cross that bridge when you reach it."

"Who knows?" Jean-Luc answered. "Palestine may even fall to the Germans. Even if it doesn't, the British have double-crossed us and are making it extremely difficult to enter the homeland they promised the Jews."

"Tell me . . . why in the world did you reveal your Jewishness to Chantal?"

"You won't believe the truth," he said.

It was an incident that had frightened as well as astonished him. All through the days surrounding the news of her father's death, Chantal had been calm, poised, in command and coping with the strain of organizing the obsequies and handling her relatives. Once the château had quieted, her "personal dam let go," as Jean-Luc put it.

Not in a prolonged crying jag, he was quick to add. But in an explosive paroxysm of anger—"aimed at me," he admitted.

The bizarre aspect was that because of the research we had collected on the ancient Celts, she had fixated on a statement that the Alemanni had been the founders of Alsace. "She read me the passage," Jean-Luc said, "and she began shouting: 'Those Alemanni were Germans! Alsatians are Germans!' And she turned absolutely hysterical, screaming at the top of her lungs at me: 'You are nothing but a German. A dirty Boche. An enemy who killed the finest man in the world. Get out! Get out!' She was shrieking. All I could think of was her mother whose fits she had described to me. I felt desperate.

"'I can't be a German,' I argued. 'I can't be a Nazi.'

"'That's it, yes, Nazi! You Nazi! Get out!' Her furious rampage grew louder. It was a good thing we were in her bedroom. Had we been in the Billiard Room, she might have thrown the balls at me.

"I shouted back: 'Do you know why I can't be a Nazi? Why I can't be a German?'

"That stopped her for a moment. 'Why not?'

"'BECAUSE I AM A JEW!' I bellowed, expecting her to accuse me of lying.

"Instead, she simply said, 'Oh, I didn't know,' and sat down.

"You see how hard I would find it *ever* to leave her," he concluded.

Advisor Eugène advised: "If you do go to Palestine, take her with you."

"I hadn't thought of it," he admitted. "I will have to give the thought consideration."

There this matter rested, ready to be revived as circumstances demanded. A month later the war would take another unexpected turn, when Hitler again surprised the world by invading the Soviet Union. December of 1941 witnessed the United States' joining the fight against the Axis powers. Most of 1942 seemed the high water mark of the dictators' triumphs. Another new twist directly affecting France was the Allied capture of our colonies in North Africa—Algeria, Morocco, and, after fierce battles, Tunisia.

Hitler responded by ordering his troops to occupy Unoccupied France. On November 10, the Nazi-mobilized columns entered Vichy and Lyon, and armored cars full of Wehrmacht soldiers rolled into Limoges. Since the next day was a Thursday, Jean-Luc and I were not at school to see them circulating around the city. But we had plenty of opportunities from then on to see green-grey field uniforms and all the panoply of Teutonic insignia, particularly swastikas. Yet Vichy still governed and civic order was maintained by French gendarmes.

No one bothered a couple of school kids commuting to and from a Lycée.

Still my stomach tightened and I'm sure Jean-Luc's did, too, when we spied the "green mice," which we had secretly dubbed them, strolling the Limoges streets. Back in Charniers, these rodents were never seen.

At the time, the full picture of what was brewing behind the scenes not only in France but for humanity on the whole remained invisible. Who could have predicted a war crime so outlandish, so unthinkable in its scope, so efficiently ruthless in its execution, that it would brand itself on history by the name of the Holocaust (or *Shoah* in Hebrew). Wartime atrocities had never been absent from the chronicles of mankind. Genghis Khan remains alive in memory because of the horrors he inflicted on entire populations. Nor have such killings, albeit on a smaller scale, disappeared since 1945. Slaughter based on ethnic identity continues merrily.

Which brings me back to the current period of writing these memoirs. I have to laugh. I am like an addict, I realize. *Out of the frying pan into the fire,*

Naansee would say. No sooner have I exited an exhausting reminiscence than I am contemplating the continuation of my "interviews." And I believe I have a perfect subject.

You'll be surprised at my choice.

Max Cohen! Jean-Luc's maternal grandfather.

The more I think about it, the more excited I'm getting. Although he had died of a heart attack in February 1939, eight months before the onset of World War II, he was so vivid to me from Jean-Luc's descriptions I literally could believe I knew him as if we had personally met.

I had been sitting at the kitchen table, finishing a light supper when this lightning strike of an inspiration hit me.

Not so much as bothering to put my dishes in the sink for Arlette to wash in the morning, I downed the last of the Sancerre I'd been drinking, wiped my mouth with a napkin and made a beeline for my study.

XV

Do you know a painting by the White Russian-Jewish artist Marc Chagall entitled *The Rabbi of Vitebsk* or *The Praying Jew*? Long before I saw the colored plate of Chagall's masterpiece, Jean-Luc had described the portrait to me. All works of this artist had been banned by the Nazis, and Chagall, himself, had fled to the United States. Jean-Luc had shown me the picture in an art book at a Limoges bookstore, before it was removed. His own framed print of it had been left in his bedroom in Strasbourg.

The incredible blue eyes of this rabbi, he said, reminded him of Grandfather Cohen.

Thus had the Alsatian begun to bring Max Cohen to life through those amazing eyes that were bluer than blue, bluer, actually, than Chantal's. Also emphasized was the utter contrast of Max's physical appearance compared to Chagall's subject. That religious Jew was absolutely Semitic in his looks. One conjured an image of Abraham's Bedouin sons or of Jewish warriors in the Arabian desert, hawk-nosed, lean-faced and black-bearded, whereas Max Cohen was round-faced, chubby, clean-shaven, and born with red hair. Said Jean-Luc: "Max—he made me address him as Max—not grand-père, opa, or zaydee—claimed his features, like mine, derived from some carrot-topped Slavic peasant who raped a Jewish girl in the midst of a pogrom but let her live to have a baby, a boy. That poor illegitimate creature, shunned by Jew and Gentile alike, managed in later years to marry in the faith and produce progeny who transmitted the traits of hair color and freckles generation after generation. Max's hair, when I became conscious of him, was already white, including his fluffy beard. During my earlier years, I thought he resembled Saint Nicholas—the patron saint and protector of children."

This crash course in Judaism needed to fill out Max Cohen for me also included the Torah, the Kabbalah, and the Hassids. The first has been referred to as "The Five Books of Moses" or what we have called "The Old Testament." Jean-Luc said, and I paraphrase, there is no higher calling in the Jewish religion than devoting a lifetime of study to the Torah, parsing every word and even quibbling about punctuation. The Kabbalah is another examination into the mysteries of God, the mystic side of Jewish philosophy, much of it contained in a literary work, The Zohar. The Hassids began as a cult of eastern European Jews, tired of the dry intellectualism of rabbinic hair-splitting and instead seeing life as joyous and expressed in song and dance, especially through the music of *klezmars*, the Yiddish version of troubadours.

Reb Max Cohen was connected to all of these varieties (*Reb* is the equivalent of *Monsieur*). Lest you think of Max as a ghetto refugee still lost in ancient dogma, forget it. Despite his religious proclivities, he was a sophisticated European gentleman with an encyclopedic grasp of Western learning, especially in literature, history and politics.

The *Pale of Settlement*, Max's birthplace, was essentially a gigantic ghetto created in 1791 by Catherine the Great, the Empress of Imperial Russia. All Jews under her rule, except for a favored few, were confined to an area comprised roughly of present-day Poland, Lithuania, Belarus, Moldova, parts of Western Russia and the Ukraine. Vitebsk, where Max's forebears settled, was within this mostly impoverished special region. His people had emigrated from a German Duchy turned unfriendly, but when an originally welcoming Russia proved to be no less anti-Semitic, they emigrated back. When Max was born in 1856, the family was in the Rhineland, in Cologne to be precise. At the age of twenty, he sought his fortune in Alsace after its capture by the Prussians. And he found gold in retail operations that *he*—not his son-in-law René Rosenstein—erected into major department stores.

Whether this superficial grounding in Judaism Jean-Luc had given me, reinforced by my own reading and research, would prove sufficient to stage the event I planned for myself tonight was anybody's guess. Undaunted, I plunged ahead, in the spirit of Jean-Luc Mueller.

Before I knew it, it was show time!

Lacking newsreel footage of Max, I simply awaited him in person.

Would he be in the prime of life? Or would he be the octogenarian he was at the time of his death? Would I hear the tap, tap, tap, of a cane?

Of all things, Max Cohen arrived dancing!

The music, out of nowhere, had a gypsy tinge to it, shrill violins but nothing mournful—nothing but happy jubilant sounds delivered at an unbelievably fast pace. Hearing such a catchy tune made you not only stamp your feet, it also pulled on you to jump out of your chair and join the whirling dervish who had just entered. Max was going around and around in circles in accordance with the Klezmer beat. A clarinet was wailing ecstatically, drums were thrumming, cymbals clashing. He caught sight of me and gestured: "Come! Come!" And lo and behold, we were suddenly twirling about.

The old white-beard with the unforgettable blue eyes was wearing a round, flat-topped fur hat that instantly summoned visions of another age in eastern Europe, a throwback to the Hassids, and I remembered Jean-Luc had told me its name—a *straimel*. Max and I had clasped each other's hands in order to make our circles. Suddenly, the music changed. If anything, the new tune was wilder. My dance partner separated himself from me and squatted, kicking his legs in front of him, keeping time to the raucous uproar, maintaining his balance as he moved across the floor on his haunches, shouting at me: "*Kazatsky! Kazatsky!* You can do it, too!"

One night, Jean-Luc after several glasses of wine, had performed this "Cossack dance" before Chantal and me in the Billiard Room to music produced by his own voice.

Neither the countess nor I had tried to imitate him. But here, alone now, I crouched down and kept my legs thrashing à la Max while the spectral Max shouted encouragement until all of a sudden the kicking upset my balance and down I tumbled backward onto my *cul*.

Laughter broke from me, holding my bumped bottom and feeling ridiculous while Max guffawing, rushed over and jerked me upright.

"I'm Max Cohen," he said. "Enchanted to make your acquaintance, Monsieur . . ." He waited for me to fill in the gap.

"Desfosseux, Eugène," I replied. "I became a great friend of your grandson's. But after you died."

Those last words came out choppily since I was trying to catch my breath. The far more elderly person seemed barely to have exerted himself. Until he removed his *straimel*, I had not seen much of that famous full white head of hair, only the fluffy beard. His hypnotic sapphire eyes fixed on me, full of pleasure at our meeting in this entirely unorthodox fashion.

Other than the fur hat, Max was clothed in a suit that probably was very expensive but hadn't been pressed for some time.

Finally, we rearranged ourselves opposite each other in our respective chairs. I started the conversation.

"*Monsieur Cohen, vous* êtes—"

That is as far as I got before he held up his chubby hands. "Hold on, hold on," he interrupted. "Even my cat called me Max. And we must *tutoyer* besides, *mon cher* Eugène."

With that formality out of the way, we proceeded to an extensive discussion about his late grandson. Max initially had used *Jean-Marc*. But when I commented he had always been Jean-Luc to me, his gracious grandfather said: "Jean-Luc he shall be then." And Jean-Luc he was throughout our talk.

There was a tolerance in his tone that told me much about the man . . . a Semitic fatalism, as it were. God's will trumped everything else. *Insha'Allah*, the Arabs say.

I abruptly stated. "You know Hebrew, Jean-Luc said. Do you know Arabic?"

His modest reply was: "I've learned some Arabic phrases . . ." Whereupon he rattled off a rapid string of Middle Eastern intonations.

"What does that mean?"

"May the camel of adversity *emmerder* on your descendants to the tenth generation."

"I guess I know the French equivalent."

"Hebrew and Arabic are not far apart. If I were in Palestine, I'd learn the latter completely. Here, I do a good job with Romance languages, including some Romanian. In German and its Alsatian dialect, I'm of course fluent. Yiddish was spoken in my parents' home. Ladino—the language of the Iberian Jews, I don't know,"

"But altogether impressive," I commented. "Outside of French, I know only English . . . the Yankee version."

We swiftly bonded, Max and I, with the same ease described to me by Jean-Luc. In Strasbourg, Max inhabited a wing of the, picturesque, half-timbered Rosenstein mansion bordering one of the Ill River side canals in the *La Petite France* section . Once his wife had died and he had sold the majority interest in his stores to his son-in-law René, he turned over the house to R. R. and Miriam but retained about a third for himself. There among his books, his religious paraphernalia, entertaining almost daily visits from his beloved grandson, Max was well-contented. Before the Nazi era, numerous synagogues were open in Strasbourg and Reb Cohen was welcome at all of them. "The Israelite factions fought each other like you can't imagine," Jean-Luc had told me, "but they all loved their Maxie." Young people today would say that he was *sympa*—the slang abbreviation of *sympathique*, which has a slightly different nuance in French than "sympathetic" in English.

"Now what about you?" the visitor said, his blue Chagall eyes fastened on me." I have some questions."

Just like that, Max gently turned the tables. The interview guest was probing the host.

"Where were you born? Myself, I was born in Germany before there was a Germany."

"In the Limousin," I answered him. "At the hospital in a nearby town, also named Charniers, the bigger Charniers-sur-Vare. My father Doctor Desfosseux delivered me."

"You have lived in this place all your life?"

"In our Charniers until it was destroyed by the Nazis. In Paris for studies and teaching French history and presently in the separate hamlet of Bregonzac."

"Under the shadow of the château."

"Ah, you saw it. Did you also note the ruins next door?"

"Only a glimpse. When we are finished gabbing, I would like you to show me them under the light of a full moon tonight."

It was consequently decided instantly without either of us saying anything that we, rather I, would attempt something entirely new. Make my show a travelling show. But before leaving the study, we still had much more to say about Jean-Luc.

"Tell me about the girlfriend, the countess, his maiden *affaire*. Was she very pretty?"

"Extraordinarily so. She could have been a cinema star."

"Where is she at the moment?"

"Growing old at an estate in Burgundy near Auxerre. On her third husband, I believe."

"Any children?"

"Not by Jean-Luc, as far as I know. We've lost touch."

Max said to himself, nodding: "The end of the Cohen red hair."

For maybe the next fifteen minutes, I regaled him with stories of the Trio's adventures, truncated narratives to which he listened with intense interest.

Then it was his turn to regale me with tales of Jean-Luc's growing up. The tall, handsome blond *schagatz* (non-Jewish male) Lucien Veynachter he often brought to visit his "Max"—was specifically mentioned. Some emphasis entailed Jean-Luc's participation in the Zionist young peoples' organization *Hashomer Hatzair* (Youth Guard). Said Max: "This movement was founded in 1913, based on scouting and preparing for life in the Holy Land. René was only too happy to allow his son to join such a dedicated Hebrew group—for spite, countering my *mischuganah* (crazy) daughter's Catholic intentions for the boy. How I loved to see him march with the other kids in their blue and white uniforms: the goyish-looking redhead in the vanguard, carrying the banner of Israel—blue and white with a gold *Mogen David* (Shield of David) emblem. René had promised to use his contacts in the Zionist hierarchy for him to emigrate to Palestine. When he was old enough, Jean-Marc—*Je m'excuse*, Jean-Luc—would go work on a kibbutz and help prepare our homeland."

"But René had no intention of procuring a certificate for him, Jean-Luc told me."

"Quite possibly. René Rosenstein, for all his brilliance, was a tricky individual."

"Your daughter's single-minded dream—making a Catholic of Jean-Luc—never came to fruition. In agreeing to come hide in Charniers-sur-Nys as a . . . you say *goy* . . . Jean-Luc swore solely to attend church and go through the motions of accepting sacraments. Plainly and simply, if it hadn't been for Chantal, he never would have stayed in our dinky little village. Fortunately for me, I have him to thank for opening my eyes to the outer world."

It was after my last remark I felt instinctively the moment had arrived to attempt the "great experiment." We would soon reach the limit of time when my spectral interviewees would start breaking apart. Up we stood. Before we knew it, we were at my front door. Left in the closet when I took nocturnal walks with my poodle Jacques, I kept flashlights and the cane I had found essential for extended walks. Thus armed, I led Max into the outdoors. When shining my light in his direction, I discerned the old gentleman right alongside. So the two of us elderly men, one mustached but clean-shaven and a bit bent over, the other hirsute with fluffy Father-Christmas-white hair, were soon edging into the evening shadows.

The château was behind and above us. Although notably a cheapskate, young Count Charlot kept a pair of lights shining by his entrance. While Max and I had briefly glanced in that direction, the clouds had moved, etching in moonlight the venerable fortress. Ahead on the footpath to Charniers, the illumination from the sky was bright enough to turn off my flash.

It was like a maze, wending our way through the charred wreckage of blasted stone walls, the jagged remnants of house foundations, the scorched beams that had collapsed onto heaps of rubble. I could point to burnt-out barns in which the men and older boys of the village had been machine-gunned. I showed Max the site of the home in which I'd grown up, now permanently demolished. I brought him to the outside of the terrible church massacre scene, to stare up at what was left of its Romanesque construction. Going inside I dared not do. We walked along the trolley tracks, beyond the grenade-savaged, bullet-ridden World War I monument. We passed what was once the Hôtel Mayon, now a pile of bricks. And we ended at the ivy-covered Pont Neuf where Max and I sat down on one of the bulwarks and talked while the moon glistened on the running water of the Nys.

"It's so peaceful," Max said.

"Tell me your impressions of what you saw, Grand-Père Max," I said to him.

His response: "It is hard still to believe in God after witnessing these scenes."

"And that is without the stomach-turning sight of shapeless bodies burnt to a crisp and the nauseating odor of grilled human flesh."

"Do you know what the Shoah is?" he asked me.

"Certainly. The Holocaust."

"Do you believe it happened?"

"What are you saying? Do you *not* believe the mass murders happened?"

"The new Nazi lovers want to deny Jews were gassed, or so much as killed at places like Auschwitz. The same with pogroms in the old country, my grandparents told me."

"We've heard that *merde* here, too, or rather that Charniers was destroyed by the Resistance wearing SS uniforms and travelling in SS vehicles.

"God allowed the Shoah. I found it hard to forgive Him."

"God allowed Charniers also. The Almighty refused to intervene. I've given up on Him. And Jean-Luc, your grandson attempted, instead, a . . ."

But I didn't finish my sentence. A beam of light was approaching from the direction of the martyred village center. Benoît, the watchman! I had forgotten about him."

Within earshot, he said: "M'sieu le Professeur, mon Dieu, it's been a long time since I've seen you at night . . . Since your poor dog died."

"There's a full moon, Benoît . . ." I was about to add "*We found it so beautiful*," when I realized no one was sitting next to me. Max had vanished.

However Benoît limped over and took the place where I'd had Jean-

Luc's maternal grandfather sitting. Benoît had been a familiar figure to me since childhood. He was the *garde champêtre*—the rural policeman. On the job for many years, and under Vichy, too. But the SS marched him off to one of the barns (Phillipons) with the other men of Charniers. Because the Nazis took his shotgun from him and found a few hunting rifles, they declared a Resistance arsenal existed in our village. The killers with the machine guns in the barns apparently had been instructed to shoot low so their victims didn't die instantly but would be burned to death once covered with straw and set afire. Benoît had gotten bullets in both legs, had fallen behind other bodies, crawled to an opening in the barn's wooden wall close to him, slithered through unseen, hid in a ditch where he covered himself with brush, staunched his flow of blood and crawled out once he'd heard the SS leave. He was the sole survivor among the males.

Need I add that following the Liberation he had been given the job of watchman at the memorial for the rest of his life if he wanted, which he most enthusiastically did.

He limped along far better than I shuffled with my cane. That was one reason perhaps he insisted on accompanying me home after we had a nice little chat about my poodle Jacques and our nightly rambles, man and dog, through the ruins together when I first moved to Bregonzac and farther into the past the mischief I'd gotten into as a young kid and how he'd looked the other way and never said a word to the honorable mayor. "But you always gave me a warning," I said, "and finally it sunk in and I've been good ever since," and we laughed.

Benoît walked me right to my door. We shook hands and he returned to his patrolling while I hurried inside to the study. I half-expected to find Max Cohen in the chair where he'd sat but it was empty and stayed empty despite my intense concentration.

Yet, and this really was strange . . . the quick conversation started but not finished on the bridge about the Holocaust and the Charniers massacre was on my mind, and I grabbed a pad of paper off my desk in order to write it down, reactivating the recorder. I sat in my armchair facing the empty chair.

"Tell me your impressions again, Grand-Père Max . . ."

Then, about to voice Max's words in answering, I distinctly made out his slightly raspy voice issuing from the empty chair. No sign of the *sympa* octogenarian, only an amplification of a statement he'd made on the Pont Neuf: "It is hard to believe still in God after witnessing these scenes."

In his dignified but warm French, his final retort was: "*J'aimerais revenir, mon cher Eugène*"—"I would like to come back again, my dear Eugène."

A contrasting thought assailed me: *My maternal grandfather Eugène Jailouneix is only a line on a despoiled nameplate. Jean-Luc's maternal grandfather— invisible on an empty chair—wouldn't I have loved a grand-père like him!*

Finally, I could wring nothing more from Max. I folded that other chair and put it away in the study closet. I detached the recording machine and stored it in its usual drawer in my desk. *C'est fini*—at least for tonight.

Retiring to my bedroom, I sat and read for maybe an hour from Jean Giraudoux's 1920s novel, *Siegfried et le Limousin*, a fantasy about Franco-German relations after World War I. Giraudoux, a native of the Limousin, was a fine but difficult writer. A few chapters at a time were all I could digest of his dense, James-Joycean-style French prose, having to go over sentences and paragraphs several times to piece together the meanings.

Eventually tired enough to sleep, I undressed, donned night clothes, did my ablutions in the bathroom, and slipped quietly under the covers until the next conscious thing I knew was that I found myself listening to the morning roosters.

XVI

I t might be the reading I did the night before of Giraudoux's *Siegfried et le Limousin* that started me thinking about the phenomenon of *coïncidence* while I sat at my breakfast table over a cup of *thé citron* after Arlette had gone. The premise of the novel is based on a fairly startling type of coincidence—one of transferred identity where a French soldier wounded in World War I suffers amnesia and is tended by a German nurse who takes advantage of his loss of memory by turning him into a German. As such he becomes a national hero in Deutschland in the period just after the Armistice of November 1918.

Giraudoux's intent was to tell a fable to help cement the common humanity of our two perennially warring peoples. By this imaginative coincidence, the French and Germans were to join together, although the books ends sardonically with the Teuton leader, his memory healed by his former French sweetheart, assassinated before his return with her to *La Belle France*.

Obviously, coincidences have varying degrees. It was certainly a coincidence that Benoît limped onto the scene the moment I was speaking with the phantom grandfather of a Charniers victim but how could the *garde champêtre* know, merely seeing Professor Desfosseux alone by himself.

Of course, a far more serious coincidence was the confusion caused by the proximity of two communities named Charniers within twenty kilometers of each other. It was likewise sheer coincidence for an SS officer to be captured by Résistants at Charniers-sur-Vare and shot dead in trying to escape his captors. Was it a coincidence his good friend Sturmbannführer Durchmann, was in a position to avenge him?

Was Durchmann acting solely out of vengeful rage? From an unimpeachable source I learned he knew for certain his comrade had been slain at Charniers-sur-Vare. The choice to destroy an entirely innocent village was therefore deliberate—the *terror* effect. Allied landings in Normandy were succeeding. Frantically, the Nazis were rushing reinforcements from southern France. Slowing them down were the Résistants along their route. The German command was calling for drastic measures. At Tulle, south of Charniers-sur-Nys, another battalion of the same SS regiment had hanged eighty French civilians on telephone poles and trees because a shot had been fired at them. Our turn came next.

My impeccable informant in this instance was none other than Lucien Veynachter, Jean-Luc's previously inseparable Strasbourg friend. Here is a more uncanny but plausible coincidence. Drafted into the Waffen SS, he was present on the Champs de Foire that day in June as a member of the 2nd Company, First Battalion, Der Führer Regiment, Das Reich Division. He also served as part of Durchmann's personal guard.

Lucien and Jean-Luc had kept in touch until the Nazi occupation of Alsace. But another irony, if not coincidence, was that as a subterfuge all Jean-Luc's letters to Lucien were mailed from Limoges in order to conceal the exact location of his hiding place.

The odds Lucien's unit would be posted in southern France were not at all lopsided. The original division, mauled on the Russian front, had been reorganized in German-occupied Vichy, incorporating a substantial number of Alsatian conscripts and some "foreign volunteers," like Romanians. Their war of extermination in the East had been mainly against an unarmed Jewish population. Those *Einsatzgruppen* veterans, who included Durchmann, had learned their trade of wholesale murder in the *shtetls* of the former Pale of Settlement.

Lucien was never involved in these previous "crimes against humanity." His training only had begun in Alsace before his posting to a barracks in Montauban, where additional grueling instruction occurred to keep him fit, handle grenades and shoot straight. But at the Charniers action, he was posted right behind Sturmbannführer Durchmann.

As an aside, the village signpost of Charniers-sur-Nys had Lucien noticed it when driving in with the armored carriers at the head of their column, would have meant nothing to him. He later told me he thought the community another collection of old, unpainted, fairly run-down French country houses. The day before, travelling the streets of Limoges, however, he kept seeking in vain for his friend Jean-Marc.

But other coincidences did pile up in that month of June 1944, events coming together: the Normandy landings, the harassment by

Résistants of the German reinforcements rushing north; the death of Sturmbannführer Lange, Durchmann's dear friend, in a place called Charniers, a tough mayor, who rejected the Nazi officer's demand for thirty hostages. Papa characteristically—I'm sure quite gruffly—announced he would only offer himself.

Standing within earshot of the flushed-faced SS chief was Lucien Veynachter, his sub-machinegun at the ready. He was seemingly indistinguishable from the phalanx of steel-helmeted SS men, anonymous, faceless, intimidating, dressed for battle in their camouflage brown, green, and yellow knee-length smocks.

The noisy entrance on the scene of Jean-Luc Mueller under an armed escort had to be an incredible shock to Lucien, the most absolute of coincidences.

But he had no other choice than to stand frozen like a statue.

Or, really, did he?

Guilt—excruciating guilt—for his passivity and failure to intervene led him that very same evening to risk his life. One compelling motive for not rebelling earlier always had been fear of harm to his parents, siblings and relatives, held hostage for his behavior as it were. No longer thinking on those lines, he slipped away in the dark of night from the 2nd Company's bivouac near Charniers-sur-Vare and after various adventures, reached the *Franc-Tireurs et Partisans* (FTP) camp in the high maquis bush country. Still dressed in an SS uniform, still carrying his weapon, he nevertheless convinced the Maquisards he was a genuine deserter.

Three days later, after helping to bury the dead and clean up the smoking ruins at Charniers, I was led to the same encampment by my old buddy Mario Cioffi, already a fighter in the hills for several months, who had snuck into our martyred village fearing his parents were among the victims, which *malheureusement* they were.

Therefore, once the blond Alsatian and I had discovered our links to Jean-Luc and bonded together in battle, we had leisure time between raids to sit and chat. Accordingly, I gradually attained a vivid picture of the last moments of both Papa and Jean-Luc.

Lucien's youthful voice has embedded itself in my memory, speaking a no-less-educated French than Jean-Luc. His picture of Papa was of an imposing bull of a man in his sixties who had impressive white mustachios, hair to match, burning eyes so deep brown they seemed ink-black, and wearing his tricolor sash of office. *A man of absolute dignity and power of character*, he thought at the time. *He is going to make difficulties for us.*

M'sieu le Maire had been summoned from his office and escorted onto the Champ de Foire by an SS sergeant and two riflemen. Upon spying him, the assembling civilians demonstrated their deference and faith in him. Some men even doffed their hats.

Brought in front of Sturmbannführer Durchmann, he stared boldly into the Nazi officer's cold grey eyes, as if to say grumpily: *Why are you bothering us?*

In fact, he even spoke before Durchmann opened his mouth.

"To what do we owe this pleasure, *mon colonel?*" He spoke in French and a runty sergeant, an Alsatian, translated but missed the sarcasm, and Lucien heard every word.

Durchmann barked out his reply in staccato German, which Lucien also understood.

"A German officer has been killed in the vicinity. Cowardly murdered by Communist riff-raff. You are to name thirty hostages. *Schnell.* Quickly. *Verstehen sie?* Understand!"

With great aplomb, Papa answered with his famous "I will only name myself" . . . and *sotto voce* added: "Is that quick enough for you?"

Before Durchmann could speak, an uproar occurred on the Champs de Foire. A lone prisoner accompanied by a rifleman, walking his bicycle, let the *vélo* drop and shouting in German, hurried toward the Nazi commander. "L'Alsacien!" several of the assembled townsfolk cried. It was Jean-Luc, screaming out to Durchmann in German he had the wrong village. Lucien said Jean-Luc was actually haranguing the SS commander, threatening him, no less, if he didn't correct his blunder, how he'd face a court martial.

The SS Sturmbannführer expressionlessly absorbed the protests of the agitated redhead. While doing so, the Nazi moved his hand to the buttoned holster of his Walther P38 pistol. Was that a signal? The same runty sergeant who had escorted Papa had been quietly positioning himself behind Jean-Luc. In Lucien's words:

"I wanted to cry out to him. But it was all so quick. Durchmann nodded. Sergeant Roos, that bastard Alsatian Nazi, smashed the butt of his gun against the back of Jean-Marc's skull. Still in the act of yelling, my old pal dropped like a stone to the ground. If only I'd had the courage to turn the weapon I gripped on both those scum. But I stood like an automaton. Durchmann raised his pistol and fired two shots in the air: the signal to start the massacre."

The citizens gathered on the Champ de Foire were promptly hurried off to their respective final destinations by brutally barking SS troopers, some of whom prodded them with gun barrels, even the women and children, even those holding babies. The females and young ones were shoved in to the church. The men and older boys found themselves herded to the barns plus the town's one commercial garage, in all of which Czech-made Waffen SS machineguns on tripods had been set up. Papa and his municipal council members were pushed in with those already at Phillipon's barn, and the unconscious Jean-Luc Mueller was lugged there also.

"I was Durchmann's puppy dog," Lucien confessed to me. "Where he went, I had to go. First to his command car. Two more shots in the air from his weapon. Then he was on the radio for an hour or more while I stood guard."

My flashback at the breakfast table did not continue much longer. The rat-a-tat-tat of machinegun fire Lucien heard, and bangs of explosions from the church, black smoke rising, distant, diminishing screams of agony. Voilà. Those noises in my head sat me upright. There in the maquis, I then remembered, Lucien wore his German military trousers and black boots but complemented by a torn horizon-blue sweater, the two of us framed in my mind by wild, quasi-mountainous scenery. Here, I rose out of my kitchen chair, stretched, and, agitated by my visions, paced for a full five minutes.

I know these moods. The best thing to temper my nerves was to change scenery, go for a walk or—better yet—a drive. But where should I head?

A busman's holiday! That was it. Rather than chase my shivers away, I would confront them. Stir up the old juices of attacking, along with Lucien who soon had custody of our unit's Bren gun, taking on the ragtag of *Wehrmacht* outfits left behind and the *Milice*, too.

My decision was made in ten seconds. I would visit the local Resistance Museum, located a few kilometers outside of Charniers-sur-Vare.

I was one of its founders and a hefty contributor to the building fund and donating artifacts and memorabilia from my service in the Resistance. My fellow townspeople—what was left of them, and relatives—had elected me the titular head of the Association of Families of the Martyrs of Charniers-sur-Nys. We were a driving force in creating this memorial, along with others in the region, de Gaullists as well as FTP. It had been half a year at least until I'd paid a visit to that modest structure we'd erected at the cul-de-sac of a scenic rural road.

The land had been donated to us. We had financial help from the Paris authorities, the Départemental government and local communities as well as individuals. When I felt blue, a trip to these testimonials to our hardships, bravery and ultimate victory would cheer me up.

Within minutes, I was opening my garage door, squeezing into the driver's seat and feeling better already by the time I swung from Bregonzac onto the *Route Nationale*.

At this intersection were billboards on both sides of the main road advertising

THE MARTYRED VILLAGE OF CHARNIERS-SUR-NYS

Like other touristic signs, it was one of a series covering all of France with stylistic drawings of famous châteaux or natural attractions or historic sites. Ours, with its depiction of gaunt, shattered walls and charred rubble was unique. So inured was I to their lugubrious presence that they represented mere scenery, no different from the roadside forests. I sped toward Charniers-sur-Vare, a ten minute drive to the turn-off where I would follow a maze of back country roads.

One might question why—except for the fact of free land—had we chosen this out-of-the-way spot for our museum. My only answer is to cite a peasant sense of ownership and heritage that seems to underlie the psyche of *notre pays*. This place is our place. If strangers find it, fine; if they didn't, that was fine, too.

Needless to say, I had my own key.

Soon, the two-story rustic building was in view. Next to it, the caretaker's cottage. And, what did you know, a car—a sleek four door Peugeot sedan—parked in the visitors lot!

I checked the license plate. Unlike in the U.S., all our *plaques d'immatriculation* look pretty much the same, their separate *départements* denoted only by the last two digits. This one was sixty-seven. I had a guide in my glove department that told me. *Bas Rhin—Alsace*.

I needn't have reached for my door key. Not only had it been unlocked by our caretaker, it had been left ajar. Upon stepping inside, I heard voices on the floor above—women—and their feminine-sounding heel taps overhead.

In the entranceway, my reaction was immediate anger. Upstairs we had exhibits from the 1953 trial of the Alsatian draftees, who, though already given outrageously minimum sentences for participation in a war crime, were afterward disgracefully pardoned by l'Assemblée National. Bitter feelings still remained. If the Alsatian ladies above were relatives of the so-called *Incorporés de Force*, that was their prerogative. We were open to everyone. But I had no intention of being friendly.

Thus I lingered on the first floor. I should now describe what I was standing in front of and start with a revelation. It was a large-scale photograph of our commander, a burly, muscular, middle-aged man, posed with his sub-machinegun in one hand and a captured German "potato masher" hand grenade in the other. Would it really surprise you to learn this scowling figure was Vercingetorix Paul, my friend and mentor (in guerilla warfare). He had formed our band with a nucleus of his workers at the machine shop. Because of his on-again, off-again relationship with the French Communist Party, our *Maquisards* were less ideological than other FTP groups, accepting anyone willing to fight the Boche and their collaborators, to the extent of welcoming an SS deserter like Lucien Veynachter into their ranks.

There was a big photograph of Lucien, as well. It was the background for a glass case containing the actual Bren gun, air-dropped to us by the British and displayed by the winsomely handsome Alsatian blond guy holding the heavy weapon with both hands.

I had only time to glance at those familiar pictures before footsteps resounded at the top of the stairs. I gazed up and to see two attractive women descending. In front was a slender lady who appeared to be in her thirties with strawberry-blondish hair. The person behind her could have been her mother (and was): chic, dignified, with extremely blonde silky shoulder-length hair. I at once suppressed my intended snub. The latter lady, I immediately felt certain, was Lucien's "little sister" Gabrielle, three years younger and often taken for his twin, he'd explained, in showing us a snapshot from his wallet.

I waited until they spied me, reached the ground level, both smiled and said "Bonjour."

"Bonjour," I replied and addressed myself to the older of the two. "Madame, are you Gabrielle Veynachter?" I asked.

"I was," she said, obviously surprised, "until I married. And you, M'sieu, are . . ."

"Desfosseux . . . Eugène Desfosseux. All too briefly a friend and comrade-in-arms of your brother Lucien. Also, in my martyred town, of his friend Jean-Marc Rosenstein, although I knew him by a different name."

A blush in her pretty features at Jean-Luc's mention could be attributed to her comprehension. "Ah, yes, he was like a brother to my brother . . . And Desfosseux. We have just witnessed the exhibit about the famous heroic mayor. Was he your relative, M'sieu?"

"My father," I told her. "And please, mesdames, for you I am Eugène."

"And I am indeed Gabrielle and this is one of my daughters, Martine."

"You have driven from Strasbourg?" I asked.

"Taking a diversion on our trip to Saint-Jean-de-Luz. I have long wanted to visit your museum since it is like a shrine to a member of our family."

Our tones struck me as somewhat stilted, unsurprisingly given that we were essentially strangers.

Gabrielle went on: "Word came to us that Jean-Marc had been one of the massacre victims at Charniers. Yet when I searched for his name among the murdered, it wasn't there. You may laugh when I tell you that red-head was my first heartthrob at twelve years old. Did you know he was Jewish? It was later estimated he had gone to live in Palestine."

"He's been listed by another name," I gently told her. "Jean-Luc Mueller, his pseudonym. Unfortunately, he *was* among the murdered."

For an awkward moment, we three stood staring at each other in silence.

"Come," I said finally. "Let me show you my favorite photograph."

Lined along a nearby wall was a row of framed individual squad pictures, exhibiting all of us in warlike poses. In ours, Lucien and mine, we were sporting our weaponry—he, his beloved Bren gun while I held up a shiny German Luger pistol taken from a Wehrmacht officer I'd shot dead. Also, slung over my shoulder, was the sniper's rifle I'd used. Between myself and Lucien, knelt Mario Cioffi, and I pointed him out as the person who had led me to the Maquis hideout and Paul the Gaul's brigade.

Martine, who had been silent but smilingly attentive after we exchanged Bonjours suddenly spoke. "It is a German pistol you're holding, isn't it?" she asked.

"You're absolutely correct, Martine," I said, deliberately employing her prénom because I sensed she didn't quite dare to utter mine. Then, I added: "There's a bit of a story of how I came into possession of it. Involving your uncle, too, if you care to hear it."

"Oh, please," she answered and cast her eyes at Gabrielle for approval and received it.

I consider myself something of a storyteller. But not insensitively long-winded. In as concise a fashion as possible, I described the battle in which I downed the Wehrmacht captain who was brandishing his Luger as he led a charge of soldiers across a local river bridge against our position. Had the Krauts succeeded in driving us from our defensive line, the way would have been open to our encampment in the mountainside behind us. Our FTP guys had been overwhelmed by the onslaught on the distant side of the bridge and were in hasty retreat. My sniper's rifle shot that dropped the German commander—I was in a tree—had a startling effect. The leaderless mob of grey-green uniforms stopped in its tracks, and sustaining casualties from bursts of Lucien's Bren gun and other fire, turned tail. In their panic, they left their captain's body lying on the bridge, the Luger still clutched in his hand.

The denouement was yet to come, and here is my finish of the story as I told it to them, if I remember correctly: "Regarding the pistol, I had joined the pursuit of the enemy back across the bridge and paid only a moment's notice to the crumpled form while running past. But one of our guys, a veteran member of Commander Paul's original recruits, whom we called Skinko—a Slovak or Slovene or Pole—with an unpronounceable Slavic name, anyway, but French, decided he wanted that highly prized weapon. It was said he had to cut off the clenched fingers of the dead man to get it . . ." I remember pausing here, fearing I might have been overly graphic. But neither of my audience had flinched and expectantly seemed eager for me to continue, which I did as follows:

"At this point, Lucien played an important role. Without telling me, he went to Commander Paul. Told him I deserved to keep the trophy gun. So I was summoned to the command tent and awarded the pistol he had taken away from Skinko, whom he said would sell it. Not only did I deserve such a memento but I would need it for added firepower in our fights to come and thus was also provided several bullet clips found in the officer's kit bag.

Martine thanked me profusely after I finished. "I have heard about my uncle all my life," she added. "You know he won the *Médaille de la Résistance*. Maman has it on display at home."

"Yes. I was present when he gained it through an extraordinary act of courage."

"Oh, will you tell us?"

However, Gabrielle interrupted, saying" "We have taken up so much of Eugène's time, Martine. And we do need to get back on the road. Possibly you can guide us, Eugène, is there a decent restaurant nearby where we can have a bite before we head south?"

I pretended to be thinking and answered in the following manner: "I know a perfect place in Charniers-sur-Vare. The Guide Michelin gives it two red forks . . . But there is one problem . . ."

"Oh?" Both Martine and her mother who had brightened suddenly sounded disappointed.

Quickly, I added: "You see, they'll be jam-packed at this hour. Since the *patron* is a friend of mine, a member of our Families Association, you will need me with you to obtain entry, and I will only agree to it on the condition that you are my guests."

I perhaps expected an argument. Instead Gabrielle responded: "We'll be delighted. That is so kind of you."

After I locked up the museum, they followed me in their car into Charniers-sur-Vare.

Instantly, at the Café Le Grand Cerf, we were guests of honor and ushered into a private room my friend Maurice kept in reserve for favored customers. There, away from the din in the main restaurant, the three of us enjoyed ourselves despite our inclusion—at Martine's request—of an eyewitness account from me of Lucien Veynachter's last moments.

Of note in our tête-à-tête-à-tête in Le Grand Cerf was not only the food, living up to its *restaurant agreeable* status in the Michelin, but also Gabrielle's revelation that she had brought a framed copy of the citation and a facsimile of the coveted medal for the Museum to own and left them with the caretaker who had let them into the building. Additionally, when Martine was in the lady's room, her mother discreetly informed me she had just gone through a divorce after ten years of marriage, fortunately with no children caught in the middle.

For you readers, I'll be briefer on Lucien's storied feat of war than I was with his family members. In short, the blond hero was killed in the act of singlehandedly attacking a German tank threatening to wreak havoc with our forces during a raid on a key mountain town. Forsaking the Bren gun whose bullets bounced off the steel hull, he ran toward the armored vehicle, jumped on the rear, and having noticed the hatch cover unsecured, yanked it open, tossed in several grenades, and slammed it shut. Then he jumped clear, but a single shot, after a fusillade from nearby German infantry had missed, hit him directly in the heart. The tank was disabled, its crew perished, and the second-rate Nazi troops opposing us were sent fleeing for their lives.

Gabrielle and Martine listened intently. Lucien's sister professed having known some of the details, but declared herself fascinated by my firsthand account. Martine had appeared as spell-bound as a child listening to a fascinating tale.

In the meantime, we had eaten well and drunk fine wine. I introduced them to my favorite Sancerre. Since they would soon be on the road, each consumed solely one glass and I, on the other hand, my emotive juices loosed, downed three glasses—no, I confess, four.

When we parted, we had bonded splendidly. I felt almost as if Lucien had been with us. Beforehand, Gabrielle casually asked me if I'd ever been to Alsace.

My answer was: "Hélas, only for a quick visit to Colmar."

We exchanged addresses. We promised to maintain our connection to each other and, I added, "To the past." Once we were out of the restaurant and they had gone, I realized I shouldn't get behind my wheel immediately. In the middle of the town, a street away, was a small park with benches and flower beds. Walking to it, I decided I was a trifle more unsteady on my feet because of age rather than due to the alcohol I'd drunk. But I reached the *jardin* without incident, proceeded along a gravel path, took a seat and watched people pass by.

I must have stayed an hour outdoors. One single memory of the stay was of a colorfully dressed family of Africans parading with their children. From Senegal, I decided. Which tribe? Wolof? Fula? Serer? Jola? I used to know all of their ethnic groups when I was deep into writing my histories of France overseas.

But for the majority of the hour, my attention was not primarily on the immediate moment, but ruminating about Lucien and about Jean-Luc, Chantal, Papa, Madame Blanchard, etc.

It was growing toward dusk when I finally dared to return to my automobile. The short ride back to Bregonzac was uneventful. At my doorstep, though, having parked the Renault in the barn garage, a most extraordinary occurrence caught me by surprise.

I had turned my key in the lock. I had begun pushing the front door open. And then all at once, behind me, a familiar voice said: "Don't forget to let me in, too."

Turning, I was sure it had been an hallucination, a trick of my wine-addled mind.

So help me, Lucien Veynachter, blond as ever, stood a few steps behind me.

Spectral vision?

True. But in my condition and state of mind, he *was* as real as the figures I conjured up for my interviews. I spoke to him. "I was with your sister today and the niece you never knew."

"Tell me all about it," he said, stepping past me to step inside.

"*This is going to prove interesting*," I said to myself as I followed him inside.

XVII

I should not have been surprised that Lucien had arrived like this. After all, hadn't I freed Max Cohen from the restrictions of my interview routine and walked with him in the budding moonlight toward the Pont Neuf? To be sure, he had vanished as soon as Benoît's flashlight beam had pierced the riverside darkness. Need I remind you that Benoît saw no trace of Max—only doddering old Eugène Desfosseux.

Would not the same thing have happened had Arlette, who was due presently with my supper, caught us together? Nevertheless, to ensure our privacy, I directed Lucien to go ahead to my study. It was inconceivable Arlette wouldn't knock first if in some barely foreseeable circumstance she needed to see me. When I entered, myself, I saw Lucien was already seated on a folding chair opposite my inquisitorial post. The recording machine was set up to run. Had I done that before leaving? Age again. Impaired memory. Actually a blank.

Remember Lucien was eighteen years old when he died. I postulated he must see me as his contemporary instead of my actual self these decades hence. But he astonished me by his opening remark in exhibiting knowledge of an event happening nine years after we buried him.

"Tell me your opinion," Lucien started right off. "Would I have been tried as a war criminal with those other Incorporés de Force?"

"If you survived the war . . ." I hesitated. "Honestly, I doubt it. With your record as a Maquisard, your Médaille de la Résistance. How could they?"

"I am told certain of the Alsatians of my group joined the Paras in Indo-Chine, yet ended in the dock on trial with the others. Hardly fair, I feel."

"From the standpoint of loyalty to France, you were unimpeachable. And less than a month after the massacre, and in the Limousin, not overseas."

"I think they would have lumped me in with the others, all those Malgré-Nous whom you people screamed should have received the death penalty."

"We would have vouched for you . . . me, Paul the Gaul, my friend Octave Bois who was already then vice-chairman of the Association of Families."

"I'm not sure I would have vouched for myself," the handsome young blond facing me countered. "I let my best friend be dragged off to his doom without lifting a finger. I let those horrid deeds proceed unimpeded because I feared for my life. At the very least, I could have shot Durchmann."

"You had reprisals to your family to worry about. Your sister Gabrielle whom I just lunched with is a delightful person and your niece Martine . . ."

I was interrupted. "Poor girl, Martine . . . a difficult marriage. But happily no children. She can start over again." Then, he asked: "Will you visit them in Alsace?"

"I don't know."

Lucien continued: "You know I was nicknamed Durchmann's puppy dog. He made me his orderly. I had to sleep in the same quarters together with him. No, not in the same bed, I promise you. He was no pédé. That was a capital crime, especially for the SS. What motivated him, I had to believe, was that I made the perfect model for his portrait painting. He was such a Nazi, such a believer in Aryan beauty and I fit the part. Never in the nude, mind you. Head and shoulders mostly or a full body pose in uniform."

Was this stuff coming exclusively from me, Lucien dressed in the spectral Maquis garb in which I'd last seen him, including the German steel-pot helmet he'd brought with him and always wore in battle? The atmosphere was uncanny. I consulted my watch. Ordinarily the ghostly personage I had subconsciously summoned would have evaporated by now. But Lucien Veynachter didn't fade away.

The recording machine was now running. I didn't remember turning it on. In addition, seemingly beyond my control, a newsreel had started on the white wall. Lucien changed the angle of his seat in order to view the black and white images that were materializing.

I recognized the scene at once. It was the exterior of a courthouse on a back street of Bordeaux. Next the interior was shown. On the dais were five military judges in their khaki uniforms and gold-braided kepis.

In the center sat the president of the court—a civilian, a distinguished jurist who conducted the questioning of defendants and testifiers. His robe was scarlet. The camera panned around the large high-ceilinged room. Marie Malinvaud, swathed in black, was on the witness stand. Facing her were several ranks of defendants—German SS men from the 2nd Company in the front rows, the Incorporés de Force behind them—all in ill-fitting civilian clothes, jackets, ties, their too-short trousers revealing white socks, with all those bad haircuts. Furthermore, they were uniformly paying anxious attention to the unforgettable victim in widow's weeds who raked them with her flashing dark eyes.

I was in the front row of the Visitors' Gallery. The audience had been pretty much restricted to those from the Limousin. Separated from us by a line of gendarmes was a small body of Alsatian spectators, relatives of the accused. I observed them now and then. While Marie delivered her hair-raising narrative of miraculously escaping from the conflagration in the church, they kept their eyes glued on her, listening with rapt, if sour-faced attention.

The trial has been written about frequently since those Bordeaux days of 1953. After several long sessions, the litany of stories, who was where, who did what, the flowing geography of death-dealing within a small town's borders, the miniscule number who survived, the drunkenness of the killers, etc., had become monotonous to me, I'm embarrassed to admit.

The verdicts were as if chiseled into stone, irreversible. Guilty all. One German sergeant sentenced to death. Roos, the Alsatian traitor, sentenced to death. Other non-commissioned officers and enlisted men received wrist-slapping sentences of as little as five years. We, the Association of Families, were enraged by the leniency shown. To add injury to our insult, the Chamber of Deputies voted pardons for the Incorporés de Force.

Therefore, the newsreel projected on my wall cut to the Gare Montparnasse in Paris. A delegation had arrived from our region. Having moved to the capital to study at the Sorbonne, I was there to greet them. Octave Bois, who had replaced me as association president (I became emeritus) led the *défilé* out of the train station in his wheelchair (he had had both knees shattered during the *Drôle de Guerre*) with Roger Phillipon by his side. The crowd in back of them was somber, silent, but the messages on their placards were not. Mario Cioffi held up a sign bearing the name of Alsace's leading politician of the 1950s:

PIERRE PFLIMLIN
MURDERERS' ACCOMPLICE

The news people present, reporters, photographers, et. al. concentrated on a singular touch of the drama. The community of Charniers-sur-Nys, awarded the *Croix de Guerre* and *Légion d'honneur* by the postwar de Gaulle government, was returning both medals to the Chamber of Deputies in a gesture of disgust. Two girls of nine or ten, dressed in mourning black, carried the enameled crosses on blood red pillows.

Back home the Association had erected two giant billboards at the entrance to the ruins, bearing the names of all the law makers who'd shamed themselves by voting for this injustice.

On my newsreel wall now were images of us on arrival at the Chamber of Deputies across from the Seine. As if a problem with the film occurred, one picture seemed stuck . . . or rather, repeating itself. It was of Mario, now like me nine years older, having sprouted a fierce Italianate mustache, waving aloft his nasty denunciation of the Alsatian politico Pflimlin.

But my mind ceased doting on our enormous hurt. It was offering me Mario for a different reason. Backtrack to the three-day cleanup of the massacre site, when I encountered him. We were circumspect about how we talked to each other. I already knew he had joined the Resistance. At the smoking village, Vichy officials were still in control. There might even be Gestapo agents among the rescue workers the prefect had sent. I remember Mario told me about his parents' deaths and then with a jerk of his thumb indicated a direction toward the distant mountains. "When you're ready?" he said. Like all the others on the scene, we wore white masks over our mouths for sanitary reasons. We had removed them momentarily to speak. At the end of the third day, he passed by me. No words had to be exchanged. As soon as the burial services ended, and it was dark enough, the two of us decamped.

My newsreel at that point, weird as it seems, rewound itself. Charniers had been restored on the "screen" to its appearance the morning of June 14. The next shot showed me and Chantal on our bikes in front of my house bordering the main square. We were outfitted for a picnic, knapsacks on our backs. After a word with Madame Blanchard, off we rode.

I know. Where's the third member, people might ask, the redheaded, freckle-faced, Aryan-looking, secret Israelite? Why, like many Jews of that era, in hiding. He called it the better part of wisdom. Some suspicious characters had showed up recently in our town, obviously working for the Nazis. French collaborators. Police detectives, most likely. Some months previously, a Jewish family at Charniers had been denounced anonymously and taken away. We learned these strangers had offered rewards for anyone who ferreted out other Jews for them. We also learned that on their visit earlier in June, someone had mentioned an Alsatian living in our midst.

An unheard alarm signal went off. Jean-Luc insisted on going alone to the hideout. If in the next few days, nothing bad developed, we could come fetch him or at least keep him company.

That is what Chantal and I were doing the morning of a gorgeous, clear, blue sky example of springtime at its best. We left at the usual hour for a Trio departure and biked in the open with nothing furtive about our movements until, safely out of the sight of everyone, we entered a side path into the forest and found our special passage to the cavern.

The problem of what to do about our bicycles once we'd dismounted had previously been solved. Rumors had been floated several weeks past about a Milice unit in the area. It was possible they might have explored parts of the cave. Therefore it had been incumbent on us to seek a safe place farther inside and away from prying eyes.

We had subsequently found a small grotto not too apart from the entrance but literally unexposed unless you knew it existed. On this June 14 occasion, we found Jean-Luc's bike there and laid ours alongside his. Everything seemed perfectly in order. The revolving wall worked fine, the ladder was where it was supposed to be, our knapsacks didn't hamper us as we climbed up. Except . . . there is always the unexpected.

In the current instance, it was that Jean-Luc was still asleep in his sleeping bag laid upon the stone floor and cushioned by a thick pad. With a cry of "Wake up, sleepyhead!" Chantal leapt upon him. Had I not been present, I am not sure what might have followed.

I glanced sideways to see if the newsreel was picturing the scene but found it blank and surmised it had been since right after Chantal and I had entered La Cav. It was thus left to me to ruminate from memory. Jean-Luc, I remember, had slept in his clothes. They were disheveled and in a sense so was he. A visible growth of red whiskers coated his cheeks, his head of flaming hair was seriously unkempt, his green eyes only slowly opening.

"*Je m'excuse*," were his first words to us. "I don't think I smell very good."

No water for washing had been available to him. Only several canteens for drinking. Not that he couldn't have climbed out of his hole and descended to a small brook in the vicinity. But, as he explained, it had seemed too much of a risk.

Besides, we learned that he had been otherwise preoccupied during the daylight hours. Among his personal items, he had brought his typewriter with him. We saw it on a rock shelf that was serving him as a table. He wouldn't tell us about the "opus," he was working on until he'd finished it. In a serious tone of voice he added: "You know what I forgot to bring? I could kick myself. Carbon paper. The result: I only have this one original set." He indicated a thin pile of papers. "I'll have to type those pages over again for an extra copy. Using carbons, I can make three or four copies at once."

"Next time we'll bring you some," said Chantal, "If I can find any."

"Somewhere in my room I have some," said Jean-Luc. All of a sudden, too, a mischievous half-smile appeared on his lips and he added: "Maybe I should go back with you two and dig it out of my trunk. What do you think? Has the danger passed?"

It was my turn to volunteer: "Through my father I heard those *flics* whose presence scared us had been seeking a different Alsatian, not you, Jean-Luc."

"Did they find him?"

"Flew the coop. Papa said they told him they'd been given wrong information about his whereabouts and should look in the Saint-Junien area."

"Then I *will* go back with you," Jean-Luc declared. "My stench may be tolerable to you but not to me. We Jews have a fetish about washing and keeping clean." A humorous wink at Chantal was included: "Not wholeheartedly pure, though."

In such a light-hearted mood did we leave La Cav, following the lunch we'd taken with us, cheese and baguettes and fruit. It was much appreciated by Jean-Luc who'd been living off canned goods until then.

In my role of historian, I will digress a moment to draw a broader picture of what was happening in our region during that historic June of 1944. The Normandy landings were taking hold, although the Boche were frantically rushing reinforcements to bolster their defenses. Partisan groups harassed them with the aim of slowing them down. Only afterward did we learn about the atrocity that took place in Tulle, not far south of Charniers-sur-Nys. A different regimental battalion of the SS Das Reich division was involved in the hangings.

When we three pedaled back to Charniers-sur-Nys in the forenoon, we were riding into a whirlwind and didn't know it.

The first shock once we neared our destination was the extraordinary sight of Big Freddi in his navy-blue Milice uniform chugging up toward us on our bike trail, as fast as his thick legs would carry him.

I hadn't seen him in Charniers for months and there he was struggling toward us, huffing and puffing, dripping sweat. With a sense of relief, I quickly noticed he wasn't armed.

It seemed to me he couldn't see us as he ran uphill. His head was lowered, his eyes on the fairly uneven path underfoot. Nevertheless, he stepped on a protruding rock, yelped and discovered the three us who had stopped biking as soon as we'd spied him.

Once Big Freddi caught his breath, he exclaimed: "Eugène!"

I wasn't flattered that he uttered my name alone. I no longer considered him a friend. He'd joined the enemy. A disjointed two-person dialogue followed:

"Freddi, what's all this?"

"They wouldn't let me warn the village."

"Who wouldn't?"

"The Alsatian guards. They're in the SS. They told me in French: 'Speak to us in German." They aimed their rifles at me. They shouted a word. *'Rowse'* it sounded like. But one did translate: *'Va-t'en.'* I'm desperate. Something terribly wrong is about to happen."

This is an approximation. *Raus* is the German term he cited, meaning "Get out of here." We parked our bikes, surrounded him and between fits of his blubbering, finally obtained a picture of what was transpiring below.

Moreover, Big Freddi knew its full and terrifying extent.

It came out of him in bursts of language. Although it wasn't easy to follow him, one salient fact was made clear. The Germans had decided to wipe out the entire community of Charniers-sur-Nys and every last one of its inhabitants. How did Freddi know? Because his commanding Milice officer told him so.

Likewise obscure was the Milice Captain Langevin's intentions in allowing his underling to rush away to his home. Warning the community of its impending peril? Getting folks to scatter? Freddi's unit, it turned out, was in the vicinity of La Cav as backup for Durchmann against any Maquisard attacks. His surprise presence on our supposed secret path might have been because he'd since discovered our shortcut by himself, maybe following us, back in his pre-Milice days.

It didn't matter. He was too late arriving at the Sirois farm on the northern edge of Charniers, which would have been his entranceway to the town; Freddi was stopped by a contingent of SS soldiers in their camouflage outfits. He cried to them in French. They responded in German. "*Halt! Hande hoch! Papieren.*" At one point during the shouting match that ensued, the corporal in charge took him aside and whispered in our language that they were Alsatians but had a German watchdog in their midst who would report them if they spoke français, which would incur severe punishment.

At the end of several minutes of fruitless pleading by the blue-uniformed Militiaman, the corporal released Freddi and sent him back the way he'd come. It was uphill and retreating he raced, afraid, he later admitted, he might be shot from behind. He needed to catch his breath from time to time, even while his flood of verbiage assailed our ears.

Chantal, deep worry on her lovely features, broke in following one of the big fellow's pauses. "Did you hear anything about the château? Are they going to blow it up?"

To her no doubt immense relief, Freddi said: "No, Bregonzac will be spared." But he added: "Only if your address is Charniers-sur-Nys are you a target."

Until then, Jean-Luc had not said a word. His comment was: "Lucky for you, chérie."

Chantal paled, however. "But what about you? Your address is Charniers."

"No, Strasbourg it reads on my *carte d'identité.*"

"And Eugène?"

"Ah, Eugène. We will need to figure something out for him." Immediately afterward, he said to Freddi: "On your way again, Milicien. Return to your fellow Vichy lovers."

No added words were necessary. Off went the lumbering, pimple-faced, outsized youth and within a minute or so was out of sight.

"We should go back to La Cav," Chantal suggested. "For Eugène's sake."

Jean-Luc shook his head. "I don't trust that tub of lard. He'll have his Pétainists scouring La Cav as soon as he returns,"

"But we're caught then," I said. "Down at Sirois Farm are those SS we must get past."

"Here's my idea," Jean-Luc offered. "You two leave your bikes here. Bushwhack through this off-trail brush that will hide you until you reach Bregonzac. And I will go down and talk in *Elsässerdicht* to my compatriots on guard . . . and don't forget, I'm also perfect in German. He spouted a long sentence in that hated tongue and translated: "Herr Commandant, the honor of the German Reich will be forever despoiled and you made a laughingstock for a reprisal against an innocent community."

"No, Jean-Luc, it's too dangerous," Chantal protested.

"Someone has to tell the Nazi commander his mistake. He'll realize they'll boil him in oil for this senseless atrocity. Even dumb Hitlerians can recognize the harm it will do their cause."

Barely had he finished his last sentence than he started pedaling away.

"No," Chantal cried after him. "No, *mon chéri*. No! No! No!"

And he shouted over his shoulder: " Obey orders, countess. You're an officer's daughter."

It will behoove me later to describe his fatal adventure after he departed us. Most of what I learned originally came from Lucien Veynachter. Naturally, there are gaps, too, where we know nothing until Jean-Luc appeared at the Champ de Foire, the redhead at ease laughing and joking in German with his armed escort who, it developed, were Romanian *Volks Deutsch* and had replaced the Alsatians at the Sirois Farm. Sturmbannführer Durchmann apparently had just finished his colloquy with Papa when, all at once he was confronted by this swaggering young man who harangued him in high-class perfect German. Meanwhile, the SS men not very gently were breaking the assembled men into groups and herding the women and children together.

But I was not present, of course. My own eyewitness account is of how Chantal and I made our way through a mass of tangled vegetation to Bregonzac and safety within the château. And the aftermath. Ignoring Jean-Luc's instruction, we walked our bikes with us. The rough going took twice as long as it would have on the secret path, itself, which was possibly too close to the Sirois Farm for us to sneak by.

Due to my taste of a rude utter disruption in my life on our return from La Cav, I could associate with the feelings of the folks all of a sudden forcibly removed to the Champ de Foire. How many of the children were crying? Mothers *were* trying to hush them. Men and boys had been formed into a massive column, as if ready to be marched.

Lucien, in his narrative to me, found it hard to describe this premassacre preparation, since it was almost impossible to see much of the noisy hurly-burly that eventually died into expectant quiet.

With the citizens sent to their destinations in the barns, garage, and church, Lucien had to follow Durchmann around. "How many chances I had to shoot him," he would wail to me. "How many? How many?"

Two shots in the air from the Sturmbannführer's Walther 38 pistol set everything in motion. Two additional shots signaled: START KILLING.

Within the château, Chantal and I had hurried up to the rooftop battlements and observed Charniers-sur-Nys in the distance. At first, we could see nothing unusual. The Champs de Foire and the town square were obscured by intervening houses and leafy trees. Beyond, rose the tower of Saint Augustine's church beseeching on behalf of all sinning Catholics as it had for centuries. The SS trucks and armored vehicles that had transported the storm troopers to our town were parked out of sight. Even with binoculars, we were missing the main action.

We finally went down to the kitchen, Chantal and I, having cups of tea, when we heard the initial gunfire, sounding tinny and unreal, followed by an audible explosion. Both of us rushed back up to our posts above. A far off white flash seen from the heights brought another vibration (a phosphorous grenade) to our attention.

"*Nous sommes foutus,*" I said to Chantal and didn't excuse my gutter language.

She was dry-eyed as she responded: "We will never see Jean-Luc again."

"There's always a chance," I tried to comfort her

Instead of the answer I had expected, a defeated *No use,* she took me by surprise. "Let's go to the Billiard Room and play. There's nothing more to look at." Smoke, both white and black, was blanketing the scene.

How long we kept at billiards, I don't know. I felt that every minute Chantal was expecting Jean-Luc to appear. Her game was paradoxically sharper than it had ever been. Finally we were interrupted by Old Marianne, the longest serving employee, telling us word had been received the Germans had driven off.

Darkness was approaching when we left the Billiard Room and glanced out a downstairs window to see a glow against the sky and lace-like drifting outlines of smoke illuminated from below. Very pretty. Very deadly.

"I should go and find out," I said to Chantal. "I don't like to leave you alone, but—"

She interrupted me. "I have been selfish, dear Eugène," she said. "I realize you have to be concerned about your father. Yes, you must reconnoiter."

At the front door, we shook hands good-bye, added a kiss on both cheeks, which I noticed were not wet with tears. She was absolutely stoic in the manner of a Greek statue. Outside, I had dropped my bicycle on the side of the front steps. I asked the doorman who let me out to put my machine away with Chantal's and proceeded on foot into the heart of a still-burning acrid inferno.

XVIII

The Vichy prefect in Limoges had to dispatch the personnel necessary to deal with the disaster: the firemen to handle the blazes, medical help in the form of doctors, nurses, etc., sanitation workers to bury the dead, police, an administration mouthpiece, and with them came nongovernmental civilians, the Red Cross, religious figures, volunteers from neighboring communities, newspapermen, photographers . . . what had transpired was a major embarrassment for Pétain's minions. All of the Limousin was soon aroused.

My first encounter was not far from the Sirois farm with a group of "stretcher bearers"—two pairs of them, carrying red wooden shutters—a body shape on each one. The obvious corpses on them were covered with torn-off window curtains.

These men all wore sanitation masks and Red Cross armbands.

I had overtaken them, walking at an ordinary pace while they had their awkward burdens to slow them down. Seeing a stranger, they halted.

A fifth man, who seemed to be the Red Cross overseer, asked me. "Are you lost, M'sieu?"

My formal sounding answer was: "I'm en route to discover what's left of my home and if any of my family, friends, neighbors, etcetera, are by any chance alive."

His reply was a bit formal, too. "It is my sad duty to tell you we know of only two survivors—a man and a woman. They have been transported to Limoges for more extensive medical treatment. May I ask your name, M'sieu."

"I am Eugène Desfosseux, son of the mayor of Charniers-sur-Nys."

I was frankly surprised by the reaction of the group. Off came their caps and berets in a gesture of respect, as if I were suddenly a person of awe.

The Red Cross leader said: "From everything we have heard, your father was heroic in his defiance of the . . ." He stopped for a moment and shared glances with his crew, as if seeking approval to proceed, which was granted with nods, "Of the beasts responsible for this crime."

His name, he told me, was Abel Ronce, a medical doctor, summoned from Saint-Junien. "I knew your father," he went on. "We did not often agree on political matters, but he was an admirable person and a fine doctor. With great regret I have to inform you he was not the one male survivor."

His news was only final confirmation of a reality I had already accepted. Papa was dead. The source of all the information they had, I learned, was Benoît. On the Champ de Foire, as a town employee, the *garde-champêtre* had been close enough to hear what Papa told the SS commander. I would have to wait for further details until I was able to visit him in the hospital. However, I could not keep myself from asking Abel Ronce: "Was there any mention of a redheaded fellow who spoke German and went to tell the SS they were making a huge mistake?"

Since the lower half of Abel's face was covered by the white sanitation mask, I couldn't make out his whole expression but it was plain from his eyes I had drawn a blank.

Then he reached into a side pocket of the long white doctor's coat he was wearing over his clothes and drew out a mask identical to the ones they all had on.

"If you're coming with us you'll need this," he said. And not simply for sanitary reasons. We must be discreet."

His men were bending to start picking up the shutters they'd laid on the ground when Abel seemed to have an afterthought.

"Perhaps you can identify these two poor souls. Are they Monsieur and Madame Sirois?"

The covering curtains were lifted. Lying face up were two old people, bullet riddled but otherwise recognizable. "Yes, the Sirois," I answered. "We called them Grand-Père and Grand-Mère Sirois. In their eighties. Sweet harmless farm folks."

One of Abel's men commented. "At least they'll have a gravestone with their names on it . . . Everyone else is burnt to a crisp."

I remarked: "I can't believe the Alsatians on guard there killed them."

Abel said: "Benoît mentioned Romanian SS—Germans who lived in Romania—had replaced the Alsatians. At least those Balkan barbarians didn't burn down the farmhouse. Simply shot the couple, ransacked the place inside, and threw their bodies into the well."

We started off back to Charniers. Our immediate destination, I soon recognized, was the local cemetery. We did not penetrate into the center of the town but veered off at Phillipon's barn, which had been burned to the ground. We should have passed by the school except no school building was visible—only charred timbers, scorched roof tiles and a mass of still warm, still smoking, stinking rubble. A light breeze distributed ashes into the early evening air. In this vicinity I saw other teams of "stretcher bearers" heading for the same place. They all carried uncovered views of human bodies burned beyond recognition.

On those canvas stretchers charred humps of what might be taken for over-fried meat were being transported to a common grave. Some of these hideous objects had retained their entire forms; others were now featureless masses of heads, arms, legs, feet, all melted together; still others were but partial human frames from where explosions had ripped off limbs, leaving protruding bones or necks looking as if guillotined. The sights were as nauseating as the unforgettable stench of burnt flesh. We deposited our two identifiable bodies to one side of the common grave pit, since they could still be buried in the ancient cemetery itself.

Knowing I had to remain incognito, I passed up a chance to visit my mother's grave. Furthermore, I had to be circumspect when an extraordinary incident caused me to feel the immense pain I was suppressing in regards to Papa.

As I stood beside Abel who was waiting for his superior to arrive and tell him how to handle the two intact bodies we had brought from the outskirts, I noticed two men approaching with a stretcher bearing a single, totally carbonized body of an obviously large man. Something caught my attention. Could it be Papa? A real jolt occurred when I spied the thick fingers on the right hand had only been singed. A gold ring glistened on the third digit—the ring my mother had given him!

I pointed this out to Abel. Instantly, he asked: "Should I get you the ring?"

The stretcher bearers were abreast of us the next moment, heading to the pit. It was the only chance I would have. The reason I finally shook my head was not any fear those men might report the action. I told Abel: "No, Maman's ring belongs with him. She might scold him for losing it when they meet soon enough in heaven."

Docteur Ronce, openly touched, put his arm around my shoulder. Briefly I broke down, wept, then quickly composed myself. "You're my assistant," he whispered to me as his superior moved into view. "I'll tell them you just came from Saint-Junien to assist me."

No problem there. The Red Cross man didn't even notice me and moved on after a few words with my protector. Later Abel told me, "You were lucky, Eugène." We had begun calling each other by our prénoms, which struck me as highly apropos since his Biblical namesake was metaphorically the world's first murder victim. That a few collaborationists were around was plain once Abel led us to the Champ de Foire. En route, it was when we encountered the town's lone auto garage whose brick walls had not crumbled. On one façade, a freshly plastered poster of Pétain met our sight. Under the lettering was the propaganda message,

LE MARÉCHAL PÉTAIN VOUS AIDE.

On the opposing wall was the identical *affiche*. Only here, an anonymous brave soul had doctored it. Over the É in PÉTAIN had been scrawled a great U, spelling PUTAIN: our Vichy *prostitute*. Fortunately, none of le maréchal's flunkies were around to hear our laughter.

In this leg of the walk to the center of Charniers, I went by where my home should have stood. All that remained was a pile of smoldering debris. The roof had crashed down into the cellar, scattering Papa's expensive blue-grey slate shingles everywhere. In addition, the outer walls had collapsed entirely inward. Anything wood or other flammables inside had quickly been swept up in a raging bonfire. Its roaring now ceased, the died-down flames lingered in red hot coals and embers.

I was alongside Abel and pointed out the mess to him. "Do you want to stop here for a moment of reverence?" he kindly asked me.

"Thank you, no . . . not tonight. Besides, there is plenty of work yet to do." Our destination was the Red Cross command tent where Abel would receive further orders.

Portable lights were being set up when we arrived. There was such a scurry of people that I fit right in—merely another rescue worker, although *rescue* wasn't our job. Preventing contamination was—a threat from those soon to be rotting bodies.

I noticed a cluster of masked men with shovels moving off to join others we had already seen clearing away wreckage so streets could become passable. Abel saw me eyeing those shovelers and said: "We could use a couple of tractors but for now we can only dig by hand."

"Should I go with them?" I asked. "

"You'd better stay close to me," he answered. "until you become a familiar figure."

He received no argument on my part although the reason I had kept staring so intently at those guys was because one of them, due to his small stature, burly build and bandy legs had seemed familiar. Could it be Mario Cioffi? We hadn't seen Mario for months in Charniers and the rumor was he had fled to the Maquisards. Afraid of attracting attention, I gave up any thought of rushing up to my old pal.

So I went tagging along with Abel while the good doctor conferred with various subordinate leaders on the Champ de Foire. When waiting for him, I began to realize I still hadn't even touched upon the mystery of Jean-Luc's fate. But if I opened my mouth . . . And the knowledge I had nothing to report to Chantal triggered another conundrum. Should I sneak off to the château and tell her I had seen neither hide nor hair of the redhead, nor even heard any mention of him?

I prevaricated. One excuse was the urgency of the need for workers here. More cogent, though, was the argument I needed more time to do a thorough investigation. Unfortunately the only eyewitness who might have told me anything, Benoît, was having his wounds attended to at the hospital in Limoges. It would take days before he was available. So, in a manner of speaking, I clung to Abel, carrying his clipboard and medical bag as we meandered from place to place in what was left of Charniers. He told me how it helped to have a guide who knew every inch of the community we had to scour.

Once darkness fully enveloped the ravaged town where remnants of the fires amid mounds of glowing debris stood out as occasional flickering flares, the artificial lights running on generators turned night into an eerie imitation of day. Another alibi I gave myself for not facing Chantal was the danger of making my way to the château in the dark without a flashlight.

But at a hurry-up supper all of us gulped down, gathered together on the Champ de Foire, I sensed a stroke of luck concerning my dilemma. Among the latest of the volunteer arrivals was my friend, the doorman at the château, Eduard, who always let me in and out. Since he roomed at the château, he'd be able to deliver my message to Chantal that I was still collecting information on Jean-Luc's whereabouts, that conceivably he could have been arrested by the Nazis or was hiding out and unable to contact her.

However, I consulted Abel first. What should I do in my predicament?

"Do you trust this person?" I was asked.

"Let me say Eduard already knows I went into Charniers," I said. "Also he's no Pétain lover. We've talked politics on occasion."

"Make sure you're not overheard," my newfound doctor friend warned me.

Albeit I thought Abel overcautious, I waited until the doorman finished eating and stood alone. He was about to put his mask back on when I approached and lifted mine.

"Ah, M'sieu Desfosseux," he replied, not overly surprised.

"Are you returning to the château tonight, Eduard?" I inquired.

As an answer, he displayed a large flashlight ."When the need for me is over."

"Did Countess Chantal send you to find me?"

"No. I'm on my own time here to do what I can."

"Does she know the horror that happened?"

"She knows something terrible took place."

"Will you take a message to her from me?"

"M'sieu, I would be glad to when I am done."

I gave him the lack of news about Jean-Luc and that Benoît might provide an answer, but not right now. Meanwhile, tell the countess I needed to remain helping with the aftermath of the massacre. He said he would either relay the message personally or have one of the female servants communicate it.

Our brief colloquy ended at this point. Eduard went off with his cohorts and their stretchers, fetching mainly the last of the roasted victims from the holocaust in the church.

Once he disappeared in the shadows, it occurred to me. Where would I sleep that night? But on my next tour with Abel, I saw cots had been arranged in various tents to accommodate the workers. Not anxious to face Chantal, I gave up any thoughts of going to the château.

Three nights and days of primitive accommodations were to be my lot, makeshift sanitary facilities, cold water for washing off the grime of ashes, cold food, wine out of a canteen with a brassy taste . . . and in the midst of a *I can't believe it, I can't believe it* nightmare of human-wrought destruction.

I'd been correct that I'd spotted Mario Cioffi. Clandestinely, we eventually signaled each other. Right away, once we met by ourselves, he told me that when he left, I had to go with him. "Agreed," I replied. In the meantime, he said, we should both continue working until he could make arrangements. No one would denounce him, he was confident. He had forged papers explaining his absence, saying he had been in Germany doing forced labor but was released for health reasons. What wasn't fiction was he had been scouting Nazi troop movements nearby when word reached him Charniers had been surrounded. Only when the SS departed was he able to rush home and find no parents, no siblings, no house, no trace of anything dear to him.

I gave him my account of why I was alive. Also of Jean-Luc's foolhardy bravery. Those strong hands of Mario's knotted into fists, his dark expressive face full of visible rage, while he descried: "We will have our revenge on those *Tedeschi* swine, wait, you will see, Eugène." And he finished his threat by adding a gesture I'd seen him use as kids whenever he was really angry, the worst Italian insult; he bit the end of his thumb and then flicked it toward his enemy, on this occasion an invisible foe—Germans.

By the third day, Abel felt I didn't have to be cagy any longer about my identity. Benoît had talked to news reporters from his hospital bed. The story of Mayor Desfosseux's heroic defiance had appeared in newspapers all over France. It seemed to be the one thing even hardcore Vichyites wouldn't make trouble about.

On the third day consequently, it was safe for Abel to introduce me to the emissary of the bishop of Limoges, Monseigneur Solignac, who had presided at the count's memorial. Indeed, the Monseigneur had sought via Abel to visit me deliberately to convey personal condolences from the bishop, as well as himself, and an appreciation of the sacrifice Papa had made.

The prelate did have a soothing voice and an eloquent manner. We met in Abel's tent, the two of us alone, since the doctor had various details to see about in connection with the ceremony that evening when the common grave would be closed.

The chat between the Monseigneur and myself proceeded well until, in his comforting approach to the subject of sudden, inexcusable death, he committed the mistake of saying: "I trust and pray, Eugène, you will accept the inscrutable wisdom of our Heavenly Father, much as you might be tempted to blame Him for this human disaster."

My answer to him was: "Did not God create us, as the Bible says, out of dust and a rib? Maybe the Almighty should go back and start all over again, use different materials. Look around you at the handiwork of His handiwork."

"You must not be bitter, my son," Solignac also made the mistake of saying to me.

"I'm not your son," I retorted sharply. "You have people address you as Father. You're no father to me. My father's out there, M'sieu, in a pit."

"Your own father was a son of the Church," replied the unflappable churchman. "There was a misunderstanding years ago, you might call it, over our differences with M'sieu Maurras. But Étienne Desfosseux never denounced us. And your mother of blessed memory . . ."

"Leave my mother out of this!" I snapped angrily, almost shouting.

Monseigneur Solignac, I had noted, exhibited a slight facial disfigurement—a *wen*—in the middle of his forehead, a protruding cyst. No doubt, it had existed for many years, maybe since birth. I kept my eyes fastened on the spot. Was he self-conscious? I acted scandalously, finally pointing to the wen and asking: "When you tell lies, Monseigneur Solignac, does that stump on your brow grow bigger and bigger? It looks to me like it could."

Most likely it was my imagination that his fingers were rising to feel the size of his deformity. Ostensibly he was trying hard to remain his equable self in the presence of my rudeness. I imagined him a schoolboy unflinching at the taunts of his classmates.

"Years from now," the Monseigneur stated pontifically, "You will find your peace in Christ and with God, and the Holy Family."

"Years from now," I shot back, "I will be savoring my vengeance." Waiting a moment, I added: "I understand killing is an instinct from the hand of HE whom, you insist, fashioned me."

There is no need to continue this re-created unpleasant dialogue between the two of us, the smooth-shaven, silver-haired, well-spoken priest and the agitated, heart-broken adolescent in grimy clothing, flailing about verbally. As it was, Monseigneur Solignac had to move on and prepare for the evening's graveside service as soon as the sun went down.

At the final interment, torches provided the lighting. A crowd stood around the perimeter of the large shadowy black hole in the earth into which for three days the unidentified jumble of the dead had been placed carefully and tenderly. Monseigneur Solignac conducted our reverent farewell to the departed, an outdoor, informal funeral Mass you might call it, bereft of the trappings of a church interior. In the warm June night, we listened to his homilies. I had posted myself next to Mario. Between us, we had planned that as soon as the religious rites terminated and we helped shovel the blanket of soil to cover the formless victims for eternity, we would slip away and trek to the Maquisard encampment Mario had taken leave of temporarily.

That new adventure of ours was briefly delayed once the massive grave had been filled. Spontaneously, all of us joined hands and we began to sing. Only many years later did I learn from Naansee the haunting song we all instinctively chose was not a French tune. It was Scottish, she informed me and called *Auld Lang Syne* in the Celtic tongue and sung every New Year's in Anglo-Saxon countries, invoking the good times fading into the past, an achingly nostalgic melody that also sought to comfort with a paean to the future.

In French, it is also sung at New Years and no less redolent of the most intense emotion of loss and hope. Here at Charniers-sur-Nys, the words and music rose spontaneously from hundreds of throats in the quiet of the breeze and the swaying of surrounding trees.

"Ce n'est qu'un au revoir, ce n'est qu'un au revoir. Oui, nous nous reverrons, mes frères. Ce n'est qu'un au revoir.

"It's just a short good-bye, it's just a short good-bye. Yes, we will see each other again. It's just a short good-bye."

Tears were in every eye and we sang on and on . . . until one last melancholy refrain burst from us:

"Oui, nous nous reverons, mes frères. Ce n'est qu'un au revoir."

The sound rose into the heavens, faded, and left only silence filled with the murmur of weeping.

I looked at Mario. He looked at me. We lingered a few minutes longer. Then, we, too, faded into the darkness.

XIX

One item I have not elaborated upon is the STO—the *Service de Travail Obligatoire*—forced labor in Germany the Nazis and Vichy decreed for all French males of seventeen and older, which we later hailed as our "best recruiting tool for the Resistance." Instead of signing up, thousands of young Frenchmen fled to the Maquis. Interestingly enough, before the massacre, I might not have been one of them. Papa had arranged my deferment through the prefect, shielding me and Jean-Luc, too. We had both entered our eighteenth year.

After June 14, 1944, it mattered not. I *wanted* to fight and fight I did. Specifically, I wished to kill Germans, SS or not, and Milice.

Psychologists have written it is not in the genetic code for humans to kill one another intentionally. Reports are offered of soldiers purposely firing over the heads of advancing enemies. Statistics cited are impressive. But let me state baldly: I had no qualms.

For example, the German officer I shot on Gamelin Bridge whose Luger ended up in my possession. I never bothered to find out anything about him, certainly nothing about who he was; his name; his home in Deutschland; his family and any photos he might have had in his wallet. Where our guys could, they usually rummaged through the pockets of a dead enemy, seeking information and, I'll admit it, cash. But on the whole, our battles weren't so much at close range as that one. My specialty was sniping, firing long distances, picking off those green-grey uniforms (or Milice navy-blue). I never kept count of the foes I downed . . . possibly a dozen.

Admittedly, my toll on the Boche didn't win the war. Just a contribution. Pinpricks that bled. Others obviously decided the conflict: American might, Russian numbers, British grit, Free French stubbornness, and the all-out effort of these and other participants in the Allied coalition.

For us inside France, in the Maquis, our struggle was a matter of honor, redeeming our country's prestige. For the most part, even the Communists in our ranks, whose leaders had a definite allegiance to the Soviets, were French patriots at heart.

Mario Cioffi had tendencies in the direction of the hammer and sickle\. We never argued the subject. Besides, he called himself "a true Socialist," not a Communist, although dedicated to Marxian principles. His family, like mine, were really "bourgeoisie," a dirty word for most of his "Comrades." In Mario's case, because of his father's anti-Fascism, they were forced to leave Italy and go into exile. By upbringing, my boyhood friend had become wholly French, not that I ever considered him anything but. In battle, we were now inseparable and linked to Lucien Veynachter en route to forming a new Trio—until Lucien was killed, *bien entendu.*

One wonders how Fate plays its hand. The thesis of Lucien's seeking his death out of guilt is decidedly not far-fetched. Neither would be the counter-claim his recklessness had simply been on impulse. Nor the accidental coincidence he had found in me a bosom friend of his bosom friend Jean-Marc Rosenstein, who undoubtedly would have forgiven him for his standing helpless in the face of the brutality on the Champ de Foire.

It was a short period that Lucien and I were together—a month and a half at most. From him, not long after we met, I learned of the ultimate end of Jean-Luc, as he had witnessed it. He described the shock of seeing suddenly on the village green a redhead who incredibly resembled Jean-Marc Rosenstein, laughing with his armed escorts and seeing them freeze at the sight of Durchmann. Lucien's order was to stand at attention, eyes front. Furtive glances confirmed this new arrival was his Strasbourg friend. "I heard the Sturmbannführer, annoyed by the interruption, bark out: *'Was is los?'* The cocky redhead had launched into his berating for the blunder of mixing up the towns. No German officer had been killed here. Referring to Big Freddi, he had the word of a Milicien that the SS officer had been shot near Charniers-sur-Vare."

An epilogue from Lucien was: "I could see that bastard Roos slipping up behind Jean-Marc. Everything within me wanted to cry: 'Watch out!' But I remained as if gagged. It happened so fast. Durchmann must have signaled Roos. Jean-Marc was struck from behind, knocked out cold. The Sturmbannführer's pistol shots in the air resounded. All Hell unleashed."

The setting for this talk was at our Maquisard headquarters, which in other times would have been a picture postcard vacation spot. Craggy mountains surrounding an evergreen forest, high above placid blue lakes and vast wilderness stretching forth below. Lucien and I were settled on soft needle-covered ground that smelled deliciously of balsam. We had come back from our first raid together and he wanted to unload his feelings. "The deserter," as some in the unit surreptitiously called him, had already been accepted by Paul the Gaul three days before my arrival.

More thrilling action was still ahead of us two. Ten days prior to de Gaulle's dramatic entry into Paris on August 25, the small Limousin city of Brive-la-Gaillarde enjoyed the distinction of being the first city in France to be liberated solely by the Maquis. This was decidedly poetic justice for on June 17, 1940, after the Fall of France, Brive-la-Gaillarde had staged the first act of resistance in France when pamphlets urging defiance were placed in local mailboxes.

The Limousin was thus from the start a hotbed of activity against the invaders and their Pétain-Laval toadies. Our fellows made things so rough for the krauts that many of the veterans of the eastern front referred to our region as "Little Russia." By the early autumn of 1944, we'd pretty much run the Boche out of our *terroir*.

In the Resistance Museum, in addition to all the photos of our Maquisard activities and martial poses of *les gars* with their weapons, it goes without saying there were plenty of pictures from our triumphant days: Germans in uniform, their hands behind their heads, marched through the streets by young men in shirtsleeves and civilian garb, sporting armbands, toting submachine guns; or of Miliciens surrendering hands held high; and, naturally, the parade of shame—French women who had cohabited with the enemy, shorn of their hair, stripped of their outer clothing, running a gauntlet of jeering civilians, the most aggressive of them females.

Ah, what euphoria!

But before this explosive termination of four years of suffering tapered off, incidents occurred. Frankly, countrywide, some nine thousand of our countrymen considered the most villainous, the most responsible for the torture and execution of our fighters, supporters and innocent hostages, were summarily dispatched. Up against a wall. Pow! Pow!

I swear on the grave of my martyred father I took no part in these understandable acts of impromptu justice. Did I not thirst for revenge, myself, against those who committed the unspeakable crimes at Charniers-sur-Nys? Of course I did. And you can be sure I did not lift a finger nor utter a word of protest against such precipitous actions.

But there was one instance where I hesitated.

We had just marched in Charniers-sur-Vare's Liberation celebration. Paul the Gaul had given us the unofficial title of the Vercingetorix Brigade. His wife had made a banner we carried, depicting the sword-waving Celtic hero against a yellow-gold background. Armed to the teeth, we proudly strutted to the cheers of crowds on both sides of the principal street. Also visible in the throng of Maquisards were the red flags of the more leftist adherents of the FTP and the blue, white and red Cross of Lorraine ensigns of the de Gaullists.

The atmosphere was that of a July 14 Bastille Day celebration, only much more warlike. We had several bands in our cortège blaring out patriotic music. Onlookers threw flowers at us; pretty girls (and some not so pretty) came out to embrace us. The only element missing from this Roman-style victory procession were prisoners in chains. We knew a group of Miliciens had been captured that morning but were locked in the local jail—Paul The Gaul's orders—he wanted us dignified, not stained by ugly scenes of townspeople spitting on the captives and beating them, justifiable though it might be.

Yet once the festivities ended and the crowds dispersed, he turned a blind eye.

I came upon the scene innocently. Not that my thoughts were innocent. There I was with my sniper's rifle slung over my shoulder, my captured Luger on display in its holster and a girl on each arm and we were headed for the small apartment I had rented in Charniers-sur-Vare. But it was innocence in the sense that I hadn't expected what we encountered. Adjacent to the *Hôtel de Ville*—the City Hall—was the jail where the Miliciens were being held. A crowd was gathering outside—I wouldn't call it a mob, but there were a lot of angry faces.

Two members of the Vercingetorix Brigade were barring entry for anyone who might try to get inside. A truck with an open back was parked at the curb nearby, its motor running. Suddenly a sound I can only liken to a collective *hoot* came from the people on the sidewalk, coinciding with the opening of the jail's front door. Out stepped two more veterans of our outfit, holding submachine guns. One was Mario Cioffi. Behind them was a defile of haggard men in torn, rumpled navy-blue uniforms, guarded on every side by more grim-faced armed Maquisards.

An outcry of guttural rage exploded from the ranks of bystanders, while others were racing to add to their numbers. "*Au poteau!*" "To the stake!" everyone began yelling.

"Don't worry," Mario said to them, drawing his finger across his throat. On the rear of the truck, others of the *gars* with automatic weapons waited for the prisoners who were being prodded along and then forcibly mounted.

At that moment, Mario spied me. "Aren't you coming to take part in the fun, Eugène?" he called to me. For an answer, I indicated the two beauties I had accompanying me, signifying I had other things on my mind. Just at that moment the lumbering figure of Big Freddi appeared among the line of captive Miliciens. He had been beaten about the face and was conspicuously limping. At once, he noticed me.

"Tell them, Eugène!" he screamed. "Tell them I wanted to warn the Germans off, tell them I tried. Tell them, Eugène."

Mario stopped the line and came over to me. "You're not going to speak up for him, are you?" he challenged me. "That bastard denounced the La Belle family. Five little kids and their parents. All dead by now, just because they were Jews."

Big Freddi was still clamoring: "Tell them, Eugène! For God's sake, tell them!"

I said to Mario: "Do what you have to do."

He asked again: "Are you coming?" I shook my head. Off he went, seemingly disgruntled, and the flow of prisoners to their ultimate destination recommenced. Several cars full of Maquisards followed when at last the truckload of traitors, in our eyes, departed.

There was some coolness between Mario and myself after that incident. We were both living temporarily in Charniers-sur-Vare and we saw each other from time to time in one of the local cafés. He would come over and we'd exchange a few words and then he'd go back to his "Comrades" in another part of the establishment. I'd usually be with one or the other or both of the two lovelies I'd met at the victory parade. In the daytime frequently, I went to Charniers-sur-Nys. Even before the Paris government voted the funds and authority necessary to erect a New Charniers, we had started the creation of the organization that turned into the National Association of the Families of the Martyrs of Charniers-sur-Nys. I made sure to invite Mario to join us on its Executive Committee. He let me know he'd be leaving the area soon but to send him a membership card. I tried to turn down the presidency of the group, arguing I was much too young. The older folks assured me my name was too important not to grace the top of our stationery. I agreed so long as I could have two more experienced deputies to guide me. One was of the Phillipon clan—Marius—a much respected man in his sixties, and the other Octave Bois, This latter person was the heart and soul of everything we did. He had been wounded in 1939 in one of the minor skirmishes of the Phony War and had both knees shattered. He moved skillfully in his wheelchair, always cheery, highly competent, and was made our secretary. Because of his pension as a disabled war veteran, he could do all of the chores of the Association for the mere pittance we could pay him. Originally, he worked out of a room in the intact Sirois farmhouse, our temporary office. I, myself, stayed overnight there when I toiled all day with Octave and was too tired to drive back to Charniers-sur-Vare.

I had bought a car—a used 1938 Renault Frégate. Papa had banked a considerable amount of money in Limoges and I was his only child and heir. Consequently, once the formalities of the inheritance were completed, I was—if not overly rich—certainly independent and able to get along nicely on the revenue from these invested funds.

It was over a number of years that l'état, i.e., the national government of France operating from its capital in Paris, did its best to assuage our village that its predecessor in Vichy had not protected. Construction on the New Charniers commenced in 1946, a year following the end of the war in Europe. Meanwhile, those two signal honors were awarded Charniers-sur-Nys, the *Croix de Guerre*, France's highest medal for Bravery, given in 1947 and the prestigious Légion d'Honneur in 1949. The year 1962 saw Charles de Gaulle pay us a visit under circumstances that were unusual. Due to the furor caused in our region by the Bordeaux trial of 1953 and the subsequent pardon of all the Alsatian draftees who had been convicted, the town had henceforth refused to receive any representatives of l'état. Only in the case of the great de Gaulle, then president of the French Republic, was this show of our implacable anger temporarily relaxed.

Long since ensconced in Paris, I did not in 1962 deign to be present at this historic occasion. Although I had been absent from my native hearth for a decade and a half, I kept my ties to it and my name on the masthead of the Association of Families, while no longer an active officer.

I moved to Paris during the summer of 1945 as soon as the first anniversary of the June 14, 1944, event was, shall we say, solemnly commemorated, understandably not *celebrated*. With the encouragement and acquiescence of my friends like Paul the Gaul and Octave Bois and other officers, along with rank-and-file members of the Association, I was persuaded to leave the area and pursue my education. The group would continue to keep me as a titular head, and I promised to come back home whenever I could and in addition serve as a liaison with the officials at various government departments in Paris and likewise with our députés and sénateurs in the Assemblée.

My own intellectual bent had been prodding me in the direction I had taken. I would become an historian—that much was preordained. But I was most inner-directed toward the puzzle that arose from the traumas that I'd lived through. The barbarity I had personally experienced challenged me to unravel the entire tapestry of military atrocities since the dawn of time, to try and comprehend the horror and cruelty that connected so many disparate crimes of war.

This inchoate mix of feelings and thoughts, which had no directive form but yet tormented me to learn, learn, learn evermore, originally sparked to life within me at Charniers-sur-Vare when I sat drinking by myself one late night in the café—Le Coq Bleu—that I most frequented. To my surprise, I looked up from the Cognac I was sipping and noted my old friend Mario entering alone. Usually, he would be accompanied by his left-wing buddies.

Therefore, I had a distinct impression my estranged Franco-Italianate friend had come deliberately seeking me out. From the moment I saw him lurch once he'd caught sight of my table, I knew he was pretty drunk.

But he was coherent after struggling to land in the seat opposite me. His voice sounded only a tiny bit slurred. His agate, deep brown eyes reflected a poorly concealed inner pain.

"You weren't there," he started. "*Non*, you were definitely not there."

Those two cryptic remarks were not so opaque to me. I knew where Mario was headed. He paused at least half a minute before he spoke again. Having ordered a red wine from the waiter, it stayed untouched while he stared at me, at the ceiling and finally at me again.

"We took them to that big meadow surrounding La Cav," he said.

It was not a profession of remorse. "Those *salauds* deserved every bullet they received," was the defiant ultimatum he spat. "D'accord?" he asked. "Do you agree?"

"Oui. D'accord." I answered him.

"Do you know Jacobi?" he asked. "He was a guy from Poland who was with us at the very end. And with the Brigade on the day of the parade."

"Correct. He was once in a Nazi camp and escaped? Kept to himself a lot. Brooding, but who would blame him? Dark beard, dark eyes."

"He told us: 'Let's give those rats a taste of the medicine the *Einsatzgruppen* gave us in Tarnow.' He was Jewish. He had a funny Yiddish accent when he spoke French. Pretty amusing. But deadly, no clown."

I had heard a general description of the executions of those Miliciens I'd seen shoved into the back of a truck and driven away. I hadn't heard any of it from Mario, though, until that night in the café. He dwelled on the role played by Jacobi who had explained the Einsatzgruppe technique—named for the German killer squads who murdered Jews and Slavs by the thousands in eastern Europe. Mario, I remembered, said: "At Jacobi's command we gave the Vichy salauds shovels to dig ditches—two lines of graves several meters deep—for these traitors to France and humanity. 'This is how the Nazis did it,' Jacobi informed us. 'Get the lot of them in the holes, make them lie face down, spray them with bullets and pile the dirt back.' We did so near La Cav. Meadow flowers will soon be growing over them. Justice done."

With that, Mario emptied half his wine glass in a single swallow. He slammed a fist on the table. "All right, you and I need to discuss our one-time pal Big Freddi."

"Dead with the others, I'm sure."

"Believe me, I enjoyed blasting a burst into that tub of lard. But he kept blabbing about: 'Ask Eugène . . . Eugène'll tell you.' The fat pig was beside himself, screaming his lungs out. 'Act like a man, Arnaud,' I yelled at him, moments before we all fired."

I thought maybe we were finished. However, Mario picked up his glass again and drained the rest of his Burgundy in another single long gulp. "War crime," he said. "Crimes of war. Is revenge one? If we'd lost . . ." He drew his finger across his throat. "All of us."

"Right, naturally."

"Crimes of war. Crimes of war," he continued. "Out in the meadow, Jacobi gave them a tribunal. Unanimous decision. *Condamné à mort.*"

"But no defendants allowed to speak?"

He assented with a nod.

"Crimes of war. Crimes of war," he repeated, stood up and staggered out of the café.

I sat and watched him weaving away on the sidewalk.

In a stage play, the curtain would have descended. We would have had an *interlude*—a space to fill. For an historian, a didactic footnote might be appropriate at this point. I am well aware I have skipped a beat in relating my story. What of the poor heroine alone in her castle, pining for her first love or happy news of him?

Chantal! I had left her on June 14th but could not get back physically, forced to depart posthaste in secret with Mario for the maquis. My message in regard to Jean-Luc, as I've indicated, was of no concrete information. But once I met Lucien up in the mountains, I had a clearer picture of what had transpired with the redhead. Although I dawdled and dawdled, I eventually made myself send a note with the help of Paul the Gaul's wife to Countess Chantal de Bregonzac-Chastain—one regarding her loved one, a sort of missing-in-action-but-presumed *mort pour la France* communication. You must understand under no circumstances could I even hint at my location.

Following the Liberation and my return to the ruins of Charniers, which de Gaulle decreed should be forever preserved in the same state left by the Germans, I immediately made an unannounced visit to the château to see Chantal and, more prosaically, retrieve my bicycle.

Eduard let me in. When I told him I'd like to greet the countess, he sort of blanched. "*Impossible*," he declared and immediately added: "She is gone to her relatives on the Côte d'Azur, taking Charlot with her."

"And she will come back when?"

In a confidential low tone, he half-whispered: "Perhaps never."

"Do you have an address where I can reach her?" I asked, not really overly surprised by her action. "I need to know if she received my news about Jean-Luc Mueller."

"We are not allowed to know exactly where she is," said the doorman. "A cousin has come from Burgundy to manage the estate. " Less formally, addressing me as "Eugène," Eduard confided: "I fear she has become a different person. More like . . . More like . . ."

"Her mother?"

"*Exactement.*"

One thing Eduard could be more helpful with was my bicycle left abandoned on the steps at the château's entrance. He had stowed it away for me in the estate's stable. Reunited with my trusty old mode of transportation, I pedaled off to my temporary quarters at the Sirois farm.

This ride was not exactly a déjà vu. Rather, a reminder to me of how fragile a steady state of existence can be and how my world had altered so drastically within less than two months. Papa was dead. Jean-Luc was dead. Chantal quite probably driven toward an inheritable madness and, in any case, indefinitely gone from the scene. Soon, too, my life and physical abode would undergo a more normal shift when I departed for Paris to attend the Université Paris-Sorbonne.

One day while still in the Limousin, when I had nothing else to do, a spontaneous, mindless urge seized me. It commanded: *hop on your bike, go out to La Cav, climb up to Jean-Luc's secret hiding place.* I convinced myself I had a practical aim to my whim. A flash of memory reminded me he'd been working at his old-fashioned typewriter with metal keys when alone. In the hurried rush to leave La Cav that June day, we hadn't taken anything, not even Jean-Luc's toothbrush. Unspoken was the certainty we would return with him to collect his belongings.

In the intervening two and a half months, whenever I mentally pictured the cave-within-a-cave interior, it was as I had last seen it, fully stocked with canned goods, ratty furniture, sleeping bag on a floor pad, books, sheets of paper mounting up alongside that woebegone typewriter. At my leisure, I could peruse Jean-Luc's final writings, stick them in my knapsack for further study, gauging his mindset before tragedy befell him, which was his own red-head tempered doing, some would argue. History in its undetected makings. Although silently apprehensive enough to fret about the revolving wall and the ladder's availability, but hearing no discouragement from Octave Bois from whom I borrowed a big flashlight, I grabbed a bite of lunch at midday and shortly afterward departed the Sirois farm via our shortcut path to pleasant and not so pleasant memories.

Hardly was I disappointed in finding any of my perceived obstacles nonexistent. The revolving wall turned easily when I pressed the camouflaged lever. The ladder I soon saw was in place. I climbed it to the upper ledge without incident. My flashlight lit the natural tunnel to Jean-Luc's inner sanctum locus of refuge.

But inside . . . My beam with the aid of illumination from cracks in the rock ceiling revealed a dumbfounding phenomenon. Nothing was visible except bare stone floor and walls. No clunky typewriter, no budding stack of manuscript pages, no boxes, no chairs, no oil lamps, no sign whatsoever of Jean-Luc's brief presence.

Except, eventually, one item . . . During my thorough examination of these now-barren premises, my eye caught a seemingly foreign object in a shadowy corner. Closer examination disclosed a book, apparently thrown by someone and landing flattened in dark obscurity. Once I picked it up, I saw the title was: *L'Histoire Indispensable du Sionisme.*

Left without even a carton to sit on, I contemplated an explanation. Dismissed almost at once was the possibility of strangers finding this spot and stealing the whole works. Fleeing Miliciens seemed a long-shot guess—anti-Semites—who took everything except a book on Zionism they jettisoned in disgust. But why Jean-Luc's papers? That didn't make sense. I could find no sign of ashes where anything might have been burned.

Which led me finally, logically, to accuse Chantal. She not only knew the route through the cavern but she had furnished the interior. It would have been no problem to bring several male servants to help her lug away the contents, swearing them to secrecy. I wondered if I should question Eduard. This thesis would explain the missing papers. But the book seemingly flung into a corner?—

A bookplate on the inside front cover divulged the volume belonged to Jean-Marc Rosenstein at a Strasbourg address.

Slowly in my initial puzzlement, a hunch had appeared, growing ever more plausible. The idea had dawned that Chantal believed Jean-Luc hadn't died. No doubt she knew of his desire to go to Palestine. What if in her distorted mental state she believed he had used a ruse to do just that . . . and, good Lord, had made me his accomplice trying to convince her he'd been killed in the massacre, quoting some *Lucien person* I'd invented.

Sitting down on the stone floor with the book under a ray of sunlight from above, I pored through the volume in search of any clues. Like me, Jean-Luc jotted annotations in the margins and on blank space of thoughts inspired in our reading or underlined passages that had especially caught our attention. I could visualize Chantal's having found a statement in his penmanship such as *How I long to be in Palestine* and in her fury blindly throwing the volume away. The results of my immediate search revealed no such quote in Jean-Luc's handwriting but several underlines in a chapter on Moses Hess, one of the earliest Zionist thinkers that linked France and the future of the Jews. Thus in 1862, Hess, who lived in Paris for the latter part of his life, wrote: "The Jewish people will participate in the great historical movement of present-day humanity only when it will have its own fatherland." Most likely thirteen years old then, the Alsatian lad also earmarked Hess' admission of respect for *la patrie:* "Since the French Revolution, the French . . . have become our noble rivals and faithful allies." At the bottom of the end of the chapter, Jean-Luc, who at thirteen thus a certified Jewish male, had penned, "Yes, we are allied with the French, thank you my dear French brothers and sisters, but we Jews need a country of our own."

I could well imagine such to have been the quote that unhinged Chantal.

Upon leaving La Cav (no problem doing so), I had the Zionist history stowed away in my knapsack for future reading. I bicycled back, had a meal chez Octave Bois et famille and drove to my lodging in Charniers-sur-Vare. Within a few weeks, I would leave for the apartment I had rented in Paris. Thanks to the SS, I didn't have many possessions to squeeze into my little car.

During much of that spare time, I debated trying a letter to Chantal and asking Eduard to have it sent. I felt I could pose a legitimate question to her. Had she taken Jean-Luc's writings from the La Cav sanctuary? Were they about us, the Trio and our adventures? If I were wrong and she knew nothing of why the hiding place was ransacked, she should excuse me, and maybe we would solve the mystery together or otherwise, just not answer me and I would understand. I hoped she was well and happy. And I left her my Paris address.

It was a week or so more after I'd arrived in the capital city and settled in when the concierge of my building handed me an envelope.

I won't reproduce Chantal's words in their entirety. Were I a psychiatrist, I surely would have tried to analyze them. They forcefully displayed the power of delusion. But who was I, an historian-to-be, to judge Chantal's frame of mind. I had guessed right, however. Her tone on paper seethed with anger—not specifically at me for writing her—but at Jean-Luc—"she referred to him as "that Jew, Jean-Marc Rosenstein," who had sneakily deserted her by his smokescreen of playing the hero and pretending to save Charniers from the destruction. Obviously he had made an arrangement with the Nazis and she included words from a newspaper article confirming there had been deals by the Hitlerians to ship Jews out of Germany to settlements in Palestine like "Hasho . . . something, which he was always chattering about." Finally, as I feared, she called me "a participant in the conspiracy."

I was not surprised in the next paragraph to learn she had burned all Jean-Luc's papers. There was no reference whatever to *L'Histoire Indispensable du Sionisme*. Conceivably she believed she had tossed it into empty space.

The opportunities to speculate on the relationship between Chantal and Jean-Luc seemed endless, but utterly fruitless. I had better things to think about in Paris.

Through Eduard on my first trip home to Charniers, I simply sent back a curt note thanking her for her letter.

XX

Paris's Rue Duguay-Trouin is a short side street angled between the Rue d'Assas and the Boulevard Raspail in the Montparnasse section of the fabled Quartier Latin. A short walk will take you to the Luxembourg, arguably the most famous public garden in the city and certainly my favorite lolling place. That odd name, Duguay-Trouin, is a play on the title of René Trouin, Sieur de Gue, a French privateer of the eighteenth century and admiral of the navy, who in 1711 captured and ransomed Rio de Janeiro. Two years previously, this former corsair, a native of Saint-Malo, Brittany, had been ennobled by Louis XIV (he had by then accounted for sixteen warships and three hundred merchant vessels taken from the English and Dutch) and he was to end his successful career as lieutenant-general of the Naval Armies of the King and a Commander of the Royal Order of Saint Louis.

So much for indulging in historical trivia. This particular street in Paris where I located is somewhat trivial, itself, merely 150 meters long, but magnificently located for a student in Paris. To be sure, I wasn't your typical rube from the country coming to better himself through education in one of the *Grandes Écoles*. My experiences in the Resistance and in dealing with the Charniers massacre had aged me—if not in years then assuredly in maturity. I was not in Paris to play but to learn and although I did not shy from dropping in on the most famed (and not so famed) Left Bank gathering places, I devoted most of my bachelor life to studies. An occasional lady love might briefly impinge upon my egghead hermit's time, yet nothing serious nor long-lasting ever developed.

My sole permanent "escape" was relaxing for an hour or two in the Luxembourg, that divine oasis of greenery, seasonal flowers, statues and an immortalized pond in the midst of a crowded bustling convergence of boulevards of hallowed note: Boulevard Saint-Germain, Boulevard

Raspail, Boulevard Montparnasse, Boulevard Saint-Michel (Boul Mich). Because I was of independent means, I also could afford pleasures my classmates couldn't, like dining at expensive restaurants such as the Closerie des Lilas at the confluence of Montparnasse and Saint-Michel and sneaking across the Seine to the Right Bank and springing for a three-star meal at the Tour d'Argent.

Another difference with the image of an aspiring youngster starting in the University world was my work on behalf of the National Association of the Families of Martyrs of Charniers-sur-Nys. Thus my interest perforce had to include the same elected député we had had in the past, a Socialist I had deprecated, who now had changed his spots and become a Gaullist. A clever opportunist, if nothing else, Hippolyte Moringe at least did know his way around in the capital. Despite awareness that Papa had been conspiring with the Count de Bregonzac-Chastain to replace him, he cultivated my friendship because he knew of the standing I had at home. Helpful to an extent when it came to the bureaucracy of l'état, particularly Le Ministre de la Reconstruction et de l' Urbanisme and its overseeing of the building of New Charniers, he advised me from time to time and we met occasionally.

What I remember most from our relationship was a luncheon we had in a small restaurant on the Quai D'Orsay, incidentally the location also of the French Foreign Ministry. Hippolyte liked it because it was cheap, but had good food. In fact, among the clientele were many workers in their blue outfits and his acquaintance with the *patron* had commenced during his Socialist days. Now that we were in the ascendance of de Gaulle and his Provisional Government of the French Republic, he was nevertheless still welcome. In informing me we would be eating at this old hangout of his, he suggested I wear the ribbon of the Médaille de la Résistance I had received as part of Paul the Gaul's Maquisard group.

If you guessed he was showing me off to our fellow diners, more than a few of whom voted Communist or at least Socialist, you would be correct. Some who came to our table to say hello to Hippolyte were curious enough to ask about my medal. That I could tell them I had served in a unit of the FTP and was from Charniers-sur-Nys made a big hit.

A sly boots, that Hippolyte, and a good introduction for me to the political gamesmanship that sank the Third Republic and was eventually to torpedo the Fourth.

The Paris of those days was also the germinating location of the phenomenon called "existentialism." Its giant was Jean-Paul Sartre who with his lady friend Simone de Beauvoir held court at the Café Flore in Saint-Germain-des-Prés, not far from where I boarded. Their sidekick, Albert Camus, in time achieved even greater literary, if not philosophical fame, and a whole coterie of literateurs formed around this nucleus.

As what my Naansee would refer to as a "grind," a bookworm, buried in my studies, I missed most of the excitement spreading from Paris among the avant-garde cognoscenti of Western Europe and the United States. I once was invited to the Flore for dinner and had the worst meal I can remember. Rarely—and not during my first years—I might stop for an apéritif at the Deux Magots on the opposite side of the Boulevard Saint-Germain, another of the meccas of French thought before it became a tourist attraction.

So, again to quote one of my Naansee's *Americanisms*, I was in those heady years after the end of World War II "all work and no play," making me "a dull boy."

In one sense, *au contraire*, well before I met my American "girlfriend," I instinctively did take one day off a week following my arrival in Paris. On Sunday, the day of rest, the Christian Sabbath, I did what any French tourist from the hinterland did, as well as Americans and other foreigners. I went sightseeing, checking out landmark attractions on both banks of the Seine. How could I not want to visit the Louvre or Notre Dame or go up and down the river in a Bateau Mouche or walk the Champs-Élysées to the Arc de Triomphe or stray in the other direction to the Place de la Concorde and the Tuileries. How could I turn my back on Montmartre or Place Pigalle or Les Halles in the evening or even travel out to Versailles? On the Left Bank, there were also other showplaces besides the celebrity cafés. Cluny, for example, the Rodin Museum, the churches of Saint-Sulpice and Saint-Germain-des-Prés, the Eiffel Tower, Napoleon's Tomb, and a sleeper that drew me back again and again—the Montparnasse Cemetery.

Ah, Le Cimetière Montparnasse . . . Here are buried world class notables, primarily but not exclusively French. Charles Baudelaire, *poète extraordinaire* is an example. Guy de Maupassant, *écrivain extraordinaire*, is another. This is the last resting place of Alfred Dreyfus, after his turbulent life. Also among other graves of prominent French Jews, Jean-Luc would have recognized Adolphe Crémieux, lawyer and government minister, who put an end to slavery in the French colonies (and was called the "French Lincoln"). His famous Crémieux Decree of 1870 received much attention during World War II. It had granted French Jews in North Africa full rights as French citizens. Vichy suspended it. De Gaulle restored it. Given Jean-Luc's interest in the history of Zionism, I'm sure he would have liked to pay homage to the grave of Max Nordau, a close associate of Theodor Herzl in starting the movement that culminated in the State of Israel. I made a special trip from Switzerland to Colmar with Naansee to show her the headstone of Frédéric Bartholdi, the sculptor of the Statue of Liberty. There is also an American who has long been buried in this cemetery—Ambassador Ambrose Dudley Mann, but I hesitated to point him out to her since he represented the Confederate States of America in Belgium and the Vatican. I knew which side Ohio had been on. When I suggested the idea, she merely laughed and said: "Sure, I'd love to see old Ambrose. The Civil War, *mon cher*, is over."

My predilection among my own deceased countrymen in these premises was Edgar Quinet, an historian of enough note to have a Parisian boulevard named after him, which is incidentally the principal street that borders the Cimetière Montparnasse. Quinet, who began his career as a Professor of Foreign Languages in Lyon came to Paris to the College de France, also in our neighborhood next to the Sorbonne, but who had to flee to Brussels in 1851 because of his strong opposition to the dictator Napoleon III. A man of action and writer of numerous histories, he teamed up with the more famous member of our profession Jules Michelet to attack the Jesuits and lost his College de France job as a result. Returning from exile once Louis Napoleon was overthrown, he was restored to his professorship and elected a Deputy to the National Assembly where he fought against a Franco-German rapprochement. I believe I dwelt on Quinet because I considered him a role model.

Walking the myriad paths of this cemetery was like a continual rich French history lesson. I would see names I had not heard of previously and delve into their pasts and how they related to France; for example: Jean Bernard Jauréguiberry (whose unusual *nom de famille* first caught my eye), an admiral and statesman, governor of Senegal, Crimean War hero, and for whom two French warships were named; or Claude François Chauveau-Lagarde, a lawyer who defended Marie-Antoinette and whom Papa would have liked: a Royalist who somehow kept his neck from the guillotine while saving other adherents of the king.

But I also have to confess my deepest interest in the denizens of such a fascinating graveyard was not a Frenchman but a Ukrainian. His name was Symon Petliura and he had the bad luck to be assassinated in Paris while in exile from the Soviets who had taken over his country he had briefly led to independence in the 1920s. Petliura was shot May 26, 1926—also in our neighborhood on a side street off the Boulevard Saint-

Michel—by a Russian Jewish ex-French Foreign Legionnaire named Sholem Schwartzbard who held him responsible for the deaths of his parents and many other Jews in a bloody pogrom. Jean-Luc had talked to me about these mass killings of his people and so I was familiar with the subject. But more particular to my own circumstances, the killing of Petliura was a drama of *revenge for a war crime.* Here it was entombed within walking distance of my apartment, readily available to me for introspection. Oh, by the way, Schwartzbard was acquitted.

I do remember, too, that whenever I took Miss Nancy Jane Henderson of Lancaster, Ohio, on our tourist visits to this repository of history in the cemetery, I never showed her the grave of the . . . shall we say . . . Ukrainian nationalist "war criminal."

Half a decade of my stay in Paris had passed before I made the acquaintance—and much more—of the bright-eyed, vivacious *Américaine* who had come to Paris to obtain a French degree for teaching our language back in the States.

It is said that historians are in love with death. "Bull . . . sh . . . ee . . . t!" my American "sweetie" would declare with theatric exaggeration and a more than a little Midwest twang. She was right. I was in love with history well before encountering sudden death thrust upon me. Nor was it only those colored broadsides of France's soldiers building an empire overseas that attracted my early interest. At the age of twelve, I was delving into Michelet's monumental *History of France.* History, in a sense, kept drawing me back to Charniers-sur-Nys. I had to be there in my capacity as titular head of the Association of Families when we first had President de Gaulle pay us a visit in April 1945. Again in 1947, I had to be present for the laying of the cornerstone for the New Charniers, a ceremony attended by the president of France who succeeded de Gaulle—Vincent Auriol. In 1948, I met in Paris with Paul the Gaul, who enlisted my aid in setting up our Resistance Museum, and I spent the entire summer in Charniers-sur-Vare helping him. A year later, 1949, the construction of New Charniers was completed and de rigueur, I cut a ribbon and also turned down the offer of a free house in the complex. Previously, though, as part of Papa's legacy to me, I did accept a payment from l'état for our family property taken to preserve the ruins.

So it was in 1950 I felt I had slowly started to become a true Parisian. I had planned to vacation starting the 15th of August *(le quinze août)* like almost all of my fellow inhabitants of the City of Lights, heading for the seaside or lake shores or rivers or mountains of France or other countries. However, it was also in 1950, a month and a half earlier that

Nancy Jane Henderson—Naansee, my first (and only) serious *affaire d'amour*, entered my life.

Prior to our accidental meeting, I was having strange dreams. I haven't talked much about my internal life at this period. June was never an easy month for me, neither consciously or subconsciously, obviously, because it was the anniversary of our "Great Tragedy." Jean-Luc had told me of a special tradition in his Jewish religion for memorializing the dead. On the date of their decease, a particular type of candle was lit that burned for twenty-four hours. He called it *Yahrzeit*—"year's time" in Yiddish—and Grandpa Max had practiced the rite to honor his own parents and so Jean-Luc had practiced the same for Max surreptitiously in his Catholic convert mother's home. Not in Charniers, however. "Only in here," he told me, touching his heart. Too dangerous during those Vichy years of the 1940s.

At any rate, my dreams in the June of a new decade had begun with—no surprise—*bad dreams*—waking me up. I would be in a dark room and two dogs would be barking, or rather growling threateningly. I could only make out their shadows, but they were big and vicious—a German shepherd and an Alsatian shepherd. Terrified, I always sat bolt upright in bed.

But as the month of June neared its finale on the 30th, the *really strangest* thing happened: I started having *pleasant dreams*.

While those snarling dogs still woke me up, showing their teeth, I had gained a protector who chased them out of the dark room and as the dark room brightened, showed himself—itself—to me.

Let me refresh your memory. In La Cav, in Jean-Luc's hiding place, we found sort of hieroglyphics on the wall. Stick figures, not sensational animal paintings. Were they Neanderthal or Cro-Magnon? Professor Forestier had never gotten really to examine them.

Briefly, my now inner self had projected onto the wall of my sleeping brain a life-sized, animated stick figure, who with flailing stick arms and kicking stick feet drove away the beasts tormenting me. Finally, by the time June ended that year, the demon dogs had thoroughly vanished and I was left with a jolly pinhead, biped dream rescuer I christened CRO-MARITAN.

Okay, back to Naansee not long afterward. July had commenced—a celebratory month for both the United States of America and France. Per usual, I went into the Luxembourg Garden each rainless day with a book and read for at least several hours.

On this particular early July afternoon, I had brought Book VI (out of forty-two volumes) of Chateaubriand's monumental autobiography *Mémoires d'outre-tombe*. The reason I had decided to dip into the oceanic depths of this eighteenth- and nineteenth-century aristocrat writer-politician was the plan I had to spend my initial August vacation near his birthplace of Saint-Malo, Brittany. The Vicomte François-René de Chateaubriand's tomb is also in Saint-Malo built at his request on the Île du Grand Bé, an islet only reachable from the city ramparts five hundred meters away by foot at low tide. In seeking this site from the city fathers, he told them in his felicitous literary style that he wanted to be where "the noise (of the sea) rocked me in my first sleep."

I had already reserved a small hotel room in the next-door ocean-side town of Cancale on the Emerald coast, a fishing port and "the oyster capital of France," in the opinion of some gourmets. Brought up about as far from the sea as possible, I had developed a late love and endless appetite for those briny bivalves, and I knew I could eat my fill, save money on Saint-Malo accommodations, and continue my newfound interest in the man for whom chateaubriand steaks are named, including his involvement in 1791 with the budding United States of America. Book VI highlights the start of his transatlantic trip to the world's newest republic and allegedly a meeting he had with President George Washington. One of Chateaubriand's most famous popular works is a novel set in the New World entitled *Natchez*, an expanded compilation of two smaller fiction pieces, *René* and *Atala*, documenting a real-life historical saga of French settlement in the lower Mississippi River Valley and its interaction with the Natchez Indians. The tale involves massacres and counter-massacres, a subject as you know, of considerable concern to me.

Chateaubriand is a fascinating writer and since as part of my schoolwork I had immersed myself in Franco-American relations during their Revolution and ours, it struck me as *fortuitous*, not merely *coincidental* that I met Naansee, the all-American girl, when I did.

I was on my usual chair under a plane tree in the Luxembourg, travelling mentally with Chateaubriand into Chesapeake Bay when I became aware of a tumult nearby—a pair of female voices raised to an angry, almost desperate pitch. I looked up and discovered this screeching was happening just across a path from me in a row of chairs like mine.

All at once, I heard a shout in English from one of the two disputants. She cried: "Is there anyone here who understands English and can help me!" Hers was an American accent, I immediately recognized and realized she had been until then speaking French to the excitable middle-aged woman, whom I knew, who was berating her with a rapid fire stream of slang-filled *argot* difficult for even me understand.

My English, which I had studied in the Limoges Lycée, practiced with Jean-Luc (who was fluent) and continued learning through private lessons in Paris, wasn't perfect but would do in this crisis.

So I intervened.

"What is your trouble, Miss?" I said as soon as I went over to the squabbling pair. I saw that part of the *américaine's* embarrassment was that all eyes of those seated in the vicinity were now on her and I also noted, all the other chairs around were taken.

"She doesn't understand my French," this not-unattractive young woman with bright brown eyes told me. "I tried to explain. This is my seat. I got to it first. She seems to want to take it away from me. But she doesn't listen and I can barely understand a word she's yelling."

In a soothing voice, I said in her language: "It is a simple misunderstanding." In French, I told the older female to pipe down, I would straighten matters out. Then, back to English, I informed the young American: "This lady is a war widow. She doesn't want your chair. She simply wants you to pay a fee for its use. That's her livelihood."

"Oh . . ." said the now blushing foreigner. "I didn't know."

"It's only a few francs," I said.

But instead of the relief I expected to see on her face, I saw her look even more chagrined. "Oh my gosh!" she exclaimed. "I left my purse at the place I'm staying. I don't have . . . how do you say in French . . . a *sou* with me."

Like Sir Galahad to the rescue, I reached into my pocket. "No problem. If you permit," I said to her, "I will . . . as you say in America . . . *lend* you."

And actually before she could speak, I had retrieved several coins and handed them to her antagonist, who smiled, sort of curtsied and continued on her rounds.

"Welcome to France," Naansee said, beaming. "And they say you people are not nice."

"We always try to be of help," I answered, in English.

Whereupon she started speaking to me in a French I would call "passable," now that she had recovered her composure. *Naturellement,* she had to repay me. If I would save her seat, she would run to the room she was renting not far away on the Boulevard Saint-Michel and return with her purse.

"Not necessary," I said in French and we continued our discussion in that language.

Here on the cusp of a budding Parisian romance, the opportunity is ripe for a more exact physical description of the lady who was about to enter my life. Her hair color, to start with. I've always thought of her as a brunette. Brown, a seriously dark cocoa hue, worn shoulder length, lustrous and straight, no curls. The eyes, already certified as "brown," were sparkling and, except when agitated, remarkably friendly. She appeared—the Americans would say—"wholesome" . . . "corn-fed" . . . "Midwestern" . . . no great beauty, good figure, though, leggy, and showing none of the sophisticated, calculating femme fatale parisienne. She was wearing a horizon blue (my favorite color) straight skirt and a non-frilly white blouse, no silk stockings, those bare lower limbs of hers ending in white "bobby sox" and the shoes known as "loafers." She wasn't in any measure overtly sexy, yet seemed desirable possibly due to her air of innocence. In time, I learned from her what a "cheerleader" was. She had been one at Ohio State University.

Since I would find it difficult to "save" her seat and keep mine simultaneously, I suggested we both go back to our reading and when she was ready to return to her quarters, I would accompany her to the "Boul Mich" and she could reimburse me, since she insisted. She laughed, told me she was delighted to learn a new French expression "Bull Mitch" and agreed to the arrangement.

Once she had re-seated herself, I asked her the title of the book she was reading. "*Le Grand Meaulnes*," she told me.

"You're reading it in French," I noted.

"It was assigned in class," she said. "It's wonderful."

"Every French schoolboy knows about *Big* Meaulnes. It's a classic." With a kind of sly grin, I uttered: "Obviously, girls read it, too."

"You're cute," she said in her native tongue.

I had no response ready for a common bit of mostly feminine American slang I'd heard in the movies, but took it as a compliment. Thus I felt buoyed once the two of us dispersed to our sitting arrangements on the opposite sides of the walking path and went back to the printed word. It might have been an hour or more that we kept up such diligence. Occasionally I caught her surreptitiously gazing in my direction. Once, when our glances met, she looked demurely down at her feet. I thought that was "cute," too.

Finally, my eyes still on a page of Chateaubriand's, I was aware she had approached.

"If you're ready . . . ?"

I didn't exactly jump right up, but nodded, folded a corner of the page I was on, shut the tome and popped it into a briefcase I'd brought.

"What *were* you reading?" Naansee asked me.

This wasn't just small talk, I sensed. She seemed sincerely interested.

"En route, I will tell you. *C'est un récit un peu compliqué.*"

Her rented room, which she not quite correctly referred to as her "pied-à-terre," was reached by leaving the Luxembourg through the main entrance and exiting onto the Boul Mich, crossing to the other side of the Boulevard and proceeding uphill toward the Boulevard Montparnasse. In a fairly run-down section, a drab courtyard opened, containing half a dozen three story tenement buildings. Naansee's was in the middle of the semi-circle.

We had meanwhile engaged in an animated conversation. As promised, I revealed that the "complicated" matter was explaining who Chateaubriand was, the author whose adventures in America in 1791 I was reading about."

Once I'd finished, Naansee said cheerily: "And I thought a Chateaubriand was a steak."

I enlightened her: "It was the vicomte's favorite cut of beef, so much so the chefs of that era honored the piece of meat with his surname."

Once this bit of trivia led to my recital of Chateaubriand's other accomplishments in France, I hurried on to his three-year stay in her newly formed country and the meeting in Philadelphia with President George Washington, which some critics have deemed apocryphal—i.e., a fiction made up by the Frenchman. Yet it appeared indisputable he had been in the Pennsylvania city that served as the first U.S. capital.

I quoted words of his I had underlined reading him today, as I always did whenever struck by something on the page, in this case: "The Quaker girls with their grey dresses, the uniform little bonnets and their pale faces, looked lovely." Also, furthering the American theme, I underscored Chateaubriand's decease on the Fourth of July, her national holiday."

"My goodness," Naansee said. "Tomorrow."

We had introduced ourselves before departing the Luxembourg, so as we ascended the Boul Mich we were already using Eugène (pronounced *Oohjen*) and Nancy (Naansee) but when I suggested we *tutoyer* each other, the American balked. Not for any love of formality but simply because it was easier for her to conjugate verbs by employing *vous* rather than *tu*.

"Ah, I should like to teach you," I blurted without realizing how familiar I was being.

"Well, Lafayette, we are here," she joked, stopping in front of one of the decrepit unpainted structures in the courtyard. "Although I'm afraid you'll have to wait outside. My concierge is very strict, the witch. No gentlemen in my *chambre*. I call her Madame Defarge."

"So, you are truly literary. You have read Dickens' grand story of our Revolution."

"Yes, and various writings, yours and ours, about breaking away from kings."

"Amazing!"

After this last exchange, Naansee left me and in the brief interlude she was away, I stood deep in thought, pondering whether I had the courage to ask if I could see her again.

I hadn't reached a decision before she reappeared in the courtyard, waving her purse to show me she had it. In a matter of seconds, she handed me the tiny sum I'd expended.

I thanked her, pocketed the small change and still hesitated saying anything more.

Instead, Naansee took the lead, not really brazenly but with shy charm, stating in English: "I hope you don't think I'm being forward. But you know, since I've been in Paris, except for my teachers, I've only been with Americans. I've so enjoyed talking to you and speaking French." Then in French, she asked me: "Do you think we could meet again soon?"

This was my opportunity and knew I must act immediately. "Tonight!" I fairly shouted. "Could we not have dinner together?"

"Lovely," she said. "Where?"

"Within walking distance for both of us," I said, "is the famed brasserie La Rotonde. The food is good, the atmosphere *très parisien* and the prices reasonable."

"La Rotonde. It's famous. I've been dying to go there."

"I could pick you up here."

"No, I'll meet you there." She gestured toward her domicile.

"Ah, Madame Defarge."

After a joint laugh, we picked a time and finished our conversation in which two new additions were made to my English vocabulary. "It's a date then?" Naansee said and my puzzlement showed. A *date*, I knew, was a type of fruit from a palm tree—and also the timing of something like a certain year or date. Neither of these meanings made sense in the context of her words to me.

Sensing my confusion, she translated: "Rendezvous."

"*Bon, je comprends.*"

But the next moment, she came right back with a second puzzler by adding: "And we'll go Dutch."

My brow most assuredly wrinkled.

Her explanation quickly cleared the air. She had used an American slang expression for each of us paying his or her own way. Where the phrase had originated, she didn't know. From the Netherlands perhaps, or maybe Germany, a play on their term for themselves, *Deutsch*. In Pennsylvania, where Philadelphia was, there were the so-called Pennsylvania Dutch, who were actually Germans.

On that note, we parted, having set the time to meet at the Carrefour Montparnasse-Raspail.

I walked back through the Luxembourg to the Rue Duguay-Trouin. Racing through my mind, obliterating the scenes I used to enjoy stopping to observe—the ornate Palais de Luxembourg now home to the French Senate with its gendarmes on guard, *les gosses*—the nicely dressed little boys and girls sailing their model boats on the pond, the rows of readers and other adults seated under the plane trees as I had been—it seemed— in a whole different world from less than an hour ago.

All I could concentrate on, repeating over and over again silently: *I have a date, I have a date, I have a date . . . à six heures, à six heures, à six heures . . .* until I could genuinely believe what had happened really had happened.

XXI

The hour Naansee had chosen for us to dine—six p.m.—was a bit early for French tastes, although as a brasserie as well as a restaurant La Rotonde served food and drink at all hours. I have to say that Naansee, all dressed up, was very much an alluring young woman, much more so than the bobby-soxer I'd encountered in the park.

That she wore a shade of maroon red in a rather tight-fitting silk outfit was, I decided, not to entice me but merely a tribute to our evening's surroundings. No doubt she had peered into La Rotonde's interior and seen its overwhelming décor was a dark carmine, with which her dress would neatly blend. More likely, I was fantasizing, figuring it was probably the only dressy piece of clothing she had brought with her to Europe.

As for myself, I had on my only summer suit—a blue garbadine, with a white dress shirt and red tie—like a walking *tricolor*—plus the affectation of the ribbon in my lapel of the Médaille de la Résistance.

La Rotonde was known for its amiable waiters and lack of "snob," although people flocked there to see movie stars and in the past notable painters like Matisse who had often paid for their meals with paintings before they gained fame. Naansee and I were given a corner table as if it were automatically assumed we wanted to be quietly and romantically by ourselves.

It also didn't hurt for the superb service we received that I was wearing my badge of bravery for fighting the Germans. Paris was chock-a-block with plaques on buildings, particularly in our *quartier* commemorating those fallen in the liberation of Paris. Bullet holes were still everywhere. But my wartime experiences were not what Naansee and I talked about.

I had brought with me a manila folder in which sheets of paper were visible. There was an air of mystery about it and when I saw her eyes wandering in its direction, I told her I would explain but we should order first. Then, we drew up a pact between ourselves—in order for us to learn linguistically from each other, we would speak in French for fifteen minutes and switch to English for fifteen minutes and so on.

"Does that include ordering from the menu?" she asked prettily in English.

"If you wish," I answered in her tongue.

"But do we subtract that from the fifteen minutes?"

"*Bien sûr.*"

"*Eh bien, qu'est ce que sont les rognons?*"

"Kidneys," I answered.

"See, keeping score is not going to be easy," she said.

And we both burst out laughing.

I do know she didn't order kidneys and my overall memory of the meal was our jollity and her reaction to my mystery *cadeau*, if that is the right word—gift—for the typed sheets I eventually gave her.

They were excerpts from Chateaubriand's memoirs relating to America.

Heading those pages I'd prepared for her was the famed writer's initial experience on American soil—as follows:

Walked toward a house . . . Black people were sawing timber, whites were tending tobacco plants. A Negress, thirteen or fourteen years old, almost naked and singularly beautiful, opened the gate of the enclosure for us like a young Night (sic)—We bought some maize cakes, chickens, eggs and milk, and returned with our baskets and demijohns. I gave my silk handkerchief to the little African girl; it was a slave who welcomed me to the land of liberty.

There in Philadelphia liberty took on a different meaning.

A boarding house where San Domingo planters and Frenchmen who had emigrated [from a slave rebellion] . . . lodged. A land of liberty offered asylum to those fleeing from liberty; nothing proves the high worth of generous institutions more than this voluntary exile of the supporters of absolute power to a pure democracy.

The disputed interview of Chateaubriand and George Washington in Philadelphia was also introduced by me. It occurred in Book VII:

After a few minutes, the general entered: tall in stature, with a calm cool air rather than one of nobility, he looked like his portrait.

Chateaubriand gave him a letter of introduction from the Marquis de la Rouenne and Washington exclaimed: "Colonel Armand!" It was the nom de guerre used by that French participant in the Americans' fight against the British. The American president also seemed astonished when Chateaubriand told him his plan of travel in the New World was to seek the Northwest Passage to the Orient. The young Frenchman's gracious reply was: "But it is less difficult to discover the Northwest Passage than to create a nation as you have done."

Invited to dinner by Washington, the two discussed the French Revolution and the traveler was shown a key to the Bastille given to the Father of my dinner companion's country.

A surprise from Naansee awaited me when I switched to the novel *Natchez*. I had introduced the section with a quote from an English travel writer grumpily describing in 1788 the American Midwest, to wit: "the country has a savage aspect, husbandry not much further advanced at least in skill, than among the Hurons."

"The Hurons! We had them in Ohio!" my new American friend exclaimed. "Fort Huron has the oldest summer theater in the state, I worked there for three years!"

I briefly put down the papers I was reading to her and asked: "Were you an actress?"

"I had small parts," she said, "I built sets and ushered. I really like the stage."

"There are groups here in Paris," I told her. "*Amateurs*. I could contact some for you."

"Wow!"

She was smiling from ear to ear. This was the first time I had heard the American slang expression *Wow*.

But she quickly brought me back to the Chateaubriand material I'd been going over once our dishes had been cleared and we were sipping cognacs. There were more "Wows" when I showed her mentions of the French nobleman's descent of the Ohio River and especially his quote of how he'd "approached the European clearings near Chillicoth."

"Wow! Oh, my God. Chillicoth is just down the road from Lancaster!"

"I guessed right. Chillicoth is in Ohio."

"You are very well read," she said admiringly.

I pretty much skipped over *Natchez*, since it's a pretty gloomy story and based on a real-life actual massacre when the Natchez Indians wiped out a colony of French settlers in Louisiana. Also, raising the subject of a massacre was not something I wanted to do with her.

However, we did discuss both eighteenth-century Revolutions, the American and the French. The differing aftermaths of each, I illustrated to Naansee, was aptly summarized by Chateaubriand's aphorisms:

Washington's Republic lives on. Bonaparte's Empire is destroyed.

A financial bill passed in the English Parliament in 1765, engendered a new power in the world in 1782 and caused the disappearance of the oldest kingdom of Europe in 1789.

When we seemingly had exhausted this subject, I handed her the folder to keep and she not only effusively thanked me for being so thoughtful and interesting and gone to such trouble but impulsively came right over and kissed me on the cheek.

After our evening in the restaurant ended, I walked Naansee back to the Boule Mich and into the grubby courtyard. Looking at the shabby dwellings, I couldn't help but comment she had taken quite a risk by leaving her purse in such a place, although she assured me she had most of her money in a safety deposit box at the American Express Office, and with the witch concierge on guard, no suspicious characters would be admitted. Besides, her door was locked and she showed me the key.

From that moment on, our conversation took a surprising turn. She did start to complain about her choice of habitation. The place was dirty and dingy enough but the worst part was the bathroom—in the hall, and no toilet to sit on—only a hole in the floor and two foot places for your feet on either side.

In fact, her week's rent was up the next day and she had planned on leaving.

"Where to?" I asked her.

"Do you have any suggestions?" she replied, rather coquettishly, I thought.

Surprised by my own boldness, I told her: "I have room."

Following my remark, I could hardly believe our next exchange. Even more rashly, I added: "Of course, it has only one bed."

"All the better."

We gazed at each other and, spontaneously, joined in a passionate kiss.

The arrangements were simple. At a certain hour the next day, I would pick her up in my car with her luggage at the courtyard. Our "alliance" was consummated that very same afternoon in the sole bedroom, and bed, of our "pad," as Naansee took to calling my Duguay-Trouin bachelor *apartement*. The complacent, fat husband of our concierge who bore the slightly comic—to the two of us—name of Gaston, helped settle her in—at any rate to the extent of holding doors open as we carried the *américaine*'s things up to the second floor. On the other hand, the wicked witch of the Boule Mich made a noisy fuss about Naansee's leaving, since she was also the *patronne*, the owner of the building and saw a financial loss in the sudden vacancy although she rented out rooms by the week and everything was paid up. A *pourboire* I provided of a handful of francs finally shut off her shrieks of protest and as Naansee was to put it, we were "out of there"—forever.

Since the incessant profusion of ever-increasingly vivid and kinky sex scenes in modern day literature has become, at least to me, a bore, I will forebear including any detailed description of our so-to-speak mutually agreed "wedding night" the same afternoon in broad daylight with the shades drawn. Personally I have always found a half-clothed female more sexually stimulating than a fully naked one with pubic hair showing.

No doubt this *pudeur* of mine can be deemed a cultural throwback to my Vendéen ancestry and Catholic upbringing. In the words of a countrywoman of mine encountered years later whom I briefly "messed with" at a Club Med in French Polynesia, I really was one of the "constipated Frenchmen" she herself rallied against while parading topless and sometimes bottomless as well on the lovely tropical beach we vacationers shared.

For the nonce, then, the "honeymoon" Naansee and I enjoyed upon the heels of our "discovery" of each other, lasted in its most torrid manifestations for approximately the next six months. This is not to say the romance of our relationship burnt out abruptly. Its physical side remained, only not so frequently as before. But the *lovers in Paris* aspect continued indefinitely throughout our first year together.

And not just in Paris.

The solitary pilgrimage I had set in motion for myself during the *quinze d'août* to the scenic seaside part of Brittany dubbed the Emerald Coast easily morphed into a duo of hand-holding smitten *amoureux* wandering as we had along the Seine, but atop the ramparts of Saint-Malo or among the oyster shacks of Cancale. Not only did we gorge on delicious *fruits de mer* but also on memories of Chateaubriand, visiting his solemn tomb on the Île du Grand Bé from which we escaped giggling back to the mainland a few steps ahead of the incoming tide and subsequently also visited the author and diplomat's childhood home of the Château de Combourg, fifty kilometers to the south. We read aloud to each other from the earliest books of his *Mémoires d'outre-tombe*, providing a French lesson for Naansee and one of historical biography for me. Saint-Malo, itself, proved instructive, especially its reconstruction from the ravages of a devastating firestorm during World War II, which on a broad scale was an example of exacting good restoration taste unfortunately not applied by the bureaucrats building New Charniers. Nor was Chateaubriand the only personality of interest in Saint-Malo. Jacques Cartier, native-born, whose statue in the Breton city shows him at the helm of his sixteenth-century ship en route to Canada, had piqued my fancy and reinforced a theme of France overseas for my life's work academically. Plus I also discovered my Admiral Duguay-Trouin to have been a Malouian corsair in the eighteenth century and an important contributor to the French empire. As for nearby Cancale, its unequaled *huîtres sauvages* eaten raw by the dozens in a gustatory frenzy were not necessary to arouse the virility of Nancy Jane Henderson and Eugène Marie Desfosseux, who in these beginning months of our courtship were continually in rut.

Naansee was quite Americanly cute about the first time we had to register at a hotel together (in Saint-Malo), and she needed to hand over her passport and me my *carte d'identité*. We were sharing a room yet obviously not married . . . something that would have been shocking and "just not done" in mid-twentieth-century Ohio.

By then—August 1950—bits and pieces of our individual autobiographies were being revealed during the hours upon hours we spent together. I learned about a "Winesburg, Ohio" type of upbringing in the middle of the Midwest and about the Buckeyes of Ohio State University and that a *buck-eye*—literally the eye of a male deer—was actually a type of tree—and she learned about the Resistance and the FTP and the FFI and, inevitably, learned from me the tragic fate of my native hearth. We also, I remember, compared hunting in our respective countries: her Dad had taken her with her older brother after those male Ohio deer on cold autumn days while my papa had included me along with his cronies and their dogs going after monstrous and dangerous wild boars. I had called these lumbering beasts *sangliers* but when we had a delicious meal of a young one in a Breton restaurant I had to explain we called this more chewable pig meat *marcassin* and the word was immediately jotted into Naansee's notebook of freshly learned French vocabulary.

Also around the winter holiday season (and school vacation time) we journeyed to Charniers-sur-Nys.

It was at Naansee's insistence she went with me. I needed to go at the behest of Octave Bois; some special meeting of the Association of Families required my presence. By now my darling knew the whole tragic story . . . Jean-Luc, Chantal, Lucien Veynachter, Papa, Paul the Gaul, Octave, were familiar figures to her, but it was as if from a work of fiction. Seeing with her own eyes *in situ* would add an entirely different dimension. She had seen news photos of the ruins, had read descriptions of the massacre, discussions of the moral and legal issues involved, but it was all still abstract; the only touch of reality was the night I cried out in my sleep and awoke shivering . . . shaken by a dream I can only remember as horrific, connected to the atrocity, but not its hideous content. Her arms around me in the darkness were also a sense rather than a vision— in this case a feeling of comfort they afforded me.

Was it possible to regard Naansee as the stronger of the two of us in conjunction with the most serious of our trips? One could argue she had no idea of what she would see while I had all too emotional a knowledge. I tried to stick to platitudes in discussing the macabre adventure projected for several months ahead.

"You know it's going to be cold on the Massif Central in December," I started off one conversation. I honestly wasn't trying to discourage her from joining me, only preparing her.

"Have you ever been to Ohio in the winter?" she shot back saucily.

"There might be snow," I rejoined.

"In Ohio, even in southern Ohio, we would always have loads of it on top of ice." Her gestures were to feign freezing and indicate how high from the floor the drifts might be.

"You will require warm clothing?"

"I always take long underwear with me wherever I go."

Thus light-heartedly, we jockeyed.

Besides, there was no cause to discuss my nightmares (there were to be several of them) In the same breath, I could see she was looking forward to staying with Octave Bois and family. She did not keep secret she had begun to miss her own clan in Lancaster and particularly more so as we advanced toward the end of December and the New Year. My friend and mentor Octave had moved out of New Charniers, having bought the old Sirois farmstead from the murdered couple's sons. Octave's brood included sons who would farm it themselves and the spacious home the Nazis inexplicably had left intact was more suited than an apartment to the renovations necessary because of his handicap. The cozy time we'd all spend together, I was sure, could recompense Naansee from being away from her folks this year.

Meanwhile, in the autumn months, we took "excursions"—a weekend now and then, sometimes a long weekend—in and around Paris like tours of Versailles and Fontainebleau and places in the city even I hadn't been to like the Arènes de Lutèce for a concert or the Lapin Agile nightclub in Montmartre to hear Francis Carco, the biographer of François Villon, recite his own poetry. On one occasion, we travelled to Switzerland and through La Haute-Savoie to Chamonix and its alpine mountains as well as to famous French spas on Lake Geneva at Evian and Thonon.

Those months after the trip to Brittany also witnessed the start of another facet of our lives together—our entry as a couple, you might say, into a social grouping. On a superficial scale, it could be seen as an *expatriate* crowd—Americans in Paris who met in various favorite cafés. But there was one subset that attracted Naansee beyond simply being with a bunch of homesick Yanks reminiscing about the good ol' USA. Naansee had told me of her experiences in an Ohio summer theater. Likewise, she had shared tales of her acting in high school and college. It was an activity appealing to me as well. Not that I'd indulged in it in the Limousin, but I had been told I had a talent for mimicry.

I have mentioned our visit to Versailles but not how we soon left the sprawling elaborate main royal palace and ventured to the much simpler Petit Trianon, built originally by King Louis XV for his mistress Madame Pompadour and given eventually to Marie Antoinette. The private theater where this ill-fated queen staged and acted in amateur productions immediately had caught Naansee's fancy.

Finding likeminded stage buffs among our ex-pat friends, plus a number of French non-professional actors, actresses, directors, etc. who were bilingual, a company was formed to put on two dramas in rented space before Christmas. One was an original play about Marie Antoinette we all agreed to do in French; the other—what else?—was Charles Dickens' classic *A Christmas Carol*, which we would perform in English.

Can you imagine? Eugène Desfosseux's first acting chore was to play the role of Bob Cratchit! And Naansee's major lead was to enact Marie Antoinette and entirely in French!

We called ourselves "The Petit Trianon Players." It was simply a fun effort and we even found a few "angels" among the émigrés to help with the finances, as I did myself.

If I told you each of these productions was not exactly a "hit show"—

un succès fous—I'm sure you would not swoon from surprise. We hammed them up, not always sticking to the lines, and straining for laughs when we thought we could get some. The adventures of the doomed queen were more or less woven into a French farce, and in fact an American was introduced, based on a true story figure, a handsome sea captain from the coast of Maine who was going to whisk her away in safety across the ocean to a Royalist refuge in Pennsylvania. However, the proud and silly lady dillied and dallied so long while on the run after her escape from the Revolutionaries that she was recaptured. Poor Captain Clough had to leave Le Havre hurriedly with only her furniture and her cats.

In *A Christmas Carol*, we tried to play Dickens' moralistic tale straight but some of our seriousness vanished before a seemingly insuperable problem that suddenly arose. The only English-speaking lad we could obtain to do Tiny Tim came down with "German" measles at the last moment. To replace him, we could have had an adorable little French boy except his English pronunciation even when coached was incomprehensible. Consequently, here's where I came in. Believe it or not, because Naansee had listened to me throw my voice, we rigged out what today would be called a lip-syncing act. Darling *p'tit* Georges would just mouth words and. standing a short distance away, (after all, I was his father in the script) I would project them from him through my clenched teeth. Thus we could adhere to the author's' immortal ending when the diminutive cripple cries out triumphantly in English: "God bless us everyone!"

Subsequent usage of my voice-throwing talent was to develop exponentially and attain the current acme of the sophisticated astral interviews I've been recently inventing.

It was a chilly enough, grey enough, late-November Parisian day when quite mysteriously I led Naansee from our quarters through the Saint-Germain-des-Prés area to the Rue des Saint-Pères, a long street that runs perpendicularly down to the embankment of the Seine in the vicinity of the Pont du Carrousel.

"Where are you taking me?" she asked several times.

But I cautioned silence. "Shhh—I have a surprise for you," and promptly ignored all other seductive little girl attempts to pry out of me any hints.

Ultimately, moving past the University of Paris-Descartes Biomedical school, we reached a short street parallel to the river, a block or two before the Quai Voltaire and the picturesque book stalls that line the Left Bank.

"You're buying me a book?" Naansee said or rather asked.

"Shhh—" My right forefinger went to my closed lips.

"Okay, you're buying me a print?"

As secretive as ever, I answered cryptically: "No, I'm gifting you a whole country."

The short side street was the Rue Jacob. We turned right onto it. Then, a few buildings in, I stopped in front of number fifty-six.

"Voilà!" I said to Naansee. "Here it is."

On a fairly non-descript, solidly built, five-story stone-façaded building was a wall plaque. Its weather-beaten surface and the fairly archaic lettering style chiseled into it seemingly indicated it had been attached for considerable time. In French, the words declared:

EN CE BÂTIMENT
JADIS HÔTEL D'YORK
LE 3 SEPTEMBRE 1783
DAVID HARTLEY,
AU NOM DU ROI D'ANGLETERRE,
BENJAMIN FRANKLIN,
JOHN JAY, JOHN ADAMS,
AU NOM DES ÉTATS-UNIS D'AMÉRIQUE,
ONT SIGNÉ LE TRAITÉ DÉFINITIF DE PAIX
RECONNAISSANT L'INDÉPENDENCE
DES ÉTATS-UNIS.

In this building, formerly Hôtel D'York, on September 3, 1783, David Hartley in the name of the King of England, Benjamin Franklin, John Jay, John Adams, in the name of the United States of America, signed the definitive treaty recognizing the independence of the United States.

"Here your beloved country was born, ma belle Buckeye," I told Nancy Jane Henderson of Lancaster, Ohio.

She was deeply moved, could not take her eyes off the inscription and ended by giving me a most appreciative and prolonged hug.

But an entirely different heartfelt reaction was my reward for another surprise I sprung on her when a bunch of the "gang" was seated in a bistro having aperitifs. I had continued my studies on early French settlement and exploration in North America and an incident I'd come across had really "tickled my funny bone," to use Naansee's expression.

The name La Salle, if it meant anything at all to the Americans present, was that of an automobile brand from the immediate past. To the French at the table, La Salle referred to a seventeenth-century Gallic explorer who "discovered" the Great Lakes and the Mississippi River in the heartland of the future USA." No doubt to focus Naansee's attention, I also described René-Robert Cavalier, Sieur de La Salle as the Frenchman who learned the Ohio River flowed into the Mississippi and could be followed more than one thousand miles to Louisiana and the Gulf of Mexico.

"La Salle had gained this bit of geographic knowledge from a Mohawk chieftain," I informed my audience. They listened but I felt were impatient for me to get to my punch line.

"And he gave Michigan its title," I went on to state, as if it were the final thrust of the monologue I was delivering.

"Michigan—boo," replied Nancy Jane Henderson, Ohioan. "The Wolverines—boo!"

I continued, seeming not to have heard Naansee's burst of Buckeye chauvinism. "Thus Michigan joined other permanent indigenous names on the American map. Yes. La Salle had been in a canoe on one of the Great Lakes with a scouting party of Abenaki tribesmen from New England. 'What is that country we now see yonder?' he had asked his companions, indicating to a mass of prominent highlands in the distance.

"'Michigan', his Algonquian-speaking escorts shouted in unison."

"So what?" Naansee questioned me. "You already told us that."

"Only afterward, once the name Michigan had stuck, did the explorer discover its meaning in the Abenaki language."

"And that is?" someone else at the table piped up.

"We French would translate it as *Merde*. In other words, the home of Ohio State's chief football rival is Shitland."

Mercifully, no *Michiganders* were in our company. Loud laughter rippled out after a moment. "I knew it! I always knew it!" Naansee shrieked. Forever after, the mere mention of her enemy state would draw a stream of giggles, if not full-throated guffaws.

This happened more than several times during out eventual drive to the Limousin. Without warning, I would shout out: "Michigan!" and Naansee would roar, doubling over, crying: "Oh, that's still so funny . . . so funny . . ." and finally, "Oh, stop, my belly hurts from laughing."

It was an auspicious entry into my poor ruined village.

You can be sure I made no attempt to convulse her in public during the days we spent *chez* Octave Bois in Charniers-sur-Nys. True, the extended Bois family would gather each evening in the living room and many a humorous story would be told. But to explain the University of Michigan and Ohio State and their fierce sports rivalry or how American football was played seemed altogether too *compliqué*. Some of these good folks might recognize La Salle as a French historic figure and beyond doubt all of them recognized the word *merde*, but the Mississippi and Abenakis and Mohawk—it was just *peau-rouge* stuff from long ago.

Among the old folks present in the *salle familiale* were a few aged couples who spoke to each other in Limousin Occitane—the Provençale tongue of ancient southern France. Naansee, whose ability in French was universally applauded, found herself, as a linguistic major, fascinated, and she charmed these septuagenarians and octogenarians by asking them to teach her elements of this not-quite-yet-dead language. She also endeared herself to all the family members one of whose grandsons was retarded in showing her sensitivity to *Le Petit Jop* (how he pronounced his full prénom of Joseph) and her success in bonding with the boy.

Here a more generic footnote applies to the celebration of Christmas and New Year's in rural France, which differs from this holiday week in the fifty states. In France, it does not universally occur on December 25th. In some regions, the date of December 6th, the birthday of Saint Nicholas, is used for gift-giving. Decorated Christmas trees were a rarity. The latter avoidance became particularly prevalent in the Limousin following World War II since it was Alsatian refugees who'd brought their custom to us by introducing balsam firs and other evergreens. At the time, the still pending trial of the Alsatian SS draftees who'd participated in the massacre had made the innovation taboo among us.

Furthermore, Octave's summons to me wasn't simply for the purpose of offering Yuletide cheer. The Association's executives needed to discuss the *war crimes* situation.

We did this at a lengthy closed meeting in a back room of the barn on the former farm property of the martyred Sirois patriarch and matriarch.

According to Octave, the private space where we gathered had been the domain of Père Sirois who, when he wanted to smoke his foul-smelling Gitane cigarettes, would go into exile to indulge his habit so as not to "stink up his wife's house," as this kindly peasant gentleman articulated it. Also, he kept bottles of his homemade *marc* brandy tucked away inside. Mère Sirois did not like him drinking in the house, either. She was a devout Catholic yet tolerant of her husband's habits as long as she didn't have them happening around her. With a twinkle in his eye, Octave also revealed to me one habit they'd discovered had been kept from the sweet lady by the *le vieux* Sirois—naughty pictures he kept locked away in a safe, where he also kept his money in cash. Like many of his neighbors, Maurice Sirois did not care for banks.

That same safe now contained the confidential papers of the National Association of Families of the Martyrs of Charniers-sur-Nys. Octave had opened it to show me. He'd made a hideaway for himself in which to do secret work and a conference room where the executive group could hold discreet meetings. The Paris government had supplied us with an official office in New Charniers in which our public *affaires* were carried out.

Amid faint odors of hay and manures, the following executive committee members met on that December morning: Octave Bois, president; Eugène Desfosseux, vice-president and Paris liaison; Marius Phillipon, treasurer; Roger Phillipon, secretary; Paul Vercingetorix Paul, member; Herve Malinvaud, grandson of the survivor Marie Malinvaud, member; Victor Proulx, member; Charles Leveau, member; and the mayor, my second cousin Jean-Martin Jalouneix.

Octave's opening remarks set the stage for our discussion. I took notes for myself and Roger Phillipon kept the minutes, or usually did. In this case, Octave said he wanted nothing on record, although we could keep memos for ourselves provided at the end we handed them to him for safe keeping. As I write now, the dialogue I produce is from memory.

Our leader started off by bringing up the name of Waffen SS Brigade General Heinrich "Heinz" Lammerding—commander of the Division Das Reich.

"That bastard," replied Roger Phillipon, who was a hothead and the soon-to-be acknowledged chief clan leader of the largest extended family in Charniers.

Said Octave: "We have received word that General Lammerding has been released from prison by the British in their zone of occupied Germany and has returned to Dusseldorf a free man to take up his prewar engineering career."

I will not reproduce the various explosions of outrage around the conference table. We all held this Lammerding as the criminal most responsible not only for the Charniers atrocity but murders of innocent civilians in the regions such as the hangings of hostages selected randomly at nearby Tulle.

Our angry chatter eventually boiled down to: "What do we do about it?"

And that line of thought, itself, boiled down to: "Shoot the bastard," expressed by Roger Phillipon.

"Are you volunteering?" Paul the Gaul confronted him.

However, my FTP commander already knew the answer. Much as he would like to pull the trigger on that bastard Lammerding, Roger assured us, he had a growing family to consider, and a business he had only recently gotten off the ground.

Octave said: "We already have an address for Lammerding in Dusseldorf, even a phone number. And we now understand Herr General will never be extradited to stand trial in France with the lesser defendants, whenever that takes place." Turning to me, he added: "Eugène, you've expressed to me your interest in the Ukrainian general buried in the Montparnasse cemetery, shot down in Paris in the 1920s by a Jew whose parents were killed in a pogrom he had incited. Do we not have a similar situation? The revenge taker was acquitted, was he not?"

I was most uncomfortable, feeling all their hopeful eyes on me. These other guys were uniformly family men, open to the same excuse employed by even a fire-eater like Roger Phillipon. Octave literally made it harder for me to refuse the justifiable assassin's assignment by referencing my Luger pistol, which he had kept for me when I'd gone to the city. Indeed, he kept it in the safe toward which he now pointed, saying: "I've maintained your captured Boche officer's weapon in perfect firing shape, oiled and loaded, ready to fire. What more suitable use than to take down the Boche murderer Lammerding than with a Boche gun."

"I can't," I protested. "I really cannot . . ." Knowing I would have to offer a reason, I cited Naansee whom everyone of them had met. I left unsaid the intimations they might reach: we were to be married; maybe that she was pregnant.

Since no one did anything but acquiesce by silence, Roger in a disgusted tone finally said: "We should contact Mario Cioffi. He's in Marseilles. He must know some types for hire in this sort of thing."

But Paul the Gaul who'd been relatively quiet until that moment broke in: "Nothing doing. No dishonoring ourselves."

At a standstill, it seemed, I offered a face-saving compromise. "Let me contact Hippolyte. Use his influence to demand our government push the West Germans to extradite Lammerding to France and stand trial. Make an international fuss if they don't."

To this suggestion, there was general agreement except for Roger who groused a while longer until finally, reluctantly, concurring. And thus our "emergency" meeting ended.

The rest of our visit to Charniers followed an expected pattern. Naansee continued to ingratiate herself. Protestant though she was (a

Methodist), she accompanied us to Midnight Mass in the New Charniers Catholic church, wowed a Christmas dinner of family and friends with a cheerleader routine—twirling a baton, doing acrobatics and leading a cheer she devised from Octave's last name of *"Bois, bois, deux fois bois, Octave Octave Bois Bois Bois,"* getting everyone to join the chorus honoring our host. She had worked up a skit with little Jop, the two of them in duet singing French Christmas carols, a feat hitherto considered impossible for the retarded lad. At *réveillons*—New Year's—she was joining the rest of us as lustily and tearfully, in the Gallic rendition of Auld Lang Syne— *Ce n'est-qu'un au revoir*, which four years earlier we had so poignantly employed in saying good-bye to our martyred loved ones.

My actress *sweetie*, (quite possibly in the near future to be my fiancée, I thought), certainly had scored a huge hit!

XXII

No, I am not a widower. The perceived nuptials never took place. *No use crying over spilled milk* (another of Naansee's homespun sayings). I blame myself more than anything. In an age where "arranged marriages" have long been out of style, except in certain Third World countries, it's the tradition a man does the asking. I never actually did—not directly. And finally, when I awoke to the fact, it was already too late.

Until 1954, when our destinies diverged, we were not unlike a married couple. No children. Our interests in this matter were unspoken but our precautions never ceased. What did flag our lust, an inevitable phenomenon, I understand, was passage of time and familiarity.

Albert Camus' cynical epitaph for modern man: "He fornicated and read the newspapers," an idea which always made me smirk and repeat silently, but no less cynically, to myself: *At any rate, I'm still reading* Le Monde.

But Camus, in his existential despair, was wrong. Speaking for myself, I was involved in far more than his two prescribed activities. Partly, this was in tandem with Naansee. We travelled a lot, again going in Europe beyond France: to Italy, Spain, Portugal, Ireland, Great Britain, Scandinavia . . . It was the time of the Cold War or else we would have definitely visited Czechoslovakia and Hungary. As it was, we ventured from Trieste into Tito's Yugoslavia for a couple of days, visiting beautiful Slovenia and the enchanting northern Croatian coast.

When at home in Paris, we were both plunged into our studies. Yet even more so almost, we indulged our taste for participating in amateur theatricals. I even had my own one-man act. I did "gigs" as Naansee dubbed them, solo performances as a ventriloquist. The American entertainers Edgar Bergen and Charlie McCarthy were still in their heyday. To be sure, McCarthy was made of wood, sat on Bergen's lap and had his movable wise-guy jaw manipulated by a hand hidden behind his back. I, on the contrary, did not go in for faux realism. My dummy, who started out as pure fantasy, was to be constructed as bigger than me and I was to act the dummy. His official title was The Good Cro-Maritan. Mine was MM, Modern Man. He had been built without a lap, where I could sit, so I had him propped on a portable stand alongside me, while seated in a chair and having him speak without opening my mouth.

On nights when our theater would otherwise have gone dark, I gave performances. They were bilingual and even allowed for audience participation. Cro-Maritan and MM didn't draw crowds but I was frankly surprised by the number of people who came.

Naansee was my confidante as I worked up my material. She made great suggestions and solved a costuming problem for me. Cro-Maritan had to have a head in order to have a mouth, and the head had to have hair, albeit artificial. Ergo, she had individual fright wigs made up that she had devised herself—color-coded to represent the three most important individuals in my recent life (besides herself)—red for Jean-Luc, white-blond for Lucien Veynachter and mustache-black for Papa. Some evenings, I would incorporate all three.

Aside from existentialism, which had its relatively brief moment in the sun, Freudian psychology was also fashionable. My attempt to alleviate my angst through such play-acting was something I saw as a sort of self-conducted therapy. Analyzing my problems through a "shrink"— (Naansee's term also)—would have taken years of sessions and the better part of my bank account. As a result of sheer pragmatic—one might call it Cartesian reasoning—I simply decided our stage act was a handy therapy to ease the tragedy I'd suffered.

For the pending Charniers war crimes trial, through my efforts with Hippolyte and his efforts with the reigning governmental powers in Paris, France did seek the extradition of General Lammerding. We were not successful in Bonn. The political climate thanks to the Cold War was not propitious. West Germany was too important an ally.

Did I ever think of going home to see Octave and asking for my Luger? I would be lying if I said Non. In one particularly vivid and unforgettable dream of mine, Solomon Schwartzbard passed me on the Boul Mich. I recognized him, saw the determined, other worldly shine of his eyes, and noticed a hand of his in a suit pocket that appeared to have something bulging in it. I followed him down a side street. A short, thin Slavic-looking man, nattily dressed, sporting a fancy cane, was approaching us. All of a sudden, a scuffle broke out. The dapper stranger was raising his cane to strike Schwartzbard, who now had a pistol pointed at his quarry. Petliura yelled some words in Ukrainian. Five shots blasted out in noisy succession. Revenge had been enacted in the twinkling of an eye. A body lay slumped on the sidewalk. I went over to look. But the dead man wasn't Petliura. The corpse was wearing a German officer's uniform. I could tell by the collar tabs he was a general. Nearby Schwartzbard calmly stood, the smoking weapon in his grip, waiting for a gendarme who was hurrying toward him. "But that's Lammerding you killed!" I shouted at the grinning assassin. And lo and behold, the gendarme rushed past the ex-Foreign Legionnaire and arrested me.

Are you expecting I woke up in a cold sweat at this point? Would I had. Other police showed up. Their van—we French call it a *panier à salade,* the Americans a "paddy wagon," was on the scene and, handcuffed, I was hustled into it. Staring out through the grill in the back door as the motor started, I saw Naansee running toward me, crying: "What about our future?" Off the vehicle sped before I could answer. Next to me in captivity was Cro-Maritan. "Why are you here?" I asked the seven-foot-tall homunculus I'd created. "I'm your Prosecutor," he said, "I mean Protector." And that's when I awoke.

Quietly, without disturbing Naansee, I slipped out of bed and tiptoed into our other room where I had my desk, also a pad of writing paper and sat down, pen in hand, and jotted a recap of the bizarre array of frightening images I'd subconsciously witnessed. I wanted to capture them before they shimmered away.

One more thing: you should know Naansee and I had planned to take a trip to the U.S. in the spring. It was so timed for several reasons; good weather in Ohio was no doubt the most essential, and not only was I taking off that entire term for school to travel, but additionally, following a route of what had been the French North American experience from Canada to Louisiana would be quite fulfilling. Indeed I would be gathering material for a book, the initial volume of the series I had contemplated on French expansion overseas. The two of us had also talked about Central and South America the following year—islands like Guadeloupe, Martinique, Saint Martin, Îles des Saintes, and on the mainland Guiana, and past French adventures in Brazil and Mexico.

Another mutually agreed-upon delay was I could not under any circumstances leave until the outcome of the trial was announced, which I would attend in Bordeaux alone. That had finally been set for late January 1953. Even if it finished by late February, Naansee had convinced me that March and April were not the best times to arrive in her hometown.

Oh, still one other thing. It happened in an instant while I was recording my dream on paper . . . a flash of thought . . . *Maybe I should wake Naansee up and ask her to marry me.*

Just a moment's intimation. And I didn't act upon it.

Big mistake.

Or maybe not.

In any event, here I have brought you to 1953 and I'm well aware I haven't given much attention or space to the trial, which opened in Bordeaux on January 12th of that year. My cynical remark about all the defendants having "bad haircuts" should not be taken for the final word. While the presence of the Alsatian draftees added a special moral conundrum to these particular war crime proceedings, an innovation in human attitudes to prosecute for criminal acts committed during operations of State, war or otherwise had now been established. It remained to be seen in the case of Charniers-sur-Nys how punishment would be meted out and to whom.

Therefore, in this present narrative of mine, I intend to present a detailed study of the event as I saw it during my daily attendance in the gallery.

Whatever the logic behind the choice of venue in an outlying district of Bordeaux at the confluence of the Rue de Pessac and the Rue de Treuils and in a courtroom of limited seating capacity, this is where the drama took place. The world was watching. Certainly most of France, had its interest riveted toward that relatively obscure location. The National Assembly and its politicians were involved. Sensationalist journalists scribbled recklessly that the newfound unity of post-World-War-II Europe was at stake.

It's too bad Albert Camus, one-time newspaperman, wasn't covering the story. The sparse setting, the cast of characters, the stifling atmosphere, while not as arid as the Algerian landscape and its woes he so well depicted, fit the same pattern of banality and grief amid howls of outrage from differing segments of society followed by an ultimate flatness of feeling that no one—and definitely not the human race—had profited by the court's decision and its aftermath.

A character in Dickens was once quoted as saying: "The Law, sir, is an Ass." To me, it seems more like a slippery Eel. Although clear-cut if frozen in time, its decisions are forever subject to change because lawmakers and enforcers have to contend constantly with unanticipated circumstances. Now I will be less abstract. We will have to start with a bill passed in 1944 by the newly-constituted French Provisional

Government, essentially exempting all French from punishment for their wartime activities. Four years later, this law was rescinded and a 1948 statute imposed the concept of "collective responsibility" for war crimes. Its Article 3 ensured French citizens could now be held responsible for acts deemed war crimes carried out by groups to which they belonged.

Henceforth, in effect, those deemed to be French citizens like the young Alsatians in the dock at Bordeaux were ipso-fact guilty of a war crime merely by their presence on the scene among the SS group that carried out the murders and destruction.

Obviously, no one could argue a war crime had not occurred at Charniers-sur-Nys.

Jurisdiction is another facet of carrying out the Law. To which court does the case go? Who is the prosecutor? In this situation, since military justice was involved, a military tribunal was decided upon and it consisted of six high-ranking army officers and one civilian, but the latter was the most important participant, the presiding judge, Monsieur le Président.

On January 12, 1953, these different civilized human efforts—judge, jury, prosecutor, defense lawyers, court officials, witnesses, families of the victims, spectators, merged on a frosty winter day to commence the long-awaited event. The rest of us were bundled up in overcoats and scarves as we filed into the court building, showed our passes to the gendarmes and found our seats. There was a balcony as well, a single tier overhead—the *paradis,* a wag in our midst facetiously dubbed it.

On a raised stage was the tribunal that would act as a jury, three on each side of the président. They were in full dress uniforms and wore their gold-leaf-decorated kepis throughout the trial. Now for a brief word about the key figure. Unlike the American judges Naansee had described to me, our magistrates orchestrate the activities even to the extent of asking questions of the witnesses and the accused. Since all French judges are civil servants, the man the Ministry of Justice had chosen to dominate such an explosive mixture as this was a seasoned veteran. His name was Antoine Roissy-Saint Georges, and his mere physical appearance seemed strong enough to cow any outbursts. He was a truly handsome male of the Jean Gabin type, powerfully built, grave yet compassionate, stern yet wise, wearing the black robe of a criminal judge on which he had pinned medals he had won including a Croix de Guerre. The better to show off his shock of striking snow white hair, which was intimidating on its own, he had dispensed with the little cap French judges sometimes wore in those days. Below him, to either side, were stands where the prosecutor and the defense lawyers stood when speaking, with aides behind them at tables. The main prosecutor here, incidentally, was a lieutenant colonel, and there were separate attorneys for defending the Alsatians and Germans.

When these *maîtres* in their black robes were pointed out to Roger Phillipon, he groused: "Our taxes are paying their salaries, aren't they? And who was defending our wives and children when those savages pounced on them?" Knowing Roger, he would have shouted his displeasure aloud had he not been quietly cowed by the august figure of the chief judge, so only those of us nearest to him could suffer his complaints.

Lest there be any misconception of the security arrangements, a line of armed gendarmes had been posted between the Association of Families and *them*—the alleged perpetrators on three rows of benches not far from us. In any event, no matter the provocation, we would have behaved ourselves.

I couldn't stop gaping at those prisoners. Our seats were on what they call "risers" in the theater so I had a clear look down at this collection of unexceptional-looking males, most of whom seemed around my age. Like me in 1944, they would have been in their teens. Not a single one, I noticed, was blond.

This observation led me to wonder about Lucien. Resistance hero or not, *would* he have been on those benches with the other Malgré-Nous? His situation perfectly exemplified the Alsatian dilemma. Some of those guys *had* deserted in Normandy and afterward fought in the Free French Army. Yet my determination to see the whole bunch of them convicted, and executed, no less, did not diminish.

The opening remarks from Court Président Roissy-Saint Georges aimed at a justification for the reason a judgment was being sought. It was "a trial of Naziism." At issue was: "blind obedience to a totalitarian state." About the Das Reich division to which the 2nd Company belonged, Monsieur le Président was scathing. They were "a group of thieves and assassins." Noted, too, was the Waffen SS classification at Nuremberg of a "criminal organization."

Such an obviously prejudicial view voiced by a presiding judge may seem shocking but the role of the attending chief jurist in a French trial, is "inquisitorial." It is his or her duty to do the *inquiring*, bring out the facts. These judges are not impartial referees. The best of them, like Roissy-Saint Georges are able to achieve a sense of fairness through the skills they use to conduct these "inquisitions."

The rest of the opening day was given over to the defense attorneys. A vociferous argument ensued when the Alsatian defense lawyers protested that their clients, although joined to the Germans under "collective responsibility," should be tried separately from them. Their position, to which our Association was adamantly opposed, raised in fiery rhetoric the *incorporé de force* defense—that with the one exception of the notorious Alsatian Nazi volunteer, Sergeant Roos, all of the young Alsatians present had been dragooned into the SS upon pain of death for themselves and their family members if they refused. The attorneys for the Germans on the other hand were just as vehement, claiming the 2nd Company had been a single unit and should be tried as such. I found myself with a queasy feeling I was on the same side as the Boche.

Monsieur le Président let these barristers ramble on before he finally intervened. His verdict on their pleas was decisive. Under the law of 1948, since it incorporated the legal concept of "collective responsibility," the defendants *could not* be separated.

The next day Monsieur le Président commenced with a recitation of the salient facts of the case; the time of the arrival of the SS's caravan of trucks, the surrounding of the village, the roundup of the inhabitants, the confrontation on the Champ de Foire (here he singled out the heroism of the mayor who refused to name the thirty hostages demanded by the SS commander and would offer only himself), the dispersal of groups from the Champ de Foire, the machine gunning in the barns and other places, the destruction of the church and the women and children jammed inside, the torching of the bodies and the houses and buildings of the town after looting them and finally the eventual departure—three hours of rampage; more than six hundred dead.

Once the judge had finished, my inner queasy feeling shifted its focus. There was a brief break and in the men's bathroom, I overheard a snippet of conversation between two of the numerous reporters in attendance. One said to the other: "You know if that mayor hadn't been so pigheaded and gave the Nazis their thirty hostages they might not have trashed the whole place." And the newsman replied: "Yeah, we could be at a café sipping Ricard and eyeing the babes."

What cynical jaded bastards those press guys were, I told myself, hurt by their denigration of Papa. But supposing they were right . . .

That was one part of my worry once I'd returned to my seat. Also bothering me was an anxiety arising from a sudden revelation. In Roissy-Saint Georges' chronology of sub-events on June 10th, 1944, no mention had been made of Jean-Luc Muller's foiled intervention attempt.

I suspect he doesn't know about it, I told myself. No one but Lucien Veynachter fully witnessed what happened on the Champs de Foire.

Benoît could probably only testify he'd seen Jean-Luc confront Durchmann and later, in the Phillipon barn, saw the red head propped up by others until the machineguns had mowed them all down. I was scheduled to testify later in the trial. Should I bring up this matter? To my people, Jean-Luc was Alsatian. Few if any knew he was a Jew. It was not a good time for one of us from the Limousin to make a hero of an Alsatian, Jewish or not.

But I would have at least several days to mull over a decision. The next order of business on the Court's agenda was the reading aloud of the indictment against those charged. The lieutenant colonel and his two assistants took turns going through the forty-page document. Their performance ended with an ad hoc addition by the head prosecutor about the SS drunkenness prevalent in Charniers after the killings and their ineffectual attempt to bury and hide the bodies.

The clerk of the court followed with a lengthy recital of the specific offenses perpetrated that beautiful day in June.

Following right afterward was, for me and many, many others, the single most moving event of the trial. The clerk announced he was going to read the names of the dead.

Everyone automatically stood and we remained standing for the next half hour until the end of the list was reached—more than six hundred posthumous entries of loved ones, neighbors, friends, etc., recognized, if only briefly. Sobbing in our section, male and female, was uninterrupted. Such grief may have reached a crescendo when the sonorous clerk's voice from the stand reached "infant of two months," "infant of twelve days" "infant of forty-seven hours"—newly born babies who had not yet been baptized, who officially had no names (but were given them by relatives for the memorial slabs in the Charniers cemetery).

This was enough emotion for the day and the session was recessed.

However, there had been one moment of illumination for me in that litany of the dead. The name of Jean-Luc Mueller had been included.

I fleetingly thought of procuring a copy of the page on which the redhead's demise was officially noted and sending it to Chantal as proof positive her lover hadn't abandoned her. But reason told me her unreason would deem it a ruse on my part that he, in Israel, had concocted.

Then, in my mind, arose the question I'd been weighing silently within myself. Did I need to go any farther on the subject? Jean-Luc would be counted among our honored martyrs. Did I have to embellish his sacrifice, true though the story might be?

It was at this moment alone in my hotel room in Bordeaux one night that I truly missed Naansee. The main reason she had to stay behind in Paris was because of an all-important role in a drama our theater group was producing—Joan of Arc in a play about Joan of Arc. By the time the weekend arrived and I could drive to Paris, my turn on the witness stand would have taken place. Phone communication, particularly long distance, in those immediate postwar years, was difficult at best. The only phone at our Rue Duguay-Trouin residence was in the concierge's office. Even if we'd talked in English, Naansee would have had no privacy for discussing sensitive matters . . . Anyway, I had to be man enough to make my own decision and I knew it's what my honey would have told me to do, too.

Therefore, in the following days I had pretty much made up my mind to tell the story of Jean-Luc's last hours in its entirety when a bombshell exploded in the nation's capital. Without any advance warning to us, the lawmakers in the Assemblée Nationale voted to exempt *any French citizens* (i.e., Alsatians) from the 1948 law. No more "collective responsibility"— not for the Malgré-Nous.

My Charniers people were apoplectic. Speaking of Jean-Luc's heroism was now impossible. The Limousin's fury against *all* Alsatians had turned white hot.

Hurrah for His Honor Antoine Roissy-Saint Georges! Nothing was allowed to get out of hand nor disrupt the trial. He handled the devastating news and its implications with exquisite finesse. Entirely calm, rational, sincere, this veteran jurist tamped down the seething ferment on both sides with a simple explanation. The *procès* would henceforth be conducted under the rules of the French Criminal Code. The defendants would be judged according to their individual acts since the Alsatians could no longer be considered culpable merely by virtue of their membership in the Waffen SS.

On that basis the essentially separate examination of the two types of accused began, starting with the Germans.

It seemed unbelievable that the highest ranking of the former "Master Race" members we had captured was a mere non-commissioned officer— the equivalent of a sergeant. Bereft of his swaggering SS regalia—the death's head, the zigzag lightning runes, the ominous black uniform and glistening bootwear, Alois Eberhardt, age thirty-five, resembled nothing more than a slightly beefy store clerk. The red splotches spread around his nose and an incipient pot belly indicated a prodigious beer drinker and indeed he was a Bavarian, an ethnicity he shared with Himmler . . . But Eberhardt, on the stand, acted as if butter wouldn't melt in his mouth.

No, he had done nothing else but walk around the village during the fatal two hours at Charniers. "What were you doing that for?" Monsieur le Président asked him. "Inspecting," he answered cryptically. "What?" he was asked. "Everything," he replied. It was like a surrealistic dialogue out of the famous *Alice in Wonderland*.

Then, Monsieur le Président got serious. He glanced at a sheet of paper in front of him. "Corporal Webbern says here he saw you tossing grenades into the church. How do you answer that charge?" the chief judge demanded.

"Webbern is going to retract his statement," was Eberhardt's response. At that moment, I could see in the sergeant's squinty blue-grey eyes the chicken-farmer cleverness of his fellow *Bavarois* Heinrich Himmler.

Roissy-Saint Georges turned to one of the other prisoners on the "German bench." In German, he asked: *"Ist das treu, Webbern?"*—Is that true?

"Ja, Herr Präsident."

In French, almost more to himself than the audience, Herr Präsident said: "I'll examine this later. I smell a conspiracy."

The next two Germans scheduled to take the stand caught my interest because they admitted to having been machine gunners in one of the barns. That is, they used their submachine guns to fire at the twenty men lined up against the back wall. Shooting alongside them were actual machine gunners who employed tripods for their heavier weapons. At first, I did not catch which barn they were in and was on the point of sending a note asking Roissy-Saint Georges to inquire if an unconscious redheaded young man held up by two others was among their targets when the président referred to the site as the Blanchard barn, not the Phillipon. As it happened, neither of the two said they could see the victims very clearly. Did they receive orders to shoot very low at the legs, they were asked. The one named Schuster answered: "I thought I aimed at their chests." Both of these bozos affirmed that a Haupsturmführer Kahn had given the order to pull their triggers. "It was all over in a few minutes," the other guy, Kraus, reported.

It is a terrible admission to make, but after the latter two witnesses, I was like a spectator at an automobile racing event . . . instinctively hoping for action—a *crash*, in other words. The defendants who immediately followed Schuster and Kraus—four of them whose names I forget— told banal tales of boring guard duty while the rattle of guns, the bursts of explosives, and finally plumes of black smoke and the crackle of blazing fires was in the distance. One guy with a sniper's rifle said he had been posted up in a tree for the whole two hours and hadn't fired a shot but when Monsieur le Président told him a male civilian had been killed by a single shot nearby, he changed his story and swore he spent most of the time on the ground playing with a dog.

Then—ta da!—Corporal Webbern mounted the stand. I suddenly played close attention.

Here, if not a *crash*, was a near miss, a car spinning around out of control. As predicted, the corporal retracted his evidence against Sergeant Eberhardt. But Judge Antoine lit into him. He had been at the church, himself, hadn't he? "Tell the truth, you were tossing those grenades, yourself, through the broken windows, weren't you?" His interrogation included a description of a favorite toy of the SS in their rampages: three or even more potato masher grenades tied by their handles, creating an enormous blast when all went off together. "We have testimony that this was a specialty of yours, Corporal Webbern."

"*Nein, nein!*" Webbern protested. "*Non, non,*" the translator echoed him, following which a string of German was shouted out by the defendant that converted to French stated: "It was Eberhardt who taught us to tie them together!"

"And those 'packages' are what you saw the sergeant tossing inside the church?"

"*Ja, ja*"—"*Oui, oui.*"

Whereupon from the benches exploded Eberhardt's furious cry in German: "You lie!"

And a gavel rap cut off any further outburst, restoring order to the courtroom.

After he finished with all eight of these German lightweights and before he brought on the Alsatians, Président Roissy-Saint Georges made an announcement. The court had received an affidavit from General Heinrich Lammerding in West Germany denying he had ever ordered the massacre in Charniers and that the responsibility was exclusively that of the company commander Durchmann acting on his own and exceeding his orders . . . also that Durchmann would have faced a court of inquiry had he not been fatally struck down in Normandy.

Said the judge drily after he finished reading aloud the general's message: "The clerk will note the communication and place it in the files."

Now the Alsatians would have their turn. Leading off quite naturally, separate from the others since he had been an out-and-out Nazi volunteer, was Sergeant Henri René Roos.

My interest became intense from the moment he appeared. Not only had I heard of Roos beforehand from Lucien Veynachter and how he was hated by his own men for his cruelty to them but also from the same source that it had been Roos who knocked out Jean-Luc on the Champs de Foire. *A troglodyte*, I told myself the moment I had a good look at him. I think we employ that term more in French than the same word in English . . . it describes a sort of poison dwarf, a creature from the nether world, a cave man more primitive than any Neanderthal, a thoroughly degraded, scarcely human person. Staring at Roos, I also could not help but compare him to the Nazi ideal of an Aryan elite. He was short, runty, well below the SS height standards, black-haired, ugly, badly shaven, surly, evil-eyed, a human freak who instantly elicited scorn and hostility simply by standing there in the dock without the camouflage of his military uniform.

The day before, I had already undertaken an action that affected him. Through one of the bailiff's assistants, I sent a signed note to Judge Roissy-Saint Georges, requesting of him at the appropriate time to question Sergeant Roos about his bludgeoning of Jean-Luc Mueller and a description of that incident as Lucien had outlined it to me.

Would Monsieur le Président follow up on my suggestion? I hadn't heard back from him.

Thus throughout the interrogation an air of suspense overlaid the ensuing discussion. To hear Henri-René Roos heatedly tell his story, you would think he was an angel, and not a fallen one, either. Meanwhile, I was remembering the surname Roos had been infamous in Alsace since the end of World War I. An Alsatian Nationalist Movement headed by a Karl Roos had agitated in the 1920s to break away from France and openly allied itself to a similar radical group in Germany who called themselves National Socialists. I wished this Roos would be asked if he were related to that other Roos who'd been executed as a German spy in February 1940.

I also was aware of a story Lucien told me about his mean-spirited, highly disliked superior. Because several men in their platoon had laughed at Roos when a local French girl had rejected his advances, the spiteful sergeant had forced all the men to don battle gear and spend an hour flopping up and down on a rainy field until everyone was covered in mud and given a limited period to clean themselves up with a dire penalty if they were even a minute late.

Not surprisingly, neither of these instances were included in the courtroom dialogue between the Alsatian Nazi and the judge (conducted in French, I will add). Roos's Alsatian accent showed that he'd been brought up speaking *Elsässisch*, the local dialect that was actually a form of low German, although he was understandable enough in our language. There was some initial jibber-jabbering from him about his being charged for treason as a French citizen while under the German occupation he was a German citizen. However, he made no effort to deny he had volunteered for the Waffen SS, nor would he renounce his Nazi beliefs.

As to his whereabouts during the massacre, he showed a true Himmler-like sneakiness. Had he fired his automatic into the church through a broken side window? He had been reported seen doing so. Yes, he had gone for a look there—only to look. A truly heinous crime was linked to him. In an oven of the burnt-out village bakery, in a baking pan, the charred body of a baby had been found. Yes, he'd gone for a look inside the bakery, but only for a look.

Finally the words I'd been waiting for from Monsieur le Président were spoken by him. "Let us go to the Champ de Foire. You were present, were you not?"

Roissy-Saint Georges pressed his point obliquely. "Were you aware, Sergeant Roos, the alleged reason for your unit's reprisals at Charniers-sur-Nys was that an SS officer, Sturmbannführer Lange had been captured by Maquisards and subsequently shot to death during an escape attempt? Was this the justification that Sturmbannführer Durchman, his close personal friend, gave you?"

"*Oui,*" Roos finally answered.

"The incident did happen, I know you know, but took place thirty kilometers away at the other Charniers—Charniers-sur-Vare. I know you also knew that."

"*Excusez-mois, Monsieur le Président . . . ?*" the Alsatian Nazi replied in some confusion.

"You learned it from the redheaded lad whom you later struck in the back of the head with your gun butt."

Here Roos betrayed himself. "But he was speaking pure *hoch deutsch,* that kid. Very fast. Very excited. I didn't get it all. About the wrong village . . . Sturmbannführer Durchmann said he was an anti-Nazi German fled to France, a provocateur, sent by the Communists."

"And you hit him?"

"It was an order."

Silently I congratulated myself, I had gotten Jean-Luc's story aired.

The interrogation of the Malgré-Nous was similar to that of the

Germans. Mostly these defendants had been sent on guard duty, always having a German with them since they weren't totally trusted. Only one confessed to having shot anyone. His name was Wagner.

I already had had my eye on him. An interesting thing had happened. Another assistant to the Bailiff (we call such a courtroom official a *huissier*) brought a letter addressed to me. I studied the embossed return address on the upper left hand corner. A momentary mystery. It was from a Madame E. L. Wagner in Selestat, Alsace. Seconds later, I discovered this was from Elsa Leibart, that long-ago timid blonde refugee girl I'd danced with and corresponded with for a year or so almost a decade past. The Wagner on the Malgré-Nous bench was her brother-in-law.

First, you should know that I'd noticed Louis Wagner before the letter from Elsa had arrived, and because of the impression he'd made when he took the stand the previous day right after Roos had been dismissed. Even earlier, my attention had been drawn to the fact he was the one defendant going bald. From my vantage point, I could gaze straight down at the widening bare patch on the crown of his skull. Yet he seemed no older than I was. True, his life hadn't been so easy—kept in prison for the last eight years. His forthright admission was that at the hectoring order of Hauptsturmführer Kahn he had pulled the trigger of his rifle on an older woman seeking to hide in the Charniers cemetery and shot her through the heart.

On the schedule of Alsatian defendants, Wagner therefore followed Roos due to the severity of the crime although he clearly had been one of the Malgré-Nous. Any clemency for him would be difficult, if not impossible to obtain, and that's why Elsa had been asking me for help. He had suffered enough, she pleaded. Only fear of harming his family, which was now her family, since her marriage had prevented him from disobeying Kahn's order. It wasn't fear for himself that he would have been court-martialed and executed if not shot on the spot. All of the draftees had been warned their loved ones would be sent to Schirmeck (the only Nazi death camp on French soil) if any one of them rebelled.

I waited until Louis Jean-Jacques Wagner had testified before writing back to Elsa, who referred to him as Luddy, from Ludwig, his prénom in German, the nickname his Wagner paternal grandfather, whose sole languages were German and the Alsatian dialect, had bestowed upon him. The convoluted history of our province on the Rhine had struck me as contained in that single bit of information and we should better understand the fervor of the people on the opposite side of our Association's positions. However, I had to tell Elsa quite honestly that while I wished her Luddy well, I didn't see what I could do. But I would keep my eyes and ears open to any possibilities.

Written like an instinctual politician, I upbraided myself. All the more so seeing, God help me, I was listening to Hippolyte, who was planning not to run again and thought I would make a fine Gaullist candidate to take his place.

That would not happen for a couple of years. My ambition would not interfere with my intention to travel to America with Naansee next spring, nor interrupt my contemplated writings and research in the pursuance of my academic career.

Very well, a few more highlights of the trial and then I will move on into its disappointing—nay, devastating—denouement and aftermath.

The parade of other Malgré-Nous prisoners whose roles were indeed truly tangential continued for the rest of the day. The next morning, Octave Bois, in his capacity of leader of the Association of Families, was asked by the président if he wished to say a few words prior to the introduction of witnesses to the crime.

Octave, who had been sitting up front in his wheel chair, answered "Oui," and proceeded to struggle to his feet, aided by two canes. He told Roissy-Saint Georges that he intended to mount the small staircase to the speaking stand on his artificial legs. Told he could address the courtroom from where he stood, he insisted he wanted to honor our blessed dead by making this extreme effort of his in their memory.

By God, he did it! Nor was he a "ninety-eight-pound weakling" as Naansee's countrymen might scoff. The suspense as he lifted his heavy body from labored step to labored step silenced every hum of noise in the room, except the sounds of his shoe heels scuffing and the taps of his canes. When he reached the summit, a spontaneous roar of applause greeted him. Monsieur le Président raised his gavel, but then thought better of banging it, and joined in the clapping himself.

Octave soon had the audience in the palm of his hand, including the Germans. What everyone remembered afterwards was the part where he not only told of the children of Charniers being led unsuspectingly to their deaths, not just how the innocents appeared coming from school all bright and shiny, but how they sounded—yes, especially the rhythmic noise of their *sabots*—the wooden shoes that almost all of the boys and girls wore—on the cobblestone pavements, clop . . . clop . . . clop . . . Octave did an incredible job of working those echoes into a cacophony of more than several hundred pairs of clogs marching in unison . . . and then he sang as well, the songs those little ones and bigger ones sang—

imitating their gentle straining voices and the ancient tunes of French childhood—and everyone agreed it was the most moving experience of the trial. There wasn't a dry eye—except from Roos—in the entire house.

Another extraordinary performance was that of Marie Malinvaud's leading off the stories of the survivors and other witnesses of the horror. Because of her wounds and her weakness from a recent illness, she had to speak from where she sat, and Judge Roissy-Saint Georges led his fellow members of the tribunal down to listen to her. Her voice was faint but magnified by a portable microphone so that all could hear the incredible saga of the unforgettable woman of the piercing black eyes and the funereal black dress of permanent mourning who began, "I am a mother who has lost all her children," and ended, "I have emerged alive out of the mouth of the crematory oven." Not many dry eyes then, either.

Farther down on the program, after Benoît had spoken along with several other survivors who'd saved themselves by running away, including a boy who was only eleven years old at the time, my turn to speak finally came. I wasn't an eyewitness to anything that had transpired within the town boundaries, but still I had witnessed the event from the outskirts and I told everything that had happened once the Trio had retreated from La Cav, how Jean-Luc had been hiding because he was Jewish, how we'd been panicked by the Milice contingent's appearance, the encounter with Big Freddi . . . All caution on my part was tossed aside. Jean-Luc Mueller had saved my life. He tried to save the entire village. He paid with his own life for the failed attempt. I also brought in Lucien's description of what he'd seen as Durchmann's bodyguard, and of Durchmann as the embodiment of evil: cold, calm and inhumanly unfeeling. Papa's martyrdom was something else I related and so was the agony of watching from the château the smoke and explosions that had risen from the near-distant town. And then on top of it all, reliving the additional agony of three days of burying the dead and cleaning up the mass of ruins. Papa's ring discovered and instantly abandoned—an incident eliciting sobs despite the fact that it had been a matter of mere moments—and at last my escape with Mario to the maquis.

I had thus unwittingly set the stage for Paul the Gaul, who followed me. His talk, to my surprise, was mostly about Lucien Veynachter. He, too, had wondered if Lucien had lived, would he be in the dock here today. Graphically he described the hidden predicament of the Alsatian draftee as he had heard it from the lips of the blond deserter, himself. Then, he painted a verbal picture of Lucien's heroic death, singlehandedly disabling the German tank that would have turned the tide of battle and dying right after he'd dropped a twine-bound package of grenades through the unlocked hatch he'd opened from outside. Our FTP commander actually had an understanding word for Anatole Wagner and the Hobson's choice he'd faced. No one but a Resistance leader of Paul's stature could have gotten away in such a climate with the tolerance he showed.

I did not stay for the sentencing. I was totally worn out. Octave urged me to go back to Paris. If the rumors he'd heard were correct, the capital was where I needed to be, working with Hippolyte. I drove straight through, arriving in time to join Naansee, who was performing the same evening. It was hard for me to stay awake during the show, but I forced myself. The gal had talent. She *was* Joan of Arc. Yet Jeanne d'Arc was defeated in the end, betrayed. That's how I was soon to feel.

But for the next two days, I did practically nothing except sleep.

XXIII

One thing was certain, once I had learned the results from Bordeaux and witnessed its ultimate conclusion. Never again—ever—would I contemplate making a run for political office. *Les Mains Sales*—that is the title of one of Jean-Paul Sartre's most famous plays. *The Dirty Hands:* what better expression to characterize the workings inside the French Assembly Building—the former Palais Bourbon—that borders the Rue de l'Université? The opportunism displayed within those venerable walls had thoroughly disgusted me.

I am referring to the actions of the majority of our so-called Representatives of the People in regard to the outcome of the Bordeaux Trial. Even so many years afterward, my blood still boils when I think of how those cowards treated our martyred dead. Not Hippolyte. I exempted him. He fought valiantly but vainly to thwart their abject surrender.

It was bad enough that the sentences handed down by the tribunal were so namby-pamby. Only two of the murderers received a sentence of death—the German Eberhardt and the Alsatian Roos. After that, for the Boche defendants, no verdict exceeded a punishment longer than fourteen years imprisonment and some went as low as eight years. For the Malgré-Nous, nobody received more than eight years' incarceration and some as little as five years.

And then, for that devastating vote to be immediately followed by the rubbing of salt in our wounds, infuriating us, demeaning us, spitting on the fresh graves in our cemetery . . . When all of the Alsatian draftees, including Wagner, were amnestied by statute.

Who would avenge Papa? Who the Malinvaud children, Jean-Luc, our faithful Madame Blanchard, the numerous Phillipons, the Sirois couple . . . ? My thoughts tightened around the vision of my Luger and would not let go.

To be sure, those murderers who had escaped the net—more than forty of them, hiding in West Germany or East Germany or South America had received the onus of *condamné à mort* in absentia, but that was a joke. Who would carry out such ersatz justice? During the trial, our Association received a death threat by mail from a group of French Nazis in Buenos Aires, promising vengeance if any of the SS were convicted. But who among us could travel to Argentina to make them rue their words?

Capping off this insult to Charniers-sur-Nys was the inclusion of General Heinrich Bernhard "Heinz" Lammerding on the utterly useless condemned-to-death-in-absentia list. He was much closer by in Dusseldorf, yet somehow still beyond the reach of a cowardly French government.

The worst we could do was include his name and guilt on the permanent plaque in our revamped, modernized memorial museum in the heart of the ruined town. Lammerding's crime was consequently exposed for all to see. As Naansee would scoff sarcastically: "Big deal."

Our actions had to be purely symbolic. A crowd of thirty thousand marched through the streets of Limoges in protest. *Big deal* again. We brought a delegation to Paris, giving back the medals. On the site of our ruins, now a national monument, we erected billboards of shame bearing the names of every député who had voted to absolve the Malgré-Nous. We turned our backs on the Paris bureaucrats. But the question of Alsatian unification had trumped our pain and thirst for justice. Even the great de Gaulle lent his blessing to "the unity of France."

So much activity of this sort took me away from my studies and my companionship with Naansee. Several times I had to drive to Charniers for an "emergency" meeting and stay over with Octave Bois and family, often for a number of days. On the other hand, Naansee was kept busy with her acting and the theater, so we didn't see as much of each other as formerly. However, I liked the true story of the night I returned from Bordeaux to Paris and our greeting to each other backstage after her performance as Joan of Arc. I imagined telling this to a group of bachelor *les gars* that it was the first time I ever kissed a female who was wearing armor. One of those fancied jokers promptly employed the double meaning in French slang of the verb *baiser*—to kiss—asking archly if I'd also done the other *baiser*—to a woman in chain mail? *"Pas de problème,"* I assured him.

Spring would soon be upon us. The trip we had planned to America was still in the works.

March commenced. The furor over the Bordeaux trial results and the politicians' intervention had tapered off considerably. At any rate, it was off the front pages of the newspapers and the "baiser" we in the Limousin had gotten from l'état was now quickly en route to becoming a fait accompli.

On March 7, 1953, after a home-cooked dinner, Naansee and I had settled into an evening activity we enjoyed—actually reading—something of a luxury for us. Heavy footsteps on the stairs (ours was a three-flight climb) telegraphed the concierge's fat husband's approach, who he revealed had come bearing a message for us. Usually, it would be for me. But in this instance, as soon as he knocked and was told to enter, he addressed Naansee. "Miss," he said—he liked to use that American word she'd taught him—and pronounced Meese—"*On vous demande au téléphone.*"

"Probably someone from the theater," she told me before heading out with him.

I kept on reading.

Within five minutes, she returned from the office downstairs and the expression on her ordinarily calm, sunny countenance was utterly changed. I arose from my chair with alarm.

Naansee kept her composure long enough to blubber her news to me: "My Dad . . . That was my Mom . . . Dad's had a . . . a . . . serious heart attack . . . is in intensive care . . . Oh, God, Eugène . . ."

And she rushed into my arms, crying, while I held her tightly and, I hoped, comfortingly.

Finally, sniffling, slowly regaining control, she blurted: "I've got to go to him. He's still alive. But fighting for his life."

"Of course. Of course," I said, still holding her, stroking her hair. "I will make arrangements for you at once."

Air France had a flight to New York the next morning. I booked it for her and made a connection to Cleveland where her father had been hospitalized. Naansee had come downstairs with me to the concierge's office and sat twisting her handkerchief and occasionally dabbing her eyes while I did the phoning in French. "I wouldn't have been up to it in either language," she told me. "You're a dear." Then we reached her family in Lancaster. She spoke to her brothers Alan and Bruce, both older, and her Mom, all of whom would meet her when she landed. Afterward, she seemed much more herself as we climbed back upstairs.

I drove her to Orly Airport. It was early morning, the streets almost bare and the traffic was never as jammed as on the *Périphérique* much later on. We made it with plenty of time to spare, picked up her ticket, checked her luggage, two suitcases, and waited together until the boarding call for her flight. She seemed anxious again and I kept doing my best to soothe her, saying her Dad was in good hands in Cleveland, one of the best places in the U.S. for heart problems. We held hands until she departed. But you idiot, Eugène, you still didn't ask her to marry you.

She would be returning to Paris, anyway, or if she had to stay longer into April, I could meet her in Ohio. My planned research trip would go on as scheduled.

That I did not hear from Naansee for more than a week did not trouble me. Her Dad's condition could be touch-and-go, requiring her entire attention.

Finally, at about the same time of night that the first fateful call had come through, I heard Fatty's footsteps outside my door, his knock and the usual: "*On vous demande au téléphone*," once inside. Indeed, it *was* Naansee, apologizing she hadn't gotten back to me sooner but her Dad had been through a near-fatal crisis and at last, that very day, the doctors told them, appeared to be "stabilizing." Still, he needed to remain in intensive care for the immediate future. She would stay in Cleveland, rooming with a relative, until his release from the hospital. Her presence seemed to do him "a world of good," she'd been told. Meanwhile her brothers had gone back to Lancaster—both had jobs they couldn't leave for long, and the same for Mom, who helped run Dad's insurance brokerage business. Finishing up this first phone call from her, she promised to keep me up to date on her father's condition whenever she had a chance.

After I hung up, I puzzled over several observations.

Had she not in recent months shown several signs of homesickness? She had installed a framed pastiche of photographs in our bedroom, taken at the old Henderson farm homestead near Lancaster. Several snapshots featured the Henderson clan posed by the rural mailbox displaying HENDERSON in bold letters. Other pictures were of a prize pig, several riding horses, milking cows, etc. One family photo, meant as a joke, formed the center piece of this montage. Her two brothers— "Albie" and "Bud," had made a life-sized cut-out of Naansee, next to the real life "Brad the Dad" and labeled it DADDY'S LITTLE GIRL, NOW IN FRANCE.

The son of farmers, Bradford Henderson was the first of his family to go to college and a descendant of poor New Englanders who had flooded into the Ohio Valley following the American Revolution. From a French point of view, his family was indisputably bourgeois.

The triangular football banner of the Ohio State Buckeyes—silver lettering on a crimson-red background—had been a wall decoration in our apartment living room from the moment she'd moved in. But now, in my absence at Bordeaux, it had been transferred to the bedroom. Along with her display from home and other Ohio memorabilia, it had seemed to me she was building a little shrine to her roots. Yet I never alluded to this. I would gaze at the Ohio State football game souvenir and briefly wonder . . . when, if ever, would I see her in Gay Paree again?

These doubtful thoughts gnawed at me that night in March 1953. A detail I did not recall until much later, however, was when, putting down the phone, how she hadn't answered my parting sentiment of how I missed her the expected response of *I miss you, too.*

There were two more calls to me from Naansee, one with news that Brad the Dad had been moved out of intensive care and the other that he was progressing so well that he would soon enter rehab. No indications when or if she would come back to France before April, which in the end caused me to write about meeting up with her in Cleveland or Lancaster, and I should know as soon as possible in order to make changes to the schedule for my American trip.

I don't know why I expected a phone call from her in reply. My principle motive in writing was that calling on the concierge's phone for a transatlantic call would be out of the question. While I could afford the cost, I ended by thinking: *Maybe she's responding by mail.*

Sure enough, eventually friend Fatty delivered an envelope to me, postmarked Cleveland, Ohio, USA. Several weeks had gone by. I'd already begun my paranoia, worrying she'd decided not to return to France. But the trip to Ohio? What should I do about that?

Once I'd read over the letter entirely, I realized why Naansee hadn't telephoned. In short, it was a "Dear John" letter.

In the 1950s, one day walking down the Rue de Bac, Naansee and I saw on the marquee of a small cinema that an American World War II film was being revived—in English with French subtitles. She had seen it when she was in high school, and for nostalgia's sake wanted to see it again. I can't remember the title but one sequence has forever stuck with me. This was my introduction to the concept of "Dear John."

In the one unforgettable scene of the movie I otherwise found so forgettable, a young American infantryman who had been showing pictures of his beautiful fiancée to everyone in between battles joyously receives a letter from his girl at mail call. His name wasn't John and the shocking message told him while he was away these many months, she had met a sailor on leave and was going to marry him. P.S. she was keeping his ring.

In Naansee's case, her liaison with Tom Ridley could be said to have started in kindergarten, holding hands in a sand box. He was not exactly *the boy next door*, but pretty close. The Ridley's home was across Oak Street from the Henderson's. At high school and Ohio State, the two of them were "an item."

Eventual marriage had been assumed, except Naansee longed to travel! Her dream was Paris. She had wild oats to sow and wanderlust and Tom got put aside in the shuffle.

The song lyrics from an American theatrical production shown on Broadway some years later, *Why Oh Why-O did I ever leave Ohio*, symbolized the struggle that had bubbled within Nancy Jane Henderson the last year or year and a half in Paris. Tom had re-entered her life again, particularly after she accompanied Dad back to Lancaster. The time of her passion with her "romantic Frenchman," she intimated, was spent, and now security, Ohio-style, had much greater appeal. Besides, Tom wanted children right away—and so did she. "He's a very decent guy," her letter assured me. "Much like my Dad."

I had been thinking of throwing all the possessions of hers remaining in the apartment into the concierge's trash bins. Yet instead, I arranged to have them shipped, paid for it myself, and asked to be reimbursed. The money came back in francs to the last sou. And the transaction begun that day with the old Frenchwoman's chair had finally come to an end.

In the days afterward, I moped, deep into the funk of *what if?* in English or *suppose* in both French and English: If only I had asked her to marry me a year ago . . . Suppose I had asked her to marry me before she got on that plane . . . Suppose I hadn't spent so much time away from her . . . Suppose Tom Ridley had gotten married to someone else . . . Suppose Brad the Dad had a healthier heart . . .

This habit of mine had always been part of my mental state, even since childhood. I have heard the phenomenon described as "the illusion of central position." That one's choice of actions had mystical powers was its underlying assumption. Suppose I had worn different shoes on June 14th, 1944, the massacre might never have happened, or on an even more ridiculous scale, suppose I'd worn my Ohio State sweatshirt she'd gifted me to Orly on March 8, 1953.

To break this chain of self-pitying nonsense, I decided upon *bold* action. My travel plans were suddenly and totally revamped.

The calendar remained the same. But not the destinations.

Now that I had been dumped and was free, I jumped at the research opportunity suddenly available to me. I would go to Brazil, a trip Naansee had nixed for the two of us. I had already outlined a first draft of an historical article about *France Antarctique*, a sixteenth-century (1555) attempt to establish a French colony in Brazil. If you want to make a *Brazilheiro* really "lose his shit," just tell him the French founded Rio de Janeiro.

One of our La Rotonde drinking buddies, Eustache de la Motte, was the chief editor of a monthly history magazine, *Les Aventures de la France Ultramar*—and sought to have me write a piece on *France Antarctique*. This remote but interesting subject had not often been covered because the colony was so ephemeral. Good writers on such a semi-exotic issue were needed. My maiden published work, in his words: "will be an ideal introduction for your entry into our club." But he was also frank in admitting he hadn't been able to enlist more experienced writers to attempt the assignment.

Despite Eustache's offer to help me start my professional career, I had kept his project on the back burner. That same evening I made my decision; I rushed to La Rotonde only to find Eustache wasn't there. He had gone to Biarritz for a "holiday" and would not be back until the following week.

That gave me time to plan if he still agreed to give me the South American assignment, which I was sure he would. I'd begin right away taking lessons in Brazilian Portuguese. I'd gather everything I could find written about the French experience in the mid sixteenth century—1555–1567. Needless to say, I knew nothing of the Tupi language of the Tupinambo tribe, the original inhabitants of Rio's Bay of Guanabara. They befriended the French, much like the Massachusetts indigenes had the pilgrims at Buzzard's Bay in the New England-to-be. These South American Gallic pioneers were also escapees from religious persecution. Huguenot French Protestants fleeing Catholic hostility. Stepping into the breach to protect his co-religionists was their top leader, Gaspard de Coligny, an admiral in the French navy, but more importantly one of France's most powerful politicians.

Geography, whether of *metropole* France or our world empire, has always been a feature of my historical writing. Those childhood images of the Foreign Legion's bashing of Algerian rebels has forever remained with me. Brazil was now legitimately within my purview! How I'd longed to see that "Green Hell" country, and in particular its setting as the first serious French movement to expand our borders beyond Europe.

After a week in the rose-colored, glittering ambiance of La Rotonde, I spied Eustache's rotund figure immediately. He was as excited as myself by the news of this no-doubt definitive turn in my lifelong fortunes, and we burbled happily about the role I soon would be filling in his publication. One of the young men at the table, a foppish Saint-Germain-des-Prés hanger-on type, seemed miffed I'd diverted Eustache's attention from him. Following a lull in our tête-à-tête, this guy mused quite aloud: "Why should anyone bother about Brazil?"

I quickly rose to my feet. Stimulated perhaps by several glasses of Sancerre I'd downed, I blatantly, knowingly lied.

"Honored Sir," I addressed the fop sarcastically, "you insult me. I go to pay homage to my Huguenot ancestors who lost their lives to spread the undying message of French culture to the heathen world. Study some French history, François." With that, I made a pantomime gesture of slapping him across the face with invisible gloves, as if I were traditionally challenging him to a duel, and purposely exaggerating my feigned huffiness, stormed out of the gilded bistro.

How Eustache and I laughed over the incident. ""Poor, pitiful François," said my soon-to-be publisher. "What a . . . What a . . ." the precise word wouldn't come.

"*Grand nullité*, I intervened.

"*Exactement,*" Eustache added.

Here is an example of history and geography intermixed. Admiral Gaspard de Coligny obviously originated from the small town of Coligny, which lies in the region of Bresse, close to the border of French-speaking Switzerland. Who in France has never heard of *poulet de Bresse*, the fanciest, most expensive brand of chicken raised in our *Hexagone*. The nearness in the sixteenth century of Geneva and the renowned Huguenot divine John Calvin, no doubt drew Gaspard de Coligny into its theological orbit. The artifact of a Calvin letter to Coligny confirms their ties.

It was also innovative Huguenot policy to establish colonies far from the reach of French Catholic power. Concurrently with the thrust of the French Protestants along the Brazilian Atlantic coast, a more feeble attempt was made in Spanish Florida. That episode ended with the capitulation of the French to the Spaniards at present-day Jacksonville and the instant massacre of all those surrendered prisoners of war.

Massacres were nothing new in the France of our forebears. You will discover the spectacle of outsiders slaughtering us has been a heavily emphasized feature of our own history. Less harped-upon have been the phenomena of the odd intra-genocidal outbursts among ourselves—like the Albigensian Crusade and its annihilation of the Cathars

The granddaddy French *crime de guerre* was indisputably the Saint Batholomew's Day Massacre that erupted on August 22, 1572. Its spark was the assassination of Admiral Coligny. Run through treacherously by a sword thrust, his remains tossed out a window to a roaring crowd of pumped-up Catholics, the Huguenot's leader's lifeless body was beheaded just to prove the great Coligny was really dead. This murder during an affair of State was the signal for a gigantic pogrom encompassing all of France that may have taken one hundred thousand Huguenot lives. In addition, a civil war caught fire, lasting almost a decade.

French *crimes de guerre* accordingly have made for a hefty individual entry into the world's almanac of horrendous human behavior. For example, in our day, as reprisal for Algerian insurgents killing of more than one hundred *pieds-noirs* settlers from the *patrie* at a place called Setif, some forty thousand natives would fall victim to the French Army's vengeance—putting our six hundred-plus fatalities suffered at Charniers-sur-Nys into an awkward comparison—one wonders whether one's fixation on that single deed, like mine, is not even a little overwrought. Unless, to be sure, you are *personally* involved.

All right, suppose I had been an American living in Lancaster, Ohio on June 10th, 1944? Years would have passed before I might have visited our martyred ruins. Would my reaction have been of the same touristic shallowness my distant cousin expressed: "*Another Pompeii?*"

A naturalized American, born in Belarus, undoubtedly a Jew, named Raphael Lemkin, coined the technical expression *genocide* following the Holocaust revelations of World War II. At last, we humans at least had a label and tool to employ in delving into a facet of our thinking species' genetics—the rage for mass murder—hitherto never open to laser-like intellectual analysis. The secret door had been pried a bit ajar for intrepid pioneer-explorers like me to enter a whole new configuration of this pitch-black cave mystery of the soul.

Meanwhile, in the real world of the Rue Duguay-Trouin, the Boule Mich, the Boulevard Saint-Germain, and the Carrefour of Montparnasse-Raspail, I hurried my preparations to escape all current heartache and flee, *à la Huguenot*, to the welcoming arms of the *Cariocas* of Rio de Janeiro.

XXIV

Imagine! No one in Brazil had ever heard of Huguenots, except a handful of library reference specialists and academics in university Romance Language departments. Right away, I learned about a peculiarity in Brazilians' pronunciation of the Portuguese tongue. I had not yet landed at Rio de Janeiro when it was brought home that my arrival would be in HIO de Janeiro.

"You will find the *Brasilheiros*, in general, a gregarious and friendly people," Eustache said in seeing me off at the Orly Airport. "They are always happy to chit-chat with a perfect stranger, even in mutually incomprehensible dialogue, as long as it's done over a glass or, better still, a bottle, of their favorite refreshment—beer."

My publisher, observing me wrinkle up my nose, continued: "But no problem. You can obtain wine. Argentina next door produces quite acceptable vintages. The reds especially . . ."

In my hand luggage, I carried letters written by Eustache introducing me to his Rio connections. For my benefit, Eustache—God bless him—had also provided a list of "must-sees" and "must-do's" in the then-capital of the nation, including my gourmet friend's own predilection, "must eat-at's."

It took less than a week of strolling around the gorgeous metropolis that had long since sprung up in place of the French Protestants' primitive huts for me to realize a salient fact. I was certainly in an *American* city, as much so as Naansee's Lancaster, Ohio. These folks I was seeing in the palm-lined streets of Rio de Janeiro—South Americans—were "Americans," too. It was a special cachet felt in contrast to the Europe I had just left. Old and new; stale and fresh—however you wanted to portray the difference. I became aware of myself—*the constipated old Frenchman*, although not yet thirty years old.

The very first of the "must-visit" assignments Eustache had given me was to visit an ordinary bookstore in the Leblon Beach area. He knew the Portuguese love of letters had survived the Atlantic crossing and I would adore going to one of these modest *livrerias*, avoiding a pet peeve we shared at home: the surliness of many Parisian sales people in such establishments. So much as ask them a question about one of the tomes on display? "*Pardon, Monsieur*, what do you take me for? I am an ornament, not a notice board."

Voilà, now I will present my "baptism of fire" at the checkout counter of a Rio de Janeiro bookstore.

While I waited in line, having chosen half a dozen volumes on Brazil's history recommended by my friend in Paris and unobtainable elsewhere, I was spotted by a sales girl who had spied, she later said, that I still had the list in my hand.

Coming right over, she addressed me: "*O Senhor?*" But I stopped her with my initial stab at the language: "*Não falo muito portugues.*"

I knew, too, from a beginner's language lesson book that *O Senhor*— literally "the gentleman"—was their polite third-person way of saying "you." The next moment, we were into "you" in English. Naturally Estrelda tried the Anglo-Saxon tongue on me first since most of the foreign customers she encountered were North Americans or Brits.

Right off the start we were on a first name basis—"American," sure enough. The young woman was enchanting. Brazilian beauties were usually pictured with shoulder-length raven hair, smoldering black eyes and large, enticing breasts. Estrelda could not have been more different from the stereotype.

Once we had established our mutual competence in English, I told her that a single item—the one I sought most, of course—had been missing at the gap on the shelves where it should have been alphabetically arranged.

Her own deep dark eyes lit up. "Oh, I am *désolé*, as you say in French. Last week . . . the last copy . . . *phfut* . . ." She made a gesture, as if the errant volume had swept itself out the door.

"*Okay.*" This little word was a bad linguistic habit I had picked up from Naansee—okay, time to describe Estrelda. Like many Brazilians, her skin was the coffee-and-cream color of the mixed blood where the Indians and Europeans had cohabited as they did all over Latin America and the Caribbean, while some, not Estrelda, showed Negroid descendance from the clusters of slaves the traders had brought out of Africa to the Rio de Janeiro area.

She was a native of one of those small *cidades* that fed its surplus population into the urban agglomeration. She was a country girl, surviving off her quick wit and innate charm, as well as her good looks. Taught that among her ancestry was an adventuring Austrian, she advertised the fact in her blondish hair and green-blue eyes. By God, she even had freckles.

No, I was not about to rush into another *affaire* thousands of miles from home and less than a month after my time with Naansee had come to a crushing end. Had I carefully leafed through the stack of introductions Eustache had penned for me, I would have discovered one to Estrelda to be on the *lookout* for a skinny Frenchman buying books, fair-haired and light-complexioned who appeared much older than he actually was.

Okay, we had connected.

If this had been a put-up job by Eustache and Estrelda I frankly didn't care. Shouting something to a young woman cashier and entrusting my packaged-and-paid-for books to a co-worker, she grabbed me and brought me into the city proper. The heat there in March was more intense than anything I had ever experienced in my life.

To make a long story short, we arrived on a street of funky shops and entered one of them, an emporium selling contemporary and ancient Indian crafts from the interior. The patron greeted us warmly. Most of the discussion between the two Brazilians was in a machine-gun-like exchange of the national language. She turned to me all of a sudden with a beatific smile. "He has the book," she said, "and you may have it as a present. He is a great friend to Eustache."

In such fashion was I inducted into an inner sanctum of young professionals inhabiting the city and its surroundings. Mario, the black-bearded, balding proprietor of the indigenous curio store was one of its leaders. He expressed himself as "very interes" in my subject of the early French in the region. Afterward, Estrelda would not allow me to buy her so much as a *cafezinho,* one of those tiny cups of coffee the Brasilheiros consume an inordinate amount of daily, but she did tell me to head to a certain café at a certain hour in early evening and drew me its location on a city map. Also, she said, she would arrange to have my purchases, plus the gift, sent to my hotel while I went unencumbered to "do the sights."

The Rio *sight of sights* in the world's consciousness is indisputably *O Corcovado.* In Portuguese, this means "The Hunchback," and refers actually to a mountain peak within city limits jutting up out of the surrounding bay and offering a truly extraordinary viewpoint. On its

summit, itself 100 feet high, a giant statue was erected in 1931—Christ
The Redeemer—another 125 feet high—spreading its sculptured arms
in a tender gesture of peace. Most first-time visitors make a beeline for
this iconic landmark that is cited by tourism publicists as one of the
Seven New Wonders of The World. Special trains carry you to and from
the location . . . And I must pause now and gather my thoughts about an
extraordinary experience I had there—perhaps even an *epiphany*, although
hardly like Saint Paul's on the road to Damascus.

All around me as I disembarked from the train and joined the crowds
on the platform were humans seemingly in a holiday mood, enjoying
probably the most unsurpassed scenic beauty they would ever see. Yet
these were no carnival throngs. The kindly piteous regard the Christ
figure cast down on us engendered a sense of decorum, not exuberance.
Nature added its own dimension of sunlight issuing through the clouds
onto unroiled blue Sothern Atlantic waters, dotted by lesser rock fingers
reaching heavenward. I was mesmerized.

Eustache had cautioned me to be careful in Rio. Most to be feared
in crowds were the *garotos*. These were only kids, thirteen, fourteen,
some even younger, but they could be deadly if they attacked you. Some
carried .45 caliber pistols, most had knives or other cutting weapons.
My publisher advised me: Don't wear conspicuous jewelry of any kind
out on the streets and beaches, including watches, and best also not to
carry a camera openly. You can buy better pictures than you could ever
take. Don't go down dark streets alone, day or night. Order cabs in the
evening. Brasilheiros are very friendly, but always be casually on your
guard (as much of an oxymoron as that might seem on paper).

All such tension had disappeared from me completely once I stood
at O Corcovado.

In hindsight, I attributed the effect of my subsequent mystic
experience to the fact I had never been in a tropical climate before Was
it a flash of light I saw? Yes. But not blinding, nor did any voice thunder
from behind it. The impression was of nothing and of everything.
Soon I had the titillating thought I could suddenly face the Romish
underpinning of my being since birth and holy water. Logically amidst
this stunning beauty, God was good and represented by a statue of His
"only begotten Son." God made the world in seven days, I was taught
from the moment of my own genesis. He declared it good. Here was
proof, whether *His* handiwork or engendered from a speck of fertile
dust billions of years ago.

Alone amid hundreds of strangers, I remained dazzled on *O Corcovado*.

As soon as I returned to Brazilian reality, I knew a change had been effected in me but neither how nor for what purpose.

Back at my hotel, to show I had not really lost control of myself, I set my first research task: to try to track down a rumor that the Christ the Savior statue had been a gift from France to Brazil. This tidbit was included in one of the pamphlets they handed out. I drew a blank, although learning the masterwork was paid for by thousands of small donations from the Cariocas who were then almost entirely Roman Catholics. However, France became involved through the sculptor chosen for the task. He was a Frenchman of Polish origin—Paul Landowski. I felt the same twinge of Gallic pride as I did about Frédéric Auguste Bartholdi and his Statue of Liberty when I took Naansee on that quick visit to his museum/workshop in Colmar, Alsace, where he was born.

Antarctica! How did the modern designation of the South Pole end up in the French lexicon during the middle of the sixteenth century? That same early evening socializing with Estrelda Dos Santos, Mario Almeida de Leite, and their assorted friends, I noticed something about the prodigious beer-drinking in the Cascavel (Rattlesnake) Bar. Only two brands were available—BRAHMA, for the bunch-necked white cattle out of India, now ubiquitous in the Brazilian countryside, and ANTARCTICA. Then and there, I arbitrarily decided the short-lived Gallic settlement had left its permanent mark.

In the welter of books—the half-dozen from Estrelda's store and a few others—I was in time able to piece together a coherent picture of the major failed French effort to colonize Brazil. Its history is complicated although the experiment lasted but a dozen years. Two main factors seemingly allowed the French to gain a foothold in magnificent Guanabara Bay, starting in 1555. The Portuguese, whose head-start of more than half a century since Pedro Alvares Cabral's "discovery" of Brazil in 1500 was tempered by two factors: first, they were too preoccupied by their own settlement efforts farther north up the coast in Bahia, and second, they felt legally covered by the fact the Spanish-born Pope Alexander VI had essentially divided the unclaimed areas of the globe into the property of the two Iberian powers, Spain and Portugal. The treaty signed in Old Castile at Tordesillas in 1494 drew up the final dividing line. Brazil fell on the Portuguese side, alone among all present-day South American countries, and King Manuel I in Lisbon and his subordinates in the field could feel their juridical rights would keep out all interlopers.

Such arrogant presumption did not go unchallenged. King François

I of France sarcastically declared he "knew of no clause in "Adam's Will" that would give such an outrageous legacy to those two kingdoms. French merchant adventurers from Saint-Malo and Dieppe had been sailing to the Brazilian coast almost as long as the Portuguese. The money product from its dense Atlantic rainforest was a tree that came to be called *brazilwood*—from the Portuguese word *brasa*—burning red coal—because of a scarletdye extracted from its fiber, much favored incidentally at the French court (c.f. the red robes of Richelieu).

It took me no time to establish an unfailingly agreeable routine in Rio. Never one much for strenuous tourism—and certainly not after O Corcovardo and Pão de Açúcar (Sugarloaf) on my first day—I would take a leisurely breakfast at my Leblon Beach hotel . . . no croissants, hélas, but lots of delicious fresh fruit, newly squeezed *suco de naranja* (orange juice), *cafezinhos* galore, home-baked bread, and creamy country butter. Then, it was off to the pool in this comfortable hostelry with books and notepads and a delicious rest of the day spent outside where cold drinks were always available, even while sitting on an underwater bar stool, and ordering light lunches. Indeed, I worked but I had never been in a relaxed atmosphere so conducive to losing some of my Limousin stiffness. I was careful not to get too much sun—Estrelda had warned me—and they had cabanas, little individual bathhouse shelters where I could find shade and nap on a cot if I wished. Everywhere music played continually, samba rhythms mostly, and a scent of flowers of a powerful fragrance such as I had never encountered before.

Yes, I stayed away from the ocean. We don't have salt water in the Limousin. Papa's Vendée did reach the Atlantic and once I stuck my bare foot in on a summer trip with him to L'Île de Noirmoutier. It left my toes and ankles aching from the cold.

Often I would say to Estrelda and Mario and their friends at the Cascavel Bar each early evening: "I could get used to this life," which I'm sure was a bromide they heard from all their visitors. After drinks, we would disperse to restaurants they liked: *churrasquerias* (barbecues) for meat and hearts of palm salad, seafood places for *moquecas* (delicious stews) and *lagosta,* lobster eaten Carioca style. The custom of sprinkling manioc flour was introduced to me—*mandioca*, the ancient and enduring staple made from a ground-up root. Sumptuous egg desserts, the gift of Portugal; my favorite inexplicably was called Molotov . . . Exotic? You bet. What a wondrous means of soothing me out of my recent sorrows and disappointments.

On the weekends, the "gang" would take me on excursions into the surroundings. Some of the phenomena were elegant, opulent, and European-inspired, like Petropolis: once the abode of Emperors, high above the coastal city. If not more fun was going to a *fazenda*—a sort of ranch and farm combined, greeted by the grandparents and parents of one of our group with unfeigned warmth as if I were a long lost son, riding horses, seeing swarms of bird life and South American animals like ring-tailed coati raccoons and capybaras (the world's largest rodents) in the wilds, not to mention swarms of colorful birds. We dined on roast wild boar and sat around a campfire telling jokes and stories, while the samba, etc. beat provided non-stop music and I was urged to pick out any of an attractive covey of young females . . . At this point, let me draw a discreet curtain and meanwhile declare: "Never have I made so much progress on a work assignment so that within two weeks, I could start writing, rather than waiting to get back to Paris.

Of the books I had bought, the first two I devoured during those lazy hours around the pool were sixteenth-century classics written about the *France Antarctique* colony. I had sought copies for myself in vain in Paris before I'd left and was thrilled to find exactly what I wanted in Rio. The two authors represented two facets of the opposing French religious picture in 1555–1567. André Thévet, a Franciscan monk and Catholic chaplain, and Jean de Léry, a Huguenot pastor trained in Geneva under Calvin, sailed together on two voyages to Guanabara Bay, financed by King Henri II of France and wealthy Huguenots in the mother country, who included Admiral Coligny.

Thevet's portion, *Les Singularitez de la France antarctique*, 1558, also contained an extraordinary set of woodcut prints depicting native Indian life and de Léry's *Histoire d'un voyage fait en la terre du Brésil*, while less pictorially sensational, has still been deemed a "masterpiece of early modern ethnography."

Admiral Nicolas Durand de Villegagnon led the expeditions. It has been charged he played a duplicitous game from the start, pretending to be a champion of Huguenots, naming the fort he had built in Guanabara Bay for his dear friend Admiral Coligny and accommodating Protestant clergy like de Léry and his followers on his ships. However, it was darkly whispered this white-bearded Knight of Malta had gone to King Henri II, who would gladly have burned all of his Protestant subjects, with the proposal he get rid of such dissenters by packing them off to the Brazilian wilds and enticing Huguenot lords like Coligny to help His Majesty foot the bill. In time, after fortifying what today is Villegagnon Island and a spreading settlement just opposite on the mainland at Henriville, now

Rio de Janeiro, Villegagnon ended a fierce dispute with the Calvinists over the Eucharist by having three of them drowned. The rest fled to the onshore wilderness and took shelter with the local indigenes, the Tupinamba.

Consequently, when the Portuguese woke up, found they'd been outflanked and the Treaty of Tordesillas flouted, they amassed a formidable force to drive the Gallic trespassers away. Three of the exiled Huguenot dissenters in the bush emerged to aid King Manuel I's commanders discover the strong point's weaknesses. A decisive battle on March 15th, 1560, dislodged the French, but they doggedly continued guerrilla warfare for seven more years on the mainland. Meanwhile, the Portuguese commander Estácio de Sá had established the ramparts for a future city of São Sebastião de Rio de Janeiro, mistaking the narrow saltwater entrance to the broad bay for a river mouth.

Reproductions of several of Thévet's woodcuts from *Les Singularitez* were a key feature of my article. For a European audience of the mid 1500s, his scenes of Tupinamba life had been a fascinating novelty. Examples that Eustache and I were to include in my article were sylvan scenes of natives gathering *caju* (cashews) to roast so that their enveloping fruit could then be distilled into a fiery liquor. Of general interest, we threw in his illustration of Villegagnon Island, plus bizarre animals—a four-footed beast with a human face, a toucan whose enormous bill was bigger than its body, and a scaly sea-monster with the body of a fish and the head of a duck. But above all the pièce de résistance was a most vivid, ghastly depiction of a cannibalism ritual. No doubt this horrendous scene of the dismembering and devouring of body parts had sold Thévet's chronicle, and my publisher-editor in twentieth-century Paris was equally exploitive in making such horror the cover of the issue in which my maiden work appeared. Concerning the Calvinist pastor de Léry, excerpts of his Huguenot point of view toward France Antarctique were included as were his perceptive observations of the original Brazilians, although in the mindset of his age, he stated his belief that "the Devil entered into their bodies and they suddenly became possessed with the Devil." A final quote, apropos of Cannibalism and the Protestants' squabbles with the expedition's leader over the Catholic rite of Communion, compared the cannibalistic Tupinambo who ate their enemy captives thinking they would thereby gain the foes' inner powers to Villegagnon who wanted the Protestants "to eat the flesh of Jesus Christ raw."

In my glorious three weeks in Rio, other Carioca ties to France emerged: some tangible, like the very sight of Villegagnon Island where a Brazilian Naval School now stood on the ruins of Fort Coligny; others intangible, like the fact that Leblon Beach where I was staying had derived its name from one Charles Le Blond, a French whaling captain who'd bought up the property in the 1840s, or that Lapa, a funky quarter of the city where we spent considerable time was nicknamed the "Montmartre of Rio." It really amused me to find in the city's municipal history a section on that swashbuckling privateer from Saint-Malo, René Duguay-Trouin. In September 1711, in an eleven-day battle in which his forces were vastly outnumbered, Duguay-Trouin had revenged our loss of *France Antarctique* by actually capturing Rio de Janeiro. Until he received a significant ransom, which he pocketed for himself, Duguay-Trouin held onto his prize, came out of the affair a very rich man and received from the Sun King Louis XIV a commission for France's highest naval post.

Call me a provincial, if you like, but these tidbits of ties to my Gallic heritage far from home tickled me to no end. In addition, it was just such fun hanging around with Estrelda and Mario, so much so I entertained thoughts of the three of us as a new Trio, off on international adventures. As with Chantal and Jean-Luc, I was the tag-along for those two, who unlike Chantal and Jean-Luc lived to marry and raise a family. We continued to see each other for many years. I went back to Brazil several times for trips around their country, the most unforgettable of which was to the Pantanal, "the world's largest swamp," and a paradise for wildlife that could make you think you were right at the dawn of creation. Following their wedding, my friends spent part of their honeymoon in Paris, from which I led them on a tour of France. I even escorted them, at their request, to my Charniers, about which I'd told them.

Mario and I passed seemingly endless hours conversing about his intellectual passion—the ethnography of the Indian tribes of Brazil (talking mostly in English until my Portuguese improved). Eventually, he was to find a post at the Federal University in Rio, developing a program of studies about these once-hated aborigines and their fascinating cultures. On several of my subsequent trips, he and Estrelda let me accompany them into the wilderness and stay on reservations the national government had allotted the tribes from their ancestral lands. What a delight for a kid who in his medieval-looking home village had read American books about the forest and plains Indians and the troubles they had suffered and suffered others to endure.

When we two males too pompously showed off our erudition on the subject, Estrelda would tease she was the only real Indian in the room, despite her great-grandfather's Austrian roots. The cannibal jokes she told, she admitted, were in bad taste, but these were her people (on her mother's side) so she had the right to be jocular about them. On the other hand, Mario was of pure European on both sides—Italian mother and Portuguese father from the northern Minho Province. In talking about this ancestral area he had never seen, he emphasized its Celtic background, spoke of Druid priests before the birth of Christ, and even mentioned an oppidum he had read about at a site called Citânia de Briteiros. Years later, when the couple's little *João* (John) was old enough to travel, we met in Santiago de Compostela and toured all of Galicia and nearby Tordesillas.

If perhaps I have dwelt overlong on this one travel experience, it's because later trips of mine to far more remote centers of former French imperialism—like Madagascar, Pondichery in India, Quebec, Louisiana, Haiti, Senegal, Mali, New Caledonia, Tahiti, Guiana, the Maghreb, Guadeloupe, Martinique, etc.—were nowhere near as much unexpected fun as Brazil had been.

Another indication of a change in me from my Rio sojourn was subtle enough—a gradual shift in appearance. It so happened one morning in my Leblon hotel bathroom, I gazed in the mirror and, totally unexpectedly, thought: "I'll grow a mustache." So I put down my razor and toweled the shaving cream from my upper lip. You may not remember I inherited my mother's fair complexion and blondish hair color and only Papa's deep, nearly black eyes. I opted for a much smaller design of facial hair than his handlebars: something neat, trim, the English aristocrat style. Several days later, Estrelda touched a forefinger to the burgeoning fuzz under my nose. "Nice," she murmured. "You will now be irresistible to the ladies." Joining her in this good-humored banter was Mario, who added: "The Tupinambo would have found you delicious." To which, I shot back: "I was always told that we paler Caucasians were too salty for anthropopathic palates." To which Mario returned the joke, stroking his hirsute ebony chin whiskers. "You may be right. We've often been told they preferred dark meat." The rolling of his eyes was like an exclamation point.

This lugubrious kidding, I assure you, was simply natural good spirits. Mario's intentions vis-à-vis the folks he studied had not a speck of disrespect. But the M.O. of my friends Estrelda and Mario was never to take themselves too seriously.

Would you believe this defender of the natives spoke up for cannibalism? It had been found almost universally among early stage societies, clearly driven initially by a basic need for food, camouflaged by mystical justifications. A twist of logic—that warrior strength could be gained by digesting the brave—took thousands of lives. The same mode of distortion led our own forebears, the Celtic Druids—this wasn't a rumor—to construct those huge statues made of straw, in which victims perished in giant bonfires. In our own sophisticated age, deliberately distorted, knowingly untrue propaganda had killed millions. Witness Hitler. Witness Stalin . . . and, in a low whisper from Mario: "To a much lesser extent, our Brazilian strongman Getúlio Vargas."

In those golden three weeks, I learned an amazing amount of Portuguese and began reading the language fluently. The single most important word in the Lusitanian language, explained to me at the end of my stay, was *saudade*, used for goodbye.

A gang of friends had come to see me off at the airport. Estrelda started the ritual once my flight was called. Wiping her teary eyes, she said in English: "I have *saudade*." Our French word *nostalgie* has a similar connotation but is nowhere near as strong. For sheer haunting melancholy, I can only liken it to the broken-hearted refrain of "We shall meet again someday" that we sang to Auld Lang Syne at the gravesite of our loved ones in Charniers. But *saudade* mingles sadness with optimism, for we do meet again, take leave again, rendezvous once more, etc., in the sweet and sour of life.

Unlike the Portuguese *saudade*, our wonderful French word *dénouement* has worked its way into other languages, notably English. If there was a denouement to my fabled 1953 Brazilian experience, it happened almost two decades later. I have already mentioned a cinema on the Rue de Bac that played "off the beaten track" motion pictures. Walking by it as I often did, I was struck by the advertising playbill for a certain foreign feature film. THE TASTY FRENCHMAN, the lettering proclaimed in English.

My attention caught, I stopped to examine the panels of publicity stills, obviously photographed on location in the Brazilian wilds since the captions and headings were in Portuguese. The film's title in that tongue was: *Como gostoso era o meu francês*—literally "How tasty my Frenchman was." Halfway through reading the principal blurb, I realized: *Oh, My God, that's Hans Staden's story.*

Que Saudade! The basis of the plot was an actual true incident by a shipwrecked German Hessian sailor named Hans Staden who was captured by the Tupinamba in the latter 1500s and held for several years before able to escape and publish his bestselling memoir, *The True Story and Description of a Country of Wild, Naked, Grim, Man-eating People in the*

New World America, 1557. This movie was a comedy, or rather a satire. The blond French actor playing the Staden-inspired key role, half naked like the natives, was throughout referred to as *francês;* nevertheless, he was eaten in the end. Yet the independently made motion picture still had to include a boy-meets-girl episode. *Girl meets Food*, I silently wisecracked.

Believe me, I had every intention of seeing the movie. However, I had to put off attending for the next few days because of other commitments. But when I finally was able to get to the Rue de Bac, I found to my great surprise and utter chagrin that *The Tasty Frenchman* had been replaced. *Quelle dommage.*

I held off writing about the incident to Estrelda and Mario, with whom I continued to communicate, although by then it had been half a decade since we had gotten together . . . I was going to add here "in the flesh," God save me.

Signing a letter to them, *The Tasty Frenchman*, something I'd first contemplated, struck me as crass. Mario might well have been offended. Thus the mocking moniker stayed hidden within me and only used silently when I wanted to pooh-pooh myself. Nor apparently did my friends in Brazil ever view the production that most certainly must have played in Rio. No mention of the film was ever made by us in any of our future letters to each other.

It was just as well.

XXV

I have to remember I am not writing an autobiography. My temptation now is to carry on chronologically from beyond 1953 to the present while I sit alone at my kitchen table in Bregonzac finishing a cup of *thé citron*. All of the effort is to satisfy my quest for an absolutely elusive truth. How could a Charniers-sur-Nys Massacre happen?

In other words, what genetic trait allows humans to slaughter other humans without the blink of an eye? Most likely this internal quirk has always manifested itself in the genus, especially expressing itself in the justifying phenomenon of war. It sole arguable good excuse was the practice of cannibalism. I picture Thevet's infamous woodcut of a Tupinamba warrior holding aloft a boiled severed leg as if it were a chicken drumstick. The mere mention of cannibalism is universally horrific these days and so extinct it can be mocked in a satiric cinematic drama.

These musings of my post *petit déjeuner* produced the usual commonplaces. Evil countered by good, or vice-versa, the Devil versus God.

This isn't history. No, the vapid thoughts I was having this morning were as vividly insubstantial as the snap vision of God (my epiphany) at the Corcovado site in Rio so very long ago.

Here, honestly, I nearly undid myself—inwardly generating a pledge to stop pure reminiscence. I realized I needed to return to the interview process, which I had more or less unconsciously abandoned recently in favor of memory introspection. Only one caveat remained before I could return to the first phase of revivifying my little self-created theatricals—choosing the next subject.

It took my breath away when I realized what I was contemplating. *Suppose* . . . there I go again . . . suppose I stage a debate between God and the Devil. The subject would be . . . *War crimes!* I would act as moderator, disguising my role as creator.

Okay. Follow my next steps. They might appear quite confusing, even a bit loony. I gulped down the rest of my tea, arose and went into my bedroom. Nothing strange there. But I headed not for my bathroom but into my walk-in closet.

I brushed aside some hanging clothes and out of the shadows reached down for a large oblong package wrapped in heavy brown paper. No one saw my expression as I glanced at a cardboard shoe box next to it on the floor. Memory produced a momentary grin. Then, I hoisted my bulky parcel and moved back into the bedroom with it. Meanwhile I spoke aloud to the inanimate bundle in my hands.

What I audibly said to it was: "*Bonjour, mon vieux*, I have neglected you far too long. However, I must have your guidance."

I laid the burden on my bed. Back to the closet, I went and emerged with a tool kit. Very carefully, one might consider *lovingly*, I unwrapped the protective covering. Revealed as the contents were what looked like half a dozen body parts.

Yet I didn't blanch. I knew they were made of wood.

With the advice of Naansee, the skill of an artful carver I hired and a professional ventriloquist we had constructed this . . . sorry, Cro-Maritan . . . detachable "*dummy*."

Assembling him in our old Paris theatre days took but a few minutes once I'd practiced enough. The tall, skinny stick figure had screw-in sets of legs and feet, arms and shoulders, torso and head and neck . . . and disassembled they fit into a carrying case that someone stole one night while I was performing with C-M. By then, anyway, my act had pretty much run its course, the Bordeaux trial date was nigh, and I wrapped the dismembered guy and tucked him away.

This didn't mean that on occasion, in Paris and in Bregonzac after I retired, I wouldn't think of a question to ask him, set him up, and throw my voice to have him answer squeakily through a fixed half-open mouth. Oh, yes, mounted on his portable stand, he was a full head taller than me.

But for a man of my years, without an audience, formerly blondish hair turned to murky silver, the discreet mustache not well trimmed, a faceful of wrinkles and the image of a grown person alone in a scholar's cushy work space, conversing with an upright wooden puppet betokened absolute *folie*—straight-out madness.

Prior to addressing my momentarily silent companion, I arranged my thoughts. As moderator, I would have to pick the question to be debated.

What I wanted to try out on Cro-Maritan was the challenge I would pose: ARE YOU, YOU GOD AND YOU DEVIL, NOTHING BUT FIGMENTS OF THE HUMAN IMAGINATION?

Before I let Cro-Maritan speak, I must insert a word about the timbre of voices. For my act in Paris, I was able to formulate a range: high-pitched, normal, basso profundo for laughs, unexpected screams (some comic), and shocking obscenities.

"I am at your service, O Master," was the initial sentence Cro-Maritan finally uttered. Banal enough, yet followed with a *tour de force*—a crackly snort.

Show-biz required a feisty character in a stage dummy, like Edgar Bergen's Charlie McCarthy. I knew better, though. This artfully contrived creation of mine really had a sweet disposition, like the Biblical Good Samaritan.

Here is a sample of the back and forth discussion I then transcribed.

C-M: Go ahead. I will be your tuning fork.

ED: You have a distinguished heritage . . . that of those first peckings of an artistic human impulse chiseled into a cave wall . . . Did your illustrated stick people invent God?

C-M: (indignantly) Stick people! Certainly I have more substance than that.

ED: Did humans invent the Devil?

C-M: Wait a minute. Do you mean Satan?

ED (nodding): Or call him Lucifer or Beelzebub. He's a fallen angel, a would-be egotistical revolutionary who sought in vain to displace the God of Love.

C-M: Oh, that inveterate troublemaker. The Lord of Cruelty. A mass murderer.

ED: My proposed debate between those two Titans would be on the question of whether or not they have any semblance of existence on their own, or are the creations of homo sapiens.

C-M: Presumptuous, is it not?

ED: But possible, n'est-ce pas?

C-M: Worth trying.

One thing I've neglected to discuss, I realize, is the original costuming for my creation. Cro-Maritan had a theatrical wardrobe tailored to fit his "naked" frame. He could appear in public just as he was, the paint on his exterior that of a garment to cover him. But in addition, large doll's clothes that Naansee had designed might be overlaid. Befitting his stage name I had given him, the two most popular outfits were: an animal skin of brownish-yellow fur in honor of his Cro-Magnon ancestry and the somewhat truncated robe of a Samaritan—good or otherwise.

We all know the parable Jesus told about the admirable action of an unknown member of the Samaritan ethnic group assisting a stricken Israelite enemy in the highway when no one else would help. From a young age, worshipping at Saint Augustine's in Charniers, that tale had made an enduring impression upon me. In my historical studies, I learned the Samaritans—who still exist especially around Mount Gerizim and the village of Kiryat Luza in the Samaria district of Israel—were bitter enemies of the Jews, and why they were on such opposite sides. I talked on this subject with Jean-Luc. He showed no animosity toward these people but claimed they had been planted, like Fifth Columnists, by Assyrian conquerors to weaken Jewish resistance.

ED: I'm going to play you a couple of my aborted interviews, dear friend. Just give me a few seconds to insert the tape.
C-M: I have nothing else to do today.
ED: Ha, ha, funny man . . . But please take me seriously. Listen.

I switched on the recording machine's playback. A disembodied voice filled the air, speaking with a German accent, which when heard again, as always, made me want to cringe it sounded so unauthentic.

"Mein Name ist Helmut Horst Durchmann," the speaker began. "I had the honor to be Obersturmbannführer in command of Company 2, 1st Battalion, Das Reich Division, Waffen SS. I do not consider myself an evil human being."

Next my voice was heard. "Most murderers never do. You Germans—and Nazis in particular—are masters at denial. There's a ridiculous story about your refusal to wear a steel helmet in Normandy, only a cloth forage cap, and, as if deliberately, got hit in your unprotected head by a shell splinter."

"So you think I welcomed suicide, Herr Professeur?"

"I think the story was *merde*," came my answer. "You supped with the Devil. You were lucky. You never had to go on trial."

"Which Devil?"

"The one with the forelock and Charlie Chaplin mustache. Your Führer."

"So you think our Hitler was Der Teufel for wanting to end the Jewish menace."

"You orchestrated the Charniers massacre of more than six hundred French women, children and civilian men. Possibly three or four were Jews, refugees in hiding."

"Cunning lawbreakers. You should have seen those Jüden in Russia. Hook-nosed demons, misers, hunchbacks, cripples, dressed in rags, smelly . . . Guilt? Don't make me laugh. We were simply eradicating vermin."

"You slaughtered French, too."

"For resisting. For treacherous behavior. Your leaders had signed an armistice."

"Were you physically attracted to Lucien Veynachter? Did you crave his body?"

"You insult me. You sound like a slimy Jew, yourself. I took to Veynachter because he was the pure physical embodiment of the Aryan ideal."

I returned my machine to the recording mode and told the big puppet: "Pretty mawkish, eh? Did I convince you Durchmann was the essence of evil? Bah—he was nothing but a self-deceiving psychopath intoxicated by power . . . Say something."

"You flopped that test and halted it. It was honest of you."

"Durchmann was thirty-one years old when he died instantly. How much more horror would he have fomented in years to come?"

"You're the one in charge. You tell me."

"Let's try another segment," I said, ignoring his remark and starting the recording machine again.

An announcer—me, my voice disguised, broke through with a shout like that of a town crier: "GOD ON TRIAL."

I sat back in my chair and summoned words to put in his mouth.

"Are you ready for this?" I demanded of Cro-Maritan.

"How God is a criminal?" he asked incredulously.

"The idea is not original with me," I answered.

"Whereupon, I related a story Jean-Luc told me he had heard from his grandfather Max. It concerned a certain rabbi in one of the *shtetls* (little villages) where Durchmann was later to perfect his art of wholesale murder. This particular Jewish man of God had a fiery temperament, great righteousness, and, infuriated by the horrors he saw God allowing all around him, determined to bring the Almighty before a court of law.

"Let me guess the outcome," said Cro-Maritan. "You ended up with a farce."

"Good guess."

As I explained to Cro-Maritan, the biggest problem I had faced in staging *my* version of the terrible rabbi's impudence was the nature of the defendant. The God the rabbi wanted prosecuted had a finite image in his nineteenth-century Eastern European world—exclusively an aged Caucasian with a long fluffy white beard and mustache, kindly enough in appearance from a distance but with craggier features in close-up that could explode into fearsome anger, dark eyes flashing, with threatening eyebrows gathered in a scowl.

To add to my difficulties, the epiphany vision I'd experienced in Rio de Janeiro was nothing of the kind. It was of sheer spirit, ineffable, visible merely as a glow of a substance easily mistaken for sunlight. How could you put *that* on the stand?

The sketch I'd had in mind included a cast of familiar characters. Max Cohen was the presiding judge. I was the prosecutor. Jean-Marc Rosenstein (aka Jean-Luc Mueller) was the defense attorney.

In point of fact, I never went very far with this fantasy. What were God's crimes? Inattention? Refusal to intervene? Smiling beneficently while mayhem raged below?

As if to goad me to stage this *comédie* in my interview style, my thoughts brought forth a prosecution witness. Her name was Veronique Tourneaux, age thirty-five, a housewife with three children, all boys, who worked in a flower shop to help with her family's needs. An imagined home for this imagined personage was at L'Isle Adam on the outskirts of Paris. Naansee and I had ridden bikes there.

The script was to be that she had lost a fourth child, a baby girl, to some unidentified malady. She would call it murder and accuse the God of Love. "I pleaded with You," she was to shriek. "Don't kill my adorable little girl! Don't kill my one and only daughter."

To wind up this interview *tragique*, I had the now hysterical Veronique reach into her handbag and then display—to gasps—two tiny hands severed at the wrists, yellowing like parchment.

Realizing I was no longer planning an interview but had edged into a bad dream, I shook my head violently.

Next to me, Cro-Maritan stood, impassive as always yet somehow reproachful.

"*Je m'excuse,*" I said to him. "I didn't mean to neglect you. Where were we?"

CM: "Something about a debate."

ED: To pit God and the Devil against each other. Resolved: Both God and the Devil are figments of humanity's imagination. Pro and Con.

CM: More than likely, both would be AGAINST. No debate. Ipso facto.

ED: All right, that's enough for you, Cro-Maritan. Time to return you to my bedroom closet.

CM: Aren't you forgetting something? Like a certain trip to Alsace.

ED: Oh, that.

CM: All the gory details, please.

ED: Not now! Not ever!

Plainly angry, I immediately set about disassembling the wooden figure into its component parts. Back he went wrapped once more in thick brown paper into the open hiding place where I kept him.

Going back to the study afterward, I intended to ponder the "debate" I'd promised myself, Cro-Maritan's cynicism notwithstanding. But I drew only a blank, no matter how I sought to focus.

Although it was growing late, I remained in my armchair, seemingly no longer in control of my thinking. Inexorably, the vision crept into my consciousness of leaving Paris for Strasbourg on a warm August day. But I fought against opening that can of worms.

XXVI

Tossing and twisting in my comfy brown leather armchair, I struggled to find an excuse to go back on my word and drop the whole idea of revealing the *true* nature of my heretofore-unrevealed visit to Alsace. This, despite the fact my pledge had solely been to an inanimate object, an effigy carved out of wood blocks. So what if Cro-Maritan reproached me? Was I not the god who gave him life? Furthermore, I'd banished him.

For a diversion, I needed only to stare across the study at the solid wall of bookcases on the other side. One particular section stood out. The volumes upon it were clothed in lavender-dyed leather. That was my eccentricity, to have a few fancy sets made of the works containing my epic study of France overseas. Some of these extravagant editions even sold, curios for collections of the rich I suspected, and were never a scholar's *must-have* since the history buffs could easily obtain ordinary print versions. The whole work consisted of twelve separate books in all, treating the French experience beyond our borders worldwide. None were shorter than four hundred pages and several of the ten geographical regions had material enough for double publications.

I will give you an example: "NORTH AMERICA, I and II!" With that audible exclamation, I sprang to my feet and in several bounds was at the stacks, reaching for the first two purply tomes. Those fat hardcovers were awkward to handle. But I removed them to my desk, laid them side by side and opened to both title pages.

The name for the overall series was simply an unimaginative, *France d'outre-mer, 1500 au présent,* since my publishers argued the enterprise had to sound somber to be taken seriously. My fight for something catchier proved unavailing.

Likewise, my title pages were kept dry and to the point:

NORTH AMERICA I
CANADA
QUEBEC, NOVA SCOTIA, ACADIA
THE GREAT LAKES
THE OHIO VALLEY
SAINT LOUIS
NATCHEZ
NORTH AMERICA II
THE LOWER MISSISSIPPI RIVER
LOUISIANA
NEW ORLEANS
MOBILE
CAJUN ACADIA
FLORIDA

And much as I dislike footnotes, using them as sparingly as possible, I insisted on an explanatory note in each of these two volumes that MEXICO, although considered located in NORTH AMERICA would await the SOUTH AMERICA, CENTRAL AMERICA, CARIBBEAN second half of the AMERICAS (particularly it would include the ridiculous but tragic Maximilian expedition at the time of the American Civil War).

So in the opening pages when I turned to bring French Canada into focus, I consequently started north and worked south, both on paper and in my actual travels. How many *français* have been to Saint-Pierre and Miquelon, those two small islands in the wild northern seas off the coast of Newfoundland that to this day still belong to France? It was no easy jaunt, I can tell you, a stomach-turning sea voyage there and back to Halifax, Nova Scotia on a trawler with whose captain I had made "arrangements" to hitch a ride. I stayed a whole weekend on these two rocky outposts, the last remnants of the mighty French New World empire that had stretched from the Arctic to the Gulf of Mexico. Once more I was in France. Gendarmes on the streets of Saint-Pierre with its gaily painted façades, wore the same kepis and cloaks as their counterparts in Paris. Likewise, the tricolor flew form the Hôtel de Ville. The French the inhabitants spoke lacked a Canadian accent. How such an anomaly came to pass has been a poorly explained fluke of history.

Here I will interject myself, *le professeur*, into my flow of narrative.

The mystery of Saint-Pierre and Miquelon can easily be explained. Since the 1763 Treaty of Paris expelling the French from Canada did leave us fishing rights in Newfoundland, it only made sense to grant these barren rocks as a place to dry cod. Moving on south, still in Canada, to Cape Breton Island, separated geographically from Nova Scotia by the narrow straits of Canso, I spent several days there, since the area is redolent of our overseas past. The famous fortress town of Louisbourg, for example. The present-day Canadian government is restoring the huge, expensive redoubt, of which King Louis XV had quipped that for the money he'd shelled out he should be able to stand on the shore in western France and see it three thousand miles across the Atlantic.

It also served as a fulcrum for French traders abroad. One of the merchant ships of the French *East* India Company that escaped the British naval blockade to enter Louisbourg was laden with tea and porcelain from China and coffee and piece goods from Pondicherry (India), Bengal, and the Indian Ocean island of Reunion. Such economic activity was even more prevalent with the French *West* Indies of the Caribbean.

Nor can I leave Nova Scotia without describing an eighteenth-century "ethnic cleansing," perpetrated by the English on the local *habitants* under their occupation in the 1750s.

What consumer of English language literature does not know of the epic poem *Evangeline* by American poet, Henry Wadsworth Longfellow, a native of neighboring Maine? The tale of the thwarted lovers Evangeline (Bellefontaine) and Gabriel (Lajeunesse), while dated, still wrings tears from its readers. An eternal human nerve has been struck by what today we would call "a war crime."

One of my bad habits as an historian is that I like to insert fiction into my work, to give it "body," so to speak. So if you want a word picture of eighteenth-century "ethnic cleansing," here's Longfellow, in part:

Where is that thatch-roofed village, the home of Acadian farmers?
Waste are the pleasant farms and the farmers forever departed?
Naught but tradition remains of the beautiful village of Grand-Pré.
List to the mournful tradition still sung by the pines of the forest.
List to a Tale of Love in Acadie, home of the happy.

Enter the ingénue Evangeline, black-eyed, brown haired,

Wearing her Norman cap, and her kirtle of blue, and the ear-rings,
Brought in the olden time from France, and since, as an heirloom.

Similarly, the reader meets her beloved, Gabriel, son of Basil the doughty village blacksmith.

Oui, happy Acadia, until the British occupied Nova Scotia in 1755 and, leery of the French inhabitants' neutrality in the Seven Years War, perpetrated the *"grand dérangement*," the uprooting of the settlers and dispersal of them into various exiles.

In the poem, Grand-Pré is burned to the ground and Longfellow graphically captures the brutality of the British action.

> Wives were torn from their husbands, and mothers, too late, saw
> their children
> Left on the land, extending their arms, with wildest entreaties.
> So unto separate ships were Basil and Gabriel carried.
> While in despair on the shore Evangeline stood with her father.

The poet's description of the finale to this outrageous act hit home with me. The pit it left in my stomach transported me instantly back to June 1944.

> And with the ebb of the tide the ships sailed out of the harbor
> Leaving behind them the dead on the shore, and the village in ruins.

The rumble of the SS vehicles leaving Charniers-sur-Nys wreathed in smoke and fire might well be substituted.

The *dénouement* of the tragic tale is that Evangeline, separated from Basil, searches for him as far away as *Louisiane*. Years later, the now aged lovers reconnect in Philadelphia, Pennsylvania, shortly before each dies and subsequently they forever lie side by side in unmarked graves under the humble walls of a little Catholic churchyard in the Quaker City of Brotherly Love.

The *Acadien* story doesn't end there. They did not all migrate to Louisiana. Pockets had remained in Nova Scotia, particularly in areas of the province that later broke off to form New Brunswick. I took a short trip in my rented car up the Saint John River, a major boundary between the United States and Canada, to an entire string of Acadian settlements on both its banks. English was rarely heard spoken in the city of Edmundston, New Brunswick, nor directly across the river in the Maine city of Madawaska. What friendly, convivial people I met on both sides of the border, so hospitable to a "cousin" from overseas who spoke with a funny Parisian accent. I only regretted not being able to stay for the Acadian Festival staged annually. My next destination, naturally, was Quebec.

Pedant once, pedant always. I cannot forebear sneaking in a snippet of background information epitomizing the difference between *Acadiens* and *Québécois*. Both have their own individual flags! My papa would have been ecstatic about the banner of Quebec, emblematic of the French monarchy, with its white *fleur-de-lis* on a background of blue, while in Acadia they sport the Republic's tricolor, albeit marked by the gold star of Notre-Dame de Lorette to lend a religious touch.

Such a dichotomy had led me to me think *nous autre françaises* of the twentieth century exhibited the same ignorance of overseas as displayed by Voltaire when he sneeringly dismissed Canada as "a few *arpents* of snow" or the indifference of Louis XV who cheerily abandoned Quebec and its surroundings to the British through the 1763 Treaty of Paris in exchange for Guadeloupe, a rich sugar colony.

Quebec fell on the Plains of Abraham. Every French schoolkid knows that fact. But what I never realized was that a French counterattack led by the Chevalier François de Levis, nearly won it back. Once General Levis' siege of Quebec City sputtered out, France lost half a continent, except vast lands, all of the area called *Louisiane*, remained to us until sold by Napoleon Bonaparte.

A final word from this region as we are about to cross in to the U.S. Anyone who has been in warmer climes will recognize the beautifully colored flowers of *bougainvillea*. Its name derives from Louis Antoine, Count of Bougainville. He was Montcalm's second-in-command when we lost Canada. Yet his later career led him around the world, giving his name not only to a floral species, but in the Pacific to the largest of the Solomon Islands and to several straits in the vicinity.

Realizing I am in danger of losing my war crimes focus, I will add here that Count Bougainville was present with Montcalm at the August 1756 capture of Fort Oswego in New York where a group of drunken French and Indians murdered British prisoners until their superiors could stop them. Another such outrage occurred a year later at the surrender of Fort William Henry where at least fifty British settlers were wantonly slain, as were seventeen patients in the fort's hospital.

Nor was the perpetuation of these excesses one-sided. A British officer, Captain Alexander Montgomery, cold-bloodedly executed thirty French civilians defending their Canadian homes after they capitulated. At Norridgewock on the Kennebec River in Maine, Yankee militiamen demolished an Abenaki village, killing everyone indiscriminately and shooting down the Franciscan priest who lived among the tribe, Father Sébastien Rasle. Attacking Saint Francis in Canada, Roger's Raiders slaughtered two hundred warriors and numerous women and children whom they burned to death by setting their teepees ablaze. Sound familiar?

But I must hurry on after a final allusion to Charles de Gaulle's rude cry of *Vive le Québec Libre* uttered from the balcony of the Montreal City Hall.

Next, my historical quest drew me into the Ohio Valley. Here it coincided with my physical visit to Ohio and, yes, seeing Naansee and staying with her family, her husband Tom and the two boys, Everett and Jonathan, all of whom had visited me in Paris. Their home in Lancaster was, by coincidence, down a hilly street from the birthplace and childhood home of the controversial American Civil War general William Tecumseh Sherman. One could argue, as we did one night, whether Sherman's *scorched-earth* rampage through the South constituted a "war crime" by his burning homes and buildings indiscriminately, albeit with no one forcibly trapped inside.

At any rate, this exotic guest from France was greeted with great warmth by the family circle and friends of my one-time *girlfriend*. They were excited about the ambitious project I outlined. We went to Columbus, the State capital, and conferred with historians who had done work on the French period in the Buckeye State.

Another excursion was a picnic at Fort Necessity, not far away in western Pennsylvania. The feature there was George Washington. He was only in his twenties when he had to surrender this outpost to the French. Previously he had been severely criticized in England following an incident in May 1754 when his militiamen ambushed a force of thirty-five French regulars. Inattention afterward by the Virginian was perhaps at fault for the tomahawking of the surrendered French commander, le Comte de Jumonville, by Half King, Washington's Iroquoian-Mingo ally. It was Jumonville's half-brother who had called his sibling's death an "assassination" now holding Washington captive. But the youthful captain of Militia was spared.

Ah, French support for the American Revolution, there was a subject I enjoyed researching. How essential it was to the embattled colonists. How often I had been to view the unobtrusive building on the Rue Jacob in which the 1783 Treaty of Paris was signed, severing the links between Great Britain and her thirteen colonies.

One sour note, unknown to me, I discovered while walking in

downtown Boston on my way home. At the King's Chapel burying ground, a small monument immortalizes a twenty-eight-year-old French naval lieutenant, le Comte de Saint-Sauveur, killed in a brawl while protecting a group of bakers producing bread for Admiral d'Estaing's fleet anchored in the harbor. Allegedly British Loyalists secretly incited a mob on the grounds the delicious-smelling baguettes were not for the local folks. The obelisk describes the victim as "The First Chamberlain of his Royal Highness, le Comte d'Artois, brother of His Majesty, the King of France."

Bear with the historian in me a few paragraphs longer. I ended the first volume of my life's work at Natchez, Mississippi, established in 1716 as the most important European settlement in the lower Mississippi Valley north of New Orleans. The present-day small city of Natchez, Mississippi, which I visited, exhibited the famed southern charm of antebellum mansions once housing the local cotton-growing French plantation aristocracy. At least a century earlier, French attempts to take Indian land for tobacco plantations precipitated a bloody revolt by the local Natchez warriors. This doleful event in which more than two hundred Frenchmen were slain later became the inspiration for Chateaubriand's classic of French literature, a trilogy under the overall title of *Les Natchez*.

Chateaubriand has been called the "founder of French Romanticism." In real life, the writer-statesman left France for America in 1791 to save himself from the French Revolution, which he had first welcomed but turned against, appalled by its excesses. His major work output from his exile in America helps detail the interactions of a budding French colonial presence farther down the Mississippi.

Arbitrarily, Book I of my North American narrative ends at this geographical point of Natchez on the Mississippi River.

Below is New Orleans, the heart of *Louisiane*, containing many other sagas of *France d'outre-mer*, plus Biloxi, Mississippi and Mobile, Alabama, and to complete Book II, a peek at a sixteenth-century Huguenot-attempted settlement in Florida, also organized by Admiral Coligny and culminating, as I have already said, in tragedy.

Having delved into my life's work in its purplish leather binding solely to put off a distasteful task, I could have gone on and on and on.

Conceivably, I might have done so had I not heard an inner voice.

I recognized I had stalled long enough. My conscience said: "Cease," although I make no excuses for giving you a sample of my opus.

"Proceed," the same voice commanded.

I arose from my desk. I headed to my bedroom. Back into the closet where I'd deposited Cro-Maritan in his disassembled wrapped state, I reached down for the cardboard box earlier mentioned.

At my age, bending is not as easy as it used to be. In addition, the box was heavier than it would have been with only papers inside.

Papers, there were. Private stuff. Even valuable documents. Where better to hide things you didn't want people to see than in this unobtrusive carton . . . How shocked they would have been to discover it contained a deadly weapon—the shiny, well-oiled, black Luger pistol I've spoken about . . . and several clips of bullets.

It was not the Luger I was after . . . it was a particular manila envelope full of typed pages.

As the saying goes: "He who sups with the Devil must have a long spoon."

In this particular document was my long spoon, so to speak, my 1972 Alsace trip I can no longer put off inserting here.

Sitting atop the closed toilet seat, I began reading it for the umpteenth time.

XXVII

This narrative of the journey was written and typed by me completely in retrospect. While it was happening, I did not keep a diary of my adventure.

At the time, I still had the same apartment on the Rue Duguay-Trouin in Paris. It was eighteen years since Naansee had gone back to Ohio, and except for brief dalliances I had lived there alone when I wasn't roaming the world inspecting sites of French influence past and present.

I had a television but barely ever turned it on. Rather, curled up with a book, classic fiction or non-fiction, I was, to use yet another Naanseeism, "happy as a clam."

Yet I was more than just a gelatinous bivalve, alive but inert. I had been badly scarred, as you know, and my wanderings around the globe and constant immersion in my history project had not erased the rancor I carried inside me everywhere.

One night, I sat reading a French translation of Johann Wolfgang Von Goethe's *Faust*. This German masterpiece had hitherto been left untouched on my bookshelf. I've guessed that what caused me to pick it up after almost two decades was because it told of a man who had made a pact with the Devil.

Ah, even then, the theme for the debate I am now considering—*God and the Devil are figments of the Human Imagination*—was germinating in my subconscious.

One night in the study, I felt a puff of wind on the back of my neck, although all my windows were closed. But I paid it no heed. Putting down my volume momentarily, I mused on the fact that Mephistopheles, the Devil, had first appeared to Doctor Faust in the guise of a black poodle. Magic incantations from Faust had brought the Evil One forth. Feeling ridiculous, I peered to see if a black poodle had arrived.

During this snapshot in time, I was a still-thin, forty-six-year-old, still-sandy-haired Frenchman with a discreet blond mustache, already settling into an academic caricature. I had to tell myself. *Of course, there's no poodle, no magic idiocy.*

Yet someone *had* entered my apartment. Even as I saw him vividly, I knew it was a spectral vision. He had the appearance of a German in civilian clothes, grey loden coat with green collars and trimming. His hair was mouse-brown, he had high cheekbones, a ruddy face. On his head was a black homburg I associated with thugs and a cane that no doubt had a leaden tip. But I wasn't afraid.

"Herr Desfosseux," he addressed me. "Do you know who I am?"

"How would I? You're a kraut, certainly," I answered saucily.

"Durchmann," he announced with a slight bow. "Heinrich Horst Durchmann, formerly an officer of the SS."

"That's not how I've pictured you," I shot back. "You are an imposter."

"My master has sent me to propose a bargain with you."

"Yes, you are dead and in Hell if you are who you say you are."

"We know in monitoring your thoughts you have more than once considered traveling to Alsace and blasting one of those so-called Incorporés de Force. That Wagner guy who shot the woman. You've never tasted revenge. I assure you it's very sweet."

"You're tempting me for a purpose. What do I get in return?"

"Remember that Jew Schwartzbard who cut down the Ukrainian not far from here? We can see to it you are acquitted like he was. You will have made a statement."

"Why should I listen to such nonsense?"

"You are curious how evil can exist. It has sorely tempted you to perform an act of outright evil, just to see what it's like."

I said nothing.

"Cat got your tongue, Professor?"

His slimy remark caused me to shout: "If I lusted for revenge, you would be my first target."

"Too late, *mein Herr.*"

He took off the homburg and what a grotesque surprise! The central part of his skull was completely bald. Moreover, its most prominent feature was a jagged hole, still crimson and wide open where he'd been hit by shrapnel, leaving a ghastly opening.

Durchmann continued: "Too bad. I'm already dead. But not Wagner."

"You ordered him to kill."

"No excuse."

I was preparing a snappy answer but no longer had an image before me. Nevertheless, I still shot back: "That's what we were saying at the trial."

Ever since this vision in my Paris quarters assailed me, I have sought an answer for why it occurred when it did. I will concede I was in a funk. For one thing, I was in the throes of a serious writer's block. This was in spite of the fact that my first two volumes were generally well received, even if one critic sniffed at my hubris in the super-ambitious breadth of the task I had announced. Originally, I was to follow NORTH AMERICA I and II with SOUTH AMERICA, THE CARIBBEAN and MEXICO. However, some quirk led me to tackle AFRICA next, and BLACK AFRICA before NORTH AFRICA.

I was eventually to think this choice had been a big mistake. But in my dabbling into our history in French Africa, I found myself fastening on a real life story that might have come straight from the pages of a Joseph Conrad novel.

Two French military officers, Captain Paul Voulet and Lieutenant Julian Chanoine, later called "two known psychopaths in uniform," were let loose in what would eventually become French Equatorial Africa to help quell a revolt of the natives. One of their actions, among many atrocities, was cited as "the worst massacre in French colonial history." As described it was: "the slaughter of every inhabitant in the village of Bimi N'Inkami . . . women hanged, children roasted over fires . . ." Photos of decapitated woolly-haired male heads and Voulet's proclamation: "I am no longer French. I am a black chieftain. I am going to found an empire." That he was shot to death the next day by a sentry, accidentally or not, hardly mattered. It illustrated how Revenge could be sweet.

My detractors would be particularly outraged by my declaration that Voulet and Chanoine were not the sole evil-doers of our countrymen in the French Empire. By featuring such a horror show in what is today the Central African Republic, I perforce cast a poor light on our IMPERIALISM of the late nineteenth and early twentieth centuries.

It was neither literary nor academic critics who pounced on me. It was the political Far Right, who among their lesser opprobriums dubbed me "a traitor to France." My status as a Résistant and sufferer from the Charniers Massacre cut no ice with them. *Au contraire*, they were types who would applaud what the SS did to my home village.

In the same time frame, the surname Wagner began haunting my mind. It was hot-tempered Roger Phillipon who inserted the germ. Following one of our Association's gatherings where he had argued again for someone to do what he, himself, wouldn't do—shoot one of the Malgré-Nous, he took me aside to confide that the target should be Anatole Wagner. The woman Wagner had murdered, he had learned, in case I was interested, had been a relative of his, a distant cousin. Roger, from the licorice smell on his breath had undoubtedly imbibed a few glasses of *pastis* before the meeting.

From then on, I gradually became fixated on Wagner. Ironically, in Goethe's classic, Doctor Faust's closest companion was a Wagner. There was also, of course, Richard Wagner, the world-renowned classical music composer, whose genius will forever be tarnished by his vicious outspoken anti-Semitism that served as an inspiration for Adolph Hitler. Then, too, the *Gauleiter* the Nazis installed to run the civil government of occupied Alsace was Robert Heinrich Wagner who earned the title of the "Butcher of Alsace." Tried and sentenced to death for his war crimes, he was executed by firing squad on August 14, 1946. Justice won in his case. But Anatole Wagner?

In 1944, I was eighteen years old. Anatole Wagner had been seventeen. I had benefited from the protection Papa had afforded me (and Jean-Luc) through his connections in Vichy. Anatole Wagner had had the bad luck to arrive at military age when the Nazis were so desperate for manpower that they opened the once elite of elites—the SS—to any warm draftable body. I doubt Anatole had thought much about the Nazis before they banged on his door and took him away to training camp.

Elsa Leibart's letter to me had singled him out among the defendants at the 1953 trial. His bad luck had ceased after serving eight years in prison awaiting trial and receiving a further sentence but having the Assemblée National pardon him.

That unconscionable act alone might have been motive enough to seek his life. Except why Anatole among the others? Here's where a shameful secret of mine must come to light.

My fantasy of presenting the Devil's emissary in the guise of an imagined Sturmbannführer Durchmann had deep roots, I confess. Evil absolutely fascinated me. I *had* kept wondering what it would be like to commit an evil act, not just exist as a victim of one. In the depressed mood I was in, the idea of doing something truly horrendous found ever-increasing encouragement.

Would pumping the Luger's bullets into Anatole Wagner constitute pure evil, I had to question myself? Could it not be considered sheer *revenge* and thereby produce *mitigating circumstances?*

That's where the coincidence of Elsa Leibart's marrying Anatole's older brother entered the picture. Vis-à-vis that nice, now-matronly girl I'd befriended in my youth, I would bring TREACHERY. Her shock at my crime and BETRAYAL should shriek to the heavens. Motivated assassination thus automatically became MURDER.

So help me God, I reveled in the thought. Moreover, I planned a trip to Alsace.

The date I chose to embark was the famous *quinze d'août*—the 15th of August, when all of Paris empties out and a journey to Alsace would seem like any ordinary vacation. My preparation, to begin with, was informing Elsa by mail that I would be in Selestat on such and such a date and could we get together? Initially, however, I would go to Strasbourg. Everyone has to visit Strasbourg.

In this connection, I hoped to see Jean-Luc's mother. There had been an article in a newspaper about this Jewish convert to Catholicism who, like the famous nun Edith Stein (Sister Teresa Benedicta of the Cross) had been incarcerated in a German concentration camp. Unlike Edith, she had survived. Referred to as "Sister Miriam," although she had not taken holy orders, she was living at a convent in the Strasbourg area. A letter went out to her there in which I requested a meeting.

I left time for both Elsa and the former Madame Rosenstein to respond and both did in the affirmative on my requested dates.

Having lined up these two principal personages, I next decided on the touristic sites I would include as decoys. The Strasbourg Cathedral *was* a must. Also, I had read about and seen photos of the Maison Kammerzell, a noted restaurant in an extraordinarily decorated sixteenth-century half-timbered building. The Place Kleber, the Rohan Palace, the canals of La Petite France section—these were other attractions I didn't want to exclude. In the latter *quartier*, Jean-Luc's childhood home was located. Lucien Veynachter's sister Gabrielle whom I phoned, regretted she'd be headed to her family's villa on the Côte d'Azur, but we had a pleasant chat. I liked to think she might understand, and, who knows, even applaud my deed.

Since I was dabbling in evil, I decided, also, to detour to the Struthof Concentration Camp en route to Selestat. From the latter spot, it was but a short ride to Orschwiller, the small town where Anatole Wagner lived and worked as full-time assistant to the mayor. My presence in this rural community could easily be attributed to the fact it housed one of Alsace's prime attractions—the Castle of Haut-Koenigsbourg.

Some years earlier, when I was flying to Bangui, the capital of the Central African Republic, with the intent also of visiting Chad, Cameroon,

Senegal and other focuses of French Black Africa, it was suggested I take a handgun along since conditions could be hairy for a white Frenchman. Accordingly, I made a special trip back to Charniers for my Luger that Octave Blois had in safekeeping for me. I even hiked out to La Cav and did target practice by myself. How Octave was able to procure extra clips of bullets for me, I never asked. In the end, learning the difficulties of trying to bring a weapon on an aircraft, I decided to take my chances in the former French colonies and go unarmed.

Ever afterward, the Luger had been in its shoe box in my Paris digs.

When, in 1972, I left for Alsace, the shoe box was on the seat next to me.

Remember, I was intending to be open about the shooting. Like Schwartzbard, I would stand over my fallen victim displaying a smoking barrel.

Before heading to Strasbourg, 489 kilometers away, I meticulously did advance work, affirming hotels, nailing down appointments with Sister Miriam and Elsa, boning up on Alsatian history and tourist attractions, even reserving restaurant seats.

Finally, the reality of the trip was upon me. I was behind the wheel. I was actually en route, although first encased in Paris traffic and the slow crawl of leaving the city until able to drive normally due east.

I was in no hurry. On the first day, as if being observed, (which I knew I wasn't), I exhibited my nonchalance by staying overnight in Lorraine, three-quarters of the distance to Alsace. Not least of my motives was the municipality's name, pronounced *Nawnsee*, not like my *Naansee*, to whom I sent a postcard from the community bearing her prénom. I stayed in the glitzy Place Stanislas, noted for its gilded and black iron grills. Incidentally, I had a marvelous fresh water fish dinner at the principal hotel and amused myself by concocting a name the newspapers might use: "The Sybarite Killer."

There would be more good cooking in Strasbourg so I was off the next morning following an ample breakfast and a cursory look at the eighteenth-century elegant Hôtel de Ville of Nancy. Another irony to acknowledge after thinking of my old amour was that I would soon encounter another Hôtel de Ville of a much different sort in Orschwiller.

I had arranged my quarters in Strasbourg near the Cathedral, which afforded me a quick walk to *La Petite France*, where I was able to locate the town house of the Rosenstein family. Needless to say, I could not go inside. It had long since been sold. Although Madame Rosenstein could have reclaimed it, I'd learned in a telephone conversation with Gabrielle how the convert Sister Miriam preferred simple convent life. I was to see her there in Schiltigheim, a suburb, the next morning. Since I anticipated an austere setting and conceivably an austere lunch, I ended that evening gorging my full at the Maison Kammerzell.

A small parlor had been provided by the nuns for our private tête-à-tête. The institutional air of sanctity, enhanced by portraits of saints on the walls, re-instilled in me a sense of my childhood attachment to the Catholic church. Jean-Luc's mother, in her seventies, was ushered in, dressed in dignified black and wearing her beautifully carved wooden crucifix. Her hair was still dark, notwithstanding her ordeal at Thersienstadt and her features reflected the Semitic traits of being Max Cohen's daughter.

Our conversation as best I can remember (I took no notes) started as follows:

"You will excuse me, Professor, I hope, if I refer to my son as Jean-Marc."

I replied. "And you will excuse me, I'm sure, if out of habit I refer to him as Jean-Luc Mueller."

A faint smile of remembrance crossed her otherwise stern features. "Yes, that was my invention. A name taken from the Strasbourg telephone directory."

"I have never quite understood your choice of our Charniers in which to hide him except that your husband and my father knew each other."

"It was a gamble," she said cryptically.

"How so?

Her long narrative in reply told a complex story. Upon the outbreak of World War II in September 1939, she began to fear for her only son. Unlike most of her contemporaries, she foresaw a Nazi takeover of Alsace. But she was reluctant to send him to the U.S. where his sisters lived. Worse, the boy, due to Grandfather Max's influence, had insisted on remaining discreetly Jewish. Yet his own father secretly would not lift a finger to help him emigrate to Palestine. Selfish man, he wanted Jean-Marc to come live with him in Switzerland. To end the impasse, she hit upon the scheme of sending him under a pseudonym to Charniers where he would be under the watchful eye of R. R.'s friend Doctor Desfosseux. Finally, she had never given up on the redhead's ultimate conversion to her faith, which would protect him as well as her, she originally thought.

"Wrong belief," she added and showed me the tattooed number on her forearm.

In a somber mood, we continued our discussion. Jean-Luc, in his correspondence with her had written about me and a beautiful young countess and our escapades as the Trio. It did not surprise her he showed no signs of wanting to return to Strasbourg nor did she press the point. Occasionally, he would ask if she had any news from R. R. about arranging his emigration to the Middle East. Such inquiries had ceased before the blitzkrieg of 1940. With the German occupation, all contact terminated.

From a small handbag she had with her, she extracted a pocket-sized photograph of Jean-Luc that had been tinted to show the color of his hair. "I've had extra copies made," she explained. "I want you to have this memento."

What could I say except *"Merci"*? In a sense, it was an unwanted gift, conflicting with the murderous raison d'être of my trip. Still, simultaneously, it was an appropriate reminder of why I was undertaking my soon-to-be shocking *attentat.*

One thing I didn't express to the redhead's mother was the notion I entertained that Jean-Luc had given his life, like her Jesus Christ, to save a portion of humanity. Was it not blasphemy to compare the two? So I kept resolutely silent on that score, telling myself unheard I would be really avenging Jean-Luc's wasted sacrifice.

After we parted and I was once more seated behind the wheel of my car, ready to turn the ignition key, I took out the snapshot of Jean-Luc and stared hard at his likeness. There was my pal, except for the freckles painted over by the colorist. Abruptly, however, I hurriedly stuck the photo into the glove compartment and drove off. Was I worried too much nostalgia might dampen my resolve?

The better part of the afternoon of the same day, I spent at the world-renowned Cathedral. This magnificent Gothic church of rose-colored sandstone bore the official title of Notre-Dame and in the past fluctuated from the control of Catholics to Protestants in the sixteenth century and back to Rome one hundred and fifty years later. Meanwhile, it had been adjudged the tallest building in the world at the time. Its statuary was extraordinary. The realistically wrought figures even included a Massacre of the Innocents, graphically showing soldiers slaughtering babies with knives. That scene especially caught my eye. With Jean-Luc still in my thoughts, I also gravitated to the full-size portrayal in sculpture of two contrasting women, representing *Ecclesia* versus *Synagoga,* the former a triumphant Christian, holding a cross aloft on a staff, the latter a Jewess, blindfolded, her staff broken, the Torah slipping from her grasp. Propaganda like that, so artfully rendered, made me think of our twentieth-century anti-Semites, the Nazis, who had used visual images so effectively.

I had not known until I read so in a guide book that Goethe had been a student in Strasbourg and frequented Notre-Dame d'Alsace. He would climb to the very top, according to the text, and summoning his utmost nerve since he had vertigo, steel himself to clutch the railing and peer giddily into the void below.

It tried this, myself, and was impressed. Was I not acting like Goethe's Faust, seduced by Mephistopheles?

A special attraction of Strasbourg was the presence of storks atop mammoth nests on rooftops. In the Parc de l'Orangerie, where I sat the next morning, you could see these giant birds all around. Thoroughly relaxed, I spent considerable time in this public garden, which also had a zoo, the historic Pavillon Joséphine, where Napoleon's wife and the future emperor secretly met, and I rowed a boat on the artificial lake.

It was amazing how calm and untroubled I felt, considering the sensational finale I had in store. There was no rush on my part to reach the conclusion but now that I was in Alsace, I intended to stick to my schedule. My next stop, however, was not to be as beguiling as the tourist days in Strasbourg. The following morning, I would drive to the concentration camp of Natzweiler-Struthof, a short distance from the town of Schirmeck.

Coming face-to-face with the artifacts of Nazi evil was taking a risk that I could lose my resolve. I needed to reason that Anatole Wagner had been on the Hitlerians' side, whether willingly or not. My reactions once I came upon the actual site were interesting.

I had booked a room in Schirmeck ahead of time and could motor directly to the preserved camp, which lay in a mountain clearing carved out of an extensive evergreen forest. The buildings had been painted a dark forest green. Why was I surprised by the presence of color in the scene? Until then, my inner vision of a death camp was always in photographic black and white. Similar feelings arose when I saw the inmates' clothing on display in vertical stripes of blue and grey. Another surprise was the drawing posted at the entrance depicting a man in the aforementioned convict uniform dangling from a gallows. Welcome to the only death camp in France. It was written that this ghastly hanging event was a reminder to the captives of their captors' power, freshly repeated every morning.

P.S. Struthof, also uniquely in France, contained a gas chamber and a crematorium.

The scenery was literally entrancing: grassy hillside meadows framed by thick stands of stately trees, sylvan beauty high above a ribbon of sunlit water streaming below, until in a hollow dipping down were suddenly those barracks and barbed wire and rows of uniform white crosses in a cemetery, all capped by a monument, a giant headstone, commemorating the victims buried at its base.

A final anomaly was the bucolic sight of three brown deer grazing ever so peacefully in the distance shortly before I entered this Hell on earth, which had been preserved, like my Charniers, exactly as it was left during the war.

A pamphlet I had taken with me described the leading perpetrators of this particular war crime and the retribution dealt out to them after May 1945. The case of Sturmbannführer Hans Huttig, who built the place, unfortunately set a pattern all too frequently repeated—a death sentence reduced to life imprisonment and a release within a decade. The same happy fate might have attended commandant Haupsturmführer Fritz Hartjenstein, had he not had a fatal heart attack after his death sentence was changed to life imprisonment. The most notorious of those who headed Struthof was Josef Kramer. As the later "Beast of Bergen-Belsen," he did not escape execution. Another vicious Nazi involved here was the SS Doctor August Hirt, infamous for his excruciating medical experiments. He committed suicide. My cynicism had been earlier initiated upon learning that Sergeant Roos, the Alsatian SS volunteer and Nazi fanatic had had his death sentence dropped and was subsequently reprieved.

Thus my visit to Natzweiler-Struthof strengthened my belief that an open act of revenge was not only appropriate but an important message for the world.

In such an exalted state, I prepared to meet Elsa Leibart Wagner the next day.

After staying overnight in Schirmeck, I was back on the road again to cover the forty-plus kilometers to Selestat. The two of us had communicated several times before I'd left Paris. We would have lunch at a certain café in her home city.

Although markedly industrial, Selestat has an "Old Town" section that is a *paradis* of half-timbered medieval edifices, some of historical significance from the fifteenth and sixteenth centuries when the city was a center for humanist studies. Against a picturesque background, amid memories of the better side of man, Elsa and I ate outdoors at a café table and chit-chatted for close to two hours. Not surprisingly, I made no notes of our conversation. She started off by reminiscing, I remember, about her stay in Charniers-sur-Nys, blushingly admitting she'd had a "crush" on me after I'd been kind to her and had enjoyed our exchange of letters until the Germans occupied Alsace. The skinny, shy young girl with blonde braids and a sensitive, intelligent face had grown into a matronly woman, mother of five little Wagners whose CV's were cited to me, the oldest now twenty-five and serving in the military, the youngest a delightful six-year-old boy with three sisters in between. Funny how those details stuck with me, but not the names of the kids. My attention expressionlessly perked up when she mentioned her brother-in-law Anatole was doing well as an assistant to the mayor of Orschwiller. His twin sons were now twelve years old and he was a devoted father.

I took note of her last remark and then suddenly we were on to a tender subject. With her intelligence still on display, she broached her awareness of how Alsace and the Malgré-Nous (she used that terminology rather than Incorporés de Force) were viewed in the Limousin. Nor were feelings any less raw in Alsace about that feature of the war and the "lack of understanding of our plight among you people," as she put it.

"Yes, I'm glad I have a Paris license plate on my car," I quipped and brought a chuckle out of both of us.

"You've been to Strasbourg," she said, changing the subject, "and seen our torment at Struthof. But you must see more. The wine country and—"

I interrupted her. "I leave in that direction tomorrow. To Haut-Koenigsbourg."

"Wonderful!" she said, brightening. "It is actually in Orschwiller. A moment later, she added: "But perhaps it is best you do not contact Anatole."

"I agree," I quickly chimed in.

There! How more hypocritical could I be!

"You must also stop in Riquewihr," she went on. "A quaint little city preserved exactly as it always has been."

But not in ruins, I thought.

Before returning to Paris, she suggested, I should also make a detour to Colmar and especially view the world renowned Triptych of Issenheim.

"Colmar, I *have* been to," I said. "A quick side trip from Switzerland. Not enough time to see the triptych."

Knowing I was lying, I promised I would take in all the sights she recommended. We finally parted after our lengthy reunion and I spent that evening alone, eating well as usual. Quite early, I was on the road to Orschwiller.

While motoring through glorious scenery, I tried to lock my mind and not think of what lay ahead a few days hence. The direction was due west on a Route Nationale, a mere forty-seven kilometers away. Sorry, Elsa, I will have to miss Riquewihr and the Colmar Triptych. At the end of my local stay, I will most certainly be in custody.

Meanwhile, once ensconced in a small Orschwiller guest house, I began reconnoitering the area. The rest of the day of my arrival, like other tourist clients, I proceeded directly to Haut-Koenigsbourg.

An exhaustive description of the castle's exterior and interior isn't necessary. The rose-colored sandstone of its exterior battlement walls and interior buildings matches the hue and texture of the Strasbourg Cathedral. Reconstructed by Germany's Kaiser Wilhelm II in the early 1900s, the fortress is a highly intricate two-story structure of courtyards, multiple antique-filled rooms and ubiquitous stairways. I had forgotten about *La Grande Illusion*, the film classic Elsa had told me about so long ago. One of the staircases of an inner courtyard had been roped off with a placard in front, identifying the location as the final scene of Pierre Renoir's classic anti-war movie.

In short order, I knew my way around Orschwiller. At the guest house, I used my own name, asserted professorial interest in the history of Haut-Koenigsbourg, which dated from 1147, thereby accounting for my repeated trips to its ramparts over the next few days. The mairie, Anatole Wagner's place of work, was an imposing building on a sloping hill, in the center of the village, adjacent to several peaked roof half-timbered dwellings. I could park nearby and watch when the employees left the premises. As luck would have it, my quarry appeared on the very first afternoon I started my surveillance.

There was a fountain below the municipal structure, bedecked by plantings of pinkish flowers and Anatole, whom I recognized immediately, walked past it en route to his car. His balding hair was still jet black, I noted, but possibly touched up with dye. He carried a briefcase. The most important observation for my purposes was that he walked alone, not with any of his colleagues.

So, too, was it on the second day. Previously, I had followed him discreetly to his parking spot and did once again. Identical parking space for me. Identical solitary exit from work by him.

On the third day, if conditions remained the same, I would strike.

Meanwhile, I continued my daily "research" at Haut-Koenigsbourg.

Each time I passed the now roped-off, labeled staircase on which the climactic scene of Renoir's film was set, I would always pause as if paying my respects through a few minutes of cogitating on the ravages and futility of war.

The sole question remaining for the third day was whether I should go by foot to the mairie or drive there in my car, park and step onto the sidewalk to confront Anatole Wagner. To be honest, I chose the latter course because I was lazy. Suppose I hiked that not inconsiderable distance from the guest house to the site and he appeared with people around him. Shooting anyone else if my aim somehow wavered would not have accomplished my purpose.

No, Anatole had nobody with him when he descended the curving sidewalk from the mairie. I was sitting in my car only several meters away. The Luger in its cardboard box was loaded and primed. I took the pistol out, hid its bulk in my hand inside my pants pocket and left the driver's seat. I approached the victim. And—

Nothing happened!

I hadn't the excuse of a malfunctioning weapon, nor did its bulk stick in my pocket and make me miss the crucial opportune moment.

We passed each other, Anatole and myself. As Frenchmen will, we politely said bonjour to each other.

It was as if a veil had fallen from my eyes. He went on to his parking spot. I slipped back to my car. The Luger was returned to its box. Back to the guesthouse I drove, checked out and consciously following Elsa's must-sees, spent a day each at Riquewihr and Colmar before returning to Paris.

XXVIII

Miraculously, once back at the Rue Duguay-Trouin, my writer's block and desuetude immediately vanished. The return to my life's work proceeded with unceasing vigor. The experience at Orschwiller established itself in my mind not as a tragedy averted but a comedy, indeed a farce. I'm convinced my initial reluctance to share this episode, despite my inner Cro-Maritan's hectoring, was due to embarrassment, not shame. But this up-to-now solely private incident has been revealed. An intent to kill *manqué*. Is that a crime? Or just plain silly?

I have often wondered since: Has this incident been recorded by all-seeing God. What about the Devil? Had he and his minions been privy to my thoughts as well?

The same year, 1972, there appeared in the United States a book with the startling title: *The Reality of the Devil: Evil in Man*. Its author was an American woman philosopher and writer, Ruth Nanda Anshen. Perhaps in late 1973 or early 1974, I first heard of this publication and determined to find a copy. It had not been translated into French but since I read English, I found the publisher in New York (Harper Brothers) and obtained the lady's brilliant work.

Considering how the question of evil in humankind (man and woman), had been my inner torment for years, I eagerly entered her fascinating cerebral and emotional territory. Had I not in Alsace in fact brought myself to the brink of a possible Goethean leap into a tantalizing, fearsome void? Unlike the Boche poet's protagonist, Doctor Faust, I'd made no compact with Mephistopheles-Lucifer-Satan-Beelzebub etc. What Ruth Nanda Ashen did was personify the many-named fallen angel of Biblical ill-fame whose quarrel with God had turned him into a hateful, destructive force. Her proposal, as paraphrased by me, was: The Devil is equally as much a recognizable model for creating humans in his image as is God. If we are descended from God and view him as a white-bearded, kindly, beneficent old gentleman who nevertheless could inflict wrath and havoc when riled, then the Devil, we may infer, could not simply disguise himself as a black poodle nor appear in the ridiculous guise of horns and tail and scarlet skin color. Instead he might resemble a fuddy-duddy clean-shaven but white mustached academic in his retirement.

There were many striking passages in the Anshen tome. One worth repeating exactly as it struck me on reading, I append in the original English: "*There is a certain type of man, the true villain, who is the Devil's bodyguard. But he stands in alliance with his master and does not need to conduct a pact with him.*" [R.N. Anshen, *The Reality of the Devil* (New York: Harper and Row, 1972) p. 41.]

At once, the name of Obersturmbannführer Heinrich Heinz Durchmann flew into my mind. What a perfect description of *a true villain*—the Devil's bodyguard.

What comes first, though, with a cold-eyed monster like Durchmann? Was he born evil; if so, why aren't we all? Or maybe all of us are?

Anshen wrote of Faust: "caught in the snares of a diabolical plot, he is unconsciously isolated and hollowed." How true of me, pre-Alsace, *isolé et creux*, in a state of mental lethargy and depression until I conceived my plot against Anatole Wagner.

Somehow in the welter of coming to terms with Ruth Nanda Ashen's thesis that the Devil was at least as real as God, I logically became interested, academically, in a confrontation between the two—now for me, at least—living personalities. The notion was planted of a debate. Presently, I will ask both of them to assess their reality.

The failure of my attempt to stage the outraged rabbi's trial of God only had discouraged me temporarily. I convinced myself that if one approached such a strenuous undertaking carefully, it could be done.

Okay, more than several decades elapsed from the time I beat my retreat from Alsace and the present. Creatively rejuvenated, it seemed, I had plunged right back into the awesome task of completing my series on the history of France's expansion—and contraction—overseas.

Volume followed separate volume. The scope of the entire work rivaled the worldwide scope of French imperialism. I have given you a taste of it in North America and Black Africa, which has covered not only the Central African Republic but also Senegal, the Ivory Coast, Cameroon and Mali with its unique Tuareg population. The plenitude of place names and people continued; whether the Maghreb countries of North Africa, Morocco, Algeria, Tunisia et. al.; or Madagascar; or Oceania, Tahiti and French Polynesia in particular; or the Caribbean, including French Guiana (Devil's Island); and Asia, tripartite Vietnam, Cambodia, and Laos; plus the French presence in India and China. The final Book XII was a reflection on lessons to be drawn and spotlights on the many massacres and untold cruelty, by both sides, as our empire-building proceeded.

In time, Paris began to wear on me. Whenever I returned to Charniers-sur-Nys for Association meetings staying *chez* Octave Bois, the idea of retirement to the Limousin gained more appeal. So it was I found my current property for sale in Bregonzac and settled into a prosaic physical life style but one full of continuous mental activity and the comfort of living among my roots. I needed only to look up in the morning, exiting my front door, and see the silhouette of the château above for a flood of memories, many of them endearing.

And for most of these years, self-exiled off in the country, I had a companion, my poodle Jacques, who lived out his length of doggy life and whom I have never tried to replace. It's plain Jacques has remained eternally embedded in my mind, as I discovered recently in a dream.

There he was, my late black pet, his shiny, Persian lamb-like coat glistening amid darkness, achingly real.

His oh-so-familiar growl, clearly indicating he was out of sorts, was nevertheless like music to my ears.

"Jacques!" I exclaimed. "You're alive. But are you upset about something?"

We had signals. Two curt barks would answer me yes. One guttural yip would be no.

Instead, an unrecognizable voice speaking perfect French responded. Clearly, I heard: "I am not the Devil! That is a damnable German lie!"

I responded: "But Jacques, you are a French poodle, are you not?"

What I didn't dare to tell the beautiful creature was how poodles, their common name notwithstanding, were originally a German breed.

I could see the change in Jacques following my words. He was like his old self, not only gorgeous and aristocratic but full of mellow mischievous humor. I half-expected he would jump on me and want to wrestle. Better still was the look in his eyes, those orbs of deep dark brown above his moist de Gaullish nose—a stare of utmost loyalty and friendship.

In my bedroom, it was pitch black. On went the end table light. It was three a.m. on my bedside clock. Sitting up, I marveled at the authenticity of my subconscious vision of Jacques and mourned that it had only been a dream.

The day chosen for my proposed debate I had plenty of leisure after my usual breakfast, since tonight's question was fixed, and I thus needed no rehearsal and had only to move in two chairs, which I would do after Arlette left me my dinner and I was alone.

What should I do with the rest of the day?

I first thought of a stroll, my usual one to the old ivy-covered stone Pont Neuf bridge of so many memories. Or I could sit inside and read, but it was a bright sunny day. The upshot proved a surprise to me. I decided I would walk to New Charniers instead. At one of the bistros, I would take a light lunch—a croque-monsieur and, again, very much unlike me, wash down the ham and melted cheese with a beer instead of wine. Feeling almost peppy, I seemed simultaneously relaxed.

The original bistro in New Charniers where my cousin and I had lunched perhaps half a century ago had long since been replaced. The more chic La Chatte Friponne was the current favorite. After as brisk a hike as I could manage with a cane, I toured the "cookie cutter" (Naansee's term) environs of the government-built community, finally arriving before the signboard image of a mischievously grinning feline and seating myself at a sidewalk table.

I was pretty much a total stranger. The *patron* of the establishment, I'd been told, was an immigré from Savoie. He came out and gave me a cordial welcome, as he would any customer. Yet while I sat basking in the sun, I suddenly heard my name called. "Professeur Desfosseux!" Looking up, I saw a lanky, blondish man maybe in his thirties crossing the street toward me and waving. He had a vaguely familiar air about him.

"You know my family," he said. "I'm a Phillipon . . . Jean-Michel, Roger's oldest son. May I sit down? I had intended to contact you. I am an *agrégé* in French History and actively teaching. I wanted to tell you how much I've enjoyed your books."

Although his father had always been a thorn in my side, how could I refuse?

So for an hour or so, we chatted away like old friends. After my beer, I changed to wine. I learned he was living in Libourne on the outskirts of Bordeaux, teaching in a Lycée there, and home for a visit. Jean-Michel told me he'd read half a dozen of my volumes and used segments in his classes. He looked forward to reading the rest of them. Like colleagues, we discussed aspects of France d'outre-mer. It was a thoroughly enjoyable use of my self-allotted leisure. Unfortunately, his schedule had him leaving for Libourne later the same afternoon and he hoped we could meet again on his next trip.

Once we'd separated and I was once more alone, I glowed inside—not only from the beer and wine, but also from his praise and the feeling I'd done good work in my life.

I still had several hours until Arlette would arrive with my dinner, having told me she was bringing her unsurpassed *cassoulet*—my favorite dish. Once I finally rose up from the café table, I found myself admitting I did need a walk. My unsteadiness wasn't solely due to age.

I was strolling considerably steadier on the hike back to Bregonzac. Out in front of my house, I paused to admire the growth of ivy on my outside stone façade. In another deviation from habit, instead of entering the usual way, I went around back. In a small orchard of fruit trees was the grave in which I had buried Jacques. No headstone, no cross certainly, but a metal plaque attached to a flat rock marked the spot and the lettering on it bore the hardly imaginative statement of *Fidèle Ami.* I stood for a few minutes, gazing down. Before I left my pet's company, the errant thought struck me that in English—*Dog* spelled backward was *God.*

Then via the rear door, I re-entered my abode, remembering I still had some work to do before tonight's session.

Setting up the two chairs for my illustrious guests, readying the recording device, checking its working order, inserting a fresh tape—these tasks would take less than fifteen minutes. Arraying the audiovisual effects might be twice as long. The remaining bulk of my preparation remained exclusively cerebral.

Before I realized it, I was having complicated thoughts about tonight's event. After all, I was the creator. *Pro* and *Con.* I recognized I had to assign those positions to the question of God's and the Devil's reality. True, rationally, both would oppose the premise. But one of them perforce would have to argue Pro—yes, they *were* figments of human intelligence.

I picked God to do so. His underlying argument would be that while the firmament existed with galaxies like the Milky Way, containing millions of stars, each with the heat of our sun and surrounded by innumerable planets, we only knew of it through our homo-sapiens brainpower. Conceivably, if all humans were blotted out, the universe would disappear as well.

Specious, to be sure. Most certainly weak.

But could the Devil speaking Con produce a more powerful rationale?

It might be in arguing against human influence, he was feathering his own nest, declaring evil the only reality.

Maybe, I thought, I'll also have them switch roles afterward and go another round, an idea that briefly intrigued me and was just as quickly rejected.

My mind felt fatigued. *Give it a rest*, I commanded.

Give me a rest, too, I added and did something I rarely did. I took a nap.

I awoke quite refreshed before Arlette arrived with my supper. With great relish, I polished off her delicious *cassoulet*, accompanied by a superb Saint-Émilion Bordeaux red.

En fin, the dishes were cleared away, put in the sink for Arlette to attend to in the morning, and I retired to the study.

I had no front-of-the-curtain announcement to make, no audience to address, so when the houselights dimmed—I shut off some lamps— the show commenced with visual images flashed on the screen-like surface of my one white-washed wall . . . rolling cottony clouds in a blue vaulted heaven; gates shining like pearls; winged creatures in the sky, big as Alsatian storks but actually angels; golden harps in an endless row, plucked by virginal-looking ladies . . . followed by the opposite side of the coin: the cavernous blackness of Hell lit up by scarlet bonfires; a gigantic pitchfork worshipped by twittering masses of creatures who resembled a flood of ravenous rats; a mean-looking volcano spewing rivers of flame-colored lava burning and burying everything in its path; the gate of a concentration camp and its sign: *Arbeit Macht Frei*.

At last the two principal figures arrived, rather theatrically. A huge golden halo accompanied the elderly, portentous gentleman with snow-white hair, trim white mustache and fluffy white beard. Incongruously, he was dressed in a handsomely tailored three-piece brown serge suit, rainbow colored tie and wearing obviously expensive handcrafted brown leather shoes. His counterpart also had on a three-piece serge suit, in this instance black and pin-striped, a flashy tie of gold lightning strikes on scarlet silk, and rich man's shoe to match his rival's, black leather, shined to equal those on a pair of SS boots.

Oh, I didn't describe their vests: yellow-gold silk brocade for God, fiery red-black trimmed silk brocade for Satan—

Editorial Note

At this point, the narrative of Professeur Desfosseux is interrupted. It was apparently his habit to make a live audio recording of what was occurring in his "interviews" and transcribe the material to his computer, from which he then printed out a manuscript copy. The actual dialogue of the "Grand Debate" he envisaged between God and the Devil was never recorded, only his welcome to the two contestants. Following this, these hastily uttered words of his were audible: "Feel exhausted . . . Catch my breath . . . Calm down . . . Wait a minute . . . What is this wave coming over me? . . . OH, MON DIEU! . . ."

—Octave Bois, Editor

Addendum

To: Mrs. Thomas Ridley
10 East Main Street
Lancaster, Ohio, 43130, U.S.A.

Ma chère Nancy,

I am writing to you in French, knowing you are fluent in our language, and I am, unhappily, illiterate in yours. I have fond memories of your visit to us in Charniers with our mutual friend Eugène Desfosseux. We were so happy to have you as our guest.

Alas, it is now my painful duty to report to you the death of our dear Eugène. It was apparently very sudden, at night alone in his study—a totally unexpected heart attack. Slumped in his leather armchair, he was discovered the next morning by the woman who brought him his breakfast and prepared other meals and acted as housekeeper.

Among his effects were three copies of this manuscript he was creating currently. In the testament he left, I was to receive one and you another, which is being sent to Ohio by separate mail. The third, of course, was his own working document. The value of his possessions was bequeathed to the Association of the Families of Martyrs of Charniers-sur-Nys with the exception of the captured German Luger pistol and the "uniform" he wore in the Maquis, given to the Resistance Museum. Any royalties from sales of his academic books have been dedicated for stipends to local students studying French history, particularly his specialty of France Overseas.

He is buried in the Charniers cemetery joining his mother and the martyrs of the massacre among whom were his brave defiant father and his best friend, the Alsatian Jean-Luc Mueller.

Should you come to France again, I hope you will honor us with a visit in Charniers and we can go together to pay our respects to a wonderful human being.

One more detail. When you read his manuscript, you will be apprised of Eugène's "hobby," shall we say, of staging "theatricals" using historical personages. We know through him of your performances in Paris and his amazing talent of ventriloquism.

His last extravaganza was nothing less than a "debate" between God and the Devil. Eugène's final utterance of *"Mon Dieu,"* indicates to me whose side he favored.

From my stationery, you can see that I am, despite my antique age, the mayor of Charniers-sur-Nys. Return correspondence is best directed to me at the *mairie.*

Please be assured of my sincere regards to you and your family. *À bientôt.*

Octave Bois, Mayor
Charniers-sur-Nys, Haute-Vienne, France

In addition to his many publications, Neil Rolde is a long-time public servant, philanthropist, Renaissance man, and gentleman. The renowned Maine historian grew up in Brookline, Massachusetts. He earned a BA at Yale and a master's in journalism at Columbia University. He worked as a film scriptwriter before moving to Maine with his wife of fifty-four years, Carlotta Florsheim, to raise their family. In York they brought up four children and now enjoy family visits with their eight grandchildren.

The author has won book awards from the Maine Historical Society, the Maine Humanities Council, and the Maine Writers & Publishers Alliance. Most of Neil Rolde's books involve the history of his beloved Maine and its people. With a wealth of historical knowledge about politics, the author has recently turned his skill and wit to blogging current political incidents in a historical context at neilroldeauthor.com.

Rolde's public service includes six years as assistant to Maine's Governor Kenneth M. Curtis and sixteen years as representative in the Maine State Legislature. He was the Democratic candidate for U.S. Senate in 1990. The author has served on many state boards and commissions, including the Maine Health Care Reform Commission, the Maine Historic Preservation Commission, the Maine Humanities Council, and the Maine Arts Commission.